THE
DISSIDENT

Nell Freudenberger

PICADOR

For my parents

First published 2006 by HarperCollins, New York

First published in Great Britain 2006 by Picador

This edition first published 2008 by Picador
an imprint of Pan Macmillan Ltd
Pan Macmillan, 20 New Wharf Road, London N1 9RR
Basingstoke and Oxford
Associated companies throughout the world
www.panmacmillan.com

ISBN 978-0-330-49344-4

1 3 5 7 9 8 6 4 2

A CIP catalogue record for this book is available from
the British Library.

Printed and bound in Great Britain by
Mackays of Chatham plc, Chatham, Kent

Visit www.picador.com to read more about all our books
and to buy them. You will also find features, author interviews and
news of any author events, and you can sign up for e-newsletters
so that you're always first to hear about our new releases.

Also by Nell Freudenberger

LUCKY GIRLS

1.

I WAS NOT MEANT TO BE A DISSIDENT. I WAS NOT SUPPOSED TO LIVE outside of China. I never intended to be a guest, for an entire year, in the home of strangers, dependent on their charity and kindness. Who would have imagined, watching me grow up in Harbin—sitting quietly with my father in our old apartment behind the Russian church, or clutching my mother's hand as she haggled good-naturedly with Old Yang over the price of scallions—that I would wind up in Los Angeles, living in the guest room of people who could not find the province of Heilongjiang on a simple English map?

I am tempted to say it was an accident. Certainly I would not have gotten involved in politics, or in the artistic community of the Beijing East Village, had it not been for my cousin, also an artist—I will call him X. (Because of his continuing activity in China, I am forced to conceal his identity here.) But it also began with my mother, who always hoped I would become a famous artist and go abroad, and with my father, who sent me to have drawing lessons with his old friend, the painter Wang Laoshi. Quite possibly it began with Wang Laoshi, who saw my early efforts, and encouraged me to pursue absolutely any other profession.

But I hesitate to put responsibility on others. In the end it's my fault that I am so easily persuaded. I have always been impressionable, skilled at mimicry. I am, as my teacher admitted, a brilliant copyist. On paper, I could reproduce Audubon's and Bada Shanren's birds; I could make my mother laugh by imitating the gestures and mannerisms of people we knew (for example, my father's postprandial expression of despair); even the pronunciation of foreign words was not difficult for me. In school, English was my best subject, not only because of this talent for imitation but because of my mother, who had been born in Seattle, Washington, and much later became a teacher of Business English at the Harbin University of Science and Technology.

My mother went to China for the first time in 1953, three days after her twelfth birthday, when her parents decided to return to their motherland and do their part for the glorious new People's Republic. My grandfather, an electrical engineer with the Boeing company, had been deeply honored by a personal invitation from Zhou Enlai. As it turned out, however, my grandfather's timing wasn't good. A little more than a decade later, my grandmother and my mother were sent to separate "cadres' schools" to be reeducated, while my grandfather eventually went to a much harsher place—a work camp in the Great Northern Wilderness—where he died, six years before I was born.

When I told this story—as if it had happened to distant relatives rather than to my immediate family—my American hosts were horrified. I think they were also a little thrilled by the tragic irony: it was as if, Cece Travers said, my relatives had been American Jews, returning unknowingly to Germany in 1939. I couldn't explain to the Traverses that a Chinese person did not think of the 1960s and '70s in this way: that those years represented a perversion of our own ideals, some of which we still cherished, rather than an atrocity visited on us from outside. The fact that my relatives had been in a work camp was enough for Cece. "Perhaps they aren't telling you everything," she said, in a way that made it clear she thought I was being callous about the sufferings I described.

In fact the opposite was true. I had my reasons for concealing my background from the Traverses, but I have never been comfortable telling the story of things that happened before I was born. I always feel that I'm making things up. In Los Angeles, I found out how much easier it was to tell my own history as if it belonged to someone else: at the end of my account, I was surprised (and a little proud) to find tears in the eyes of my American audience.

After the end of the Cultural Revolution in 1976 (and incidentally my birth, in 1975) my mother became an English teacher, if a reluctant one.

Her former passion for literature, in particular the Romantic poets, was not relevant to the business English courses she was assigned, and she never returned to the original poems and translations she'd begun as a university student in the early 1960s. Her talents as a teacher were thus primarily focused on me, so that by the time I was in high school, I already spoke English more fluently than my classmates and even my teachers. My mother and I used to laugh at the book I used in school, *Idiomatic English,* which purported to teach us how to speak like real Americans. The book was full of dialogues between John, Mary, and (inexplicably) someone named "Batty," of which the following is an approximate but unexaggerated example:

> *John:* I am thinking to get a gift for our friend Batty. Monday is her birthday. A necklace or a bracelet would truly fit the bill.
>
> *Mary:* No one knocks on the gift horse's mouth. But you had better not have a chat with Batty before the big day. That is to say, you are a chatterbox. You will certainly let the cat out of the bag.
>
> *John:* Mary, you are a strict taskmaster! Why do you say that I am a bean-spiller? I am as silent as the mouse, and also the grave.
>
> *Mary:* Because right now, John, you are talking my ears off!

When I finally met my cousin X in Beijing, I found him studying from this same textbook, practicing John, Mary, and Batty's lines quite seriously. This was midway through my first year at Beijing Normal, when my cousin still imagined he might go abroad and study. He had come to Beijing after being dismissed from the well-regarded Hubei Academy of Fine Arts for taking part in a controversial performance piece, *Buried Alive No. 1.* In that project, a group of students had interred themselves in a kind of mass grave, breathing through lengths of hospital tubing. The audience was led to the site (a fallow pasture lent by a local farmer), where they found only a crop of suspiciously rubbery hollow vegetables poking out of the disturbed ground. I didn't see this piece myself, but I've heard that people gasped and covered their eyes, when the first students began to claw their way out.

Buried Alive No. 1 took place in the spring of 1987, two years before the student protests; after Tiananmen, the authorities would recall it as a dangerous precedent. By that time my cousin was a member of Beijing's artistic avant-garde: living illegally outside the work unit system, moving frequently among the tenuous communities on the city's edges. From the original artists' village near the Summer Palace at Yuanmingyuan (where he was associated with the internationally recognized "cynical realists"), X went to Songzhuang and, after a hiatus in the maximum-security facility at Qincheng, to the industrial dump between the Third and Fourth Ring Roads, which became known in the 1990s as Beijing's East Village. Although we'd met as children, the East Village is where I really got to know him.

Between the fall of 1993 and the spring of '94, we produced two issues of a new artistic journal, *Lu Kou*, or *Intersections,* which was later referred to by the overseas Chinese scholar Harry Lin as "the best new journal of Chinese experimental art." (It was, at least, the newest.) After the East Village was broken up, I did not communicate with my cousin for several years. By the time we finally reconnected, he was living and working in Dashanzi, the fashionable new art district in northeastern Beijing. My cousin was one of the first to set up a studio in Dashanzi's abandoned Joint Factory 718—once the largest military electronics complex in Asia— when the rents were cheap, before the gallery owners, foreigners, and fashion designers discovered it.

Throughout my life, I have been either in very close touch with my cousin or completely estranged from him. But in the spring of 2000, when he contacted me about the fellowship in Los Angeles, our relations entered an awkward, lukewarm phase. Even though we professed our friendship and loyalty to one another, there were still certain subjects we couldn't talk about, and that added a strained and uncomfortable element to our discussions of, say, the continuing relevance of painting, or the architectural transformation of Beijing, or the possibility of artistic collaboration in twenty-first-century China. In the past there have been times when I called him "older brother," and also when I declared him my enemy; those abrupt reversals make the relationship we maintain today feel both precious and false.

I met my cousin as a child only once, when I was seven and he was thirteen. I showed him the paintings of bamboo, birds, and lobsters that I had made with my teacher Wang Laoshi, and X taught me to fly my new kite in Stalin Park, beside the river. Although he was kind to me, the distance between us seemed hopeless and exhausting; when we met again, ten years later in Beijing, this gap hardly seemed to have narrowed. My cousin had talent, political conviction, style, and (naturally) success with women I couldn't hope to imitate. Nevertheless I think even he was sometimes lonely and frightened in Beijing, which is one of those cities that can make you feel like a local or a stranger, but very rarely anything in between.

From that first reunion, we were both hoping for some kind of genetic connection, and in spite of the differences in our personal styles, his black Mao suits and avant-garde hairstyles compared with my eagerness to fit in, people said they could see the family resemblance. I treasured those compliments, and once I had lost some weight courtesy of Beijing Normal's abysmal canteen, I could see that there was something to them. On the inside, however, my cousin and I were completely opposite: he was a leader in everything, and I was the perfect follower. At least for a while, I felt privileged to take his directions.

There is only one area in which I have historically felt superior to my cousin, and this has to do with our family backgrounds. My cousin's father, my uncle, was a boatman on the Yellow River, whereas my father, because of the accidents of politics, rose from a traveling oil driller to become one of the elite cadres at our nation's largest oil field. And while my mother would certainly have completed her translation of Keats's lyrics had her education not been interrupted, X's mother sold fried snacks in a village outside Taiyuan.

Because of his humble origins, when he came to the capital my cousin did not know about the West. He soon began to claim strong preferences (for German photography, Italian fashion, French cheese) and biases (against Hollywood and American food) but these attitudes were culled from his friends, many of whom came from more exalted circumstances. My cousin didn't know where "Hollywood" was, or that ordinary people actually lived there. Like many Chinese, he was allergic to dairy products, so he was hardly an authority on Brie or Camembert. And although he tried to cover it up, my cousin spoke almost no English. He pretended not to be interested in the language, and even when I caught him studying, I was careful to save face for him in this matter.

"Won't they be surprised by your English?" he giggled, delighted, a few months before I left for Los Angeles. We were lying on our backs smoking in his beautiful studio in the Factory, with its arched Bauhaus ceiling, whitewashed brick, and fashionable big character slogan painted in red on the south wall: "Seek Truth from Facts." In fact that slogan, from the post-Mao period, was not one of the authentic ones famously preserved in other parts of the Factory ("Chairman Mao Is the Red Sun in Our Hearts," for example) but was chosen by my cousin to illustrate his aesthetic philosophy. He painted the characters in the same neat, blunted style as the originals and cleverly distressed the red paint so that you couldn't tell the difference.

This was in March of 2000. The weather was still cold, but X's studio was comfortable, warmed by the electric heaters he had once used in his famous performance piece *Something That Is Not Art.* In the distance we could hear the chugging and clinking of the radio transmitter workshop next door. I told my cousin that I didn't think my English would be very impressive to a native speaker.

"Sure it will," X said. He was in high spirits that day, as if he were the one going off to America in a couple of months. "Yuan Zhao, genius painter and speaker of English!" he exclaimed.

"Hardly," I said.

He thought I was being modest, but in fact the Traverses were not at all surprised by my excellent English. If anything, they were disappointed by the force of my accent, which they assured me I was losing almost from the day I arrived. To them, English wasn't really a language. It was a genetic gift, present in everyone but unfortunately latent in some people, like biceps. It only had to be strengthened and drawn out.

I apologize in advance for the long-windedness of this account. It's a particular trait of exiles that they are constantly having long conversations in their heads with imaginary friends. When they finally meet someone sympathetic, they tend to exhaust that person with weeks of stored-up dialogue—that is to say, they talk your ear off. In order to explain what happened to me in Los Angeles, and absolve myself of guilt in the events of the year 2000–2001 at the St. Anselm's School for Girls, I have to tell another story at the same time, set in China in the late twentieth century. I assure you that although on the surface, this might seem to be a story about politics and art and even death, it will touch on those topics in only the most superficial ways. As I've said, I am an expert in just one thing; and so this will be a story about counterfeiting, and also about the one thing you cannot counterfeit.

2.

CECE SHOULD NOT HAVE BOUGHT THE BEAR CLAWS. SHE WAS ALREADY regretting the purchase when she rang Joan's doorbell; her effortlessly slender sister-in-law probably wouldn't want one. It had been a spur-of-the-moment inspiration in front of the bakery case: Cece had felt like celebrating. She wasn't sure she could explain why she was so excited about the famous dissident, nor could she articulate, even to herself, the salutary effect she hoped Yuan Zhao might have upon her scattered family.

Cece was about to turn around and take the white pastry box back to the car, when she saw Joan coming toward the door. Through the frosted glass panel, Cece could make out just the shape of her sister-in-law, stopping for a moment to examine something on the hall table. It was uncharacteristic of Joan to interrupt her day for a coffee date; Cece couldn't remember the last time the two of them had socialized alone.

"I hope I'm not interrupting."

"Don't be silly."

Cece stepped into the house, which was dark and smelled of books. Or maybe she just imagined that it smelled like books: her sister-in-law was a novelist, who also taught graduate creative writing by correspondence. She lived in a perfectly nice two-bedroom Spanish bungalow across from the Rancho Park golf course, which Cece thought might be immeasurably improved with a simple renovation. She'd even made some suggestions: about ways the furniture might be rearranged to encourage circulation, and the type of blinds that would maximize the light. Her sister-in-law wasn't especially interested in interior decoration, however, and the house always felt haphazard to Cece. There was also something about being there that made her hungry.

"Here's just a little something left over from brunch. They're good if you warm them up."

Joan looked inside the box. "How many people did you have at brunch?"

"Oh, well, I thought Maxwell and his friend would be hungry."

She trailed after Joan into the kitchen, which was full of bright blue tile. It reminded Cece of a trip they had taken once, to Istanbul, where Gordon had given a talk. This was just after he had published his important work *Manias and Obsessions: A Symbiosis.* The book had propelled her husband to academic stardom, for a time, and made him the youngest psychiatrist ever to be tenured by UCLA.

This, of course, was many years ago, and Gordon's subsequent books, on bulimia, trichotillomania, and the family of maladies that fall under the rubric "OCD," did not cause quite so much of a stir.

Joan had asked about Max's friend.

"She's very pretty," Cece said. "Almost a bit much—for Maxwell, I mean. Well, girls develop more quickly of course. I was trying to think what it was about her, because she's very sweet, very polite . . . but it may just be that she wears these colored contact lenses, and they change depending on the day. None of the colors match her skin, so it's a bit disconcerting—"

"What color is her skin?"

"Oh well, Joan. It's brown."

"Dark brown?"

"You think I'm racist," Cece said.

"I'm teasing," Joan said. "Is she black or Hispanic?"

"Hispanic. The mother is from El Salvador. But Max says her stepfather is black. And she has two very cute little black brothers. I saw them once, when her mother picked her up."

"What's her name?"

"Jasmine. That's pretty, isn't it? They're both involved in community service. That's how they met—although it seems that Jasmine was involved in it before Max was. Or at least, that's what I gather." It was amazing that her tendency to babble got worse around Joan, one of the people she wanted to babble in front of least. Around her brother-in-law Phil, who was at least as smart as Joan, she had always felt perfectly articulate.

"He met her doing his community service?"

"Mm-hm."

"So what did she do?"

"What do you mean?" But she knew what Joan meant. She meant: What did Jasmine do in order to get herself assigned to the graffiti-eradication project? It was something Cece had wondered herself more times than she would've liked to admit.

"I mean, did she commit a crime?"

"Oh, I don't think so. She's very quiet."

"But then how—?"

Sometimes Cece had the uncomfortable feeling that her sister-in-law was asking questions in order to gather material, or simply stockpiling facts in case she found a use for them in her writing. At those times Joan became unnaturally conciliatory and empathic. She nodded sympathetically and made her voice even softer than usual, as if she would like you to forget she was there.

"I don't know," Cece told Joan firmly. "Maybe she's just community-oriented."

"I would love to go out and see the project," Joan said. "Do you think Maxwell would mind?"

"You can see it driving west on the ten," Cece told her. "Just look for the painters' scaffolds."

Joan looked disappointed. Good, Cece thought: it was important that her sister-in-law get her priorities straight.

"The important thing is just that Max has such a nice girlfriend," she continued, fabricating a little, in the service of Joan's priorities. "Jasmine is his first." It wasn't that Jasmine wasn't nice, only that Cece couldn't tell what she was. She was closed off, sealed up. Joan would say it was a cliché, but as far as Cece was concerned, eyes were the windows to the soul, and Jasmine's windows were covered over with incongruous, bright blue Venetian blinds.

"I'm surprised that you and Gordon let her sleep over."

"We don't. She just came over early this morning—although, you know, if they're going to, they will."

"That's very enlightened, Cece. I'm impressed."

She tried not to feel that Joan was being condescending. It was only that she had an acerbic manner, which was maybe more pronounced because of all those years of being independent. Joan had been married and divorced in her thirties. Although she had dated a reasonably desirable succession of men since then, she had always chosen to live alone. As far as Cece knew, her sister-in-law had never expressed any interest in having children; now it was too late. Cece tried to imagine her life without Olivia and Max, and failed completely.

"As long as I know where they are," she said quickly. "I have to drive Max everywhere now anyway."

Joan shook her head. "What a hassle."

"Oh, I don't mind." The idea of once again giving Max the mobility and freedom that came with a learner's permit was too terrifying to contemplate. "It's not as if I have anything else to do."

"You do things." Joan paused for several moments. "You do career counseling."

"That's not definite," Cece said. In fact she was reconsidering her offer to volunteer as the internship coordinator at St. Anselm's School. There seemed to be so much to do at home. "It would just be coordination," Cece said. "Putting girls in touch with St. Anselm's parents who work in particular fields."

"That would use your people skills," Joan said. "God knows, I could never do it." Cece could not help feeling that what Joan was saying was that she would never *want* to be the internship coordinator of St. Anselm's School. Nor did she necessarily blame her.

Joan made a face: "I can't believe I just said 'people skills'—what an idiotic expression." She arranged three of the bear claws on a plate that Max had made for her years ago, and put them in the microwave. Cece remembered when she would take her children to the store where they could decorate paper circles, to be turned into plastic plates. Other children had focused on stars and moons, or dinosaurs, or simply filling the entire white space with color; Max had drawn a bright green stick figure in the center of the circle, and then almost obscured it with punishing black dots, like rain or snow or (now it was impossible not to imagine) bullets, and then printed his name in large red letters, larger than the drawing, marching around the edge of the plate: "Maxwell T., age 7." She had almost told him he couldn't give the plate to his aunt—but of course you couldn't tell them that.

"I can't believe you still have this," Cece said.

"I love this plate. It always reminds me of *Thirty-three Short Films about Glen Gould*. You know at the end? When Glen Gould is just a speck in all of that snow?"

"I don't think I saw that," Cece said. Joan thought Max's problems were evidence of some kind of depth, or even artistic talent; she thought that they signified something. But Max's depression wasn't "creative"; it was a sickness. It meant nothing. It sucked all of his energy away—that was how she thought of it, the good particles fighting the bad particles, like on antihistamine commercials—so that he was listless and tired, and even his eyes looked fluey.

"How does he seem?" Joan asked. "Apart from Jasmine?"

"I don't know, to be honest," Cece said. "I've been trying to stay around the house, in case he needs anything. But he never does, really."

Joan didn't say anything, but Cece knew what she was thinking: her sister-in-law thought that she was too involved with her children. Cece was willing to cede ground to Joan in many areas, but not in this one. Joan had never had children; she could not know what it was like to have a teacher begin a conversation, "We aren't sure what to do with him anymore." She didn't know how it felt to find out about the birthday parties he hadn't been invited to, and then to see him spending hours on weekend afternoons in the den with the shades drawn, sitting four inches from the television, hunched over a control pad, with which he was shooting aliens, or mafiosi, or cops, his body jerking to the rhythm of the robotic digital soundtrack.

The accident with the gun had happened nearly five months ago. They called it "the accident" because it had happened in a car, although it was not a traffic accident in the strict sense of the word. The officer had pulled

Max over for driving in two lanes at once (a beginner's mistake) and found that he had a learner's permit, which did not allow him to drive without a licensed adult over twenty-five. Then the officer had asked Max to open the glove compartment—to check for the registration—and that was how he had discovered the gun.

"Should we have our coffee in the garden?" Joan asked.

Cece followed her out the back door, latching the screen a little more vigorously than necessary. She would have liked to explain to Joan what it was like being Max's parent: to surprise her with some of the things she didn't know—but it wasn't worth it. Joan would be fascinated; she would want to talk about articles she had read on gun shows and the NRA in the *New York Review of Books*. Joan liked it when you could attach real people to big themes; what she didn't understand was that it was never the same when it was your child. You could not consider your child in the light of the *New York Review of Books*.

"So when does your dissident arrive? It's any day now, isn't it?"

"On Monday," Cece said. "Just before Livy." Her daughter Olivia had been in Paris and the Dordogne for ten weeks, studying French. It had seemed like longer. "I shouldn't even be sitting here—there's so much to do."

"What do you need to do?"

"Well, we wanted to leave some art supplies in the pool house. Some watercolors, and one of those wooden manikins, you know, for figure drawing. It was supposed to be for Max, but all he draws are cartoons. And we put in a skylight," Cece continued. "The guys finished yesterday, but they've left a mess of course."

"A skylight!"

"For painting, since it's going to be his studio for a whole year."

"Well that's generous," Joan said.

Her sister-in-law implied that it was too generous, over-the-top, but Cece thought it was the least they could do. She had always had a problem saying no to foundlings. Now they were down to Salty, Spock, the four cats, the blind guinea pig Ferdinand, and Freud (the single surviving bunny), which was progress. When Cece thought of the dissident, alone and in America for the first time, she felt a kind of anxiety that could only be alleviated by doing something. It wasn't generosity so much as a kind of habit.

"We want him to be comfortable," Cece said. "Did you know that he's never been outside China? It's like a miracle that the government is letting him come."

"Is he that big a deal?"

"There's an article about him." Cece had forgotten about the article, which Max had printed off the Internet for her, and she had put in her purse. But had she switched purses? She could feel her sister-in-law watching as she sifted through her bag, where she'd dropped the article in a hurry, folded into squares.

"Here!" she said, finally uncovering it. "It's fascinating—from the *Taipei Times,* so it's less biased."

She had not expected Joan to be interested; she was pleased to see her sister-in-law skimming the article and examining the badly reproduced picture. Cece had looked closely at that picture, trying to get a better sense of the person who would be living in their house for the next nine months, but the image was frustrating. It gave you a certain impression: a defiant young man standing in Tiananmen Square, his hands in his pockets and a line of flags snapping in the wind overhead, but you couldn't make out much of an individual expression.

Joan looked up from the article. "Can I keep this?"

"Of course," Cece said. "And you'll have to come and meet him."

"All right," Joan said, surprising Cece again. "When?"

"Sometime next week." She decided not to mention the dinner party yet. She had invited Professor Harry Lin from UCLA, a colleague of Gordon's and the one who had arranged the dissident's visit. Her sister-in-law did not like to be introduced to eligible men, or at least not the eligible men Cece suggested; she'd made that clear on a number of occasions. And yet in this case, Cece couldn't help being a little sneaky. Harry Lin was a leader in the field of Asian art history, obviously extremely intelligent, and in their (admittedly brief) interactions, Cece had found him modest and kind as well. His wife had passed away several years ago, and as far as Cece knew, he was still single.

"I'll give you a call. Max and Livy will be glad to see you," Cece added, although both her children tended to make unkind jokes about Joan, occasionally referring to her as "Auntarctica." Joan did have a tendency to be a little chilly, especially around family: something that would happen, Cece imagined, if you spent most of each day alone.

Joan was getting up from the table, clearing the remains of the bear claws and the cups. "This will be the last year they're both at home, won't it?"

It was like Joan to focus on the negative. But Cece wouldn't let it ruin her mood. On Monday she would pick up the dissident, and Thursday was Olivia's homecoming. By next weekend, the house would be lively and busy again.

"I'm thinking about this week," Cece told Joan firmly. "I'm not thinking any further than that."

"You're going to have a full house. I can't believe I just said 'full house,' " she added. "Clichés are insidious."

Cece sighed happily. "We're going to be packed to the gills."

3.

WHEN SHE GOT HOME FROM JOAN'S, MAX WAS SITTING ON THE FRONT step with Jasmine. They were just back from the freeway, splattered with paint—although the clothes Jasmine was wearing didn't seem appropriate for outdoor work. Her jeans were so tight that Cece wondered how she could climb the scaffold, and she was wearing a sleeveless pink T-shirt with the words "Baby Doll" in rhinestone-studded cursive across her breasts.

"Hi guys," Cece said. She was holding two bags of groceries, and there were six more in the trunk, yet neither child got up to help her.

"Hi Mom," said Max. Jasmine stared at her knees.

"If you could just—" Cece began, but Lupe was already at the front door, hurrying to take the bags. On the way back into the house, the housekeeper stopped:

"Maxwell—your lunch." She didn't acknowledge Jasmine in any way, confirming Cece's suspicion that there was something going on between them. The first time Max had brought Jasmine home, Lupe had pulled Cece aside, with one of those urgent confidences she could never quite understand:

"Missis, that girl . . . is from El Salvador."

"I know," Cece said. "Max mentioned that." Although she had employed Lupe for ten years as live-in domestic help, Cece realized that she didn't know anything about El Salvador beyond the fact that it was troubled, and that America was somehow involved with those troubles. "Is she from the same region as your family?"

But Lupe had shaken her head impatiently, as if Cece was missing the point. "No good for Max," she said.

"Lupe!" she said. "You don't even know her."

"Missis," Lupe said, "I *know*."

Whether Lupe meant that she did in fact know Jasmine, or that she knew Jasmine's type, or whether the housekeeper was simply repeating the last thing Cece said—a strategy she used when her English failed her—Cece had no idea.

"We're not hungry," Max told the housekeeper.

"There are still some bear claws," Cece said. "I was hoping you'd take them to your friends at the freeway."

At this Jasmine smiled. Today her eyes were hazel with streaks of yellow, like a cat's.

Max sighed. "They're not our friends."

Cece returned Jasmine's smile, although it had clearly not been for her. "They're not great for your waistline—but they're delicious." She was trying to bond with Jasmine, but she wondered if it had sounded as if she were criticizing her figure. There was certainly nothing wrong with Jasmine's figure, except perhaps that it was a little too much on display. "Not that you have to worry," Cece said quickly. "I meant, 'you' as in 'one.' Or really, 'me.' I'm the one who has to worry."

"*Mom*," said Max.

Jasmine looked at Cece with a combination of alarm and disbelief. Her ears were pierced all the way up the sides; one long gold earring spelled out her name. Cece was struck by the difference between this girl and Olivia's friends, who were only two years older, but had a completely different style. Tight and revealing clothes were "nasty" or "totally tacky." The used or inherited T-shirts and jeans they favored showed off their bodies, but in a covert way. Olivia spent more money on lingerie than Cece did, and would often go to school with a black lace bra underneath her regulation white blouse. Cece had been concerned about it, and once even asked Gordon whether he thought they ought to say something, but Gordon had said that exhibitionism in an all-girls school was a way of trying on adult sexuality in a safe arena, and that it was perfectly normal.

Jasmine said something to Max so softly that Cece couldn't hear it.

"I'll come with you," Max said.

"Where are you going?" Cece asked.

"I'm just going home," Jasmine said.

"Do you need a ride?"

Jasmine shook her head. "I'm waiting for my cousin."

"I'm going over to Jasmine's for a while," Max said casually, as if he didn't know that he had an appointment with his therapist. Cece didn't want to mention the therapist in front of Jasmine.

"Not this afternoon," she said meaningfully.

Max looked at Cece so blamefully that she started to get angry back. What had she done, except try to be friendly and offer the two of them a snack? "Help me with the rest of the groceries, Max."

Without looking at her, Max said, "Lupe'll do it."

"Lupe will not—" Cece began, just as Lupe returned for the rest of the groceries.

"For Livy?" the housekeeper asked.

"Yes," Cece conceded. "We're having a welcome-home dinner on Friday. Don't forget," she told Max. "For your sister and Mr. Yuan."

Max made a face.

"Max?" said Jasmine. "Friday?"

"Oh yeah." Max turned to Cece: "We're busy Friday night."

Cece tried to be patient: you didn't gain anything by losing your temper. "Busy with what?"

"A party," Jasmine unexpectedly volunteered. "For my cousin Carlos's birthday. He could drive Max home afterward."

"Oh, no," Cece said. "Someone will take you after dinner, and then pick you up so that you're home in time for curfew."

"Livy?" Max asked.

"We'll see."

"One o'clock, right?"

"Eleven-thirty."

"I don't want you to have to come pick me up," Max said. "Since it's far."

"Where is it?"

Max began to speak, and stopped, conscious that he'd made a mistake.

"Echo Park," Jasmine said.

Had Max asked her privately whether he could go to a party in Echo Park, Cece would've said no immediately, citing a recent article in the *L.A. Times*. Apparently the area was practically ruled by the local gangs who, on weekends, engaged in turf wars with one another. Of course she kept quiet now, because of Jasmine.

"I can just stay at Jasmine's," Max said firmly, as if it was settled. "Since you don't want me coming home late."

The reason Cece had been able to impress Joan with her laid-back attitude about sex was that she didn't believe Max was actually having any. She'd assumed that Jasmine was using Max for whatever advantages he could provide—the swimming pool, the house, perhaps even the black Nissan Pathfinder, which Max had been slated to inherit before the incident with the gun—and that Max was deriving a parallel benefit from having such an obviously desirable girlfriend. The idea of a party followed by a sleepover at the house of Jasmine's older cousin changed things; it was not something Cece was willing to consider.

"We'll talk about it later," Cece said.

Max responded to this discouraging signal by pretending he hadn't heard it.

4.

IT WAS A RELIEF TO STEP INTO THE DARK INTERIOR OF THE HOUSE. EVEN without air-conditioning, their house seemed to regulate itself perfectly. The stucco kept it cool in the summer; in the winter, such as it was, they barely had to use the heat. It had been built in the Spanish style, with a red tile roof and a long balcony across the second floor facing the driveway, grown over with dark pink bougainvillea. There was another balcony off the master bedroom in the back, from which a dressed-up, nine-year-old Olivia had once called out "Romeo," and Maxwell, age seven (misunderstanding but thinking he was being included), had enthusiastically responded: "Polo!"

Max had been too young to understand the difference between the rental in Westwood and the house Cece's inheritance had helped them buy, but Olivia was not.

"Are we rich?" she had asked, one of the first nights Cece had tucked her daughter into bed in her new room.

"We're comfortable," Cece had said. "We don't have to worry, which is nice."

In fact she sometimes wondered whether they hadn't been, literally speaking, more comfortable in the old house. They had occupied the top half of a duplex in Westwood, a two-bedroom apartment that belonged to the university and was reserved for junior faculty. That house had been small, without any special style or luxury, and yet, especially recently, Cece had found herself missing it.

It was the house where they had lived when the children were born, for one thing. It was the house where Gordon had written *Manias and Obsessions,* a book he now described as "immature" but nevertheless the one that had made his reputation and secured his position at the university. Writing it had also seemed to make him happy. Cece had not been working then, and no one had expected her to. When she took Olivia out in the stroller, neighbors would help her up and down the front stairs, which were steep and painted a handsome brick red. It was in that house, up those very stairs, that Gordon's little brother, Phil, had appeared one day out of nowhere, and very soon made it impossible to imagine he hadn't always been a part of their life.

That was in the early fall of 1983. Olivia was two, and Cece was seven months pregnant with Max. It had gotten to the point that she couldn't pick Olivia up, which was inconvenient. They'd been sitting on the beige wall-to-wall carpeting in the living room. She had been crawling after Olivia (getting up was too much effort), who was toddling resolutely away, when the doorbell rang. She remembered feeling embarrassed—a pregnant woman crawling on the floor—although no one could see her. She had hoisted herself up, expecting the UPS man.

The man standing at the door was carrying a dirty green hiking backpack. He had light brown hair and a blondish beard. He was wearing wire-rimmed glasses with tape on one side, a madras plaid shirt, hiking shorts, and a pair of leather sandals. He was very tall and thin. At first she had thought he might be a homeless or a crazy person. ("I *was* homeless and crazy," Phil had said later, when she told him that.) But even after he had showered and shaved, and put on clean clothes, she had not been able to find any resemblance to Gordon. She had looked through the little window in the door, and seen a perfect stranger looking back.

"I'm Phil," he told her. "You must be Cece."

"I don't know you," Cece had said, holding Olivia by the hand.

"I'm Gordon's brother, Phil," he repeated. "I'm sorry not to have called first, but my flight got in too early."

He had brought them awala ponchos, a set of bowls made from stiff, hardened leather, and heavy wool hats it would never be cold enough to wear. He brought alpaca sweaters, and a brightly colored wooden mask of a bear that made Olivia cry.

"The only choice was a bear or the devil," he apologized. "I thought the bear would be better."

Cece had taken the bear away into the kitchen, using it as an excuse to examine Gordon's brother unobserved. (She had once referred to Phil as Gordon's "long-lost brother." Her husband corrected her: "He's not lost. We're just not looking for him.") Standing in the kitchen, she could see that unlike Gordon, Phil was losing his hair on top, that unlike Gordon he had strong, developed muscles in his calves and thighs. The hair on his arms was sun-bleached, and he was wearing two silver rings on his right hand. Gordon refused to wear even a wedding band because he felt that jewelry was feminine; since she'd never had any doubts about Gordon's fidelity, Cece hadn't insisted.

She had noticed that Olivia stayed with her uncle in the dining room even after Cece went into the kitchen, an extremely rare demonstration of trust. She had sat on his lap, and dropped the delicate bowls one by one onto the floor. Phil had picked them up and given them back to her, so that she could throw them on the floor again.

She made Phil a turkey sandwich and a bowl of soup; while he ate, he explained that he had been living with a girlfriend in the Bolivian rain forest. The girlfriend was a biologist writing a dissertation about leaf-cutting ants. She and Phil had lived in the jungle for six months, in a forest camp with Indians. The Indians had been involved in illegal logging, which Phil felt was their prerogative—since the land had been stolen from them in the first place—and which the biologist felt they had a responsibility to report to the local authorities. She and Phil had had a terrific fight, during which Phil had also been suffering from dysentery. When he arrived at their door, he hadn't slept in four nights.

"I don't sleep well either," Cece told him, uncharacteristically. She usually tried not to complain about her insomnia. Nobody liked to hear about someone else's ailments, particularly psychological ones.

"Really?" Phil said, as if it were a terrific coincidence. "When did yours start?"

"It's no big deal," Cece had said, suddenly embarrassed. Then she had insisted that Gordon's brother take a nap in their bed.

When Gordon got home that afternoon, she had put her finger to her lips. He assumed Olivia was napping, and a sudden apprehension kept her from immediately telling him the truth. She waited for him to find Olivia, playing quietly with the bowls on the living room floor, and to notice the filthy backpack, slumped against the wall by the door, a relic from another world.

"Guess who's here?" she said, pretending a certain stupid cheerfulness.

"Who?"

What had she thought—that he would be thrilled? That nothing but geography had kept them apart? That their family would now simply grow by one member, just as easily as Olivia had climbed into the stranger's lap and played with his silver rings?

"Who?" Gordon had demanded, although by then he must've known. She remembered the look he had given her (as if it were her fault) and the way he had turned away from the bedroom, where the door was closed but not tightly shut, and the white noise machine was making its soft, sandy sound.

"It's your brother," she had said. And even after Gordon didn't respond—didn't even change his expression, she was dumb enough to continue in the same excited tone: "Your brother Phil. He came this morning all the way from Bolivia."

5.

AFTER PHIL MOVED TO NEW YORK, NEARLY TEN YEARS AGO NOW, THEY had talked intermittently. He preferred to call her, especially after he moved in with his girlfriend, Aubrey. Cece would have felt funny about dialing Aubrey's number anyway. And so a part of her was always waiting. Sometimes it would be three times in one week, and then months would go by in silence. Recently, there had been a particularly long hiatus, and she had wondered whether their conversations might be finished for good. When he called the other day, it had been the first time in almost nine months.

She had just finished dropping Max and Jasmine at the freeway and doing some errands. Another minute at the drugstore, another red light, and she would've missed him. She had come in the front door holding a bag of prescriptions (Gordon's Lipitor, Max's Serzone, Olivia's erythromycin, her own Ambien, and Ptolemy's insulin), but when Lupe came running from the kitchen, calling "Missis, Missis," she had dropped everything she was carrying. She was always ready for another crisis with Max.

"Merry Christmas," Phil said.

Her relief was so great that, for a moment, she didn't say anything.

"Do you know who this is?"

"It's *August*," said Cece.

"Wrong," said Phil. "Hey, who's August?"

"I meant that you missed Christmas by about nine months."

"I'm a little late. As usual."

There was a pause. There were always long pauses with Philip. At first they were unnerving, and then you got used to them, and then phone conversations with other people started to seem artificial and rushed. Being on the phone was a pleasure for Phil, even apart from talking. Cece suspected he liked the attenuated intimacy of it.

"Where are you?" she asked.

"Well, you're not going to believe it, but . . ."

"Phil!"

"What?"

"You're—are you here?"

"No," said Phil. "I'm in Chinatown. The one in Flushing, not Manhattan: it's more authentic."

In that one second, she had scheduled and prepared herself for a reunion. She was relieved and intensely disappointed at the same time.

"I just came from a film production company," Phil said. "They're going to buy my play."

"Phil, that's wonderful." Outside, the automatic leaf blowers relentlessly whirred.

"It's almost seven figures. They were talking about a 'big summer movie,' whatever that means . . ."

"Phil!"

"That's only if they make it, and they probably won't."

"Don't say that!" Cece said. "I'm so happy for you. You deserve it."

"Well, I'm not sure about that." Phil sighed. "It's a lot of money, though, and I could use it."

"Of course you deserve it," Cece said firmly. "Tell me all about it. Is it a play I've read?"

"No."

"What's it about?"

"It's sort of hard—"

"Tell me the title, at least."

"*The Hypnotist*—but the title might change. Cece, it's so weird. It's great, but I don't feel great."

"You're in shock."

"I don't think that's it."

"No?"

There was a long silence. He was on a payphone; she could hear the line, clicking down their minutes.

"Phil? What is it?"

"Oh Ceece," he said, using an old nickname. "Nothing, I don't know. I think I might be breaking up with Aubrey."

Cece experienced a joyful feeling of déjà vu, like turning on the television and finding an old favorite movie playing. She had been through so many breakups with Phil. She cradled the phone between her shoulder and her ear. "Oh no," she said. "Philip, why?"

Phil didn't say anything.

"Is she there with you?"

"Not right now. No."

Phil's girlfriend was a successful corporate lawyer, of Turkish descent. She had dark, almost black hair and was very thin, because of all her nervous energy. That was the only description Phil had given her, and so it was strange how often Cece seemed to see her. In the supermarket, in a car stopped next to her on the freeway, at the cosmetics counter in Neiman Marcus. Aubrey lived in New York, and was very unlikely to be any of those places. Even if she had been in L.A., how would Cece have recognized her? Yet these pretend Aubreys continued to catch her eye. Often, it seemed that they were also looking back at Cece.

"I feel so far away from her. I don't mean distance."

"I know what you mean."

"Talking to you, for example—it feels like it hasn't been any time at all."

She had not yet told Phil about Max's accident, but the mere possibility of confiding in him was soothing. For the first time since it happened, she felt as if everything might be OK.

"What are you doing in Chinatown?" she asked.

"I'm at the market. In the exotic animal section."

"They have animals at the supermarket?"

"It's an outdoor market. They have everything."

Cece tried to imagine an outdoor market that carried exotic animals, but in her mind, it kept turning into the shops at Century City.

"What are you doing there?"

There was a long pause. "Picking up Fionnula."

"Who?"

"I can't talk about it now."

"Does this have to do with the problems with Aubrey?"

"Totally separate," Phil said.

Cece felt slightly sick, while reminding herself that Phil was free to be involved with a whole brigade of Chinese animal lovers. Was it possible to be a Chinese woman named Fionnula? She thought of telling Phil about the dissident, and decided against it. Suddenly all of the excitement had gone out of the plan.

"Well, I'm sure you'll figure it out."

"I'm not." Phil sighed. "What do I know?"

There was a long pause. "You know the dinosaurs," Cece said.

Phil laughed. She *loved* making him laugh. "That's true," he said. "I do know the dinosaurs."

"Diplodocus?"

"Up to ninety feet long, with a muscular whiplike tail."

"And the seismosaurus?"

"Two hundred thousand pounds: the earth-shaking lizard."

"Pterodactyls."

"The pterodactyls," Phil said solemnly, "had hollow bones."

In the old days, when Phil was still trying to be an actor, working nights at a trendy restaurant on Melrose, they would sometimes take the kids to the La Brea tar pits. Max especially loved the dinosaurs, and Phil had become an expert, going back and forth with his nephew for what seemed like hours: *Did you know that most dinosaurs were birds? Did you know that most dinosaurs were vegetarians?* One of the reasons it was so hard to say "affair" was that it had never been like an ordinary affair; for one thing, it had always involved the children. It had started because of Gordon's book, *Manias and Obsessions*. On the weekends he needed the house to be quiet, and so every Saturday (and nearly every Sunday) she and Philip had taken Max and Olivia on an outing. They had gone to the zoo and the beach and the tar pits. And several times to the Griffith Park Observatory. Philip had been so enthusiastic—running after the children, seeing to their needs, and keeping them entertained—that other women looked at her with envy. No one would have guessed that he wasn't her husband.

"That was *great*," Phil said.

"You knew all of them," said Cece.

"That's because I was an unhappy kid. A sad, fucked-up little kid."

"What does that have to do with it?"

"Sad kids love dinosaurs. Everything else disappoints them."

"What do you mean—everything else?"

"You know," Phil said. "Santa Claus, the tooth fairy, winged monkeys."

"Winged monkeys?"

"Dinosaurs are monsters, but they're real. They're the only ones that pan out."

"I thought it was that they're extinct."

"Sometimes I feel as if I'm extinct," Phil said gloomily.

Something to remember about Phil, when you thought you might be in love with him, was his incredible narcissism. Once she had told him that she had menstrual cramps, and Phil had said: Sometimes I feel as if *I* have menstrual cramps.

"New York is like an enormous tar pit," Phil was saying. "Full of dinosaurs. They come here, and then they never leave."

"Especially the whinosaurus," Cece said. "I bet there's a surplus of those."

"They have to shoot us to keep the population down," Phil said. "But at least we don't have the sarcastosaurus."

"At least we don't have the jerkosaurus."

"Bitcherotops."

"Misogynosaurus."

"Cece?"

"Yes."

"I adore you."

"No you don't."

"When you're around, I'm the adorosaurus."

You were annoyed, and then he said something like that.

"I—"

"It's OK," Phil said. "Because the adorosaurus is extinct."

There was the sound of Gordon's car in the driveway—a sporty, cherry red Cadillac Allante—his "midlife crisis car." Gordon wasn't having enough of a crisis to buy a German or Italian car.

"Phil?"

She heard the kitchen door slam, and then Gordon saying something to Lupe.

"I have to tell you something."

"Hello?" Gordon called from the kitchen.

"Max—"

She had never said it clearly before. She had said: *Max bought a gun.* And even: *Max was caught driving with a gun.* But she had never said, "My son Max bought a gun because he was thinking of ending his life."

"Cece?" Gordon said, from the dining room.

"Cece?" Phil said, from the rare animal market in Chinatown.

"He told the police he wanted to kill himself." There was a silence at the other end of the line. Somehow that helped her continue. "He bought a gun. He told us it was for his comic books—did you know he draws comic books? But then when they stopped him, he said—"

Gordon's voice interrupted on the general intercom: "Anybody home?"

"If they hadn't stopped him—"

"Oh, Ceece."

Gordon knocked once and opened the door. "There you are. I brought the mail."

"Do you want me to come there?" Phil asked.

"Mostly junk," Gordon said.

"I could get on a plane tonight."

"Here's Gordon," said Cece.

"Who is that?" Gordon asked.

"Well," said Phil. "I guess not then."

"Is that—"

"I love you," Phil said. "Good-bye."

The line took a moment to disengage.

"It was your brother," Cece said.

"Is he still there?"

"I didn't think you would want to talk to him."

"You were right," Gordon said. He was staring at her. She put the phone back in the cradle.

"He says to say hello."

Gordon did not question this obvious lie.

"We just chatted for a few minutes." Something kept her from telling him Phil's big news. Maybe it was just that she was used to defending Phil to Gordon; her impulse was to try to evoke his pity. "He's been going through a hard time lately," she said.

Gordon put on an expression of exaggerated surprise. "How is Phil having a hard time?"

"He's having a midlife crisis."

"Phil is having a *lifelong* crisis. He just happens to have gotten to the middle of it."

"Gordon, I'm serious."

"So am I," Gordon said. "Don't you have to have arrived at midlife, before you start your crisis?"

"Phil's forty-five."

"Technically, yes." Gordon dropped the mail on her desk. "A midlife crisis usually entails the consideration of one's responsibilities—those one has met as well as failed to meet."

Cece wished Gordon would not use the pronoun "one." It made her feel itchy.

"With regard to one's children, for example. Finances. Career. Marriage. As I understand it: a person confronting the specter of what is yet to be done." Gordon looked past her, out the window at the driveway. "Aren't those leaf blowers illegal now?"

"I think so," Cece said. "They're supposed to be very bad for the air." She felt slightly guilty, as if she'd betrayed Phil. Which was ridiculous. If there was anything she should feel guilty about, it was talking to Phil at all.

"I'll say something," Gordon said. He started out of the room.

"Gordon?"

"Yes?" He turned back, blinking his eyes behind his glasses.

"How are you?"

"I'm fine," Gordon said patiently. "How are you?"

"I'm fine, too."

He nodded, and put his hand on the doorknob.

"Gordon?"

"*Yes?*"

She knew she was annoying him, but she couldn't stand for him to leave the room. There was a conversation she knew they had to have; she just didn't know how to start it.

"Why do children like dinosaurs?" Cece asked. "Did you ever read about that?"

Her husband visibly relaxed. "Not that I remember," he said. "But it's logical. Children are fascinated by dinosaurs because dinosaurs are manifestations of their fears."

"Oh," said Cece.

"And yet they're extinct—they can't hurt them. By learning the names of the dinosaurs, children feel that they control their fears."

"That's what I thought," Cece said.

6.

AS SHE SAT IN OLIVIA'S BEDROOM, IMMACULATE AND READY FOR HER daughter's homecoming, Cece thought that her longing for the old house was more than simple nostalgia. There had been something about living in a rental that had made the future seem open and indeterminate. Then her father had died, and their financial worries had ended. *Manias and Obsessions* had been published, to great acclaim, and Phil had moved to Manhattan. She and Gordon had looked around for six months, and finally found this house on Mountain Drive; all at once, without warning, everything had become permanently, irrevocably fixed.

There was the sound of a car outside, and a rhythmic drumming; when Cece looked out Olivia's window, she could see an old brown Chevy sedan, with the finish worn off but the hubcaps and tires replaced. She wondered if that was the cousin from Echo Park. The driver honked gently three times.

Max and Jasmine were standing together at the top of the driveway. She could hear her son's voice, but not what he was saying. All of a sudden, he leaned in and kissed Jasmine. It wasn't a long or particularly passionate kiss, two dark heads bumping together for just a few seconds, but Cece took a step back from the window. She felt strangely childlike, startled by something she'd heard of but never seen.

A moment later, Jasmine was tripping down the driveway in her high-heeled sandals. When she opened the car door, loud music overwhelmed the quiet street. Then the door slammed, and the sound was only a heartbeat again. It was one of those uneven days, weather-wise; when the sun was out, it was hot, but clouds kept passing in front of the sun. The four trees Felipe had planted along the driveway had bloomed yellow, and the tiny flowers shivered in a light breeze.

A moment later Cece heard Max's not-delicate tread on the stairs. She turned away from the window, but when he saw her in his sister's room, he stopped. Cece felt the urge to defend herself.

"I was just making sure everything was ready for Olivia."

Max looked around the room as if he were assessing her work. He glanced at the ceiling, and then down at his sneakers. He put his hands in his pocket, took them out again, licked his lips, and said: "I think it's hard for Jasmine."

The confidence was so unexpected that, for a moment, Cece didn't respond. She had the urge to stay absolutely still, as if a rare bird had flown into the house and perched on the bedpost right in front of her.

"Because Carlos can't always drive her," Max continued. "When he can't drive her, she can't go paint."

"Was that Carlos?" Cece asked carefully.

"Yeah."

"Couldn't one of her parents drive her?"

"They're at work," Max said. "And anyway, she usually stays with Carlos. She doesn't really like her stepfather."

"Why?"

Max shrugged. "He makes her uncomfortable."

"Uncomfortable, how?"

"I don't know."

"Well, but I mean she must've said—" But Cece didn't want to push it.

"Carlos takes care of her," Max said. "He's working so Jasmine can go to college."

"Why not her father, or her stepfather?"

"Her father's in El Salvador. She hasn't seen him since she was a baby. And her stepfather . . ." Max shrugged.

"Well, thank goodness she has her cousin," Cece said.

Max nodded. "That's why we have to go to his birthday."

Cece was disappointed: was this whole conversation about a party? Or was it possible that the party was an excuse, that Max wanted to share with his mother the disturbing things Jasmine had told him? Cece looked at Max, who had taken the Raiders cap off his head and was crushing it in his hands.

"Max," she said. "I hope you've told Jasmine she can always come here."

Max looked at his sneakers, which were some sort of futuristic new thing, without a tongue or laces. "Yeah."

"Any time of the day or night, she should feel free to call. And if it's that she can't get to the freeway, we could even pick her up at home."

"Yeah."

"It's only about twenty minutes out of the way, and the traffic isn't bad by that time—"

But by that time, Max was already halfway down the hall to his room.

7.

THE LAST TIME I SAW MEILING, SHE WAS LIVING ALONE IN A SMALL
apartment in the hutongs between the Drum Tower and the Bell Tower.
This was in the early spring of 2000, and I was staying at my cousin's studio in the Factory at Dashanzi. At that time X both lived and worked in
his studio, a brick and concrete industrial space without heat or running
water. That suited my cousin, then. Although it wasn't comfortable (the
toilet and antique communal shower were in another building), the arrangement allowed me to stay for several weeks in Beijing while I finalized
the details of my trip. My cousin had helped me organize everything with
Harry Lin, the professor who had once come all the way from America to
see our work in the East Village.

I would leave from Shanghai in August, just before the start of the
American school year. In Los Angeles, I would be a visiting scholar at the
St. Anselm's School for Girls, and live with one of that institution's most
committed families: "patrons of the arts," who were delighted to have the
opportunity to host me for the year. I would also receive a small stipend
from UCLA, through a fund called the Dubin Fellowship, which "encouraged artists to cross borders and challenge their thinking as they engaged
with artists of other cultures and disciplines." In return, I would present
one solo show of oil paintings (paintings that had already been shown at
TFAM in Taipei, but which would be new to an American audience) and
another of new work in the spring. At that time I would also give a lecture,
in which I would place my project "in the context of Chinese contemporary art and the development of freedom of expression."

"Longxia Shanren will have to come out of his shell," my cousin joked.

He had always teased me about being a hermit, a mountain man like my favorite Song painter, Zhao Cangyun. Zhao Cangyun was called "Cangyun Shanren" (Gathering Clouds Mountain Man) for his habit of wandering the Anhui hills, and I became "Longxia Shanren" (the Lobster Hermit), after the childish paintings I'd once shown my cousin in Harbin, as well as a tendency to get red in the face when I drank.

"You'll want to bring some Chinese clothes," X suggested. "For meeting important people. They love that in Los Angeles."

"Like yours, you mean?" My cousin was fond of silk pajamas, which he often wore for interviews with the press. I couldn't picture myself in that kind of getup, strolling around Los Angeles like some sort of Ming courtier.

"I think you can handle the big university VIPs," he continued. "It's all those teenage girls I'm worried about."

"What will I teach them?" I asked, trying to get him to be serious for a moment. But my cousin was characteristically unconcerned with practical details. According to X, I would be an ambassador for all the artists we knew—especially those of us who'd been displaced when the East Village broke up, and were now living as far away as Xian, Ürümqi, and Inner Mongolia. There was nothing more important, X began; then he got a silly, infuriating expression on his face.

"You'll be taking the old work with you," he said, indicating the canvases stacked against the walls of the studio, which I had just retrieved from a storage facility near the You Yi Shopping City. "But maybe you'll be bringing some new work back. I'm so eager to see what the painter-in-exile will produce."

He was reminding us both of my long period of inaction, during which I had been working a comfortable job at my father's office in Shanghai. I couldn't deny it, but I thought it was unfair of him, of all people, to bring it up.

"It's not an exile," I said. "I'm choosing to go."

"In pseudo-exile," X agreed. "Even more interesting."

"Why don't you go be an ambassador yourself?" I demanded.

The question had the effect I'd intended. X shrugged and mumbled something, turning away from me.

"What?"

"Harry Lin wants you," X said impatiently. "He's seen your work—*Drip-Drop*, for example."

"That was a collaboration, if you remember," I said. "And does he know what I've been doing since?"

X waved that away. "An artist is an artist, no matter what he's doing."

I didn't believe that. In fact, I believed the opposite: an artist is someone who's making art, and I had not done anything more than pencil sketches for the past five years.

"What about when he comes to see my work?" I asked.

"He won't do that before the show," X said.

I didn't see how my cousin could be sure of that. "Won't he want to introduce himself?"

"Trust me," X said. "He's going to give you 'space' to complete your project."

"That's what I'm worried about," I said. "Completing a project."

"And you speak English," X continued, as if I hadn't spoken. "Think of how valuable that will be."

"There are translators. Harry could translate for you himself."

"Americans don't have the patience to listen to translators," my cousin said.

I couldn't understand it. Publicly X had always said, "Keep Chinese art in China"—a slogan the foreign journalists particularly liked—but even my cousin knew that in order to become really famous, you had to show abroad. I was sure that was why he'd gotten in touch with Harry Lin in the first place, and inquired about the Dubin Fellowship. Why wasn't he envious now?

"You'll go," X said, "and then you'll tell me about it. That way we can"—he switched to English—"have our cake and eat it."

"Too," I corrected.

"That's right," X agreed. "Two cakes, one for each of us. You'll go, and I'll get to hear all about it."

We were standing at the big worktable in the middle of the studio, and my cousin wasn't looking at me. He was helping me choose the work I would take on my journey, holding a sheet of slides to the light and frowning. I could see that most of the film on this sheet had been exposed, but X continued looking at the slides, as if there was something hidden there—and all of a sudden I understood that my cousin was afraid. X, who had come from Shanxi with two hundred yuan in his pocket, who had cut, burned, and frozen various parts of his body in the name of art, and now lived in an abandoned factory for the same dubious reason, did not want to leave Beijing. He did not want to fly seventeen hours across the ocean, or live as the guest of strangers. He did not want to shake hands and smile while people discussed his work in a language he couldn't understand.

I had admired X's individuality, his integrity, and his passion for so long that his fear, apparent in the gallery that afternoon, was a revelation. It startled me, although perhaps it shouldn't have. A lot of people are afraid to travel. There is the discomfort, the strange food, the inevitable failures of plans. There is the fear of flying, and the possibility of getting lost. It helps to have a talent for making oneself agreeable to strangers, something that has always come easily to me. I see what people want, and I give it to them. Maybe that's a bad quality; in any case, it isn't one my cousin has ever shared.

8.

I HAD COME TO STAY WITH X IN BEIJING AFTER A THREE-YEAR ABSENCE, without knowing what my plans were regarding Meiling. My cousin and I didn't talk about romantic matters, but the thought of my ex-girlfriend was always in the back of my mind. I didn't do anything to engineer a meeting, which I both hoped for and feared; rather, I imagined it might simply happen. We were circling one another, and one day we would come together like magnets, naturally and inevitably. I didn't think of what would happen after that.

On the last day before I was scheduled to return to Shanghai, I visited a new gallery near the Workers' Stadium. When I returned, my cousin was still out. I was leafing through a pile of miscellaneous cards on his worktable when I came upon a red postcard. On the front of the postcard was a photo I recognized; I picked it up and examined it, as if I might have made a mistake. But it was certainly her. She was standing next to a model in a white, Western-style wedding dress, but Meiling didn't suffer by comparison. She wore her hair in two neat plaits, a style that contrasted with her tailored army jacket (not PLA surplus, but a knockoff she'd designed herself) and her knee-high black leather boots. On top of the photo was the company's logo, a design that incorporated her initials in English and Chinese.

I was still holding the postcard when my cousin came in the door behind me. He saw the card in my hand.

"Have you seen that yet?" he asked casually.

I shook my head.

He laughed. "Professional, right? She was always a businesswoman."

"Are you in touch with her?"

"Some," my cousin said. "Not much."

"She lives with someone?"

X shook his head. "Alone. Near the Bell Tower." He hesitated for a moment: "Will you go and see her?"

"No."

"She'll be sorry," he said. "I know she wanted you to come."

He turned away as he said it, giving me my privacy. He must've known it was the very thing I'd come to Beijing hoping to hear. Still, the thought of Meiling and my cousin discussing me together—wondering whether I would have the courage to visit her—was painful and humiliating, and I didn't want X to know I was already considering the possibility.

"I know she'll be around tomorrow morning," my cousin said. "The address is on that card."

"I won't have time before my flight," I told my cousin—a pretense that deceived neither of us. My flight wasn't until the afternoon, and there was nothing special I was returning to in Shanghai anyway.

"Take that just in case," my cousin said, indicating the postcard. "I have too many of them."

This was in March, and Beijing was cold and windy, as if winter and spring had combined in their worst aspects. Nevertheless, the following morning I found myself biking east from the Factory, toward Houhai. I had thought that the ride would be invigorating, and prepare me for a difficult meeting, but as I rode east I got colder and colder, so I was almost tempted to turn back. By the time I reached Meiling's lane, I was shivering, and my stomach was uneasy. These physical ailments were at least a distraction from what was ahead of me: my thoughts felt frozen, locked up and inaccessible, as if I were one of the ice sculptures at the famous festival held every winter in my hometown.

I let my feet take me down the lane, following a jog in the path, past a tiny hutong shop selling ice cream and telephone cards, to her building. I could see what had attracted her to this house right away: the entrance was made in the traditional way, with two overlapping walls forming an S shape, so that a visitor was unable to see inside from the street. I could hear my own pulse as I stepped around the second wall, but the courtyard was empty. There were some loose, cracked concrete paving stones, a plastic laundry line, and some plants along the wall, huddled in their red clay pots. The staircase was dark, but some lights were coming from the apartments on the second floor. I could hear a pair of female voices, although I couldn't make out what they were saying.

I climbed the stairs in the same numb way I had turned in to the lane; I felt insubstantial, as if someone coming down the stairs in the other direction wouldn't see me, would pass right through me like a ghost. On the landing I stopped and listened: the voices had also stopped, replaced by a CCTV news anchor: *"Scientists are planning to investigate a lake in the Xinjiang Uigur Autonomous Region, where local farmers have reported sightings of an aquatic monster. Could China challenge Scotland with its own homegrown 'Nessy'?"* This information was coming from apartment two, and Meiling was in number three. I knocked tentatively; a woman's voice (not hers) called out:

"Come in, come in!"

At first I didn't see anyone in the room; then I heard, quite literally, a pin drop. I looked up: the most glamorous young woman I had ever seen was staring down from the landing of a steep flight of wooden stairs, an "international-type" beauty, tall and imperious, with large eyes and long, gangly limbs. She was wearing a white jacket with epaulets, and slim, midnight blue pants. Kneeling at her feet was a figure all in black, her hair in a knot on top of her head, her mouth full of straight pins. I stared at that tall, beautiful girl the way you might stare at anything—a newspaper, a map, or your watch—to avoid making eye contact with a stranger.

Meiling, on the other hand, looked right at me, until I had to look back. She couldn't smile (her mouth was full of pins), but she nodded briskly. She put another pin in the hem of the model's slacks and then removed the rest of them from her mouth.

"Take a rest," she told the girl, who jogged down the steps and brushed past me with the smile of the very beautiful, who imagine their every glance to be a kind of largesse. I had no eyes for her. But neither could I look at Meiling, who was coming down the steps slowly, supporting herself on the railing. At that time it had been almost three years since I'd seen her, and the shock of being in her presence was such that I didn't notice the most important change in my old lover until she was standing right in front of me.

"You're—" But there was no need to state the obvious.

Meiling laughed. "People told me you were in town. I didn't think you would come, but when I heard someone in the corridor, I knew it was you. Will you have some beer? Someone brought it, but I won't drink it. Or some tea?"

She was wearing a loose black dress and a man's white linen shirt with the sleeves rolled up, but even this modest clothing couldn't conceal the fact that Meiling was going to have a baby. Why hadn't my cousin told me?

"Or lychees?" Meiling suggested. "I'd like some lychees myself."

"All right," I said. "Anything is fine."

Meiling laughed gently. "Sit down, have a rest. Get ready for your big journey."

"I'm not leaving until August," I told her, but I sat down obediently. While Meiling got the fruit, I looked around the room: there was a pair of pink plastic slippers outside the bathroom door, lined up perfectly along with sneakers and several pairs of the traditional cloth shoes she liked to use on her models. An intricate Tibetan rug, turquoise, red, and green, decorated the floor, which was the same polished wood as the table. On the wall above the table was a small photograph of Meiling's grandparents, in a gold frame hanging from a red plush ribbon.

Of course I wondered about the baby's father. But my cousin had said that Meiling was living on her own, and there was nothing in the apartment to indicate otherwise. In fact the extreme neatness of the room was characteristic of her; although the outside of the building was decrepit, and the common spaces ill cared for, Meiling seemed to take pleasure in reversing that entropy here. The one thing that surprised me was a pack of Red River cigarettes on the table next to my left elbow; although everyone had smoked in the East Village, Meiling had always said the habit was disgusting. I credited her with the fact that I'd never taken it up.

"I can't believe you smoke now," I said to Meiling's rear end, which was facing me as she rummaged in the cabinet for a plate.

"They're the model's," Meiling said, straightening up and looking at the girl, whom I could see standing on the roof, staring out toward Yong-hegong, her arms crossed over her chest. "Isn't she lovely?"

I made a face: you could see that my response pleased Meiling. There's a funny kind of camaraderie between women and the men they've dropped. Perhaps because I wasn't threatening, she allowed herself to talk intimately with me—not only as if we had been speaking every day, but almost as if we were still together. It was flirtatious, and at the same time the very purpose of the flirtation seemed to be a warning, that whatever had been alive between us was now quite dead.

Meiling came and sat in the chair opposite mine: "Are you nervous?"

I was fantastically nervous, but not about my trip. I felt as if I were onstage or in a difficult exam; my mind seemed to have flown out my ear like a sparrow, and escaped through one of the kitchen casements. In its place was a small hole and an empty, buzzing sound.

"Yes," I said.

"What you're doing makes everything possible. People here are still making their projects—blowing bubbles and howling." Her scornful tone pleased me, and I didn't remind her that not so long ago in the East Village, she had applauded those same projects: the fish-frying, the bubble-blowing, and the collective primal screams. Some of these performances we called art; others were just pranks; but we noticed that the critics often couldn't tell the difference, and sometimes I wondered whether we knew ourselves.

"People have seen these things already," Meiling said. "And who cares about a performance nobody sees? What you're doing, on the other hand . . ." She gave me a smile so radiant that I hardly noticed how her voice trailed off. Like my cousin, Meiling was vague on what I would actually be doing in America.

I looked at the poster above her head, from the late 1960s, when my grandfather was breaking rocks in Heilongjiang. It was now a fashionable collector's item. The poster showed a boy and a girl in red neckerchiefs holding hands: the boy is launching a toy rocket, while the girl waters a hole in the dirt next to a tiny potted sapling. Perhaps it was the factory smokestacks in the background, or the lavender color the artist had chosen for the sky, but there was something unnatural and sinister about the image (undoubtedly why Meiling liked it). Underneath the children, a caption read: "Revolution Improves Productivity."

Meiling sighed: "Sometimes this place is like a pigeon coop." I couldn't tell if she was talking about her apartment, or Beijing, or all of China. "You're lucky to be going away."

"Come with me."

She laughed, and glanced down at her belly.

"I'm serious. How are you going to do it alone?"

"My mother will help." Meiling sounded casual, but I thought I heard a false note, a crack in her confidence.

"For how long?"

She shrugged. "It'll be all right."

"I could take care of you," I said.

Meiling half-smiled and shook her head. "Why are you so nice to me?"

The answer to that question was fairly obvious.

Meiling blushed, and tried to turn it into a joke: "A pregnant woman traveling with you . . . that'll help with your visa application for sure."

She picked up the cigarettes and turned them around in her hands, frowning at the label. Was she considering my suggestion? Suddenly I thought everything might change; the present seemed to crack open, revealing a potential future I had barely allowed myself to imagine. It's funny that in this moment I didn't think of the baby's father—who certainly did exist somewhere, even if he was no longer part of her life.

"He could be an American citizen," I said.

"How do you know it's a boy?"

Then, without thinking, I did something that surprised us both. I reached out my hand and put it on Meiling's round, black stomach. The skin there felt tight, the flesh of an unripe fruit.

Meiling sat still for a moment, tolerating me, but her expression changed. She stood up from the table.

"I'm sorry." But I wasn't. I was glad to see that playful ease drop away, even for a second.

The model stuck her head in the door. "Miss Xu?"

"Come in, come in. What are you waiting for?"

Meiling turned to me, composed again. "The fact that you would do this for us . . ."

For *us*. The collective pronoun startled me, and I looked up, as if there were someone else in the room I had missed until now.

"For everyone, I mean. Not just East Village artists, but all young Chinese artists. You'll be part of a whole international *movement*."

There was a new glibness in Meiling's voice; this kind of rhetoric was uncharacteristic of her. She'd always been suspicious of groups, even of our East Village, and I knew she didn't believe in the idea of artistic "movements."

"This is the Chinese century," Meiling said. "Everybody says so."

If it was really the Chinese century, I wondered why I had to go abroad. But I didn't say that to Meiling. If she was encouraging me to go to America, then I had my answer. My ex-girlfriend might remember me sometimes with nostalgia, but her feelings were no more than that. How could I have imagined otherwise?

"Thank you," I said, and Meiling smiled. She thought I was responding to her flattery: that I really believed in myself as an ambassador of Chinese art.

"This could be the beginning of something big for you," she told me.

"Yes," I said. At least I knew it was the end of something else.

9.

A RECURRING TROPE IN THE LANDSCAPES OF THE OLD MASTERS IS THE passageway between this world and the other. In the Zhao Cangyun scroll *Liu Chen and Ruan Zhao in the Tiantai Mountains,* the border is a stream the two pilgrims wade across to meet the immortal ladies on the other side. In paintings like Zhang Feng's *Stone Bridge,* it's a rocky arch the pilgrim comes to suddenly on a mountain path. Sometimes, like Liu Chen and Ruan Zhao, you pass through easily, but cannot return. Other times, like Zhang Feng's solitary pilgrim, you stay on the bridge, locked in place, unable to go either forward or back.

I thought of this arch as I stood by the gate of the American consulate on Wulumuqi Nan Lu, in a long line of applicants. Everyone had warned me to get to the consulate early, and I'd had only a glass of tea before leaving the apartment. By the time I reached the striped sentry platforms, with their two stone-faced guards, my stomach was growling. It was not only hunger I felt, but a kind of anxiety, similar to stage fright. My cousin had promised that there would be no problems. I would simply explain that I had been working in the Shanghai office of Ditian Petroleum for nearly three years, and that I wanted to perfect my English, my greatest contribution to the company. In exchange, I was happy to share with the American students some of the glories of the Chinese landscape tradition, which I had studied with a master painter as a child.

I arrived at the consulate with my passport, the receipt of my CITIC application fee, and my forms (DS-2019 and DS-156-158) neatly completed in English and Chinese. I had a letter from my father, president and CEO of Ditian Petroleum, and one from my painting professor at Beijing

Normal, who spoke of my mastery of traditional technique. Just to be safe, I also had brought along my old portfolio—a body of work that had not been updated for some time. More important was the letter Professor Harry Lin had sent from Los Angeles, verifying my invitation from the St. Anselm's School for Girls, and offering the stipend I would receive from UCLA as proof that I possessed sufficient funds to complete my stay in Los Angeles. I had wanted to see those letters, to be sure that all of the information was correct, but my cousin told me to relax; he had checked the paperwork himself before forwarding it on to the consulate.

In addition to my qualifications, there was the evidence of my parents' apartment, our car, and the fact that I was an only son with a profitable career ahead of me. I had no relatives in the United States, and would be staying with strangers. There had been some question of applying for the "O" visa: Nonimmigrant Temporary Worker of Distinguished Merit, but my cousin and I had judged that needlessly complicated. I was a natural as a J-1 Exchange Visitor, and so we would aim for that.

After nearly four hours, I was admitted to the courtyard, where I joined the "pre-screening" line. These days the U.S. visa section is located in the five-star Portman Ritz-Carlton Hotel complex, but at that time they were still operating out of the old consulate, a beautiful walled house that had belonged to the last Qing finance minister. Ginkgo trees cast lazy shadows; outside the canteen, a small stone bridge spanned an artificial pool, stocked with frogs and lotuses. It was almost lunchtime, and the American employees strolled casually in that direction, as if they had nothing particular to do. Those of us in the visa line watched their progress. Someone had told me that the visa windows were actually in the Qing minister's former stables; I thought of a joke about the officers "stalling for time," but I did not think my compatriots in line would understand it.

Finally I reached the pre-screening window, where a young Chinese consular employee—hiding a bad case of acne behind a curtain of hair—looked over my documents, stamped my forms, and sent me to the second window, where I had to wait again. Outside I noticed people had been chatting and joking with each other, but in here everyone was silent, as if we were students in an examination where only a certain number of passing marks would be awarded. One man had what looked like a photo album under his arm, to demonstrate "strong ties" to his family, and the girl standing behind me in line was carrying a violin case, as if she might at any moment take out her instrument and begin to serenade the officer.

For his part, the visa officer looked uncomfortable behind his plastic partition. As I got closer, I could see him more clearly. He had sparse, fair hair, more colorless than yellow, and the kind of skin that suggested he didn't spend very much time outside. His manner was very serious, but there was something funny about it too: his expression made me wonder how long he had been in Shanghai and whether his more experienced colleagues liked to tease him. I had the feeling he was younger than he looked, especially when he motioned for me to step forward to the window and pass my documents through the partition.

"Hello," he said, glancing at me sharply, as if he knew what I'd been thinking. "Would you start by telling me who will sponsor your stay in Los Angeles?"

"I will be co-sponsored, by the St. Anselm's School for Girls, and Professor Harry Lin of UCLA."

"Will you be staying with the professor?"

"No. I'll stay with a family called Travers, whose child attends the school where I'll be teaching."

The visa officer seemed to relax slightly. "You speak English very well," he said. "Where did you learn it?"

"My mother was an English teacher."

The officer looked at his screen. I wondered how much information he had about my background, my mother's exotic history and my grandfather's death in detention. Whatever he knew, he didn't seem to want to discuss it with me, and I didn't blame him. I myself had never liked to hear about how my mother's father, who suffered from a congenital weakness in his lungs, had perished laboring in the frozen fields north of Harbin—where the air is so cold it hurts to breathe—or about my father's family, boiling grass to make soup during the famine of '58. As a child I had rebelled instinctively against those stories, which seemed to me a way of letting ghosts into our house.

"You're currently working for your father—is that correct?"

"Yes."

"At his office here in Shanghai."

"It's in the Shartex Plaza."

The visa officer sifted through my documents and extracted one, I couldn't tell which. "Excuse me for a moment," he said, getting up from his desk. He disappeared through a door the same color as the wall behind him, and I was left listening to the murmur of the officers and applicants on either side of me, who kept their voices hushed, as if they were conducting secret transactions. A wall clock ticked loud seconds. I wondered if there was something in my past that neither my cousin nor Professor Harry Lin had anticipated, which would prevent me from making this journey after all.

I don't remember when I first learned that my mother had been detained; it was something that seemed obvious in retrospect, one of those things you both know and don't know at the same time. My mother never had to remind me not to talk about it outside the house; I was conscious as a child of the fact that we were being watched, by our neighbors, the leaders of my mother's work unit, my teachers at school. It wasn't the malevolent kind of watching so much as the stern "for your own good" kind. People thought they could understand our family just by looking at it: my father was a rising star in the Party, who could never have hoped to win a woman like my mother without his newfound connections, and my mother was an elite intellectual, who had sacrificed her dignity so that her child would never suffer the way she had.

In spite of all that, I know my parents' marriage was not one of convenience. I can tell because of how disappointed the two of them are now. My mother must have thought that her sacrifice would be rewarded by the kind of love you read about in English poems; my father, when he saw that he couldn't make my mother happy—no matter what promotions he received, or what material comforts he could provide—sank into a kind of chronic, low-level depression. In some unhappy marriages I've heard the child is ignored, but in my case, it was the reverse. Both of my parents watched me with the intensity of a pair of gamblers, waiting with clenched hands to see whether I might find the satisfactions that had eluded them.

For much of my childhood, my father lived in the workers' compound at Daqing, while my mother and I stayed in Harbin. During that time, I refused to admit I hardly knew my father. I often lied to my classmates, making up stories whose purpose was not to cover up the truth so much as to get away from it for a little while. For example: my father had been sent on a secret mission to Moscow, where he was getting technology secrets from Chairman Andropov, unknown in the West, which would allow China to triple its oil production within five years. My father was working with a team of scientists to refine a specialized jet fuel for use in the first Chinese spaceship to the moon. I once told a new student that my father had died in an oil well, where he was drilling deeper into the earth than anyone had previously ventured. I remember promising myself that I would tell this boy the truth, once I was sure he believed me. I left him by the Ping-Pong tables, with the image of my father's hand disappearing slowly under the bubbling black liquid. I then forgot about the story, until the new boy told the others, and someone who knew my situation reported me to the teacher.

"How could you not be proud of your father, when the whole of China looks to Daqing?" my teacher demanded. "What kind of person makes up lies, when the truth is so glorious?"

I was sent to think about these questions while I cleaned the lavatories; worse than the punishment was something else my teacher told me, quietly, when the other students had dispersed: "Don't you know that lies like that can come true, if somebody says them out loud?"

That night I thought of things I might carelessly have said, and forgotten. My father, on one of our visits to the compound at Daqing, had given me two plastic soldiers, one red and one white; sometimes, before they set upon each other with brutal ferocity, I allowed them to engage in a bit of pre-combat dialogue. Had the things I said while I held these soldiers—a PLA infantryman and a Japanese officer, who threatened each other with methods of torture I had learned about in school—become true without my knowing it? Would someone somewhere have his fingers crushed, his skin branded, or his eyes cut out, because I snarled these horrors in the voices of my soldiers? Would my father decide to take a nighttime walk, trip, slide, and be sucked down between the giant iron birds, kowtowing to one another in the freezing field?

The visa officer came back through the unmarked door and sat down in front of me. He picked up the letter from Professor Sui at Beijing Normal and frowned at it.

"It says here that painting was only your minor in college. Why do you think this American school invited you?"

This was a question I hadn't prepared for, and my hesitation must've shown on my face. The officer's momentary friendliness slipped away; he seemed to be taking pleasure in my nervousness.

"Someone must have recommended me?" It sounded as if I were begging. I thought of my cousin and how he would've handled this situation, with only his few phrases of English. Of course, my cousin had not put himself in a position to find out.

"I have friends who—" But I didn't want to mention X or any of our friends in Beijing. I had the feeling that I was in a dream, in which a child in adult clothing had suddenly assumed complete power over me.

The visa officer waited.

"I think they must've thought of me because of my experience with traditional technique," I said. "I studied with a well-known painter as a child, specializing in landscapes. If you'd like to see some of my work, I have . . ."

But the officer was shaking his head, as if he'd already gotten what he wanted. "You can go to window number seven, now," he told me. "They'll stamp your passport with the visa."

Clearly he expected me to thank him, but somehow those words stuck in my throat. He watched me struggle for a moment, and then looked past me impatiently to the next applicant, the girl with the violin. As I turned toward the final window, this very young girl glanced at me; I was surprised to see a shadow of envy and distaste in her clear black eyes, as if I had somehow obtained this piece of good fortune unfairly, through no particular gift of my own.

As a child, I had a fantasy about disappointing my parents, who had always done everything for me. One day, I thought, I would stop doing my homework, or purposely fail my college entrance exam. Even once I was a student at Beijing Normal, I would sometimes cut my classes, walk out to the plaza with the fountain (which they filled in winter, to make a skating rink). I would sit on the edge of the fountain and imagine going farther, getting on a train to Ürümqi, Kashgar, Lhasa—I didn't care where. I would stare at the faces in the crowd going past outside the gate. Their quick movements seemed guided by some inner purpose, in contrast to my own inertia. Those on foot or bicycle would glance in at the elite campus as they went past, thinking, perhaps, of their own sons and daughters, and yet none made eye contact with me. Our mutual envy was misinformed, and willfully so: we didn't want to know the truth about each others' situations. We wanted to imagine that paradise existed just outside the gates of our own lives.

That evening, my mother cooked a celebratory dinner, and my father got out an atlas with a map of the United States, to pinpoint the exact location of Los Angeles, California. I found his questions and my mother's enthusiasm oppressive, and after dinner I told them I was going out. I wandered for almost half an hour, not sure of where I was going, and eventually found an anonymous, smoked-filled public call shop, populated by teenagers hunched over antiquated computers. Because X believed our phone lines were never entirely secure, we spoke in an amateurish kind of code—certainly something the authorities could have figured out, if they were in fact listening. But this type of theatrical secrecy was typical of my cousin.

"How is the new painting?" he asked me.

"It's coming along."

"I mean, today in particular. No snags?"

"I'm starting to think the whole project is too ambitious," I told him. "Maybe it wasn't such a good idea in the first place."

"Oh, it's good," X said. "Trust me. You can't see it yourself, because you're standing too close to the canvas."

My departure date was set for the fifteenth of August. In the intervening months, during which I obsessively visited my favorite spots in Shanghai— the museum, the Jing'An Si, and the bar at the J. W. Marriott hotel—I never quite believed that I was going. Even once I was at the airport, I was waiting to be stopped by a customs official, or one of the doctors who can quarantine a passenger at the last minute and keep him back for examination. On the plane, my anxiety did not abate: I thought I would be apprehended as soon as I disembarked in Los Angeles, by a conscientious team of ground crew, customs officials, and police, who would put me on a plane right back to Shanghai.

If it still seems unbelievable that all of these people would support me, given the name I had established for myself, and that I would be allowed to leave the country on any premise, given my political history, I would ask you to suspend your disbelief a little longer, so that I might tell my story in order, not chronologically, but as it falls out of my memory, through my fingers, and into this laptop computer. The computer—manufactured by the American company Dell but made in China—was a gift from Cece Travers, who noticed how much of the time I was supposed to be painting I actually spent filling up yellow legal pads. I used my own language at first, in case anyone found my diary; but once I had the computer, I thought I might try writing in English.

"Does this have to do with your project?" Cece asked me kindly, when she found me poking at the American keyboard, one-fingered, my horsehair brushes languishing soft and unused in the spectacular studio she had prepared for me.

I explained to Cece that I was planning a special project, something different from all of my previous work, which would include text as well as images. Of course that was another fabrication. In order to keep lying convincingly, and hold on to your sanity, it helps to have a private place where you are simultaneously either speaking or writing down the truth.

10.

JOAN'S TELEPHONE DID NOT RING IN THE MORNING, ORDINARILY. EV-
eryone who knew her was aware that she didn't like to be disturbed before
noon. It was her habit to sit down to work from seven-thirty until eleven.
Then she would go for a jog, fix a light lunch, and read the newspaper
while she ate. In the afternoons she would return to her desk, either going
back over what she had done that morning or taking care of other tasks:
university paperwork, her students' stories, or the occasional book review.
These days her schedule hummed along as usual; a book of her short stories came out in paperback; but she couldn't ignore the fact that it had
been two years since her mornings had produced anything really new.

When the phone rang on Wednesday morning, she thought she might
as well answer it.

"Joan," Cece said. "I don't like to call in the morning—"

"That's OK," Joan said.

"I just wanted to invite you to dinner with Mr. Yuan. It'll be simple,
maybe a tomato salad—the Santa Monica market has heirlooms now—
and a pappardelle I've been making with Peekytoe crab. I don't know if
you have plans on Friday, but I'd love it if you could come."

"I don't know," Joan said. "I wouldn't want to intrude."

"Harry Lin is going to be there, too," Cece said casually. "Did I mention him before? He's the one who organized everything with Mr. Yuan.
He's the chair of the art department at UCLA, published very extensively,
Gordon says. Divorced, I think—or widowed? And he's unusually tall, at
least for a Chinese—"

"Cece?"

"What?"

"Are you trying to—"

"No! Joan, I swear. I'm not even positive he's single. It's just that he's an interesting man, and I'm always a little intimidated around him. I thought you would add so much to the conversation."

"I don't know about that," Joan said. Cece's flattery was blatant, but it was also hard to resist.

"Think about it," Cece encouraged her, and then expertly changed the subject: "Did I tell you who called the other day?"

"Who?"

"Phil. From Chinatown, of all places."

Joan was seized by a sudden apprehension. "You mean, Chinatown in New York, don't you?"

"Of course," Cece said.

Joan relaxed. She'd been relieved when her younger brother had left Los Angeles ten years ago for New York. They had never gotten along particularly well. Phil was manipulative, depressive, and needy, qualities the whole family indulged to an extent she had never been able to understand. There was also a sort of competition between them, perhaps because of their closeness in age. Gordon, who was five years older than Joan, had always been untouchable, but against Phil she felt she had to prove herself again and again. Maybe this was her own fault: she did tend to measure herself against others. But who didn't? She had always worked harder than her younger brother, but no matter how irresponsibly he behaved, things seemed to work out for him. Part of that was his looks, his chiseled features and childlike blue eyes; he could be very charming, especially with strangers. It was difficult to explain to other people what aggravated her about Phil.

"It's great news, actually—"

But Cece had covered the phone and was saying something to someone on the other end.

"Cece?"

"Sorry, the cats are getting into the slides."

One thing that had brought Cece and her brother Gordon together was their love of animals: a suspicious character trait, in Joan's opinion.

"I'm finally organizing all our slides," Cece was explaining. "I'm labeling them with dates, so that if you want to look at Max's sixth birthday, say, you can just find August 1991 without having to go through the whole—" Cece cupped her hand over the phone, but Joan could still hear her chastising, gently: "Ptolemy! You *know* that's naughty."

Joan did not like animals, but if you were going to have them, at least they should not be named after historical personages. This was obviously her brother's doing. Cece was inclined toward the innocuous sort of names that people ordinarily gave their pets, but most of the animals were saddled with her brother's attempts at cleverness. On more than one occasion, when he and Cece were entertaining, Joan had heard Gordon chastising the animals: "Freud—control yourself!" or, "Retreat, Napoleon—bad cat!"

"It was so funny to talk to Philip," Cece continued. "He sounded better than he has in I don't know how long."

Cece was the only person, besides their mother, who had ever called her brother Philip. Joan wondered if she was aware of it.

"I almost didn't answer the phone, actually, because I didn't think it would be either of the children—Livy just called yesterday from Paris, and Max was at the mural—and I was in the middle of brushing Nixon's teeth."

"You brush the cats' teeth?"

"Only the ones who have gum disease," Cece said defensively. "Anyway, I was right—it wasn't either of them. It was Phil."

It was Cece's vagueness that bothered Joan. She thought that if her sister-in-law could find something to do—an actual job, as opposed to the errands, compulsive childcare, and scattered intellectual enthusiasms that filled her days—she would be able to focus. Cece was far from stupid. She was a serious reader of books that other people didn't have time for, particularly multivolume works; she was the only person Joan knew who was able to say that her favorite novels were *Remembrance of Things Past* and *A Dance to the Music of Time* without sounding pretentious. "I like to get immersed," she explained.

"But what did Phil say?"

Cece lowered her voice to a confidential tone: "He had just come from the studio. He was signing a big contract."

"He got a part?" Her brother had auditioned for movies and television for years, securing several commercials and a few bit parts in films, before he left L.A. and moved to New York "to be a playwright." As if writing was something you could only do in certain places, like surfing or skiing. As if you could suddenly decide to become something that other people had been working at every day, for their entire lives. He still did commercials and institutional videos, and some grantwriting on the side, but Joan suspected that her brother's Manhattan lifestyle was financed mostly by his girlfriend.

"No," Cece said. "It's a writing contract."

People said that your stomach fell when you heard certain kinds of news, but Joan found that hers tended to rise. It seemed to bob up into her throat, like the plastic bath toys Cece's children had had when they were young.

"Although, I mean, it seems like it's for something he's already written, so I don't know." Cece had a very effective way of being mysterious— probably the result of intense mental disorganization. "I'm not sure if he'll have to actually *write* something now, or just—"

"Cece!"

"What?"

"What is the contract for?"

Cece sounded slightly offended. "That's what I've been trying to tell you. They're paying Philip a million dollars to turn his play into a big summer movie."

Joan looked out the window. The Epsteins' daughter, Sheila, was hitting a tennis ball against the garage door. Sheila wasn't especially accurate, but she was persistent; she sometimes hit for over an hour. Watching from her office window, Joan often wanted to tell the girl to stop. It wasn't worth it. She was never going to be a natural, and if she was going to work this hard, it ought to be at something more practical, a field not quite so crowded with naturals.

"He said as soon as he was finished with the movie people, he went straight to Chinatown. Not Chinatown, Chinatown, but the one in Flushing. Did you know Queens had a Chinatown?"

"No."

"Neither did I! It's supposed to be the most authentic in the world—I mean, not counting in China."

"I don't think you call them Chinatowns in China," Joan said.

"He was at the rare animal market."

"What was he doing at the rare animal market?"

"He didn't say. It was so nice to be talking to him—I don't know when the last time was."

"Looking for a companion, maybe. A nice Bengal tiger."

"A while, anyway," Cece said.

"Pricing dodos," Joan suggested.

"Aren't those extinct?"

"You never know."

"I think it's time to become a family again," Cece said. "I'm sure Phil agrees with me. It's time to put the past behind us."

"I don't think the past is ever very far behind Phil," Joan said. "He brings it along with him, like Linus with his blanket."

"PTOLEMY!" Cece said. "You get out of there!"

"Cece?"

"Sorry—it's the cats. So we'll count on you for Friday. Around seven?"

When she'd gotten off the phone with Cece, Joan went downstairs to the kitchen and replaced the phone in the charger. The worst thing she could do today would be not to write. That would be letting her brother get away with something. Still, she could not quite go back to her office. She stepped out the screen door into the backyard: an empty rectangle of grass that she had slowly transformed into a garden. Now there were ferns, impatiens, and a few birds-of-paradise, along with her big purchase—a Meyer lemon tree. She had been proud of the garden, startled that her efforts had yielded something tangible. Now, suddenly, the yard had become a negative quantity, a colorful representation of the work she had failed to do.

It was not that Joan was envious, or not only that. After all, she'd never wanted to write a play, a form that forced you to give up control to a terrifying extent. It was more the fact that her brother's achievements seemed to go against the natural order, in which years and years of labor finally produced something acceptable to its creator, usually ignored by the larger world. Instead, after years of ostensible "writer's block," there was suddenly a play, which was now going to be made into a "big summer movie." Standing in the garden, Joan realized that she hadn't asked about the subject of Phil's play. She was pretty sure she already knew.

11.

FOR A LONG TIME, JOAN HAD IMAGINED WRITING A NOVEL ABOUT CECE and Phil. Her ex-husband Frank had suggested it a long time ago, when they were still married and had socialized with Gordon, Phil, and Cece on a regular basis. According to Frank, you could no longer write a novel about adultery, both because the nineteenth-century precedents had exhausted the genre and because the social taboo that had once made it a great subject was gone. Incest was still available, but it was sensational and hardly sympathetic. The situation with Gordon, Phil, and Cece, on the other hand, was perfect: even in late-twentieth-century Los Angeles, people ordinarily refrained from sleeping with their spouses' siblings.

Joan suspected that Frank had found Cece attractive, and reveled in the contradiction between her perfect housewifely persona and the very clear evidence (although it was never discussed) that she and Phil had been engaged in a long-standing sexual relationship. Joan had agreed that the idea had potential, but of course she could never use it. Now that their parents were gone, and Phil was essentially out of touch, Gordon and his children were the only family she had left. Even a new novel wasn't worth losing them, she told herself. And anyway, who knew whether it would work?

There was the question of Gordon, for example. In a novel, you would have to specify whether or not Cece's husband knew about the affair. His condescension toward Phil, which had culminated in essentially dismissing their younger brother from the family, suggested that Gordon was well aware of what had been going on for all those years. On the other hand, when Joan was getting divorced, Gordon had called her up one day to tell her very seriously that no marriage was perfect. He and Cece had had their difficulties too, he said, as if that fact wouldn't be completely obvious to Joan. If she had been forced to articulate it, Joan would've said that her brother both knew and didn't know. But you couldn't do that in a novel: that was why real life was both more complicated and less satisfying than fiction.

She had worried that Frank would take on the project himself, but luckily her ex-husband hadn't been interested in "domestic themes." "That's your department," he'd been fond of saying, as if by granting Joan family life, he was entitled to stake his claim on everything else. When they'd divorced, Frank had been at work on a very long, heavily researched novel set against the backdrop of the Spanish Civil War, a magnum opus under which Joan imagined he was still laboring.

She hadn't listened to Frank, and now she strongly suspected that her brother had gone ahead and written it. Of course, someone might argue that the story belonged to Phil, whereas it wasn't Joan's to write. But Phil was not a writer! He was someone who dabbled in literature, the way he dabbled in theater, in women, and in life in general.

On her way up to her office, Joan came across the article about the dissident, on the kitchen counter underneath the toaster oven, where she must've left it yesterday. She picked it up and toed the foot pedal of the trash can, preparing to toss it out. It was just a photocopy of a printed article—a copy of a copy of a copy—from the *Taipei Times*. The quality was poor, a pixilated newsprint version of a photo that had probably been dark and grainy in the original, and the dissident's expression was hard to make out. Joan had to squint to read the accompanying text.

Yuan Zhao was one of the leaders of the democracy movement. He was arrested in June of 1989, and spent six months in Beijing's notorious Qincheng prison. He was reported, upon his release, to have commented that the food in jail was better than in his university canteen. In the late winter of 1990, he had moved to an artists' community near the Beijing Summer Palace, where he had lived in close proximity to some of China's most famous contemporary artists, of the internationally recognized "cynical realist" school. Two years later he moved again, this time to the far east side of the city, an area that would soon be dubbed Beijing's East

Village by the shabby collection of painters, photographers, and performers who began to take up residence there.

The East Villagers lived where the rents were cheapest, among filth and industrial waste just outside the Third Ring Road, where they began publishing an underground journal of their work called *Lu Kou*, or *Intersections*. During this time, Yuan Zhao stopped painting and began staging increasingly daring performances, often in collaboration with his friends. These performances attracted the attention of foreign media, as well as of the government. In June of 1994, exactly five years after the Tiananmen Square crackdown, Yuan Zhao returned to prison briefly, this time at a detention center in Changping.

Joan went into her office, and was clearing off the space around her computer—a pile of receipts marked "taxes," a copy of *Family Happiness and Other Stories* overdue from the Beverly Hills Public Library, an ancient glass of water with a dusty skin on top. She realized she was still holding the article, and pinned it absently to her bulletin board. You never knew what might be useful. Sometimes it scared her, how unpredictable these things were: you were annoyed about being disturbed, and then that very interruption dropped something precious in your lap.

12.

I CLEARED U.S. CUSTOMS EASILY, THROUGH THE DOUBLE DOORS MARKED "Nothing to Declare." The officer, an older, heavyset black man with a mustache, barely glanced at my passport. He asked me the purpose of my visit (cultural exchange), my occupation (teacher), and whether I was transporting any weapons or farm products. When I showed him the small pocketknife with the mother-of-pearl handle I always carried, he waved me through, all the time continuing a conversation with another officer.

I proceeded through the passageway, out into a light so bright that initially I was blind, and saw only an indeterminate mass of people crowding the barrier between us and the main terminal. The terminal was all glass and blue steel; outside you could see the cars gliding peacefully by, like silvery fish. I looked around, and saw the characters "Yuan Zhao" on a sign, above which was a halo of yellow hair, some large gold earrings, and a smooth, eager face.

"Hello," said Cece Travers. "I'm so relieved that you made it. I could barely sleep last night—although I'm sure it was much worse for you. Was it very uncomfortable?"

"Hello," I said. "No, thank you."

"Do you remember which baggage claim you are? I never do—oh, wait, here, we'll just ask. Sir?"

"Baggage claim two," I said, but Cece was already getting the answer from a member of the ground crew.

"I meant to bring my son to help with the bags, but he was busy today. That's Max; his sister Olivia will be home on Thursday. And I didn't even introduce myself properly. I'm Cece Travers."

"Yuan Zhao."

"Well, I know who you are. I copied your name from the museum catalogue. I know how if you just get one line wrong, it means something totally different."

This idea about the mutability of Chinese characters was one I heard over and over again in America. There was also some confusion about the Chinese having multiple words for *snow*, which I eventually determined was a corruption of a similar misconception about Eskimos—one of those interesting ideas that achieve their currency through repetition, and take hold in people's minds in spite of clear evidence to the contrary.

"I know that your first name—I mean the name that comes first—is your family name," Cece was saying. "Do you prefer to be called Mr. Yuan?"

On the plane I had been planning to give Mrs. Travers my childhood nickname. My mother had called me Xiao Pangzi because I was an enthusiastic eater, and it was a name I still felt comfortable answering to, particularly among people who didn't understand its silly connotations. However, the whole point of this trip, at least according to my cousin, was to enhance the reputation of modern Chinese painting in America. Meiling was even more optimistic: we were at the outset of a whole new movement in international art, and Americans should associate that movement with the name "Yuan Zhao."

"Mr. Yuan is fine," I told Cece. We proceeded toward the baggage claim, where Cece set the sign down casually on the ground. That was something a Chinese person would not have done, although it was a relief to me to have the large, embarrassing characters out of sight. The crowd around baggage claim number two was almost entirely Shanghai people; I was nervous that at any moment someone I knew might appear and ask what I was doing in Los Angeles.

Cece saw me looking at the sign and misinterpreted my reaction.

"Please forgive the calligraphy. I did make a mistake, didn't I?"

"It's perfect," I said. "Thank you very much."

"Thank *you*—for being patient with me. I love Chinese painting, and you were coming, and I thought I might learn some characters. But of course, it's very difficult. I was consoling myself with how different the languages are—and now here you are. I have to admit, I didn't expect you would speak such beautiful English."

"You're too polite," I said automatically, but Cece took me literally.

"No," she said, touching my arm. "I'm really not being polite at all."

I almost said that my mother had been born in America, and then caught myself. One of the things I had been doing in the months leading up to my trip was practicing how I might answer certain questions, so that nothing I said would contradict the things my hosts might already believe about me. I was surprised to have almost slipped so soon.

"Chinese schools must be excellent," Cece remarked.

My bags arrived all together, and the process was just as simple with the paintings: a clerk at the office for oversized baggage assured us that they had arrived safely, and confirmed our authorization of the graduate students from UCLA who would pick them up.

"I don't want to embarrass you, but I have to say—I'm a huge fan of your work," Cece said. "Harry Lin gave us the catalogue from the Taiwan museum."

"Thank you," I said, but the reference to Professor Lin startled me. All of my communication with him had been through my cousin, and X had promised me that I wouldn't have to meet the professor for months, until I had established myself in Los Angeles (and hopefully made a start on my "project"). I was disturbed to hear Cece mentioning him so casually, as if he were a friend of the family.

"They just took my breath away, even as reproductions. I'm so impatient to see the originals."

"That work is very old," I said.

"Oh, I know that," Cece said, just as we passed through the last set of automatic doors into the street. For a moment, the air caught me off guard. It wasn't the heat—I'd expected that—but a certain softness, which I would later learn to associate with the desert cities of the "Southland": Santa Barbara, San Diego, Palm Springs. In between the traffic sounds, you could hear small birds. Looking up, I saw a slim tower, topped with a futuristic, circular glass room, a miniature version of the new Oriental Pearl TV headquarters in Pudong.

"Someone once told me that's the sign of a real artist—they don't care about their work after it's finished," Cece continued, pressing the button for the crosswalk and searching in a large leather purse, the color of butter, for her keys. Palms waved in slow motion all along the pickup zone; across the street, orange and purple birds-of-paradise shared a bed with red azaleas in front of a pink stucco parking structure. I thought of my cousin with regret: these were his colors, his palette. X would have loved to be where I was now, looking up at the round restaurant rotating lazily on its narrow spire.

"We can be excited about the work, whether it's ten years old or two hundred," Cece said. "But for the artist, it's always about the next thing."

"Yes," I said gravely. There were hummingbirds in the flowerbeds: I had never seen a real one before, and my hand itched to draw it.

"Not to put pressure on you," Cece said. "I know you'll need lots of time just to settle in with us. For tonight—I didn't know whether you'd be hungry?"

I hadn't felt the emptiness in my belly until she mentioned it. "A little."

"You should try to eat, if you can," said Cece. "I made some tomato soup, and a parmesan bread, and there's all kinds of fruit. We're having tuna steaks for dinner—my family likes it practically raw, but I still eat it the gauche way, all cooked through—and a pesto risotto, and of course I'll make a salad. There's a tart I did last night that came out pretty well, with apples and currants." Cece glanced at me. "I have to admit that my Chinese cooking isn't up to snuff. But maybe you could help me?"

It was amazing to have come so far, and land in the midst of a family that, at least in its emphasis on food, was very Chinese: for the rest of the ride to Beverly Hills, Cece and I discussed the dishes we might prepare together.

As we left the airport, I was hungry enough to eat, but by the time we pulled into the Traverses' driveway, I was so tired that I worried I wouldn't be able to make it from the car into the house. Cece guessed this, and suggested she take me straight to my room.

"Our housekeeper will bring your bags," she said. "You shouldn't sleep more than a few hours, but maybe you'd like to lie down until dinner? We eat around seven—I hope that's not too early for you?"

Two eight oh five Mountain Drive was even more lavish than I'd expected; what I didn't expect was how familiar it seemed, from the moment I walked in the door. It was nothing like my parents' apartment in Shanghai, where money often buys space or ornamentation before comfort. Nor was it like the apartment I considered my true home, in Harbin, which was extremely simple. (Even after my father began to succeed at Daqing, he was understandably frugal, inclined to hide rather than display his newfound wealth.) Nevertheless, I thought I *recognized* the Traverses' house, as if I'd dreamed about it before I arrived.

The only thing that surprised me was the presence of a sort of domestic zoo: as soon as we got inside, a large white dog was leaping affectionately onto my chest; Cece managed to grab his collar, but by then two cats were twining in and out between my legs in their quick, unnerving way.

"Sorry," Cece said. "You don't dislike animals, do you?"

"No."

"I just learned my Chinese zodiac sign. Lupe! Come help with Mr. Yuan's bags. I'm the sheep or the goat—depending on which book you look at."

I was startled. Assuming she hadn't made a mistake with her sign, Cece was forty-four, seven or eight years older than I would've guessed.

"What's yours?"

I hesitated only for a moment. "The dragon," I said, upgrading my sign from the humble rabbit to the fiercest and most beautiful of the animals. I remembered how X had called me "Longxia Shanren" for a joke, the Lobster Hermit; in Chinese, a lobster is a little dragon.

"That's the best one," Cece said. "So you were born in—"

Before I could answer, a very fat Hispanic woman, dressed all in white, came into the foyer and took my bag. When I protested, Cece shushed me.

"Mr. Yuan, this is Lupe. Lupe, Mr. Yuan. Please ask her if you need anything, and if she doesn't understand, ask Maxwell to help you; he's our Spanish speaker." Lupe said something in an obliging tone, which I didn't understand: I was distracted by a bright orange and purple pattern, projected on the floor by a high stained-glass window above the stairs. I thought again of my cousin, almost as if I were seeing everything—the house and Cece and the mysterious Spanish woman—through his eyes.

"You'll meet Max and Gordon at dinner," Cece said. "Now I want to leave you alone to rest for a while—if you're sure you don't want a snack?"

"I'd like to lie down," I said: things were beginning to slide away at the edges of my vision, and I was conscious of how often I was blinking.

"You poor thing," Cece said, taking my arm and guiding me down three polished wooden stairs. We went through a vast living room, with cream-colored wall-to-wall carpeting, matching cloudlike drapes, half drawn, and an overstuffed, armless sofa that extended across an entire wall, upholstered in blue-and-cream-striped silk. Over the plaster fireplace was an Andy Warhol print of Marilyn Monroe, in orange and purple; on the opposite wall was a painting I preferred, a large oil abstraction in pale colors that seemed to run down the page, almost like a watercolor.

"Mr. Diebenkorn, of course," Cece said. "My favorite thing we have is in your room, though. It's a Frankenthaler; you'll have to tell me what you think of it."

By the time we had passed through the copper and mahogany bar, with a big-screen TV and a glass-fronted liquor cabinet, gone out the sliding glass doors, and crossed the breathtaking lawn, I knew what was familiar about the house. I had seen it in the movies—not this particular house but similar ones, where nothing that isn't beautiful has been allowed to stay. Everything with a necessary function, from telephones to garden tools to toilet plungers, has been designed to add, or at least not detract, from the overall pleasantness of the rooms.

In spite of my exhaustion, I couldn't help admiring the pool, with its unusual cusped shape and dark violet-blue bottom. My arms and legs were cramping, but my upper body felt light, as if a part of me might detach at any moment, leave its battered skin (still fifteen hours ahead of itself), and sail newborn above the trees.

Cece unlocked the door of the pool house, and all I absorbed of the two rooms were their shuttered coolness, and the large inviting white expanse of the bed.

"Someone will come to wake you for dinner," Cece said. "There are towels and things in the bathroom, if you'd like to wash up first."

I may have washed my face then. All I remember, after the door clicked closed behind her, was stripping off my clothes and climbing into those cool sheets. The last thing I thought of was an article I'd seen in a magazine at home, about the different kinds of sleepers (side, stomach, back, fetal) and what each position said about the sleeper's personality. Someone who is outgoing (what we call *wai xiang*) will sleep on his back, open to the world, while an introvert (*nei xiang*) will face down, or curl up into himself. I thought that if my illusion were going to be complete, I would roll over onto my back. It was just an idle thought; I've never been able to sleep exposed like that, and I dropped off that first afternoon in Los Angeles the ordinary way, on my stomach, my face crushed into an overwhelming mass of pure white goosefeathers.

13.

FIONNULA WAS CHITTERING AGAIN. PHIL HAD BEEN FORCED TO SEDATE her before they left the ground; now, in the middle of the flight, suspended above the indeterminate dark rectangles of the midwestern United States, the drugs were wearing off. She had started vocalizing the moment Phil settled her under the seat, a detail he hadn't considered when he'd imagined transporting an exotic African primate by air.

"She'll calm down once we're airborne," Phil had promised the stewardess, who was watching them.

"You've got it all zipped up in its case?"

"It's a cage, actually. Even more secure."

The stewardess, whose nametag said "Karen, Portland, OR," looked wary. There was one bombshell of a flight attendant on the plane: southern, very tall, with waist-length red hair, freckles, and an absolutely perfect, heart-shaped ass. Most stewardesses now were unattractive. Karen was squat and jowly, with a self-satisfied expression that he associated, probably unfairly, with the Pacific Northwest. You could imagine her going on hiking trips on the weekends, with a bunch of equally smug, middle-aged "girlfriends."

"I certainly hope so," Karen said skeptically.

"She's happy," Phil said. "That's why she's, um, making sounds." Fionnula did sometimes chitter when she was pleased, if you rubbed behind her ears or gave her a melon rind. Those sounds probably meant something different now. He had brought her home from Flushing in the same case two weeks ago, in a gypsy cab, just after he had resolved to go to L.A.

Aubrey was not impressed, even when he showed her the biography of the bush baby, also known as a lesser galago (*Galago senegalensis*) in "The Online Encyclopedia of African Wildlife."

"We talked about getting a pet," Phil reminded her. "You said you'd like that."

"I was envisioning a French bulldog," Aubrey said.

That was a lie. What Aubrey was envisioning was not a French bulldog, or a bush baby, but an ordinary baby, with a fuzzy head, spindly arms, and a fat, round body, containing a set of underdeveloped, unpredictable intestines. She was envisioning hats with little cat ears, stuffed giraffes, and an expensive stroller from Japan, which a more perfect version of Phil would manipulate skillfully into different configurations, depending upon the weather.

The lesser galago required no such props. Omnivorous, arboreal, and nocturnal, he could subsist happily on a diet of fruits, vegetables, and field mice; he lived in nests or tree hollows in the bush and woodlands of sub-Saharan Africa, an environment that Phil could imagine reproducing in Cece's large and exquisitely maintained backyard. At only seven to eight inches long (excluding the tail), and weighing in at only five to ten ounces, the lesser galago was a practical pet. Except for self-defense and, among females, fierce protection of the young, bush babies were not aggressive. They could reproduce the cry of a human infant, whistle in response to predators (including eagles, owls, snakes, and genets) and cover ten yards in seconds. They could leap twenty feet, and live in captivity up to fourteen years. Aside from his airline ticket, Fionnula was the only thing Phil had purchased in the month since his fortunes had so dramatically improved.

A woman he had never met had changed his life. Phil Travers, struggling actor/playwright/grantwriter, was now Phil Travers, Hollywood screenwriter, with a million dollars (almost) in the bank, and a coproducer credit on what promised to be a hot summer movie. The transformation had happened, as they say, "overnight." There was now no reason why Phil should not quit his grantwriting, give up his apartment in Queens, and marry (and then swiftly impregnate) his girlfriend Aubrey, who had been dating him with this expectation for the past four years.

The woman responsible for these reversals was arguably not yet a woman at all: her name was Darcy Feyth, and she was nineteen years old.

Darcy Feyth first appeared as the gap-toothed little sister on a short-lived network sitcom in the fall of 1986. She then disappeared for ten years and was effectively consigned to the Arts and Entertainment section of Trivial Pursuit, when along came *The Big Blow*, a tornado movie produced on the cheap which swept up its hitherto unknown star and dropped her gently down onto the covers of several glossy magazines, as "The Comeback Kid" and "Darcy Feyth—the Return of the Girl-Next-Door." *Jane of Hearts, Cassiopeia*, and the phenomenally successful *Black Dagger* trilogy followed: films set in rural Idaho, outer space, and feudal Korea, respectively. Although none was Oscar material, critics concurred: "Darcy Feyth continues to transcend her material," and "Hollywood's Darling Is a Diamond in the Rough."

Phil read about Darcy's meteoric rise (to which he was now attached, as a kind of flaming, orbital debris) on the Internet, while Aubrey pored over his contract. The contract was with Karl Niedbalski, an old friend from the Albatross—an off-off-Broadway venue where Phil had acted and Karl had been the dramaturge in a series of original productions staged by mutual friends in the late 1970s. Karl had obtained Phil's play through one of those friends (now the artistic director of a respectable downtown repertory company), who had passed on it. Karl assured Phil that the artistic director had made a terrible mistake.

They had negotiated the contract at an alcoholic dinner in an "illegal restaurant" above a glue factory in Red Hook, where Karl had invited Phil and Aubrey to eat a Polish delicacy called *kiszka*. Karl described himself to Aubrey, whom he was meeting for the first time, as "a man with a knack for transforming unreadable novels into unwatchable films." Aubrey had pushed her *kiszka* politely around on her plate.

Karl offered Phil a generous five percent of the film's net profits. He then cheerfully explained that the only two of his eighteen films to secure distribution had lost money: "Of course, I won't make you pay five percent of the debt," Karl joked. (Aubrey hadn't laughed.) They were the only people in the restaurant. Karl's wife hadn't been able to make it to the dinner, and so the filmmaker had brought his hundred-and-forty-pound

Pyrenean mountain dog instead. It was pouring, and Phil's primary memory of the night was the absolutely unique and probably irreproducible smell of *kiszka*, glue, and wet dog.

The evening was one more indication that he and Aubrey were not right for each other. Aubrey belonged with a man who conducted his business in the daytime, in Manhattan. She should be dining at Montrachet or Babbo, drinking a spectacular vintage. Aubrey's friends did not go to illegal restaurants. (They were, after all, lawyers.) Phil had felt for a long time that it was necessary for one of them to leave the other, and that the best person to effect this change was Aubrey. It was one of the rare points on which he and Aubrey's family were in complete agreement.

It was almost a month after they'd gone out to Red Hook, when Phil had practically forgotten about the cinematic version of *The Hypnotist*, when the phone rang. Karl was breathless:

"I sent it to some agents. It was a joke, really, you know—Julia Roberts as Celine."

"Julia Roberts is going to play Celine?"

"Better," Karl said.

"Good," said Phil. "Because Julia Roberts isn't at all the kind of actor I had in mind."

"Funny," Karl said. "But we're not talking about Julia Roberts. We're talking about *Darcy Feyth*."

"Who's Darcy Feyth?"

Karl sighed. "How did I know you were going to say that? She's the new Julia Roberts. Or I mean, I guess she's the new Meg Ryan. Unless she turns out to be the new Nicole Kidman. You never know—she's nineteen."

"She's nineteen?"

"She has more money than you and me and everyone we know put together, and she can't even buy a beer. We live in a funny country, Phil."

"Celine is in her thirties," Phil began. "A mother of two. There's no way that a nineteen—"

Karl didn't let him finish: "The point is—she wants to do it."

"Is that good?"

"That depends who you are," said Karl. "If you're you, you're currently under contract for five percent of the proceeds of a film with a star whose movies have previously grossed between four and four hundred million dollars each. So yes—I would say that this has the potential to be very good news for you."

Everything around Phil, the computer, the bed, Aubrey's clothes on the floor, seemed to get soft and fuzzy. He experienced a momentary feeling of ecstasy: he might slip out. He might simply extract himself from this life, like a splinter, letting everything heal up nicely behind him, as if he'd never been there.

"That's if you're you," Karl continued. "If you're *me*, you've just been paid a five-thousand-dollar finder's fee, and invited to 'stay in touch.' "

Phil was indignant. "They can't do that to you. I'll call them. Who do I have to call?"

The filmmaker started giggling. He giggled for so long that Phil got annoyed.

"After all, I wrote it."

"Oh, man, you're funny," said the filmmaker. "You'd better get a lawyer."

Of course, a lawyer was the one asset Phil had.

Aubrey renegotiated the contract with the production company in Los Angeles. She took a morning off from work to do it. When she finally made the phone call, he couldn't listen. He went into the bedroom and did some breathing exercises that his therapist had shown him, which were supposed to combat his borderline social anxiety disorder.

"Phil?" Aubrey called him from the living room: "I'm done."

Her voice was tearful: clearly, she hadn't succeeded. He too was getting only five thousand dollars. If someone had told him a month ago that he was getting five thousand dollars for nothing, he would've been elated (at least for a few minutes). Now he felt like giving it back. He felt like crawling into the closet and hiding among the shirts.

"Phil?"

He went into the living room (Aubrey's living room) and listened to his girlfriend tell him, with bashful pride, that he was now a "coproducer," and that someone from a company he had never heard of was going to send him a check for a million dollars.

"You did it," Aubrey had said, throwing her arms around his neck. "I *knew* you would. Now are you finally going to let me read it?"

He had written the play over a period of three months, in the middle of the night, while Aubrey slept. He had not ever intended to show it to anyone, but then his vanity had gotten the better of him. This success seemed to confirm something. But what was good about it, really? It was hardly original. He had written a play about a man who falls in love with his brother's wife.

14.

THE STUDIO HAD NOT EXACTLY ASKED HIM TO COME. THEY HAD MEN-
tioned something about flying him out "at a later point" to meet the writers, and when Phil had expressed confusion—he'd been under the
impression that he *was* the writer—the executives had explained that with
a project like this one, it was always good "to have a couple of extra hands
on deck." Phil hadn't mentioned this conversation to Aubrey, who believed he had been summoned urgently to L.A. and was going under du-
ress, in order to secure their future together.

He didn't want to keep things from Aubrey. But once you'd kept one
thing secret, Phil had discovered, it was often difficult not to conceal others. Aubrey wouldn't understand why it was so important for him to make
a triumphant return to Los Angeles, the city he had left in shame and anger ten years before.

He had resolved that it would be different this time. He'd planned to
finalize all of the arrangements beforehand, to leave nothing to chance.
Then Cece had told him about Max. Phil believed that there had always
been a bond between himself and his nephew. From the early days, when
Max had begun to ask him questions about the dinosaurs (and Phil had
essentially memorized the encyclopedia in order to answer them), he was
startled to find that his nephew looked up to him. He took Phil's hand
and listened with a kind of enamored fascination. No one had ever listened to Phil that way, before or since. When Max had stopped eating everything except for strawberry yogurt, peanut butter, and plain pasta (and
only the kind shaped like pinwheels), Phil had been able to relate. It was
nice to know what you were getting. He had been the one to carry those

snacks on their frequent outings, secured in little baggies. He had been the one to reassure Cece that Max would be fine.

He knew from Cece about his nephew's problems in school, but school wasn't for everyone. (It hadn't, for example, been for Phil.) At five, Max had known the difference between the brontosaurus, stegosaurus, and triceratops. He had known the pterodactyls. Phil had missed a good deal of Max's childhood, admittedly, but the kid he'd known had been destined for greatness. He had always meant to get in touch with Max, in an avuncular way, perhaps by mail, but it had never been exactly the right time. There was also an element of pride involved. Ten years ago, his brother had essentially banished him from the family; and if they didn't want him, he certainly didn't need them.

Of course, ten years ago, Gordon had had his reasons.

"We have a problem with your *lifestyle*," his brother had said. This was after Gordon's book had been published, and his brother had spent nearly a year lecturing all over the country. He had even been to Europe. Phil was working at the restaurant on Melrose, waiting tables and tending bar. He was supposedly auditioning during the day, but it was hard to keep that up, especially after he'd started spending time with Cece and the kids. His shift at the restaurant ended at one in the morning, and he often went out afterward; if he occasionally enjoyed a line or two of cocaine, that was a part of the scene. It wasn't like he was snorting it in front of the children, or mixing up their little baggies with his own. Phil told himself it was Gordon's dishonesty that bothered him. There was only one reason his brother had asked him to stay away, and it had nothing to do with Phil's lifestyle.

They never determined how much Gordon actually knew. There were certainly never any dramatic scenes of discovery, or any demands about where Cece had been on such and such a day, at such and such a time. Phil sometimes thought it was the friendship Gordon had resented more than anything else. He had a vivid memory of coming in the front door of their old house in Westwood late one afternoon. Cece was carrying Max, and he had Olivia by the hand, and they were laughing about something, he couldn't remember what. They had the same dumb sense of humor. Gordon was standing in the kitchen doorway, holding a mug of coffee. He looked at Phil as if he were seeing him for the first time in years, as if he were just now coming to the conclusion that his little brother had grown into a fully functional adult.

Three weeks later, Gordon had asked him to go.

If his brother had accused him in a straightforward way, it would've been different. If he had threatened him or hit him, or worse, asked how Phil could have done it—he would have been ashamed. He would have been sorry, and he would've wondered himself how such a thing could've happened. He might even have gone away on his own.

As it was, however, Phil had not been able to feel sorrow or regret. He had been too angry. His brother had a way of making him feel like a disappointment: a combination of disgust and pity that was very familiar.

"I don't want you around my children," Gordon had said. It had been his brother standing in front of him, but he had heard his father's voice. And the worst thing was, when Phil repeated it to Cece, she hadn't been indignant. She hadn't rushed to his defense, reminding Gordon of all of those weekends at the observatory, or the tar pits, or the museum, while they had amused the children so that he could have peace and quiet to complete his Great Work. She hadn't even argued. When Phil told her that her husband had spoken for her ("*We* have a problem . . ."), Cece had nodded and said:

"Well, maybe it's best."

15.

PHIL HAD DECIDED TO TAKE THE RED-EYE TO COMPENSATE FOR THE EX-
tra expense of an open return. It wasn't like he was rich: a million dollars
wasn't so much anymore, especially after taxes. He had tried to explain
that to Aubrey, who of course didn't hear him. With her salary, and the
promise of Phil's new career, they ought to be able to get started right
away. Aubrey was coming to visit him at Thanksgiving, by which time
Phil knew he was expected to have procured a ring.

He booked an in-cabin animal passage for Fionnula, who was traveling as a "kitten." Every day before his departure he had thought of cancel-
ing the ticket; every day he had put Fionnula in her case (so that she might
get used to it) with a square of sheepskin that had been rubbed against her
mother in Flushing. He wanted her to be prepared either way. He'd been
petrified about the airport—surely someone would ask to see her—but in
fact the only time he was required to take Fionnula out of her case was at
the X-ray machines.

"It's a newborn kitten—the runt of the litter," Phil had said when he
lifted her out of the case. He held her against his chest, shielding her body
from the eyes of the guards.

"Aw, a kitten," the security guard said. The man in front of the X-ray
monitor hadn't looked up.

It was only once he was on the plane that he encountered suspicion.

"What is that anyway?" Karen, the Portland-based stewardess, asked
him.

Phil did not like to lie. He occasionally fibbed, in order to make life
more pleasant for himself and the people around him, but he tried not to

do anything that *felt* dishonest. In general he tried to go by his gut feeling. Because they were still on the ground, where rules could be put into effect, he decided to be evasive. "A cat. Sort of."

"Sort of a cat?"

"A kitten. She's a rare breed. Have you heard of the Singapore shorthair?"

"I've heard of Siamese."

"That's different," Phil said.

The stewardess shook her head. "Just make sure you keep it in its cage."

A businessman stared across the aisle at Phil.

"She qualified as a cat," Phil reassured him. "Slipped in under the cat wire."

The southern stewardess began the announcements, from behind the curtain in the first-class gallery: *"Fasten your seatbelt by inserting the metal fitting into the buckle. Pull on the loose end to secure the strap."* Voice, Phil thought, was one of the key things about a woman. It was rare that you found a truly gorgeous woman with a comparatively appealing voice. Fionnula Flynn, for example, his favorite NPR correspondent, was a large woman with a long face and a practical haircut, who favored shapeless blouses and bright-colored shawls. Her voice, however, could make in-hospital interviews with mutilated Chechen militants sound sexy.

It figured that the best-looking stewardess would be working first class. Phil might have flown first class himself, or at least business, if he had waited for the studio to fly him out. Everything would have been arranged in advance: a car to meet him at the airport; a fancy hotel; a schedule. He would've disembarked first, fresh and well rested, and his family would've been waiting for him at the gate. His brother would've given him a real, fraternal hug—which would've signified love, forgiveness, and the fact that blood was thicker than water, which was under the bridge anyway. His niece and nephew would've been jumping up and down, asking whether he'd brought them anything, and when he looked up from their eager caresses, he would've seen their mother standing there, waiting her turn. Cece wouldn't have said anything, but she wouldn't have had to: everything would've been right there in her goddess-gray eyes.

Of course, his family did not know he was coming. His niece and nephew—it was difficult to remember—were now teenagers, hardly likely to rush out to the airport to meet him. Nor was his brother Gordon, famously unable to sit through a commercial film without falling asleep, likely to be impressed by the screenplay deal. His brother would be sure to ask discouraging questions, such as:

When will they actually make this film?

What exactly does the coproducer do?

And:

How much will be left, after you've paid off your credit-card debt?

It had been ten years since their falling-out, but it was very possible that Gordon would still not welcome him with open arms. It was even possible that Cece was annoyed with him after the conversation about Fionnula, whom she had mistaken for a new girlfriend, a misunderstanding he hadn't been able to correct, since he wanted the bush baby to be a surprise. If Cece and Gordon turned him away, where would he go? He loved hotels, but you couldn't live in a hotel for months, even if you were a millionaire.

"Pardon me?"

It was the businessman across the aisle.

"Yes?"

"You said that was a cat?"

"Yes."

The man spread his magazine facedown on the seat next to him. It was the in-flight shopping guide. He was looking at page after page of chocolate truffles, Soloflex machines, and Brita at-home water filtration systems.

"What kind of cat?"

"Just the ordinary kind," Phil said. When you were fibbing, it was better to keep things as simple as possible.

"That's funny," said the businessman. "Because I'm allergic. Usually."

"She's nonallergenic," Phil said. "A special breed."

"Is that right? My wife would love a cat, but the dander's a problem. Knocks out my sinuses."

Somewhere in the front of the plane, a baby was crying: a grating, depressing sound, varying in pitch, like a siren. Why was everyone so focused on the well-behaved and unobtrusive Fionnula?

"She shouldn't bother you," Phil said.

"That's the funny thing—she isn't. Wait now, I should write down the name of the breed."

"Singapore shorthair."

"That's like a Siamese?"

"Much rarer."

The man nodded, as if he'd expected this. "I guess they cost a fortune?"

"The earth," said Phil. "Excuse me—I think I'll take a little rest now." He had the second half of last night's Ambien in the pocket of his jeans, wrapped in paper. Even the Ambien wouldn't be effective protection against the baby, who was letting out long screams separated by nerve-racking intervals, worse, to Phil's mind, than the screams themselves. Even more ominous was the unmistakable scraping sound coming from underneath his own seat. Fionnula was turning in circles, beginning to panic. He knew the feeling.

"Hang in there, little lady," he implored her: "Just a few more hours." He'd hadn't fed her for twenty-four hours before the flight, as the breeder in Flushing had instructed, but it was still possible that she could soil the cage. He hoped not. He had promised her a big meal when they got to Los Angeles, anything she wanted—figs, melon, field mice.

In a way, Phil had decided to buy Fionnula for Cece years ago, because Cece had said she wanted a monkey. Or perhaps she hadn't *said* she wanted one—not in so many words—but she had implied it. They had been at the San Diego Zoo. Max had been afraid of the orangutans (Phil hadn't blamed him), and Olivia had refused to go into the Monkey House at all, because of the smell, but Cece had been characteristically delighted. She dragged them all over to the chimpanzees, so that they could watch the animals grooming in pairs, picking the tiny nits from each other's coats.

"They're so gentle, really." Cece was holding onto Max, whose face was buried in his mother's thighs. "You can see the way they care for each other—I love that."

"I'll get you one," Phil offered.

("No!" Max had cried.)

"They're like people trapped in animal bodies," Cece said.

"They're our animal selves," said Phil.

Then Cece had blushed. With that blush she had told him that she would like to have a monkey.

The curtains parted and one of the first-class passengers appeared with the baby, now whimpering in a threatening way.

"Sorry," the father said. "Just trying to quiet the little monster down." He was one of those enormous Scandinavian men, a Norwegian or a Swede. His child seemed, to Phil's untutored eye, similarly oversized. The gorgeous flight attendant—up close you could appreciate her luminescent skin—was right behind them. Phil was grateful for the plastic nametag: "Julie."

"Could I bring you more milk?" Julie asked the baby's father sympathetically.

"You've been too kind," the Scandinavian said. He was just as tall as Phil, but with massive shoulders and thick blond hair—real boons if you happened to be after the stunning young flight attendant. Of course, the Scandinavian was not after a flight attendant. He was a father taking care of a cranky child. He smiled apologetically at Phil: "God forbid she should sleep."

Then he continued down the aisle. Julie seemed inclined to follow him.

"It's a long flight to have a baby in your section," Phil said. "That must make it difficult for you."

"He's such a good daddy!" Julie gushed. "He's been up with her the whole time."

"Do you work this route often?" Phil asked.

"Excuse me, sir?"

"Do you fly from New York to Los Angeles very often?"

"Three times a week," Julie said. "The baby's called Britta—isn't that sweet?"

"After the at-home water filtration system?"

Julie looked confused. "I think it's because they're from Denmark." Then, more encouragingly, she leaned over him (a pretense, he hoped) to take his glass. The fabric of her uniform, a navy blue straight skirt, stretched taut. "His wife died in a terrible automobile accident," she whispered, barely concealing her excitement.

"That's terrible," Phil said. "I'm Phil, by the way."

The baby Dane howled.

"Chee," Fionnula protested. "Chee, chee."

Julie frowned. "What is that?"

"What?" said Phil.

"That noise."

Shut up, Phil communicated silently to Fionnula. *Just be quiet, and in Los Angeles you'll have beetles and bananas.*

Fionnula chattered her teeth.

"There!" said Julie.

You'll have figs and papayas. You'll have strawberries and avocado and spiders. "Oh," Phil said. "I'm traveling with a kitten."

"That's a kitten?"

Luckily, at that moment the pilot came on the loudspeaker to give them their coordinates. As far as Phil could determine, they were smack in the middle of nowhere, near absolutely nothing at all. The Dane returned with his baby and, smiling cordially, slipped through the velveteen curtain into first class.

"Excuse me," Julie said, hurrying after him. On the upside, she had lingered a long time in economy. On the downside, she had clearly not been lingering because of Phil. It occurred to him that he was witnessing a biological phenomenon: women were programmed to respond to creatures with large eyes and heads, such as babies, puppies, and kittens—not to mention many types of monkey.

As soon as Julie disappeared, Fionnula chittered again. Probably the medicine was wearing off. Phil was rooting around in his carry-on for the drugs the breeder had given him, which came in a red plastic pillbox with Chinese characters on it, and needed to be fed to Fionnula inside a chunk of banana, when he had an idea. If walking was good for babies, why not for bush babies? He didn't especially want to draw attention to her, but it would certainly be worse if she started howling. If he wrapped her in a blanket, no one would know. And who could help loving the bush baby, with her large, ringed eyes? He was sure that in the right circumstances, even practical Aubrey would have come around.

Phil crouched down in front of his seat and unlatched the cage. Fionnula stopped whining and stared at him reproachfully, flicking her long tail back and forth. Her translucent, triangular ears were cocked.

"Want to take a walk?" Phil whispered. Luckily, the man across the aisle had put away his magazine and was sleeping soundly. Although Fionnula hadn't defecated, the sour smell of galago urine was unmistakable.

"That's right," Phil coaxed her. "We're going to get a little air." He held the blanket in front of the cage and carefully slipped the latch. Fionnula stayed where she was. "Come on," Phil said. "Come to papa." He sat back from the cage, on his haunches, so to speak, giving her a little space. When she flattened her ears, Phil was ready for her. He held his blanket in front of the cage, like a net; Fionnula leapt gracefully into it. They were in sync, like a pair of circus performers.

"Good *girl*," he whispered. He clasped her tightly against his chest; Fionnula whistled, an alert to other lesser galagos of nearby predators— such as the eagle, owl, snake, or genet. Phil felt slightly offended.

"What do you think I am?" he asked. "A genet?"

With the bush baby in his arms, Phil stood up, banging his head on the underside of the overhead bin. He suppressed a groan and, holding her more tightly than usual, carried her down the aisle to the bathroom, patting her lightly on the back. It was unlikely that she would burp, but the gesture gave him a certain satisfaction. He was surprised that people didn't seem more interested. When he was a child, air travel had been a different thing: you arrived early, all dressed up, as if for an adventure. You made eye contact with fellow passengers, as if to confirm that you'd all be looking out for one another. Now it was almost like getting onto the subway; no one chatted up their seatmate, or offered to share food or reading material. He wondered what would happen if there was some kind of accident. Would people suddenly turn to comfort and touch one another? Or would they continue staring fixedly at their tray tables, struggling alone with their ambivalent attitudes toward God?

The lavatories were occupied.

"Shhh," Phil said, because it seemed appropriate, not because Fionnula was making any noise. Nor was she moving. He released his grip a little, feeling for her breath. It was hard to do through the blanket. Was she getting enough air? What if she were dead! He lifted the corner of the blanket, as he'd seen the Dane do with his baby, and whispered her name. She was a warm little bundle in his palm, all eight ounces of her. Could she be sleeping? He wanted to reassure her that there were no eagles, owls, genets, or snakes around.

"Fionnula," he whispered.

There was nothing.

"Fionnula!" A woman in the last row turned to stare at him; he didn't care. "Hey *please*," he said. "Fionnula—*wake up.*"

Fionnula's ears popped up; he felt a faint pressure on his palm and, as his heart expanded with happiness and relief, his baby leapt easily out of the blanket, onto the headrest in front of them. Before Phil could grab her, she had leapt again: three and four rows at a time, across the aisles, landing not only on seatbacks but on shoulders, laps, and one tousled, newly awakened head. Fionnula cried out at full voice, exulting in her newfound freedom: *Chee! Chee! Chee!*

Someone screamed. Other people got to their feet. The flight attendants pushed past him. Fionnula stayed at seat level as long as possible before dropping to the floor, evacuating three rows in one stroke. A steward pushed past the passengers in the aisle, knelt, and peered under the empty seats.

"Excuse me," Phil said. "That's my—kitten."

"Well, then, you'd better go get it." It was Karen from Portland; she was right behind him, and she sounded less than pleased. Phil took the banana out of his pocket and unpeeled it. He hurried down the aisle and handed it meekly to the steward.

"Oh, thanks," the steward said. "This is great." Not yet aware of Fionnula's provenance, he obviously believed that Phil was the kind of helpful passenger who always brought a supply of potassium-rich foods on board, in case of emergency.

"Excuse me, ma'am. If you'll just step back a moment." Under his breath Phil heard him say: "What the fuck?"

"She's not dangerous," Phil said.

But the steward didn't appear to hear him. He was cajoling Fionnula, stretching out his hand with the banana in the palm, the way you might feed a horse. "Here, here. C'mere now, buster."

Buster?

The steward shook his head. "You're supposed to be prepared for anything—but this? E-fucking-T, two hours from LAX?"

"She's a galago!" Phil said. And then more softly, "A lesser one." By bending down and turning his head he could just make her out: her sensitive pink ears were quivering. She didn't know the word *snake* or *owl* or *genet* (what was a genet, anyway?) but some code deep inside her was alert to them. She had captured a bag of peanuts and her enormous nocturnal eyes shone, as bright as the foil wrapping, in the darkness underneath the seats. What was she thinking, assuming she was thinking? Was she imagining talons on her back?

"Fionnula," he whispered. "Here, girl."

The steward turned to him in disbelief. "Is this *your* animal?"

"He's traveling with a *kitten*." Karen was standing above them. "It's a very *rare breed*."

Phil looked up, as if for guidance: suddenly, materializing in the doorway of the first-class cabin, towering over passengers and crew alike, was the Dane. He had retrieved Fionnula's cage from Phil's row; holding it under one arm and his suddenly docile baby under the other, he strode triumphantly down the aisle, like the Beowulf warrior, and set the cage in the middle of the center aisle. As if harkening to a silent command, Fionnula trotted between the pillows and carry-ons, still holding the shiny bag of peanuts in her mouth, and hopped delicately into the cage. The steward latched the cage and stood up. Someone began to clap. All around them, one by one, and then row by row, others joined in, building to an ovation.

A moment later, Phil heard Julie's honeyed voice coming from the intercom at the front of the plane:

"Ladies and gentlemen. We're sorry for the disturbance in the economy section of the aircraft. As you have no doubt noticed, a domestic animal brought on board by one of your fellow passengers was temporarily loose in the cabin. I am happy to report that your steward, Rick—assisted by a very helpful first-class passenger—now has the situation under control."

People were looking at Phil. "Was that a monkey?"

"A ferret?"

"It was a mink, wasn't it? My grandmother had one."

"I'll take her back now," Phil said.

"Just have a seat," said the steward. "We'll return her to you at the end of the flight, when we pass back the coats."

"But she needs to be with me!"

"With the coats," the steward said firmly.

There was nothing to do but return to his seat. Phil stared out the dark window and saw his own face reflected, its familiar expression of dumb hurt: What was wrong with him? They had confiscated his baby—his bush baby, but still. They had basically declared him unfit. If he couldn't take care of a seven-inch primate, he certainly could never be a father. That was something Cece must've sensed from the beginning, although she'd been too kind to say it. And yet, she had confided in him. She couldn't ask him to come, not in so many words, but he had heard it in her voice.

The sky divided itself, opened along a fold. There was a very faint gray horizon. Phil leaned forward in his seat, as if urging the plane to go faster. It had been ten years, and his nephew needed him. Or if not his nephew, then maybe she needed him herself.

16.

WHILE I WAS WITH THE TRAVERSES, I HAD A HABIT OF GETTING UP EARLY.
I liked to exercise in the mornings, before it got too hot. Sometimes Mrs.
Travers would be out there too, swimming her laps in the pool.

"You are an inspiration," she would say to me, after she had wrapped
herself modestly in a large beach towel. "Those are tai chi, aren't they?"

"Only calisthenics," I told her, but perhaps she didn't hear me, because a few days later I heard her describing to a friend how I got up every
morning "at sunrise, to practice *qigong*."

When I was finished with my morning routine (three sets each of fifteen push-ups, sit-ups, squats, and lunges), I would go into the kitchen
and make my tea, and then carry it to the rose garden, where I could be
quiet for a few moments and let my mind drift, without anyone wondering why I wasn't getting down to work in my elegant studio. The studio
was windowed on all sides, like a glass tank. Cece and the housekeeper
were constantly knocking on my door to retrieve things they'd forgotten
there (and, conveniently, to check up on me). I had seen a room I would
have much preferred—a small, private guest room in the back of the
house—but after the Traverses had gone to so much trouble with the pool
house, I could hardly ask to move.

"It will take you a week or two to get settled," Mrs. Travers had said,
but before the end of the first week, she was remarking on how eager she
was to see the work I would produce, and looking at me in a funny way
when she came into the den and found me watching television.

"Is everything all right out there?" she would ask. "Is there enough
light?" I thought of my cousin's studio at Dashanzi, with the dirty win-

dows and the dirtier sink, the old brushes stuck into coffee cans and the oilcloth on the floor, the bare cot and the unwashed dishes on the table, drawing insects. I assured Mrs. Travers that her pool house was not only the most beautiful studio I had ever had the opportunity to use (very true), but also the most beautiful I had ever seen.

"Sometimes it's so beautiful that I get distracted," I told her. "I just sit there and look out at the garden."

Cece nodded, unconvinced. "You're homesick," she said. "It will wear off."

It was early Friday morning of that first week that I spent with the Traverses, at the hour when pale sunlight bleaches the gravel walkways of the garden, and the only sound is the breeze in the dusty rosebushes. I was reading the names of the flowers from small plastic stakes—the delicate pewter-colored Blue Girls, the Belle Amours, and my favorites, the creamy, cakelike Perditas—when I spotted the intruder, lurking in the bluish shadows behind the garbage cans.

The strangest thing was that he seemed to be trying to catch my attention.

"*Ss,*" he seemed to say. "*Ss, ss.*"

He was a very tall, thin man, with large blue eyes like an actor on television. His clothes looked slept-in, but decent: he wore khaki trousers and a not very clean white linen shirt with wooden buttons. There was a yellowish stain on the left pocket. You could see that he hadn't slept; his red, bloodshot eyes gave him the appearance of a drug addict. I admit I was nervous, but I didn't want to wake the family if I could help it. This was my first chance to do something in return for their kindness to me, and I thought I could get rid of the intruder on my own.

The man moved toward me sideways, like a crab. Every few seconds he looked back at the garbage cans, as if he thought someone was going to come after him from that direction. "*Ss,*" he said. "Hey, you! Are you the gardener?"

So, he thought I was a servant—even though I was wearing a pair of designer trousers from Hong Kong, and a fine shirt of Egyptian cotton that Cece had given me (in spite of my protestations), since it was too small for Dr. Travers.

"No," I said coldly. "I am not."

The intruder looked startled. "Then what are you doing here?"

He was asking me this question.

I put my hand into my left pocket, where I kept the small knife with a pearl handle that my painting teacher, Old Wang, had given me when I was sixteen years old. I took it out and flicked my wrist, and the blade snapped open. The intruder was startled.

"Christ," he said. "Put that away. I need you to do me a favor."

"All I have to do is yell," I said. "The housekeeper will release the dogs." (He did not have to know the particulars about these animals: the sheepdog Salty, who needed to be fed by hand, ran sideways with a limp, and cowered if you raised your hand at her, and the whippet Dr. Spock, who had recently reached his adult weight of six and a half pounds.)

"Salty?" the intruder said. "Give me a break."

At that point I had to wonder whether he was a real burglar. In spite of his decrepit appearance, I didn't really think he was homeless. I had a sudden fear that this was one of Dr. Travers's insane patients, coming after his psychiatrist in a murderous fit, as in a movie I had recently seen on Cinemax.

"Put your hands up," I said, but I sounded tentative.

"For the love of God," said the intruder, but he put them up. "Is this all right? Will you come over here for a second and let me explain?"

That the intruder was moving toward the driveway was a good sign; that he wasn't the slightest bit afraid of me and my knife was not so good.

"All I need you to do is deliver this note—d'you mind?" He waved the fingers of his right hand, and against my better judgment I allowed him to reach into his own pocket, from which he withdrew a folded piece of white paper. "Give this to your employer."

"I don't know whom you're speaking of."

"I'm speaking of Cece," the intruder said. "You know who that is, don't you?"

"Mrs. Travers is not my employer."

The intruder looked at me curiously. "Maybe you're her boyfriend." He was not even pretending to keep his hands in the air anymore.

"I am her guest," I told him, in as curt a voice as I could manage.

I expected him to apologize for his mistake, but the intruder simply nodded: "Then you can give her something for me."

"If I give her the note, will you go?"

The intruder nodded. "And a small gift." He retreated behind the garbage cans, where he retrieved a square sort of suitcase, covered by a black cloth. I became aware of a high, twittering sound, which was nevertheless not birdlike. "Carry it by the handle, here," he said. "And if you could just take the cloth off when you give it to her. Not like a magician or anything—don't make a big production—but so that she knows it's a gift. Here, look—"

But before he could remove the cloth, a sound made us both freeze; I realized that by allowing the intruder to stay and talk, I was now responsible for his presence in the rose garden. Not only had I been unable to expel him, I had failed to raise the alarm.

I am sorry to say that I swore at the intruder then, and called him a name, although of course he did not understand Cantonese. We were both staring at the door to the den, which was opening, first the sliding glass panel, and then the screen. A moment later Mrs. Travers, wearing a one-piece green bathing suit, stepped onto the lawn and walked barefoot across the grass. She didn't look in our direction but headed directly to the deck; she disappeared for a moment into the pool house, and re-emerged with a striped towel, which she spread out carefully in the sun. Then she climbed onto the diving board and hesitated for a moment there, bouncing very gently on her toes.

As I have mentioned, Cece was forty-four years old. In Harbin a forty-four-year-old woman is finished being a mother, and is very often already a grandmother. In Los Angeles, however, time moves more slowly. Particularly with the morning light in her expertly highlighted hair—gold, butter, caramel—and on her carefully protected skin, Cece was a young woman. The bathing suit covered her hips and lifted her ample breasts (the nipples of which—it would be dishonest not to mention—were prominent underneath the worn green cotton). The conservative cut of the bathing suit emphasized her still-slim waist and the swell of her hips and bottom. The reader can, perhaps, forgive me for this description of my hostess, or at least remember that I was very far from home, surrounded by strangers, without a lover or the prospect of finding one.

That morning among the rosebushes I watched the intruder, who was looking at Mrs. Travers on the diving board in a way that made me think he might be in the same situation I was.

"That's Mrs. Travers," I said, glad to show my intimacy with the family.

"Cease," he said.

His response seemed unfriendly, as well as unnecessarily formal. "You ought to get out of here now, before someone calls the police," I told him. But before I could make good on this threat, three things happened: Mrs. Travers dove into the pool; whatever was in the black box began to make an unsettling noise; and the screen door opened again. A young woman stepped onto the patio and called out:

"Mom!"

The girl was wearing a pair of men's striped pajamas and her long, dark hair was messy from sleeping. I guessed that this was Olivia Travers, who had arrived the previous night from France.

"Hello," I called, and then, because I didn't know what to say: "You have a visitor." Perhaps I was trying to save my own face, by turning the intruder into a guest.

Olivia climbed the three brick steps to the rose garden. "Hey," she said. "Uncle Phil. Long time no see." She wrinkled her nose. "God—what is that?"

"How was Paris?" asked Uncle Phil.

Olivia hopped up the steps and stood with one bare foot on top of the other. One of the first things I had noticed about the Traverses was that they often walked outside without their shoes. "It was awesome," Olivia said. "Almost everyone from Dance Directions was there."

"Dance Directions?"

"That's my school's company. I'm a principal this year."

"Livy?" Her mother was standing in the shallow end of the pool, shading her eyes against the angle of the sun.

"Hi Mommer!" Olivia called. She ran across the grass, suddenly childish. Mrs. Travers squinted at us. She was not wearing her glasses.

"Oh, Jesus," the intruder said softly. "Here we go, here we go." But he stayed right where he was.

"Hello?" Mrs. Travers climbed out of the pool, one hand on the railing. She wrapped the towel firmly around her body and made her way toward us. "Mr. Yuan?"

Then she suddenly stopped short. Water was dripping from her hair, slicked back now, into her eyes, but there was no mistaking what was happening. There is something about watching a blue-eyed person cry (if you are a black- or brown-eyed person, then you know what I mean) that inspires sympathy. Maybe it's just that their tears are less easy to conceal.

"Cease," the uncle said for the second time. Still crying, Mrs. Travers threw her arms around his neck in a way that I will admit made me jealous—not because I had any romantic feelings for Mrs. Travers myself, but because, far from being an intruder, this person was clearly more welcome at the Traverses' than I was. I looked away.

Olivia might have had the same impulse, since she chose that moment to crouch down in front of the cage. She pinched her nose with one hand and lifted the cover with the other: there, blinking its large eyes in the light, was a small monkey. Or a large rat—it was the size of a rat, but it looked like a monkey, with prehensile hands and a long, simian tail. Its coat was gray, with a white bib under the chin, and its ears were lined with delicate pink fuzz. You could see its tiny black snout working frantically as it tried to figure out where it was. I felt sorry for it, exposed that way: everyone could see the mess of yellow-green turds it had just deposited in the corner of its cage.

"Sorry," said Phil, whose hand was still clasping Mrs. Travers's shoulder. "She was penned up for the whole flight. I was going to take her to a hotel, but it turns out they don't accept pets. And then I just thought if I could come here and wait until a reasonable hour—and then I saw Mr.—"

"Yuan," Cece supplied. "Oh—I haven't introduced you. This is Mr. Yuan, an artist whom we have the honor of hosting for the year."

I shook Uncle Phil's hand, and then his niece's—but Olivia was clearly more interested in the animal at our feet. She frowned and said something in French, which made Mrs. Travers and the uncle laugh. I had never studied any languages other than English, and a little bit of Russian as a child.

"I was trying to bring you a present," Uncle Phil said. "I guess I fucked it up, as usual."

"She's just gorgeous," Mrs. Travers knelt down. "Aren't you? Aren't you a gorgeous little monkey? Aren't you a gorgeous little girl?"

"She's not a monkey," Phil said.

We all looked at Phil. It was hard to imagine what she was, if she was not a monkey.

"She's a bush baby."

"A bush baby!"

"She's from Namibia, originally. I bought her from a Chinese breeder in Queens."

"At the rare animal market!" Cece exclaimed. "Is *that* what you were doing that day?"

I thought the uncle seemed embarrassed. "Some people say Flushing is New York's real Chinatown." He looked at me.

"I've never been to New York," I told him. I still felt a little annoyed about the way he'd failed to identify himself, putting me in an awkward position. At the time, the hypocrisy of this sentiment wasn't clear to me.

Both mother and daughter were crouched in front of the cage now, and although I was only looking at the bush baby, a type of animal I had never seen before, it was impossible not to notice that Cece's towel had fallen open, and her generous cleavage was exposed. Her daughter might have noticed it too, since she suggested that the two of them go inside and change.

"All right," Cece said, standing up. "And then we'll all have breakfast."

"I'm not sure I can stay," Uncle Phil said, glancing at the house.

"Don't be ridiculous," Cece said.

"Too late," said the uncle.

Mrs. Travers only shook her head and smiled. "You must be exhausted."

"I might lie down in the pool house, just for a minute."

"Oh—" said Mrs. Travers uncomfortably, and I could see the problem. I could also see the solution to one of my problems, dropping right into my lap.

"I will move my things."

"No," Mrs. Travers said. "Absolutely not."

"It's no trouble."

"That's very kind," Mrs. Travers said. "But Philip isn't staying."

"No," Phil agreed.

"Really," I said, "I insist." But Mrs. Travers was firm. She thought that I was employing a particularly Chinese form of politeness: refusing what you want until it is forced upon you. Of course, in any country, politeness is often just a way of getting what you want.

"I'm leaving anyway," the uncle said. "I just wanted to drop off the bush baby."

"No!" Mrs. Travers and I said together. "You can at least stay for breakfast," she added, turning to Olivia. "Honey, could you tell Lupe I need her help here?"

Olivia started in the direction of the kitchen. Her mother looked at Phil, and then suddenly called after her. "Livy, honey? Sorry—I'll talk to Lupe. You go tell Daddy that Phil is here."

Phil began to say something, but Mrs. Travers interrupted him.

"We'll have to keep her away from Salty and the cats—that's the only problem. Unless you think she should be outside?"

"Maybe in the pool house?" Phil said. "That is, if Mr. Yuan doesn't mind."

Mrs. Travers shook her head. "The cats sleep in the pool house."

There was an awkward pause, in which I had my brilliant idea:

"The problem is my allergy."

"You're allergic to the bush baby?" Cece asked.

"No one's allergic to the bush baby," Phil said. "She's nonallergenic."

"I'm allergic to cats," I told them. "So you see—"

"More and more people are developing allergies," the uncle contributed helpfully. "Because of all the carcinogens. It's like an epidemic."

"Oh, no, why didn't you say something?" Mrs. Travers looked genuinely distressed, and I felt sorry for lying. But there was no other option.

"I am sorry to cause you so much trouble," I said. "But perhaps that guest room?"

"I guess that's a possibility," Mrs. Travers said. "There's a back entrance, so at least you wouldn't have to go trooping through Max's room all the time." At that moment, Olivia reappeared, followed, a moment later, by her father.

"Gordo," Phil said softly, although Dr. Travers was all the way across the lawn and could not hear him. "Long time, no see."

"Mom!" Olivia shouted: "Lupe wants to know, how many people for breakfast?"

"At least stay a couple of hours," Mrs. Travers said softly, as her husband and Olivia approached us across the large, very bright green lawn.

The uncle protested, but with less conviction: "I just wanted to drop off Fionnula."

"Fionnula!" The name seemed to mean something to Mrs. Travers. Once again, I thought she would cry.

"You can change her name if you want," said Phil. "She's yours now."

"No," Mrs. Travers said. "Fionnula is perfect."

17.

WHAT DID ONE WEAR TO MEET A DISSIDENT? JOAN HAD CHOSEN A LONG,
gray silk skirt, a white T-shirt, and comfortable black sandals. Going
through the scarves in her closet, she had found one with Chinese characters on it and cringed inwardly. From childhood she'd had the habit of
inventing mortifying situations for herself and playing them out in her
mind: Cece introducing her to the dissident, and Joan edging in to say,
"Oh, hello. Did you notice my scarf? It's Chinese! I thought I would wear
it tonight, and you could tell me what it means."

Even when she allowed herself very little time, Joan was always early.
As she stood on Gordon and Cece's doorstep, she admired again the yellow flowering trees along the curving driveway, the thick bougainvillea
growing over the balcony, and the tiled eaves, casting sharp, rectilinear
shadows on the house's bright face. She wondered whether Gordon
minded that the money had come from Cece. No matter how expertly he
managed it (husbanded it, Joan thought) and no matter how much it in-
creased (her brother's investments had grown with an admirable steadiness throughout the 1990s) she knew Gordon would never forget that
their fortune had begun with Cece's capital.

There were some ways in which she and her older brother were alike.
They couldn't stand to fail. Even to succeed wasn't enough, if the success
wasn't spectacular. Both of them tended to diminish their own talents to
others, not out of modesty but in order to make those strengths more
brilliant when they did appear. Both of them liked to go through the
proper channels, to jump through hoops; only then could their achieve-
ment be meaningful.

There was thundering on the stairs inside the house, and then a voice calling, "I'll get it." Before he opened the door, she heard Max behind it: "Mom! Aunt Joan is here!"

"Hello, Max."

"Hi," Max said.

She didn't try to kiss him; she didn't like kissing hellos, and she was pretty sure Max didn't either. "How's it going?"

"People are in the yard. Having drinks." Max made a face. *"Even the children drink wine in France."*

His imitation of his sister was good; Joan laughed. Immediately Max's face darkened, as if he'd been tricked into something.

"Joan? Is that you?" Cece hurried breathlessly across the living room, holding a glass of champagne. She was wearing a white sundress with red and pink flowers splashed across it, a white sweater knotted over her shoulders, and sandals. The dress seemed to match the living room, carpeted and upholstered in white, with a red amaryllis in a crystal vase on the piano, beneath a drippy Diebenkorn horizon of pale pinks and greens.

"You look wonderful," Cece said. "How do you stay so skinny?"

By worrying, Joan thought. "So do you," she said.

"My arms!" Cece looked genuinely horrified: "I just saw them in the bathroom—they're all cottage cheesy. Like I *am* cottage cheese, not like I've been eating it. What could have possessed me to wear something sleeveless, do you think?" Cece put her glass down on the piano and embraced Joan. "I'm so glad you're here," she whispered. Then she stepped back, glancing behind her in a nervous way. Joan wondered if something had gone wrong with the dissident already. There were reasons that people didn't just take strangers into their houses.

"Is he here?"

"Harry Lin? No, but I'm sure he'll be here any minute."

"The *dissident.*"

"Oh, yes," Cece said. "He's outside. Gordon is showing him the blight on the eugenia."

"Mom?" Max called from upstairs. He was hanging over the banister.

"What is it, sweetie?"

He seemed to be leaning dangerously far. "Can we eat now?"

"We're finishing our drinks," Cece said. "I would love it if you would come downstairs and join our guests."

Joan wondered whom else Cece had invited. She planned to avoid being seated next to the eligible professor.

"When can we then?"

"If you can hang on for just a half an hour," Cece began.

The problem, Joan thought, was that Cece was too lenient. Often children who rebelled were just asking for more discipline. She had heard her brother say that parenting was all about treating children with respect; Joan sometimes wondered whether Max might want his parents to treat him with *less* respect.

"A half an *hour*?"

"I'm sorry," Cece said. "If you come downstairs, you can ask Lupe for a glass of champagne. Just tell your father it's ginger ale."

But Max was apparently not interested in socializing, even with the promise of alcohol; Joan heard his sullen footsteps retreating toward the back of the house—what Cece and Gordon referred to as the "children's wing."

"Is everything OK?" Joan asked, as Cece rejoined her in the living room.

"Fine," Cece said. "Better than fine actually. Mr. Yuan is absolutely lovely."

"That's good," Joan said.

Cece took a sip of champagne. She was getting up her courage.

"What's wrong?" Joan said.

"You're so perceptive. Because of what you do, I guess—or you do what you do because you're perceptive? Were you always perceptive?"

Joan would not allow herself to be steamrollered by flattery. "Cece?"

Cece smiled weakly.

"Is there something wrong with the dissident?"

"Well, um, no—although he's allergic to cats."

"That doesn't seem insurmountable," Joan said. "Maybe you should get rid of some of them."

Cece managed to nod agreeably, and at the same time dismiss that suggestion as ridiculous. "And so, of course, he can't sleep in the pool house."

"Isn't there a guest room upstairs?"

Cece nodded: "That's where he's staying now, but it's so small. He seemed to be just fine until yesterday, which makes me wonder—"

"Mom?" Max called again.

"For Christ's sake, Max! Give us a minute!"

It was extremely unusual to hear Cece yell at one of her children. Joan wondered if it was the champagne, although it was also unlike Cece to have more than one glass of anything at a time.

Cece looked as if she'd surprised herself too. "I'm sorry," she said to Joan. She went to the bottom of the stairs. "Max?"

"Forget it."

"Max, please come down here."

Max came halfway down the stairs and stopped.

"That's better," Cece said. "What is it?"

"I was just wondering, since I have to *stay home* tonight—is Mr. Yuan staying upstairs?" He glanced at Joan, and then quickly away. "Or is Uncle Phil?"

"What?" said Joan.

"Max!" Cece's ears were suddenly bright red. She turned to Joan, and as if blushes were communicable, like yawns, Joan felt her throat and her neck getting warm.

"Phil is—" But there was no reason to continue. It was very clear from Cece's expression, not to mention her dress and her heels, and the champagne cocktails, that Phil was here. He was right out in the backyard.

"Go outside now," Cece said to Max. "We'll be out in a minute."

Cece's voice was calm, but Joan could see a reflection of her anger in the shamed way that Max was picking at the varnish on the banister. He must've been told not to mention that his uncle was here when he answered the door. Gordon must've been occupying their younger brother in the backyard, while Cece did the delicate work of telling Joan. Why hadn't they at least called to warn her?

Cece descended the three steps into the living room, walking with the accommodating swivel that was natural to some women in heels, and not to others. She picked up her drink from the piano and ran one finger around the lip of the glass. "I wanted to say something before tonight, but . . ."

Joan couldn't help herself. "You knew he was coming?"

Cece looked shocked. "Joan—no. I swear. I tried to call you today, but your phone was turned off."

That was true, unfortunately. Joan liked to turn the ringer off while she was working (or trying to work), and she sometimes forgot to turn it on again.

"I had a feeling, I guess," Cece continued. "But he said he was in New York. He mentioned another woman," Cece blushed and corrected herself: "Another woman besides his girlfriend, I mean. But then it didn't turn out to be a woman at all!"

"Who did it turn out to be?"

"A monkey."

Joan looked at Cece.

"Actually, she's not a monkey: she's a rare Namibian bush baby! He brought her as a present—isn't that sweet?"

"Just what you need."

Cece nodded. "We've never had anything like her."

"Where is Phil now?" Joan asked.

Cece gestured toward the backyard. "He was eager to meet Mr. Yuan. Gordon and Livy are out there with them."

Probably Phil was doing research for a new play, on the subject of Chinese dissident painters. Or maybe her brother was so gifted that he didn't need to do any research—probably he'd already sold the screenplay for a million dollars, while Joan had been reading student e-mail and staring at a blank screen.

If she had known she was going to see her younger brother, Joan thought, she would've invented some recent accomplishment, or at least prepared the facts of her life into a more convincingly successful pattern. For example: she had published four books, was on the faculty of a respected college, owned a semi-valuable house in Cheviot Hills, and had been involved with two or three interesting men in the not-too-distant past. Or alternately: she was a divorced, middle-aged woman who taught in a correspondence writing program that she secretly despised in order to keep her health insurance.

Cece was looking at Joan with a hopeful expression. "I'm so sorry," she said. "I know your feelings about Phil are—lukewarm. But it's OK, right? We can all have dinner? I'm so eager for you to meet Mr. Yuan, and Harry Lin should be here any minute."

Cece broke off as Gordon opened the sliding door. Behind him, bending slightly to compensate for his height, was her brother Phil, involved in an intense conversation with a person who could only be the dissident.

18.

YUAN ZHAO WAS A YOUNG MAN OF SLIGHT BUILD, WITH ROUND, JOHN Lennon–style glasses and a long, sleek ponytail. He was wearing a dark purple collarless Chinese shirt akin to the scarf Joan had rejected earlier, dark gray pajama pants, and black cloth slippers. Joan wondered if these were the kind of clothes he wore at home, or if he had bought them especially for Los Angeles. It was rare that someone corresponded so exactly to your image of him. In fact the dissident wasn't what she'd been imagining, for exactly that reason.

"I see," Phil was saying. "But if the art scene went from zero to sixty like that, there must be a lot of junk too?" Her brother knew Joan was there, but he was going to finish his conversation with the dissident before he even looked at her. This was an old trick: Phil would wait several moments after he'd entered a room to make eye contact, a peculiarity that could seem pretentious, until you realized it was just a way for him to prepare. Her brother was one of those people who manage to transform their own awkwardness into a surprisingly successful social routine.

"A lot of junk," the dissident agreed. "More junk than not-junk."

Finally Gordon interrupted them: "Mr. Yuan, I'd like to introduce my sister, Joan."

Joan and the dissident shook hands. She was struck by the smoothness of his complexion, clean-shaven and unlined: he looked even younger than his photograph. She supposed that different people's bodies responded differently to the sorts of extreme hardships Yuan Zhao had endured.

Phil looked up, as if he'd just noticed her: "Joanie!" he exclaimed, and grinned. "Oops—do you still hate that?"

"As ever," Joan said.

"I've been telling Mr. Yuan a bit about our name," Gordon said. "Did Cece tell you I've turned up a new lead?"

"Hail," Phil said. "Noble Travers!"

"What my brother doesn't realize is that before the revolution, the name was quite plausibly 'de Travestère'—*ci-devant*, as they say."

Phil coughed suspiciously and frowned at his gin and tonic. Historically it had been difficult for Joan not to laugh when Phil did. Luckily Gordon wasn't paying attention to them.

"I'm searching for our crossing ancestor. I turned up the family I mentioned, in France, and also an unlucky gentleman who succumbed to fever somewhere in the middle of the Atlantic. There's also a family of obviously English origins—Travers, or alternately Travis—from Lancashire, who settled in Newfoundland in the mid-eighteenth century."

Mr. Yuan's expression was one of polite interest, but Joan wondered how trivial this conversation must seem to someone who had recently been jailed for his political beliefs. The article had given a little information about conditions in Qincheng, the "extremely isolated" facility where the dissident had been detained and the only prison in China run by the Ministry of Public Security. In addition to political prisoners and high-level Party officials, it had also once housed Puyi, the last emperor of China. The journalist who wrote the article wouldn't have been allowed inside Qincheng, located in a remote county outside Beijing, and so of course he could not describe it. How interesting that there was someone standing on Cece's dazzling ivory carpet, underneath the stunningly subtle Diebenkorn, who could.

"Of course," Gordon was saying, "my attraction to the subject is not entirely personal. What is it about our collective psyche right now, in America in the year 2000, that makes us so interested in digging up our roots?" Her brother looked like he was going to continue, but just then the phone rang: a shrill double tone from every corner of the house, like an alarm. Mr. Yuan jumped, spilling some of his white wine on the rug.

"Excuse me!" The dissident looked wildly around the room. "Is that the door?"

"Just the phone," Gordon said.

"My God," Phil said. "Is that really necessary?"

"Not in the children's wing," Gordon said. "They answer it the second it rings. It's impossible to get anyone to pick up the main lines, though."

"Please forgive me," said Yuan Zhao.

"Are we expecting someone?" Phil asked.

"Harry Lin," Gordon said. "A friend of Mr. Yuan's, and a colleague of mine from UCLA." He gave Joan a significant look: clearly he was in on Cece's plan. She thought she would die if Phil knew she was being set up.

But Phil's attention was focused on the dissident. "How do you know Harry Lin?"

"Very slightly," the dissident said. "We met once in Beijing. He came to see an art project. I was a performer."

Joan wanted to ask about the project, but Yuan Zhao's expression stopped her. He seemed as glad as she was that the professor hadn't arrived yet.

There was the clicking of heels in the dining room; a moment later Cece appeared in the archway between the living room and the foyer.

"That was Harry." Cece turned to Mr. Yuan. "I'm sorry to say that Professor Lin won't be joining us tonight. Something came up with his work at the last minute."

One glance at Mr. Yuan confirmed Joan's suspicions. The dissident noticeably relaxed, and even smiled a little.

"Harry's a *very* bright guy. But he's consumed by department politics. And it's not his fault. He's a fantastic scholar, first-class—and so what do they do with him?" Gordon shook his head: "They give him an endowed chair, and turn him into a glorified administrator. The tragedy of American academia." He looked at Yuan Zhao. "Harry's from Beijing, isn't he?"

"Originally," Yuan Zhao said. "But he married an American. When I met him he was doing research in Beijing, for a book about the Southern Song. We had an interesting conversation about the monk painter Fanlong."

"I thought he wrote about contemporary painters," Gordon said.

Yuan Zhao nodded. "In Beijing that year his focus changed. Now I believe he is writing about even more recent work—about performance art."

"Including yours?" Joan asked, making an effort to steer the conversation away from Harry Lin.

"Mine and others," the dissident said modestly.

Perhaps that was why the professor made Yuan Zhao uncomfortable, Joan thought. No one liked to be studied. She wondered if there was a way to write about people without unnerving them. Of course it was different for fiction writers than it was for scholars. If Joan sometimes began with a real person in mind, the character would either cleave from the real-life model almost immediately, or die on the page. Since you could never set someone down on paper as they really were, it didn't make sense to ask permission.

Phil stepped closer and put his arm around her: "It's great to see you, you know that?"

"It's great to see you too," Joan managed.

"How are you really? Are you seeing . . ." Phil looked around, as if he might have missed Joan's date until now.

"No."

"You're lucky." Phil sighed. "It's more trouble than it's worth."

"It's better for me at the moment," Joan said. "I'm at a point where I have to prioritize my work."

Phil smiled knowingly. "What are you working on now?"

"My book just came out," Joan said. "I'm getting ready to do some readings for the paperback."

"Oh, the paperback," Phil said. "I thought you meant a new book. The—wait a minute, I'll get it—Honest Truth?"

"Half Truths," Joan said. " 'Honest truth' is redundant."

Phil laughed. "That's right. Well, you should get me a copy—or don't get me one. I'll buy it from the bookstore. Can you get it at any bookstore?"

"I've been meaning to ask you about your play," Joan said.

Phil did an impression of someone who was feeling bashful. He wiped an imaginary smudge off his glass, looked at the floor, and shook his head. "I'd be embarrassed to talk about it with you."

"Why? What's it about?"

"Not because of what it's about." Phil raised his eyes demurely from his glass. Her brother had incredibly long, thick eyelashes, one of the many things that had inspired her envy as a teenager. "Because you're the real writer."

It was not a compliment. It was a way for her brother to be the underdog, a tactic he'd used all through their childhood and adolescence. While she and Gordon had struggled and strived, Phil managed to make everything he did look like the product of luck and grace.

"You didn't answer the question," Joan said.

19.

JOAN DIDN'T GET A CHANCE TO TALK WITH THE DISSIDENT UNTIL AFTER dinner, when the children disappeared upstairs and the adults retired with their coffee to the deck around the pool.

"You must be exhausted," Joan said, pulling up a chair next to Yuan Zhao's. Cece and Phil sat down a little distance across the deck: they seemed to be having their own conversation. Gordon had left to walk the dogs.

"I'm not used to so much wine," the dissident said.

"And you must still be suffering from the jet lag," Joan said. "I always found it very hard to speak a foreign language when I was tired. Your English is excellent, though."

"I went to a good primary school."

"That was in Shanxi Province?"

The dissident looked surprised. "Excuse me, how do you know that?"

"You'll have to forgive me—I read an article about you. From the *Taipei Times*? It was the only one we could find in English."

"I'd like to see that article."

It hadn't occurred to Joan that Yuan Zhao might not have had access to foreign press about himself until now. "I'm sorry, I left it at home. But I'd be happy to bring it for you another time."

"Was there a great deal about my early life?"

"Not much," Joan said. "It was mostly about the protests at Tiananmen Square."

"Ah," said the dissident, but he did not offer any more information.

"I'm interested because of my own political involvement in college," Joan said. "Which was very minor compared with yours, of course. You'll have to forgive me all of these questions. The news wasn't very complete here."

"The news was not very complete there, either."

"But you were one of the leaders," she said, flattering him a little.

"I wasn't a leader." Yuan Zhao looked profoundly uncomfortable, whether because of modesty or simply from the pressure of his memories, Joan wasn't sure. She was afraid she'd gone too far.

"We heard about the hunger strikers a great deal," she said. "Going without food makes a big impression on Americans." She was trying to make a joke, but the dissident didn't get it.

"When you talk with Americans, the conversation always begins with June 4, 1989," he observed. "That or the Cultural Revolution."

He seemed to be suggesting that they were only interested in the horrors of Chinese history, a criticism Joan was afraid had some merit. She wanted to prove him wrong: she wanted to be the kind of person who knew the right questions to ask.

"The article said that you were arrested again, in '94."

The dissident looked concerned. "I haven't read this article."

Joan knew she should stop pressing him, but something encouraged her to keep asking questions. She had a feeling she hadn't had in a long time, as if her brain was working involuntarily. It seemed to be mechanically sorting the information Yuan Zhao was giving her into larger and smaller piles. The pieces would have to be put together, and then cut up another way, and then half of them would have to be discarded. Very likely nothing would come of it: what did she know about China, after all? As she cautioned herself, however, she was getting more and more excited: an idea had appeared out of nowhere, like a puzzle, and one hand had begun to manipulate it, almost without her noticing.

"I was just asking about the arrest in '94. That was when you were involved with the Beijing East Village?"

"It was an accident that I got involved with the East Village artists. I was never very interested in performance art."

"What kind of accident?" Joan asked.

"A woman," said Yuan Zhao. "My fiancée, at the time."

"I didn't know you were married."

"I'm not," the dissident said. "We were—how do you say it?—going to be married."

"Engaged," Joan said. It seemed odd that the dissident would know *fiancée* but stumble over the word *engaged*.

"Engaged," Yuan Zhao repeated studiously.

There was an awkward silence. At the other end of the deck, Cece and Phil were talking softly. Salty dozed at their feet. Gordon had returned with the dogs, but he hadn't come back outside.

"It's so hard to balance work and relationships," Joan ventured. "I was married once, to another novelist. We joked about it, of course, but there was always an unspoken competition." She looked at the dissident; his expression seemed to encourage her to continue.

"I knew it was a bad idea, even then. I don't think married people should have the same career, but the problem is that often that's who you meet. Was your fiancée also an artist?"

"She was a fashion designer."

"But you went to jail together?"

Yuan Zhao waved his hand, gracefully dismissing his own ordeal. "She was the one who suffered. Chinese prisons can be—uncomfortable. In addition it was summer, very hot. And there is the question of disease."

"Did she get sick?"

He nodded.

"But she's all right now?"

"She was not especially strong, unfortunately."

He was so calm that it took Joan a moment to understand what he was saying. She was horrified.

"I am so sorry," she whispered. "The article didn't mention—please forgive me."

"Never mind," said Yuan Zhao.

He didn't seem upset, but Joan guessed that was cultural. She had pushed him out of stupid curiosity, and blundered into a tragedy. Even the journalist from the *Taipei Times* had been sensitive enough to leave

Yuan Zhao's dead fiancée out of the story. And here, in Joan's first conversation with him, she'd forced him to disclose it.

"Is my sister telling you about her heyday at Berkeley?" Phil said, from across the deck. "Hey, hey LBJ, and all that?"

Joan had never been so glad to be teased by her brother. "I barely mentioned it," she said. "But I think we've been keeping Mr. Yuan up too late."

Cece stood up. "You're absolutely right. Mr. Yuan, if you'll just come with me, I'll take you up the back stairs so we can avoid Max's room. He's furious with me for saying no to this party tonight," she added, to no one in particular.

"Thank you for talking with me," Joan said to the dissident. "I hope I didn't—"

The dissident gave her a little half-bow, and started across the lawn. Joan thought she'd rarely met someone who captured her imagination so immediately. It was a good argument for getting out more. Maybe people like Mr. Yuan were everywhere, just waiting to be discovered.

"Strange, isn't he?" Phil wandered over to her side of the deck, holding some sort of after-dinner liqueur.

"I thought he was fascinating," Joan said.

"Oh, yeah?"

"He was telling me about being arrested. Did you know he's been imprisoned for his work?"

"No," Phil said, watching the house.

"It's a paradox, I guess," Joan continued. "Of course it's better for artists to live in a free society, but I wonder if political pressure can sometimes be good for art?"

Phil smiled.

"What?"

Her brother shook his head. "Nothing."

"Why are you smiling?"

"I was just wondering"—he looked up innocently—"if you're thinking of writing a novel about him."

That right there, Joan thought, was the infuriating thing about Phil. Why was there never anyone around to witness it?

20.

THAT NIGHT, DESPITE MY EXHAUSTION, I LAY AWAKE FOR HOURS. I thought of the Traverses (particularly the nosy lady novelist), and of Harry Lin. Why had the professor failed to show up at the dinner party? Would he really continue to leave me alone, as X had promised? I wondered if Professor Lin remembered our conversation, during his visit to the East Village in the spring of '94: we had discussed the monk painter Fanlong, and his *Sixteen Luohans,* a scroll whose demon subjects are so persuasively human that you feel as if their faces have been copied off of people you know. There were few young artists, he had said, who were interested in the old masters today. When I got up onstage and did my part in the performance piece *Drip-Drop,* I heard the professor call out, "Bravo!"

Even if I'd impressed the professor then, however, it had been years since I'd participated in anything like *Drip-Drop.* I didn't doubt that I could teach schoolgirls to paint with ink, or that I could give a talk at the end of the year convincing the board of the Dubin Fund that I was "crossing borders and challenging my thinking," as I "engaged with artists of other cultures and disciplines." However I certainly didn't want to engage with any actual artists, and especially not art professors, who would be sure to determine very quickly that I was making absolutely no new work at all.

My cousin had dismissed these worries. Even if I didn't produce anything, he reasoned, I still had the *DNA-ture* paintings, which would comprise my first show. Once that was over, I would have plenty of time to decide what to do next.

I was not convinced. "Those paintings are more than ten years old."

"American collectors are at least ten years behind in Chinese experimental art," X told me. "Something that was made in the '80s is really cutting-edge for them."

I thought of X (it was early afternoon in Beijing) and wondered if he was working, or lazing around his studio, smoking and drinking tea. I imagined my parents in their apartment in Shanghai: my mother cleaning up after lunch, while my father sat on the sofa with its pink protective cover, watching Italian football on CCTV. Maybe I was homesick, because even the thought of the girls in my father's office gave me a pleasant nostalgic pang: their jackdaw voices complaining about their boyfriends and the traffic, as they snacked on hard candy and watermelon seeds. Although I was officially their boss, they managed me. They brought me small gifts, but only in order to lecture me. Why was I staring out the window instead of working? Did I think I could goof off, just because I was the boss's son? And why wasn't I married, they would like to know? They were all "after me" in the most obvious way; at the same time I had a convenient reputation as a man with a broken heart, and so in the serious sense, I was left alone.

That night, for the first time since I'd arrived in Los Angeles, I allowed myself to think about Meiling. I wondered about the story I'd told (or at least strongly suggested) to the novelist. I thought I'd straightened out exactly how I would present myself to the Traverses, and I was a little disconcerted to find myself inventing new lies so early in my stay. However, there are various types of lies: an outright attempt to deceive another person is different from a story that feels true, and only needs to be translated into another form to be understood.

What I am trying to say is that I lay in bed in the guest room in Beverly Hills, imagining Meiling dead. It was comforting. I thought of her martyred, in the pink-and-white printed cotton blouse I had bought her (which she later stopped wearing, in favor of a PLA army jacket and a pair of knockoff Adidas sweatpants), her face smooth and untroubled, her bangs brushed out of her eyes, the coiled jade pendant resting in the hollow of her throat. Her mocha complexion—a great flaw, in her eyes—would be pale and perfect as the Pond's Whitening Cream girl in death.

The sadness I experienced, laying Meiling out in my mind, felt pure and satisfying, unalloyed by jealousy or anger. My thoughts moved backward from the pregnant madonna, past the radical troublemaker, struggling against policemen from the Chaoyang Branch, and settled on the practical student whom I met on the third day of our first year at Beijing Normal University.

We met in the library. For our English class we had to listen to a cassette in the language laboratory; to borrow the cassettes, however, you needed to leave your library card with the clerk; to get the library card, you needed a student ID. All of the new students were falling behind since our red identification booklets were still stacked up in some office, waiting for their registration stamps.

I listened to Meiling explaining this to the clerk. I noticed the way her short haircut exposed her elegant neck and shoulders, her neat blouse and sweater, and her cheap jeans, made of thick cotton washed to look like denim. Her belt was the kind you could buy anywhere on the street: imitation leather in a variety of gaudy colors—hers was lime green—designed to add a bit of style to an ordinary outfit. Five years later, working for my father's company in Shanghai, I would be able to take out girls who worked for foreign companies, who wore genuine designer clothes and drove their own mopeds, wearing white surgical masks to protect their delicate lungs from the city air. But what my roommates and I each wanted then was a girl to study with, to steal kisses from late at night, when the library was deserted, a girl who would be happy with a date at the Dongbei restaurant in a lane behind the music building, which was a treat for us, and one of the only places we could afford.

Meiling looked and sounded like this kind of girl, based on what I could glean from the back of her head. Even from that limited vantage, I could see she was stubborn. She pretended to agree, and each time came back with an argument.

"It's hard for me to do my job," the clerk grumbled. "Everyone always asking me to break the rules."

"Hard is hard," Meiling said. "Although you don't want to stand in the way of the students' progress."

"I don't give a fart about the students' progress," the clerk said. "You think I got everything handed to me? You don't know how easy it is for you kids—sleeping in your dormitories, eating in your canteens, sitting on your bottoms in your classes all day."

I felt that the reference to bottoms was unnecessary. Meiling ignored it.

"The canteen has been closed by the district sanitation inspector," she said calmly. "Women's Dormitory Five is infested with flying ants."

Women's Dormitory Five: I made a mental note.

"It's not possible," the clerk said.

"We have a test next week," I told the clerk, stepping up to join Meiling at the counter. Then I was able to see her face for the first time. Meiling has the kind of face that short hair flatters; the way she had it cut then, the ends curled up a little underneath her ears. (On the postcard with the model in the wedding dress, Meiling wears her hair long, in braids—a style that is supposed to be more authentically Chinese—but I think she looks much less pretty, strange and unlike herself.) Her nose isn't especially wide, and it turns up a bit: she has a small mouth with a full lower lip—a mouth that can easily look unhappy. That might have been why her smile was always so sudden and spectacular: every time it was like she'd been storing it up, waiting for the right moment (or the right person) to release it.

You could see the clerk losing patience; already he was looking past us, to the next pair of students pressing forward.

"Here is my ID." Meiling handed the clerk a letter on official school stationery. "I didn't want to give you my only identification, but I suppose I have no choice."

"Move back, move back!" the clerk said to the students who were now standing all around us, pushing their library books across the desk. "What is this?" he said to Meiling, holding the letter between two fingers, as if it were trash.

Meiling looked startled. "My temporary ID," she said. "By order of the university president. Until the permanent IDs are stamped, all new students will use their Confirmation of Student Housing letters in place of identification."

The clerk gave her a suspicious look. "I haven't heard of that."

"Effective until the stamped IDs arrive."

Meiling sighed. "They say not to part with it, no matter what. Now there's no way to verify that I'm a student at all."

"I'll have to confirm—"

"Oh yes," said Meiling. "The head librarian will know all about it."

The clerk looked back toward an open office door, from which we could hear people chatting and having their lunch. There were good aromas: of tea and boiling soup, and meat frying on a hot plate. Even before the canteen had closed down, anyone who could had brought their own food; as new first-years we heard stories of insect legs floating in the soup, or the student who'd found fingernail parings scattered, like a garnish of leeks, across the top of a bowl of noodles.

To my surprise, the clerk accepted Meiling's letter. "We may not have the correct tapes," he warned, but when he returned, a few moments later, he was holding the complete set. "This is the last student," he announced, pointing to me. "The rest of you come back after lunch." He looked at me. "And make it quick. I've already wasted a quarter of an hour on this one."

"I'm with her," I said. "Thanks anyway." Meiling was still standing there, perhaps astonished by her success. "I need those tapes too," I explained. The crowd around the desk was still waiting, even though the clerk had gone into the back and closed the door. I followed Meiling away from the desk.

"I didn't know about that letter. I'm not sure I still even have mine."

"Oh, I just said that. I don't think it would work on anyone other than that goon. Although, when you think about it, we *should* be allowed to use those letters."

There was an awkward pause, in which I tried to think of some way to continue the conversation, and Meiling looked at the ground, embarrassed. This was at a time when I was beginning to think I might attract a girl, and paying attention to my personal appearance for the first time. I had seen some of the art students from CAFA hanging out at a particular teahouse near the Confucius Temple, and I'd admired the special way they dressed: there was one who always knotted a bright silk cravat underneath his army jacket, and another who used a strip of white bandage to hold back his shaggy hair. In imitation of those young men, I stopped getting haircuts (an economy measure, I told my roommates); and although I was intimidated by the headband, I bought a little scarf that I tied cravat-style underneath my jacket, prompting my roommate Little Gao to ask whether I was getting a cold.

A part of me wanted to bolt from the library, but I stood my ground. Often this is the only way I can manage to do things; I have to be forced into the position where doing *something* is inevitable. Often then, I acquit myself pretty well.

"That was really impressive," I told Meiling. "I wouldn't have thought of it."

"Don't be silly. That guy just wanted to have his lunch."

"What do you do, now that the canteen is closed?"

Meiling made a face. "I never ate in the canteen. Did you hear about the guy who found a button in the red-braised beef?"

I nodded. "But how do you eat?"

Meiling smiled proudly. "All five of us roommates are Chongqing people. We cook Sichuan food on a hotplate in our room."

"But aren't you afraid of getting caught?"

"Not as much as I'm afraid of the canteen."

"That makes sense," I said. "We mostly eat buns."

"That's unhealthy," Meiling said. "That's why you're so skinny."

I must've blushed then, and she obviously felt sorry for me. "You can share the tapes," she said. "You can even use them first, if you want."

"I don't really need them," I said. "My mother was an English teacher, so that class is easy for me."

Meiling gave me a slightly mocking smile. "So then why are you majoring in English?"

"I need to maintain my skills." For some reason I felt compelled to tell her the truth: "Also, I didn't get into art school, so I'm concentrating on that as my minor subject here."

We were standing in the middle of the library floor, students bumping around us. I was trying desperately to think of some justification for staying in touch; now that I'd stupidly admitted I didn't need the tapes (bragging, in order to impress her), I had eliminated my one sound reason to see her again.

"So you want to be an artist," Meiling suggested innocently.

"Oh no," I said. "But my cousin is a successful painter. He even teaches."

"Really?" Meiling asked. "What are his paintings like?"

"They're abstract," I said. "Sort of hard to describe." I had been supposed to go and see X the minute I arrived; now it was almost October, and I hadn't even found his address. I believed (wrongly, as it turned out) that he lived in the dormitory at CAFA, where he was an assistant teacher. If you want to study art someday, my mother had said, he is your connection, but I didn't want to tell anyone about my ambitions in that regard. I realized I'd been delaying getting in touch with X until I had something to show for myself, so that I wouldn't be coming to my sophisticated older cousin as a blank slate.

"I'm not a good artist, but I'm interested in fashion design," Meiling told me. "Where does your cousin teach?"

"At CAFA," I said. "Have you ever been there?" I was trying to change the subject, but Meiling misunderstood.

"No," she said. "But I'd love to. We could go next weekend, if you're free?"

Because that first encounter with Meiling could, on paper, give the impression that she took an immediate interest in me, I should correct any suggestions too flattering to myself. Meiling had a way of giving you the feeling that she was taking care of the conversation, that there was no need to be nervous and you should just relax and enjoy yourself; then, suddenly and casually, she would ask a question that edged dangerously close to the one thing you were trying to conceal. After Meiling and I split up, I sometimes wondered whether the secretive tendency I'd developed as a child was the thing that had attracted her to me; if you are a hider, you have to be careful of seekers, who are drawn to you simply for the challenge of discovering something. But of course, hiders are drawn to seekers too; there is always some part of us that yearns to be found out.

21.

I WOKE UP WHEN MAX GOT HOME. IN MY DREAMY STATE IT TOOK ME A minute to recognize the sound that came next: the mechanical bleeps of the alarm system, which someone was turning off from outside. The code was punched in, and a robotic voice pronounced, *"House Alarm Off."* The digital clock by my bed read 2:47. I got up and looked out my window.

The back staircase led up to a narrow landing. There was a heavy wooden door that opened into the hallway between Max's room and my own. I could see two figures in the shadows on the landing: he was with a girl. I knew that the Traverses didn't allow Max to come and go as he liked, and I hoped he wouldn't be punished for disobeying them. I listened for the sound of footsteps in his parents' end of the house, but all I could hear was the wind in the tree outside my window, knocking the dry brown seedpods against the screen.

Now that I was out of bed, I had to use the bathroom, but I was afraid they would hear me if I went into the hall. I waited, and because there was nothing else to do, I listened:

"It's too cold."

"It's heated. It's like, ninety degrees."

"I can't go naked."

"Wear your underwear."

There was a pause here, for some moments, then a giggling voice:

"In your parents' pool?"

"It's my pool too."

Another long pause. Then squealing.

"Shh," Max teased. "The Chinese guy."

"Is he in there?"

"He's asleep."

"Give me my . . ."

I really had to go to the bathroom. To distract myself, I looked through the window: Max had taken the girl's shirt, and was holding it over her head. The girl was grabbing at it. She had large breasts, a small, soft belly, and her jeans fit tight on her hips and bottom. She was wearing a white leather belt; in the light from the driveway, only the belt and her white bra stood out. The bra wasn't one of those lacy things you saw in magazines: it was thick and solid, something like the ones Meiling used to wear. This girl's skin was darker than Meiling's; she blended into the shadows.

"If you come swimming . . ."

"I don't want to anymore." The girl suddenly turned her back and sat down on the top step. "I gotta go home."

"Now?"

"Carlos only lent me the car for a little while. And I want to take her home."

I wondered whom she was referring to, and I strained my eyes, looking for someone else in the dark. But Max and his girlfriend were certainly the only ones on the landing. Max let his arm drop, defeated, the shirt in his hand like a kite when the wind has suddenly gone. They seemed to be continuing a previous conversation.

"You better not tell her."

"I won't."

"Yes you will. You tell them stuff."

"No I *don't*."

"You better not."

"I won't. Just come in for a second."

They came in through the hall to Max's bedroom. I waited until the door shut and I heard the music. Then I got up (noisily, on purpose), went into the bathroom, and locked the door. I turned on the tap. I took off my pajamas and stepped into the glass shower. I closed my eyes, leaned against the cool tile, and let my imagination take its course. Faintly, on the other side of the wall, I could hear the *thump thump* of the music.

Perhaps there is something wrong with what I did in the bathroom of my hosts. But at least I wasn't thinking of Cece, or her daughter, or the girl I'd just seen leaping around in her underwear. I was imagining Meiling—not in her army jacket and boots, nor (God forbid) in the thin black maternity dress she wore the last time I saw her, but the first night she let me kiss her, underneath the overhang of the closed-down canteen.

I've had many first kisses since then, but with Meiling it was different. It felt familiar from the beginning, as if everything I'd loved my whole life had been incarnated in a strange and exciting new body. At the time I was inexperienced, and I wasn't suspicious of this feeling; in fact, I felt it was my due, exactly what I'd been anticipating throughout my uncomfortable, ordinary adolescence. By the time I knew Meiling well enough to be wary, it was too late: my whole happiness was cupped in her casual hands.

The elation of that remembered kiss stayed with me while I got back into my pajamas, crept down the hall (which was dark and silent now—maybe they had gone to sleep?), and locked my door. But once I'd gotten into the narrow guest bed, and pulled the stiff, unfamiliar coverlet over me, I had a sinking feeling. I worried Meiling had been wired into the part of my brain that fell in love. I was afraid I would never be free of her. I'd traveled ten thousand kilometers, and I hadn't lost her; in fact, once I was alone among strangers, I missed her more than I ever had before.

22.

MAX HAD GONE OUT. CECE HEARD THE ALARM BEING TURNED OFF WHEN he came in at three, and she knew immediately. Probably he'd gotten a friend to drive him, or else Jasmine had come to pick him up in her cousin's car. Now she would have to ground him for going to the party. Grounding, a practice Cece hated—why would you make being at home a punishment?—had worked its way into their family code. Gordon agreed with her, but somehow he'd managed to show his distaste for it without actually offering an alternative.

She figured that Max had slipped out around eleven, just after she'd said good night and before they turned on the alarm. Gordon had already been in bed, wearing his Brooks Brothers pajamas and reading the *AJP*. Her husband had thick, prematurely white wavy hair. He had a receding hairline, but wasn't otherwise balding. He was one of those men who get better-looking as they get older; if he had once been a little on the skinny side, disinclined to exercise (he believed exercise outside of organized sports to be intellectually moribund), he now looked solid and confident, in a way that inspired respect from service people and maître d's. Since he'd bought the convertible Allante, he even had a bit of a tan.

Cece's friends found Gordon distinguished-looking, even handsome—why then did the sight of him, there in bed with his journal, provoke in her only a mild feeling of distaste?

"Anything interesting?" she asked.

"Some letters about the APA Ethics Conference," Gordon said. "I wonder if I should've gone."

There was a pause, which reminded her of how she'd once worried that they wouldn't have enough to talk about. Now she believed that the problem had more to do with communication than with an actual lack of topics. Her parents had been silent on all but practical matters for the better part of forty years. On the other hand, her parents had been married in 1952; they hadn't *expected* to talk much. Perhaps it was realism, rather than innocence, that Americans had lost in the last fifty years? Everyone's expectations were now so high.

"It's fascinating, actually," Gordon continued. "Less than ten percent of respondents claim to have received more than six hours of ethics training in the course of their education. More than seventy percent believe that training was sufficient. And yet, eighty-three percent report at least one boundary violation in the years they've been practicing."

"What's a boundary violation?" Cece asked, hurrying into her nightgown.

"An instance of inappropriate contact between therapist and patient," Gordon said.

"Physical contact?"

"Well, yes. In extreme cases. But not necessarily."

"Have you ever had a boundary violation?"

Gordon looked up from his magazine. "No."

Cece sat down on the plush settee. She did not feel ready to get into bed. She wondered what the authors of that study would make of this marriage, the last ten years of which had contained very little physical contact, hardly a single violation of either of their boundaries. You could make it twelve years if you didn't count a brief interlude in the early spring of 1990, when they had gone to "couples" with Cece's therapist, Dr. Plotkin. That was just after Phil had moved to New York. Three months later, the sessions had ended abruptly, when Gordon decided that Dr. Plotkin was underqualified.

Cece had been relieved to stop the intensely awkward sexual encounters that characterized those three months, which Dr. Plotkin had referred to as "experiments in intimacy." Coming down in the elevator, after one of the final sessions, Gordon had remarked: "I think the sexual realm may perhaps be closed to me for good." Then he had pressed the button; they had descended to the lobby; her husband had held the door for her into the bright street. In the car on the way home, he had talked about how computers were revolutionizing genealogical research.

Cece wondered if this feeling of dissociation was particular to her marriage or common to lifelong bonds in general. She would've liked to take a poll, to do research among her tennis partners and the parents of Max and Olivia's friends, but if you said something like, "It isn't at all like they told us it would be, is it?" or, "We were so naive," everyone would just agree with you right away. But we do not have sex, she would have liked to say. Not *ever*. Would they be shocked? Or would they smile knowingly? She wondered if every relationship had a secret in it, something too embarrassing to reveal to anyone.

Gordon closed the journal and put it on top of the stack. "Are you ready to turn out the light?"

"I thought we were going to talk," Cece said.

"I'm sorry," Gordon said patiently. "Did I forget?"

"No," Cece said. "But I mean, we haven't talked about Phil."

"What?" said Gordon.

"We haven't talked about the thing with Phil."

"The thing with Phil," Gordon repeated, in an uncomprehending monotone. It was a teacher's tactic: a way of allowing a student to recognize his or her own error.

Cece fought a sudden urge to cry. Crying had a predictable effect on any negotiation with Gordon; he would immediately stop the conversation and do whatever it took to calm her down. His strong response to tears was one of the things that had reassured her before their marriage, when she had sometimes worried that his extreme rationality signified a cold and unyielding aspect of his character. *He loves animals,* she remembered telling her friends. *He is eager to have children.*

"I mean, with him staying here. I was surprised that you—"

"Would you prefer that he didn't?"

"No," Cece said.

Gordon nodded, as if it were settled.

"No. I just remember that you said—" She stopped.

"Yes?" Gordon asked patiently.

These conversations were bizarre. It was as if they were working from two separate sets of data, as if their memories had been formed in two different marriages. Gordon did not seem to remember the things that she remembered, and therefore those things did not seem quite real. He acted as if they were discussing a kind of hysterical fantasy of Cece's, which he was doing his best to curtail. He seemed slightly embarrassed for her.

"I just thought we should talk about it," she said.

"Phil is your—concern," Gordon said cheerfully. "I leave it in your capable hands."

Had he started to say "affair"? Had he stopped himself?

Gordon patted the space next to him. "Are you coming to bed?"

Although Phil had been central to many of Cece's private appointments with Dr. Plotkin, she and Gordon had talked about him only once in the couples counseling. Dr. Plotkin had asked Gordon whether he was concerned about his wife's close friendship with his brother. Gordon had looked startled.

"Could you be more clear?"

"Are you afraid that your wife is having an affair?"

"She wouldn't do that."

"Because she wouldn't want to hurt you," Dr. Plotkin suggested.

"Because my brother is a loser," Gordon said. "He's not Cece's type."

"Can you remember what made you ask your brother to stop spending so much time with your family?"

Gordon nodded pleasantly. "Of course. I thought he might be a bad influence on the children."

"On the children, rather than on your marriage?"

"Yes." Gordon turned to Cece. "Is *that* what you thought I was worried about? Why didn't you say so?"

It was lucky that these questions were rhetorical, because at that point in the session, Cece had been unable to speak.

23.

CECE HAD THOUGHT OF SEPARATION. SHE HAD EVEN SPOKEN THE WORD "divorce" out loud, in Dr. Plotkin's office, and to a few of her closest women friends. She and Gordon would not be like other divorced couples, she firmly believed. They did not have money problems, for one thing, nor was either furious with the other. Were Gordon to move to an apartment—perhaps temporarily, on a trial basis—Cece imagined that the four of them would often have dinner together, and go to the movies; there would be no question of the children's spending holidays anywhere but in this house.

She had not been quite so concerned about Olivia, whose perfect grades and devotion to the dance troupe were augmented, now that she was entering her senior year, by an impressive social life. She wanted to go to Berkeley, and although they were going through the whole production with the other applications, Olivia was practically guaranteed admission, as the child of a professor in the UC system.

It was lucky that she didn't have to worry about Olivia, Cece thought, since worrying about Max took up so much of her time. She had worried even before the accident. In middle school his grades had hovered in the C range, in spite of the fact that all of his teachers said he could do better. He didn't like art class, but he liked to draw. Looking over his homework, she found odd-looking superheroes: men with cars, weapons, and sometimes wings, next to masked women with the kind of breasts you drew if you did not get to see many real ones.

Max had never liked to read, but he had been a devotee of *National Geographic* from the age of ten; his science report card always said that if it were not a question of so many missed or late assignments, Max could be getting As. Cece didn't think that grades were very important—that was one of the values she and Gordon shared—but the problem was that another one of their values was the importance of college, and you could not be a white kid from a private school in Los Angeles with no extracurriculars and a C average and expect to get in anywhere decent.

Apart from his grades, however, Max had been doing better. Last year he had made two new friends—Chris, a quiet redhead who had gone all the way through St. Matthews with him, and an Indian kid named Ashok, who had just moved from Teaneck, New Jersey. The first time Cece met Ashok, he had told her he was planning to become a writer of best-selling "espionage-themed" thrillers, and that if she wanted to read a sample of his prose, she could log onto his Web site: ashokundercover.com. Chris and Ashok were perhaps not the coolest kids in the class, but they seemed to really like Max. The three of them spent many afternoons upstairs in Max's room, working on the "zine" they were designing, which would be called *The Mole*. When Max had shown his mother a draft of the cover—a precisely rendered pen-and-ink drawing of a surprisingly appealing rodent—Cece thought that perhaps everything would be OK. She had decided that it might be time to talk to Gordon.

She did not think her husband would be in favor of a separation, nor did she think he would argue. She imagined him being disappointed in her, more than anything else. The thing she came up against, again and again, was telling the children. She couldn't picture what they would say in such a talk, or even determine *where* they would say it; she was sure, for example, that the living room would be the wrong choice. No one was comfortable in the impressive but much too formal living room: she regretted the white carpet, which made guests feel they had to take off their shoes, as well as the piano that none of them knew how to play. The conversation would happen much more easily in the kitchen, except for the fact that the only seating in the kitchen was the stools at the counter—and they could hardly have the conversation like that, in a row, as if they were a bunch of regulars at the local bar.

In the end none of it had mattered. After Max's accident, there was of course no question of a separation. They had conducted a series of very different conversations, in Max's room, where there was only one chair, so that someone always had to lean uneasily against the window frame or the bathroom door. Max had explained that he'd been "just kidding" about blowing his brains out, and that the only reason he wanted the Beretta Cougar handgun was so that his drawings for *The Mole* would be more accurate.

"But why didn't you just tell the officer *that?*" Cece asked.

"They still would've arrested me," Max said calmly.

"But why would you have said—what you said?" Cece found that she couldn't repeat what Max had said.

"I was *kidding,*" Max said. "How many times do I have to tell you."

"Try to put yourself in our shoes," Gordon said. "Can you understand why we would worry?"

"It was a joke," Max hissed, not looking at either of them.

"It wasn't very funny," Cece said. She was sitting at Max's desk, while Gordon sat on the bed. Max was leaning against his bookshelf with his arms crossed in front of his chest, staring out the window at the balcony, where a staircase led down to the driveway. His body language was the equivalent of a fortified tank; at any moment, she expected him to plow right past them toward those stairs.

"That cop was an asshole," Max said. "He thought I was psycho. He thought I was, like, Dylan Klebold or something."

"I don't think Dylan Klebold was psychotic," Gordon had intervened.

That got Max's attention. He stared at his father.

"I mean, don't all teenagers have those feelings? That they'd like to blow up their entire high school?"

"Yeah," Max said. "But most people don't actually go and do it."

"Did you think about it?" Gordon asked.

Cece could not believe they were talking about Dylan Klebold. They were talking about the *news.* Dylan Klebold came from a troubled family, in which the parents kept guns. It was a tragedy with profound social consequences, but what did it have to do with them?

"I can't *believe* you think I'm Dylan Klebold too," Max exclaimed. "I was going to draw a fucking *cartoon*. I didn't even have any fucking bullets for it."

"There's nothing wrong with being angry," Gordon had said.

"I'm not fucking angry!" Max screamed, tearing past them out of the room.

24.

THEY SPENT THE WEEK BEFORE SCHOOL STARTED AT HOME. ON THURS-
day morning, Cece came down to the kitchen to make muffins. Salty was
resting on his plaid flannel bed, with his nose on the floor and his big, wet
eyes open, blinking up at her. Dr. Spock was trotting through the downstairs rooms, making his rounds, Gordon called it.

Cece made two batches of blueberry yogurt muffins and sliced oranges to squeeze for juice, which she wouldn't do until everyone was
awake because of the noise of the juicer. Her children never ate eggs, and
she and Gordon were watching their cholesterol, but she had started buying them, just in case Phil or Mr. Yuan wanted some. That was the thing,
both exhausting and wonderful, about having guests: having to guess
their needs. It was almost like having small children again.

Once she had taken care of the human breakfast, she started in on the
animals: wet and dry food for Spock, who needed to gain weight, and diet
kibble for Salty, who had an old dog's belly. While she watched Spock eat
(otherwise Salty would shoulder in and finish the bowl), she administered
Ptolemy's insulin, pinching the skin at his neck in a way the vet promised
would feel normal to him, since it was how his mother had once carried
him in her mouth. It had, however, been a long time since Ptolemy was a
kitten; as soon as Cece released him, with a gentle caress, Ptolemy turned
around and bit her ankle.

There were footsteps above her head, and Cece heard girls' voices on
the stairs. Olivia's friend Emily had spent the night. Emily and Olivia had
gone to school together for years, but it was only after Olivia joined Dance
Directions last year that the two of them had become close. St. Anselm's

was known for its arts programs—Mr. Yuan was an addition to a long line of visiting scholars—but among the arts it was the dance department that distinguished itself.

Cece was proud that Olivia had been accepted into this elite troupe, but she lamented the new friends who came with it. There was a great deal of talk about body shapes and sizes, under the auspices of dance. Whose waist was thinner, whose breasts were shapelier, whose butt looked the best in the leotards? If she were honest, Cece didn't much like modern dance, which always looked a little melodramatic to her. She thought the Dance Directions routines ("choreography," Olivia corrected her) were a bit sexual for high school: last year she had seen a poster hanging right in front of the school, which had been vandalized, the "Di" replaced with a large "E." It was easy to see why the boys from William O. Douglas, St. Anselm's brother school, never missed a performance.

"At school some people think we're bitches," her daughter explained, over lunch at a restaurant in Brentwood the day after she'd returned from Paris. ("Bitches" surprised Cece, but she concealed it.) "But we're not. It's just that we don't like to be around people who aren't interesting—Emily can't stand anything *pedestrian*." (Perhaps as a mother you accepted "bitch" in exchange for "pedestrian" used as an adjective?) She could tell how important it was to Olivia that she understand what was special about this new friend, and Cece tried hard to keep an open mind.

"What do her parents do?" Cece asked.

Olivia shrugged, impatient with such a pedestrian question. "I don't know what her dad does, but they lived in Paris when Emily was a kid, and so she speaks French really well. I think maybe her mom does some stuff at school."

Cece was conscious of the fact that she was not an embarrassing mother, as far as mothers went—that she wore the right clothes, drove the right kind of car, and acted neither older nor younger than her age. When she had told Olivia about the possibility of working at St. Anselm's three days a week, Olivia had said she thought it was a good idea. Her daughter's approval meant more to Cece than the job itself, and Olivia's encouragement was what had made her finally call Ms. McCoy to accept.

In fact, everyone had been extremely enthusiastic, from Gordon, to

Joan, to Pam and Liz and Carol, her Thursday morning doubles partners. Why did so many people think it was important that she do a job, a job so nonessential that the head of school had told her to let them know "a few weeks" before the term started whether or not she would be joining them? Once she had accepted, Gordon had brought home a bottle of champagne, to celebrate her new "career." Of course there had never been any question of the job being paid; everyone knew that Cece didn't need the money.

The girls came from the front hall, blinking and stretching and exaggerating their exhaustion.

"Is it really only eleven-thirty?" asked Emily, entering the dining room before Olivia and glancing, aghast, at the grandfather clock.

Emily had blond hair, pulled up into a messy chignon. She had green eyes, a button nose, and the kind of pink and gold skin that had once been called a "healthy tan." Emily wasn't any taller than Cece (five feet five inches, rounding up) and in fact had similarly symmetrical features; any stranger coming upon the three of them would've guessed that it was Emily who was Cece's daughter, and Olivia who was the friend.

In Cece's opinion, Emily was nothing special, especially compared with Olivia. Her daughter had inherited her height from Gordon's side of the family (both Joan and Phil were very tall). She had long, dark hair with a hint of red in it, a high, pale forehead, and dark brown eyes. She had strong, striking features that made you look again; if she was not conventionally pretty, there were moments when you would have called her beautiful.

"Good morning," Cece said. "How did you sleep?"

"Comme ci comme ça," said Emily.

"That means 'So-so,'" Olivia informed her mother. "Emily speaks French way better than me."

"I have a bit of insomnia," Emily said.

"Really?" said Cece. "That's terrible, at your age."

"My mom says it's from drinking coffee when I was little. My au pair used to give it to me." Emily glanced around the kitchen. "Speaking of coffee," she said.

"I'll make a pot," Cece said. "The blueberry muffins are still warm."

"Thanks, Mom," Olivia said. Blueberry muffins were her favorite.

"That sounds wonderful," Emily said. "But if you don't mind, I think I'll stick with coffee. And maybe an orange or something, if you've got one?"

At that moment Spock tore into the breakfast room, making a beeline for Emily. He circled the newcomer twice, barking: Emily backed against the wall.

"I'm sorry," Cece said. "You're not allergic, are you?"

"No—it's just—"

Spock licked Emily's knees.

"I'm not crazy about dogs."

"Spock, get OUT," Olivia said. She grabbed Spock's collar, opened the door, and shoved the dog out into the yard—something Cece tried not to do now that Fionnula was living in the rose garden. In this case she didn't say anything, although she wondered about people who said they didn't like dogs. What was there not to like about a dog like Spock?

"We have fresh-squeezed juice," she told Emily.

Emily went to the sink and washed her hands. She stooped and wiped her knees, where Spock had lavished his affection.

"So of course we do have plain oranges," Cece conceded. "If that's all you want?"

"That would be perfect." Emily smiled, and Cece suddenly remembered the girl's mother: Felice Alderman, an angular woman with a beach club tan who organized the Christmas Wassail Party, a traditional fundraising event for parents. Last year there had been a debate as to the appropriateness of a wassail party at a nonsectarian school. (St. Anselm's had discarded its religious affiliation after World War II, although it was not until the late 1970s that the school had admitted its first Jewish students.) Emily's mother was of the opinion that abolishing the wassail party was "politically correct nonsense." In fact what she had said was, "Mr. Alderman can't stand this politically correct nonsense."

"I just remembered that I know your parents," Cece said. "Felice and Tad—is that right?"

Emily rolled her eyes. "Of course you know Mom. She's always fucking around that school—pardon my French."

The girls looked at each other and cracked up.

"We would always say that in France," Olivia said, through giggles: "Pardon my French."

Emily recovered her composure first. "Sorry, Mrs. Travers. I adore Mom. But she really needs to find something to do with herself."

Olivia shot her mother a nervous look. But of course Emily didn't know that Cece was about to start fucking around St. Anselm's on a regular basis herself.

"I'm going to go out and feed Fionnula," Cece said. "Would you mind giving Freud some lettuce, when you get a chance?"

"Freud?" Emily said.

Cece was sorry she'd mentioned it, although you couldn't censor everything. At least once in every conversation you were going to be embarrassing to your children: it was inevitable.

"Freud is a rabbit," Olivia muttered. "My dad is a shrink. The rabbit is supposed to be my brother's responsibility, but Max never has to do *anything.*"

"Your brother is still asleep," Cece said. "It would be nice for you to do it this once."

"My brother is grounded," Olivia told Emily, evidently relieved to be off the subject of pets.

"For what?"

Olivia glanced at her mother. "Going to a party."

Cece could see that her daughter would have liked to tell the whole story to her friend, and probably would, once Cece was out of earshot. She wouldn't have minded so much if Olivia had needed comfort—if it was her sorrow for her brother, or even a desire for sympathy, that had made her want to confide in Emily. But it was not. It was because the story of the gun was sensational. Olivia had something she knew her friend would find interesting, and she wanted to impress Emily at her brother's expense.

"Which party? Dave Bemish's?"

"You wouldn't know," Olivia said. "I think it was in Echo Park."

"Your brother goes to parties in *Echo Park?*"

"No," Cece couldn't help interjecting. "This was a one-time thing, and he was certainly not supposed to be there."

"His girlfriend is from there," Olivia explained. Cece was surprised to hear an edge of pride in her daughter's voice.

"Wow," said Emily. "*Ça c'est vraiment le barrio.*"

Cece would've liked to have heard the rest of the conversation, in all of its dazzling multiculturalism, but she was afraid that if she stayed, she might commit some truly unpardonable offense—such as asking the girls what they knew about Hispanic gangs, unlicensed handguns, and the possibility of a white kid from Beverly Hills with a history of depression getting mixed up in one.

Instead she gathered Fionnula's vegetables (remains that Lupe collected during the week, and left in a bowl in the fridge) and put them in her gardening basket. She put on her clogs and canvas gloves, which were useful for handling the bush baby, and took her shears from the shelf outside the back door, in case the roses needed attention.

"I'll see you girls later," Cece said. She kept her voice cheerful, to conceal a sudden onset of emotion. "Help yourselves to everything."

25.

THE ROSE GARDEN ENCOMPASSED THE NORTHEAST CORNER OF THE
backyard. It was secluded on three sides by the ailing eugenia, connected
to the lawn by a short set of stone steps. Cece hadn't been particularly
fond of roses when they bought the house, and had clipped them from a
sense of duty: the garden was already mature, and it would've been crazy
to let it go. Soon, however, she found herself spending more time pruning
the existing plants, and even putting in new varieties, until the rose garden became her special province. (They had always had Chinese tea roses,
and in her last order she'd thrown in a Tipsy Imperial Concubine, on a
whim.) From the top of the steps she could see the pool house: two of the
blinds were raised, which meant that Phil was probably awake, lying in
bed. She thought about knocking and telling him there was coffee, but
Phil wasn't very sociable in the mornings; she guessed he would prefer to
stay clear of the house until the girls were gone.

The bush baby must have hidden herself among the ferns, because the
rabbit hutch appeared empty. Gordon had built the hutch years ago, from
plywood and chicken wire, and Cece had planted the ferns, so that there
would be places for the bunnies to play and hide. It was an enormous
space for one animal; if only Freud weren't so aggressive, she could have
put Fionnula in there with him. Instead she had (somewhat guiltily)
moved the rabbit to a smaller cage in her already overcrowded study, re-
serving the leafy paradise of the hutch for the bush baby.

"Fionnula," she called, kneeling outside the cage. "Here, sweetie—are
you hungry?"

"Good morning."

Cece started: the dissident was standing right behind her.

"I'm sorry to disturb you."

"Oh no," she said. "I'm sorry. I didn't see you there."

Mr. Yuan's hair was pulled back in its customary ponytail, and he was wearing khaki pants and a white button-down shirt. She had noticed that Mr. Yuan usually wore Western clothes around the house; it was only when he went out for his walks or to the library that he changed into his Chinese costume.

"She doesn't seem to want to come out this morning," Cece said. "I'm just going to leave this for her."

"Allow me." Mr. Yuan put down his empty mug, and knelt beside Cece. The mug, from a seminar Gordon had attended last year at Stanford, said "Shrink Rap" in red letters across the side. She wondered if the dissident got the joke.

"I think I should do it," Cece said, "since I have the gloves. Phil warned me she might scratch."

"You take good care of your pets," Yuan Zhao said.

"Gordon and I are both fond of animals," she said. "It's one of the things we have in common."

"Is Dr. Travers at home?"

Gordon had been taking Mr. Yuan to the library in the mornings, where he was doing research for his project, and picking him up on his way home from UCLA. Although the university had much better collections, Mr. Yuan had insisted that he preferred the public library. Gordon had a theory that the freedom of information represented by a first-class American research university was initially intimidating to someone who had lived under communism for so long. Personally Cece thought that anyone would've preferred the public library, with its big windows and low shelves for children, its friendly volunteer librarians and new turquoise-and-gold-tiled dome, which looked like a Disney version of *The Thousand and One Nights*. By contrast, UCLA's grim study carrels and intimidating stacks—did anyone really understand the Dewey decimal system?—were much less appealing.

"I'm so sorry," Cece said. "Gordon isn't back from tennis yet."

"Never mind," said Mr. Yuan. "I can walk."

"Oh no," said Cece. "It's too far. I would drive you myself—it's only that I don't want to leave Max alone." She glanced toward the lawn. The girls had finished their meager breakfast, and were heading for the pool. "It isn't that I don't trust him," she told Mr. Yuan. "But it's tempting for him to go out now that he's grounded. And sometimes I wonder if Gordon even notices—" She stopped, embarrassed. She knew she shouldn't be complaining about her husband to their guest, but there was something about Mr. Yuan that made Cece want to confide in him. Maybe it was only that he had to listen harder, in order to understand what she was saying.

"What do Chinese parents do, to punish their children?"

"Sometimes they tell them to stay at home to study," Mr. Yuan said. "Of course if a child knows that he's making his parents unhappy, he'll feel guilty, and want to stay at home in any case."

"That's the difference," Cece said. "Our children are taught that they *have* to make their parents unhappy, that it's part of growing up."

The dissident took a step down, so that they were standing on the same level. Mr. Yuan was only an inch or two taller than she was; although he was too slight to be conventionally handsome, at least in an American way, there was something pleasing about the symmetry of his features. His presence was comforting. It seemed possible that people who were leading particularly honest, clearheaded lives would radiate peace: a kind of human feng shui.

"You know what—Phil can keep an eye on him. It's not asking much, is it? I'll go talk to him. You stay right there. Can I get you anything else for breakfast? A muffin?"

"I've had my tea," the dissident said. "I'm fine, thank you."

Cece hurried down the steps, reflecting that the blueberry muffins were going to waste. She put her gardening tools by the back door, and was about to go around to the pool house, when she saw Phil in the kitchen. He was standing by the French doors, drinking coffee. He turned around as if she'd startled him, and then smiled broadly.

"This is great coffee," he said.

"Good morning," she said. "I almost came to see whether you were awake—"

"You did?"

"But the girls—are they still out there?"

"I think so." Phil moved away from the window.

"I'm going to drive Mr. Yuan to the library. I wonder if you could just keep an eye on Max?"

"Isn't he a little old for that?"

"He's still grounded," Cece said. "I just want to make sure he doesn't go out."

"Is Gordo—"

"Here? No, he's at tennis. He'll be home soon, but I can't count on him. For discipline," Cece added quickly. "He grounds him, and then he buys him presents. Have you noticed that? A Bose stereo to replace the one Max—sold, and now this video camera."

"He sold his stereo?"

When the officer from the MPU had asked where Max had gotten the money to buy the Beretta Cougar handgun, they had had to tell him about the missing stereo. The officer had smiled faintly, noting it down. Clearly, to those policemen, the fact that she and Gordon had money made their near-tragedy into something more like a farce.

Cece didn't feel like explaining any of that to Phil. "Before the accident," she said.

"He's not grounded because of that?"

"Of course not," she said. "No. It was for going to a party the other night. Jasmine's cousin's party. Jasmine is his girlfriend."

"I remember you mentioned her."

"She's very sweet," Cece continued. "But the cousin is an adult. There's a mother and some sort of stepfather at home—he sounds like bad news—and of course there's no supervision. I understand about the freeway project: it's wonderful for kids like Jasmine. But to expose Max to this kind of lifestyle" (her voice broke, she couldn't help it) "when he's already at risk? It doesn't make sense to me."

Phil left the window and came around to Cece. He put his hands on her shoulders, and bent his head almost to her level. "I'll watch him," he said softly. "Trust me."

"Oh, look at me," Cece said. "It's not even noon."

"What does that have to do with it?"

"You can't cry before noon. It's . . ." Cece wiped her eyes.

Phil squeezed her shoulders; for a second all of Cece's worries seemed to be concentrated in the small area that Phil was authoritatively sooth-ing. "I didn't know that rule," he said.

"*You're* barely awake before noon."

"That's because there's a high risk of crying," Phil said. "Especially if you go outside. Before noon is when you're most likely to see effective people scurrying around. It can be very depressing."

"I know what you mean," Cece said.

"Sit down," said Phil casually, as if the two of them sitting in her kitchen while he gave her a backrub was a normal, everyday thing. "But you are one of the effective people."

"You must be getting me confused with someone else."

"Impossible," said Phil lightly. The feeling of Phil's hands on her shoulders was amazing. It allowed her to postpone thinking about any-thing else. "You're one of the most effective people I know. This morning you've made these muffins, which are delicious, done some gardening—"

"I was only feeding Fionnula. She didn't come out, though—I hope she isn't sick."

"And taken care of a menagerie," Phil continued. "A burden, I might add, that's been thrust on you by your inconsiderate relatives—"

"I love Fionnula!" Cece said. "She's not a burden. And anyway, that's different from doing important things."

"What's more important than taking care of your family?" Phil said.

Cece felt the warm rush of having your deepest beliefs confirmed by others. "That's what I think," she said. "But everyone—" She heard the door at the top of the outside stairs open. Mr. Yuan was coming down.

Cece stepped away. "Thank you—that relieves a lot of tension. Did you know that in China massage is a part of the traditional medicine, as op-posed to just a luxury? Blind people are trained to do it, from an early age."

"Why blind people?"

"Maybe because—" but she stopped. Was this a conversation she could have with Phil if Gordon had been in the room? Maybe that was a good barometer. "I'm afraid Mr. Yuan is waiting," she said. "I'll just tell the girls I'm going."

She could feel Phil watching her as she struggled with the stiff latch on the old French doors, and as she made her way across the lawn. The idea that he could still be attracted to her was unreasonable. He'd come back to L.A. to resolve the dilemma of a woman who was desperate to be with him—a woman seven years younger than Cece. So it was important that she not slip into some kind of old pattern with him, of familiarities. What was familiar wasn't necessarily good: that was something Cece had learned from Gordon. "Chemistry is pathology," Gordon sometimes said, only half jokingly. He meant that if people were attracted to each other right away, it was probably because each fit into an emotional pattern familiar to the other. She often wondered how Gordon thought about the two of them, when he said things like that.

The girls were lying on deck chairs on the opposite side of the pool. They had discarded their pajamas (such as they were) on the deck. The sun was so bright that at first Cece thought her eyes were playing tricks on her. She shaded them with her hand, until there could be no mistake—Olivia was lying on her stomach and Emily was on her back, but neither girl was wearing the top half of her bathing suit.

"I think he's kind of cute," Emily was saying.

"You're a nympho!" Olivia twisted her head around when she heard Cece approaching, and then quickly put her face back down in the cushion. "Hi Mom," she muttered.

"Of course it's gross to you," Emily said. "Hi Mrs. Travers. This is a great pool."

Emily's breasts, medium-sized, with the elasticity of only the very young, were oiled and brown, without any evidence of tan lines. Cece suppressed the urge to turn her back (the same impulse as her daughter's?) and talk to the girls that way. She felt that Emily could see her discomfort, and was enjoying it. She noticed that the pool-house door was slightly ajar. Obviously, Phil had walked right by them.

There were several things Cece wanted to say, but somehow none of those came out. "What is gross?"

"What?" said Emily, although Cece had been talking to her daughter.

"You said that something was 'gross.' "

"Oh." Emily pushed a pair of white plastic sunglasses back on her head. She was wearing a very small, black bikini bottom, for which she had obviously been professionally waxed. "Olivia thinks it's gross that I said her uncle was cute."

"Did you two speak with Phil?"

"Is that his name?" Emily asked. "He didn't introduce himself. He sure had a lot of questions, though."

"What kind of questions?"

"He asked us whether we'd had breakfast yet," Emily said. "Then he asked what we normally had for breakfast in Paris. How we got around. Did we go to discos? Did we have boyfriends? What kind of classes did we take—did we like The History and Culture of Francophone Africa, or did we think it was"—she looked at Olivia—"what?"

"A politically correct nod to the postcolonial perspective," Olivia told the cushion.

An involuntary shiver started between her legs, and ran through Cece's body. It was unmistakably sexual, and it was looking at Emily's body that had done it—looking, not as herself, but as Phil.

"Does your brother live here now?" Emily asked politely.

"My husband's brother," Cece said. "No, he's just passing through."

"Really?" Olivia said.

How could the child she remembered—a toddler, eating Cheerios from a plastic baggie—have transformed herself into the tanned, athletic body on the chair? Why hadn't there been any warning? For many years, Olivia had been the same little person; only the wrapping had changed. Then all of a sudden the inside was different—or if not different, then impenetrable to Cece, so that all kinds of things could be going on in there, and she would have no idea.

"I have *always* wanted to be a screenwriter." Emily sighed, shifting her oiled body in the chair. Her breasts gleamed. Cece had rarely felt so angry with either of her children. At the same time, she wondered what specifically was making her angry, and whether any of it was even Olivia's fault. She looked at her daughter and said the first thing that came into her head:

"You have to eat some breakfast."

Olivia made a sound of exasperation.

"I can't tell Emily what to do, but Dr. Meyer said you need to gain some weight."

"Lucky duck," said Emily. "I wish I did."

"It wouldn't kill you either," Cece said. "I'm taking Mr. Yuan to the library. Your uncle is going to keep an eye on Max. I would ask you—" she began. Maddeningly, her voice broke: "Please put on your bathing suits. Mr. Yuan is from a completely different culture, and if he were to walk out here . . . I imagine he might even decide to leave us."

Olivia sat up and scrambled into her racing top: what Cece had interpreted as natural modesty was, of course, simply a desire to hide her underdeveloped chest. She would've been mortified when her uncle came out. She needn't have worried, Cece thought, Phil would not have been looking at her.

"We're so sorry," Emily said, reaching lazily for the bit of black spandex on the deck beneath her chair. "It's just that we're so used to it."

Olivia glanced at her mother. "In France—" she began weakly.

"It really is so different from America." Emily leaned forward to clip the bathing suit behind her back. "Just completely unpuritanical."

"Do you think it's puritanical to respect the traditions of the country you're in?" Cece asked. "What would you think if Mr. Yuan came into our house and started spitting on the floor? They do that in China, you know." (In fact she wasn't sure whether educated people like Mr. Yuan actually did any spitting, but it was one of the things they warned you about in *Culture Shock! China*.) "Would you think he was doing the right thing, even though in his country it's OK?"

The girls were quiet.

"*Would* you?"

"No," said Olivia tensely.

"We really are sorry. We apologize."

For the first time, Emily looked almost contrite, and Cece wondered if she'd been too harsh. There were certainly many worse things a teenager could do than take off the top of her bathing suit in front of a houseguest, even a Chinese one.

"You don't think he saw us?" Emily said.

"No," Cece said. "I'm sure not." She noticed a tag Emily had forgotten to remove, still hanging off the side of her suit. "Here," Cece said, moving to help her.

Emily flinched.

"You have a tag."

Emily reached back and felt the tag. She looked past Cece at the house, as if she were appraising it: "Thanks," she said coolly. "I'll take it off with scissors later."

"I think I have some in my purse," Cece said. She fished around in the large side compartment where she had always carried Tylenol, Band-Aids, Kleenex, and at one time crayons, in case some child—her own or another—was bored.

"That's OK," Emily said.

"Here," Cece said. "Just hold still a second." She knelt down next to Emily, but what she'd taken for a price tag was actually a small plastic anti-theft device, impossible to remove.

"I guess they forgot to take it off at the store." Emily was staring defiantly into the distance, but it was a childish kind of defiance—a put-on. Children were like decks of cards, one face showing at a time. In every seventeen-year-old, there was a fourteen-year-old, and even a twelve-year-old, who, depending on the circumstances, could be shuffled to the top.

"They do that all the time," Cece heard herself saying. "Deactivate them, and then forget to take them off."

Emily looked at Cece with her sharp, slightly slanted green eyes. She had a splash of freckles, very faint, across the bridge of her nose.

"And then it's so inconvenient, having to take it back."

"We could take it back today," Olivia said. "If we can use the Pathfinder—can we?"

"I'm taking Mr. Yuan to the library," Cece said.

"After?" Olivia asked. "When you get back?"

"Don't worry about it," Emily said. "Knowing me, I probably won't."

"Sorry?" Cece said.

"Take it back."

Both Olivia and Cece looked at her.

"I mean, I'll barely use that part of it"—Emily giggled—"unless I'm here again."

"But you *will* be here," Olivia pleaded. "Mom?"

"I'll be back in twenty minutes," Cece said.

26.

WHAT IS MORE COMFORTING THAN A LOBSTER? ONE LONG LINE SEG-
ment, the length of the brush, fanning slightly at the bottom. Three or
four hook strokes, on the diagonal (three for a small lobster, four for a big
one). With a wet brush, three dashes, nearly but not quite joined at the
base, like an inverted bouquet. A dot of pure ink for the eye. Then, with a
clean brush—rinsed, dried, and separated, so that a few long bristles stand
apart from the rest—four firm lobster legs. Then the magic.

I remember the first time I watched my teacher, Wang Laoshi, pull a
hair from his own head, dip it in tincture (three parts ink, one part water)
and draw it lightly across the page. At once there was a lobster and the
ground the lobster stood upon; suddenly the lobster seemed to cast a
shadow, although there was nothing to indicate rock or seabed beneath
him. I cannot explain, except to say that a lobster without antennae is a
specimen, dependent on his dead, stalked eyes; with the antennae, he is a
creature in motion. (It is possible to paint the antennae with the very tip
of the brush, but not, I think, with the same freedom.) Occasionally, when
I have something important to do—such as tell the story of my first days
at St. Anselm's School for Girls, and about one student in particular—I
will procrastinate, and paint a lobster.

My mother had a grudging respect for Wang's talent, although her
opinion of him as a man was less favorable. She objected in particular to a
collection of postcard-sized images, pasted to the wall next to my bamboo
and lobsters, almost all of which had been cut with a small, pearl-handled
knife from an English guidebook to the Kunsthistorisches Museum in
Vienna. I was particularly taken with an eighteenth-century Spanish

flintlock gun, made of steel and tortoiseshell, and I often flipped past the Picture Gallery (full of holes, as if it had been burgled) to the Arms and Armor section of the guide.

"Look at the paintings," Wang would instruct me, smacking the side of my head very lightly for emphasis. "You don't know how lucky you are."

"Ow!" I would yell, although my teacher barely touched me.

Wang softened toward me when he realized that I could translate the captions of his favorite pictures. The translations were difficult, full of foreign names and places, and in order to maintain my interest, Wang allowed me to choose the paintings we would discuss. My mother talked about Old Wang's dirty mind, but in fact it was my fault that almost all of the pictures hanging on the wall above his table were of beautiful young women in various stages of undress. There is one I remember best, maybe because it relates to the story I'm telling now. Like most people, I think, the works of art that have stayed with me have always been the ones that accidentally corresponded to people and events in my own life.

Titian's *Violante*, a typical Venetian *bella*-portrait, was painted sometime between 1515 and 1518. It captures the Venetian courtesan Violante, a young lady who came back to me with particular force once I started teaching at the St. Anselm's School for Girls. Violante is dressed in rose and blue silk; her impossibly white shoulders are set against black velvet; her hair is so brilliantly gold that it seems laced through with metal wire. If there is a flaw in this picture, it's in the saturation of the colors: so rich and strong that they leach glory from the girl beneath them. Perhaps that's why she always looked (to me anyway) so angry.

If you had compared Wang's small gray room with Violante's marble palace in the Kunsthistorisches, if you had seen the two of us sitting at the scarred wooden table, gazing up at this portrait—an infirm, politically disgraced old man and a fat, pimply boy—you might have understood her irritation. "How dare you look at me," she seemed to say, lightly, but with an edge of fury: "Take care, take care—because I am not for you."

Before the war, Wang Laoshi had been one of the most famous artists in China. In his beautiful house in Shanghai's French Concession (not far from the residence of Sun Yat-sen) there were reproductions of works by

Italian masters: Leonardo, Caravaggio, Titian, and Parmigianino. As a young man he had even traveled to Florence on a government exchange, visiting the Uffizi and studying with a restorer of Renaissance altarpieces. He returned to China with the intention of devising a parallel methodology for the restoration and preservation of the landscape scrolls that were his passion. It was my teacher who first introduced me to the work of the Southern Song loyalists—including the hermit painter Zhao Cangyun—who fled Hangzhou in 1275, abandoning their court to the barbaric Mongol horsemen.

"Those were real painters," my teacher would say. "Where are the real painters now?"

When I began studying with Wang Laoshi, my teacher was living like a young student, in a room with a table, a hotplate, and a bed that was rolled away in the morning and propped against the wall. Our brushes were ancient (they were losing their hair), and we used only newspaper, so that sometimes I would be painting rocks and clouds and pine trees over the faces of Deng Xiaoping, Li Peng, and even old photos of the chairman himself.

"It can't be helped," my teacher would say sadly, passing me another page from the *People's Daily*. "Perhaps the shame of defacing our dear leaders will inspire you to do better."

"Wang Laoshi is crazy," I would tell my mother when I got home.

"Wang Laoshi is a great artist," my father would say. "That's what great artists are like."

I studied with Wang Laoshi until 1991, when I was sixteen and preparing frantically for my college entry exam. Because of my respectable grades and my excellent scores in English, my parents hoped that I would be admitted to a university in Beijing. When I told them I wanted to go to CAFA, the Central Academy of Fine Arts, they did not say, as others did: "How can you be sure of your future as an artist?" or "Why not study engineering right here in Harbin, so that you can get a good job with your father?" Instead they encouraged me, praising my landscapes, lobsters, and birds.

"So exact," my father said. "Like a scientist."

"As if they're about to fly off the page," my mother concurred.

At that time I particularly liked drawing birds—not the swallows that nested in the roof of our apartment building, or the crows you could see in the People's Park, but exotic species from a book my mother had given me: *The Pocket Guide to North American Birds*. I drew thrushes, thrashers (brown, sage, and California), hummingbirds (rufous and ruby-throated), the American redstart, and even the elusive ivory-billed woodpecker. I learned that the possibility of spotting one continues to lure birders deep into the old-growth forests of Louisiana, where they are almost always disappointed; the problem, of course, is that the ivorybill's existence depends on the accounts of the very people who want to see him most. They're able to dismiss a crimson crest in the female, or the absence of a characteristic note in the call—according to ornithologists, like a child's tin horn—not because they're lying, but because the passion that inspired their quests in the first place has ultimately clouded their judgment.

When Wang Laoshi looked at the portfolio I meant to send to CAFA, which included both Chinese-style ink paintings and reproductions of the European masters, he said I was a brilliant copyist. But he was also the one who reassured me a year later, when I failed to be accepted. It was almost as if he were a little bit relieved.

"Better to copy sounds than shapes and colors," he said. "Make your English perfect; then you can do anything you like."

What he was telling me, in the kindest way possible, was that my talent was for mimicry, nothing else; and as long as that was the case, I should use it for something more profitable than painting. I took his advice. I majored in English at Beijing Normal, where I worked hard for perhaps the first time in my life. I might have abandoned art altogether, never making another painting, and been perfectly happy. And then I discovered my cousin X.

27.

THE WEEK AFTER I MET MEILING IN THE LIBRARY, WE HAD OUR FIRST real date. It was her idea. We were going to the Central Academy of Fine Arts to see if we could find my cousin.

We stopped in the open reception area outside the Main Office. There was no one at the desk, but in the center of the space a student was doing a strange performance. He was standing on a chair, balancing on one foot with the other hovering in the air, raising his arms above his head. Every few seconds, he would clap dramatically once or twice, all the time muttering to himself. Other students passed by without paying any attention. Apart from this peculiar behavior, I was surprised to see no indication that the art students were different from our friends at Beijing Normal. The young men and women hurrying through the reception area were dressed in ordinary shirts and slacks; unlike the crowd I'd seen hanging out at the Kongmiao teahouse, few of them even wore their hair long. It occurred to me that I might step into the passing stream of students, attend a lecture—perhaps even spend a day as a CAFA student—without anyone suspecting a thing.

While I was daydreaming about this possibility, Meiling had approached the young man standing on the chair.

"Excuse me?" she said tentatively.

"Greedy little sluts!" he exclaimed.

"Hey!" I said.

The student put his other foot down on the chair, and turned toward us; when he saw Meiling, he blushed:

"Sorry. These mosquitoes have been snacking on me since this morning."

Meiling giggled. The student grinned. I could see that if Meiling were to become my girlfriend (a prospect still too overwhelming to picture clearly), there would be many such irritating instances with other men: she had a kind of personal magnetism that drew people in immediately.

"We're looking for a student," I said sternly. "Maybe you can help us."

"No problem." The young man smiled, mostly at Meiling. "I have a directory right here." He went behind the desk and pulled out a thick, spiral-bound book. But when I told the student X's name, his expression changed. He closed his directory and began busying himself with the cap of a leaky thermos on his desk.

"He's in the department of painting," I said.

"Why are you looking for him?"

"He's my cousin."

It didn't surprise me that this student knew my cousin, but I couldn't understand why he was being so unfriendly. He looked as if he didn't believe I was telling the truth.

"If you don't believe me, you can ask him yourself."

The student smiled. "Doubt it," he said. "Because he's not a student here anymore."

Just then a young woman came out of the office, carrying an armload of green file folders. "Hey you," the student said rudely. "Is Fang in there?"

"Where else would he be?"

"There's a guy here who wants to see him."

"The person I'm looking for is named X," I told the girl, who laughed. Then she put down her folders and opened the door to the office, calling someone inside. She looked me and Meiling over, and waited in the doorway; clearly she wanted to see what would happen.

It's hard to remember meeting the important people in your life for the first time. Everything you learn about the person later conspires to supplant your earliest impression; it's very difficult for me to think of Li Fang as the rat-faced, messy-haired, camera-toting whirlwind who emerged grinning from the office that day—as opposed to the serious assistant photo editor of our magazine *Lu Kou,* or the morose, suspicious Fang who would not return my phone calls after the crisis. But even if there had been no crisis, and the authorities had allowed us to go on publishing unmolested, we might have fallen out. Although X and Tianming got most of the credit for *Lu Kou,* it was Fang who made the deal with a printer; Fang who did the photocopying; and Fang who managed to distribute our little magazine to a few people who mattered. What began as a collaboration, before any of us were sure it had value, turned into something else once people started offering us money and taking our picture. All of a sudden everyone wanted to own what he himself had made; paradoxically, it was our very success that doomed us.

But that afternoon at CAFA, it was as if Fang had found his own long-lost cousin. Before I could even introduce myself, he said:

"I know who you are. From Harbin, right? Studying at Beijing Normal?"

Despite Fang's strange appearance—his greasy hair was pulled back in a headband, and he was wearing a dirty flannel shirt over a T-shirt that said "Happy Day"—I was proud that a CAFA student was identifying me in front of Meiling. This was the kind of student I'd seen hanging out at the teahouse, and the fact that he'd recognized me made me imagine for a moment that I was an artist myself.

"Yeah," I said. "I meant to look him up earlier, but—"

"He told me about you. He wrote to your parents to ask where you were, but he hadn't heard back yet. You're lucky—I'm going to see him right now."

"What's new?" the girl with the folders said.

"It's true." Fang grinned: "If I'm not here, I'm at your cousin's place; if I'm not there, I'm at Cash's."

"Who is Cash?" I asked.

"He's the one who hosts the Wednesday Art Lunches. When it started it was just your cousin and Cash and me; now there're usually about ten of us. You should come sometime."

"That's a strange name," Meiling said.

"He named himself after his favorite American singer." Fang grabbed an imaginary microphone and began to croon in English: "*Well, you won-der why I always dress in black . . . Why you never see bright colors on my back . . .*"

"Please," said the secretary. "I beg you."

Fang stopped obligingly. "Cash does it better anyway. He might be there today—we should hurry, or we'll be late."

Suddenly I felt nervous. "He's not expecting me. I was just going to leave a note."

"Don't be so polite," Fang said. "Man, is he going to be surprised."

28.

THE APARTMENT WE VISITED THAT AFTERNOON WAS IN A NEW COMpound just west of the Asian Games Village, in the northern part of the city. A uniformed guard let us in downstairs, and called Fang's name into an intercom receiver. You could see he was unhappy about letting us up: Meiling and I looked fine, if undistinguished, but Fang's sloppy, none-too-clean clothes made a bad impression. Although I liked him immediately, I have to admit that Fang never smelled very good.

The elevator opened onto a long, softly lit hallway, with peach-colored walls and very large fire sprinklers. Along the walls at intervals were glass-fronted alcoves; resting there were imitation Ming vases filled with silk flowers and ceramic horses in dramatic postures, their manes blowing in a fierce, imaginary wind.

"Your cousin lives *here?*" Meiling whispered, but not softly enough because Fang turned around and corrected her. It was the first time he used a tone with us that was anything less than accommodating.

"This is *nothing* like where he lives. It's his girlfriend Lulu's apartment—the setting for the project they're working on."

"His girlfriend is working on the project too?" Meiling asked.

"All his friends help him out," Fang said. "We consider it a privilege. After all, he's going to be really famous one day."

While we were chatting, the door was opened by an old lady in well-tailored modern clothes; she barely nodded, and then retreated down the hall toward what I imagined was the kitchen. I wished we were going that way; I could smell the delicious aroma of fried pork and scallions. But

Fang motioned us down the hall in the other direction, from which I could see a very bright electric light and hear several voices arguing.

Fang knocked sharply on the door; a moment later someone opened it. I was glad the hallway was dark, because I felt myself blushing; Meiling, too, did not know where to look. There were three people in the room. The man who opened the door (he was a man, from the bulge in his skin-tight black-and-white-striped jeans) had a female face—a real woman's face, rather than a transvestite's. He was wearing a tasteful amount of makeup and his shoulder-length hair had been blow-dried to shiny perfection, as in an advertisement for Rejoice 2-in-1 shampoo.

"You're late," he said to Fang, and stepped aside: we were standing in a luxuriously appointed bedroom, in the center of which was a queen-sized white bed. Standing to the left of the bed, wrapped in a pink-and-white-checked sheet, was a very tall, thin young woman. I assumed this was Lulu. She was not beautiful so much as exotic, with high cheekbones and widely spaced, almost Tibetan eyes. She didn't appear to be wearing anything under the sheet except for white tights and a pair of pink silk ballet shoes. On the other side of the bed was my cousin, who had grown lanky, dark, and strong since I had seen him last. X was wearing absolutely nothing at all.

"I don't think we should see any bush," said the womanish man. (This was Baoyu, whom I would later count among my friends; at the time he seemed as foreign to me as a circus performer.)

"What a surprise," Lulu said. "You, against bush."

"I've got bush, sweetheart. Wanna see it?"

"Shhh . . ." Lulu said, tilting her head toward the kitchen. "My *waipo*."

The woman who had opened the door, then, was her grandmother. Later I learned more about Lulu's exotic family history: she was the product of a tryst between a Hong Kong businessman and a well-known television actress. Her mother was now married to a high official, who supported Lulu generously while she studied at Beijing's famous Academy of Dance. Once she finished her training (Lulu would tell you, given any opportunity), she had always planned to go to Hong Kong, where she would find her real father and star in martial arts films. Then she met X, and everything changed. My cousin had convinced her that Chinese artists who left the mainland were betraying not only their country and their fellow citizens, but themselves.

"Just two asses on a bed: one dark, one artificially white. It's perfect," said Baoyu, but my cousin wasn't paying attention to him. He was staring at me, trying to figure out who I was. Even though he was the one who'd been caught naked with a ballerina and another man, I was nervous in front of him. I couldn't look at his face, so I stared at the floor: I was strangely relieved to discover that my cousin had ugly, misshapen feet.

"I'm sorry I'm late," Fang said. "But look who I found!"

"I know you," said X, but he could not place me.

There was no help for it. "Xiao Pangzi," I said.

Meiling giggled. Needless to say, I had not repeated my embarrassing childhood nickname to her before now.

"Cousin!" X said. Then, to my great discomfort, he came across the room and gave me a hug. He stepped back and noticed Meiling. "Excuse me," he said, grinning, but Baoyu was already handing him a bathrobe. I noticed that neither this man nor Lulu was looking at me with any particular fondness.

"My uncle's son from Harbin," X explained. "Little Fatty! A great scholar and speaker of English!" I didn't know that my normally abstemious cousin had prepared for this particular project, an exploration of bourgeois decadence in the New China entitled *Modern Dance*, by snorting three fat lines of cocaine, but it contributed to my very warm reception. He was not normally so effusive. "Permit me to introduce my girlfriend, the lovely and talented Miss Lulu. And this is my good friend, Baoyu."

Baoyu inclined his head slightly in our direction. "Lovely and talented as well, of course."

"This is my classmate, Meiling," I said. "We don't want to intrude."

"You're too polite," my cousin said. Lulu and Baoyu didn't say anything. "But it's true that we're in the middle of something."

"But the middle of *what*?" Lulu said. "That's my question."

"*Modern Dance*." X smiled at me. "What else?"

"Could I use your bathroom?" Meiling whispered.

Lulu gestured lazily, although it was obvious. The door was open, and the bathroom was lit up like a stage dressing room, with high-voltage bulbs around a large, oval mirror.

"That's your girlfriend?" my cousin asked, giving me a little wink.

"Just a friend," I told him, in case Meiling could hear us from the bathroom.

"She's cute," he said. "Seems a little shy though."

"Not usually."

X laughed. "Yeah. Hey, it's so good to see you. I thought I was going to have to come hunting for you."

"I found them," Fang reminded him.

When Meiling came out of the bathroom, she looked calmer. I could tell she had heard us talking from the way she refused to look at X. "Sorry," she said to me. "But we should go. Remember we have that mandatory study session?"

X was staring at her. Suddenly he slapped his palm against his forehead. "That's it!" he said. "Miss Meiling, you're a genius."

Everyone looked at him.

"We're starting in the wrong place," my cousin said. "I realized it when I saw her coming out of the bathroom, in all the light. The pictures should begin in there, in the tub, and then we would be wet when we got into the bed."

"That's a great idea," Baoyu said. "Let's try some different combinations too." Lulu sighed and sat down on the bed.

My cousin turned to Meiling. "You've helped a great deal."

I didn't know about any mandatory study session, but I felt it was time to leave. "We have to go," I said.

X nodded. "Here, wait a second." He looked around Lulu's bedroom: on the imitation mahogany dresser, which matched the bed and night tables, was a stack of invitation cards. He handed one to Meiling. "You two should come to my performance next week. Then afterward we can all go eat together. I'm going to be hungry," he said, grinning at the others.

"It's at his house—in the East Village," Fang said. "I can pick you up, if you give me your address."

We gave Fang directions to my dormitory. When we left, the three of them were in the bathroom together with Fang, who was taking test shots and checking the light.

"See you next week," my cousin said. He was already untying his robe.

"They're crazy," Meiling said, once we were in the elevator.

"They're artists," I said. "That's what artists are like."

Meiling glanced at the card and smiled. "Are you sure?"

"Just because something doesn't hang on the wall, doesn't mean it isn't art."

Meiling shrugged. She handed me the invitation; underneath my cousin's name, in large letters, was the following:

"Something That is NOT Art"
LANE 7, HOUSE 19, APARTMENT 2
THE EAST VILLAGE, BEIJING

November 7, 1993
11 o'clock

It was the first of many surprises my cousin had in store for me.

29.

A WEEK AFTER HARRY LIN FAILED TO SHOW UP FOR THE DINNER PARTY,
I received a letter from him. Dr. Travers brought it home from the university, in a plain envelope without a return address or a stamp. During a dinner of swordfish and corn-on-the-cob, I kept the letter next to my plate. The uncle watched me suspiciously, and I could tell that Cece was interested in the envelope's contents, but I didn't want to risk opening it in front of them. I couldn't imagine why the professor would write to me: was it possible that he'd decided to revoke my fellowship so soon?

After dinner I took the letter up to my bedroom. I sat at the desk for several minutes before opening it. What was I afraid of? In Beijing the idea of the Traverses had been abstract, and I'd barely given a thought to their opinion of me. Now that I was in Los Angeles, however, with real people entertaining the idea of me as a working artist (an idea I once had entertained seriously myself), I didn't want to disappoint them. I thought that if Harry Lin would just leave me alone, I might be able to produce something that would satisfy my hosts, as well as the trustees of the Dubin Fellowship.

My dear Zhao,
You must be wondering why I didn't show up the other night. I owe you an explanation. (I owe one to your hosts as well, but with them I don't plan to be quite so forthcoming). I've given some thought to your original suggestion, and I believe it's a good one. I am going to leave you in peace to do your work.

Part of the difficulty with these fellowships is the isolation of the

*fellow within the university: he sees the university culture, and little
else. Let me assure you, a university is not America! And so I propose
that we quarantine you. You'll work on your project, teach at your
school, and live like an ordinary Angelino (if a privileged one). Then
let's see what you come up with. It's an experiment, but an exciting
one I think.*

*Perhaps this should be our last contact before the show in Novem-
ber? I am reluctant to deprive myself of your company for so long—but
we all make great sacrifices for art. Who knows that better than you
do? Until then,*
Your friend,
Harry Lin (Lin Rui)

Of course I ought to have been pleased once I read the letter. Everything was fine, just as my cousin had promised. And yet I couldn't help
being stung by the line about "great sacrifices." There was a time in my life
when I might have made sacrifices for art, and chose not to. Afterward I
spent a lot of time wondering whether I had behaved sensibly, knowing
that I didn't have enough talent, or whether I'd simply been too frightened of failure to try. Of course, a great deal of what happens in a person's
life depends on chance, and at that time, when I was a student involved
with the Beijing East Village, several things happened to set me on another course.

I was rereading the professor's letter when I heard the double tone of
the telephone, and Cece's voice over the intercom inviting me to pick up
line one. "Fanlong" was on the phone for me. I was surprised to receive a
phone call at the Traverses'—not least from a practicing Buddhist monk
who'd been active in the Southern Song school of academic painting
around the year A.D. 1100.

I picked up the phone.

"Hello and Welcome to Beautiful Beverly Hills, California!" said my
cousin, who had obviously been practicing a new English phrase. "How's
it going over there?"

"Fine," I said. I found I was not as happy to hear a familiar voice as I'd
expected.

"What's the family like? How's the weather?"

"Both very nice," I said. "The Traverses are good friends of Professor Lin's, did you know that? He almost came to dinner the other night."

"Almost?" My cousin's blithe tone annoyed me. I thought it would serve him right if Professor Lin had shown up, against his instructions.

"Luckily he had some university business."

"See?" X said. "I told you it would work out. I said you'd want to be left alone to conceive your new project." He paused. "Have you conceived anything yet?"

"I'm glad you're amused," I said. "Did you know he wrote me a letter? He said I'd made 'great sacrifices' for art."

"Who hasn't?" X sighed. "Did I tell you that my new performance is going to have to be scrapped? And the rent just went up at the Factory again. I don't know how much longer I'm going to be able to stay here. All kinds of *artists* are starting to move in."

Ever since my cousin had become well-known, he'd begun condemning artists loudly—calling them boring, and professing that he'd rather hang out with anyone else. This behavior was confusing, especially if you remembered how assiduously he'd courted the famous ones, before he became an artist himself.

"I envy you, I really do," my cousin said. "Is there a swimming pool?"

"I don't have time for swimming," I told him. "I have to come up with an entire show by the spring."

"Plenty of time," X said. "Just do your teaching and sit in the sun. Something will come to you."

After we hung up, I noticed I'd been doodling on the yellow pad in front of me. A lobster had appeared, complete with a pair of long antennae. I thought of my cousin's nickname for me, the Lobster Hermit, and of the famous "mountain men" in our history. Each time a dynasty was overturned, some loyalists fled to the hills, living in remote monasteries, or even caves, taking comfort in the clouds and rocks, and expressing their alienation in poignant painted scrolls. These artists suffered a double loss: not only were they banished, but the court to which they'd devoted themselves was gone. After the defeat of the Southern Song, for example, Hangzhou had never again been an imperial capital.

And yet that capital had hardly been free of corruption. Some of the Song mountain men had been wealthy dilettantes, lounging on silk pillows, consuming rare delicacies, refining their calligraphy in order to write love poems to young women and boys. It is interesting to note that in Zhao Cangyun's single extant scroll, *Liu Chen and Ruan Zhao in the Tiantai Mountains*, both the village of the two Han gentlemen and the paradise into which they stumble are located close to Hangzhou. Perhaps the ambivalence of those gentlemen, hesitating between two worlds, reflects the artist's feelings as well—almost as if his home had to be destroyed before he could begin to paint it.

30.

PHIL HAD ORGANIZED HIS SCHEDULE IN LOS ANGELES IN ORDER TO AP-
pear as busy as possible. In the morning, around ten, he swam laps, a
habit he'd instituted after learning that Yuan Zhao practiced tai chi in the
early mornings. (Phil was not awake early enough to observe this first-
hand, but he had seen other people doing tai chi on television: it did not
look very hard.) When he was done with his swim, he would take a shower
and go into the kitchen. The housekeeper would offer halfheartedly to
make his breakfast; Phil declined without hesitation. Everything that took
up time was a good thing. If he got up at ten, swam from ten-fifteen until
eleven, and had coffee and a bagel at eleven-thirty, he was capable of
stretching the newspaper until one.

Since he'd arrived in L.A., Phil had begun reading the real estate section; he could not stay at his brother's forever, and a rental apartment
(preferably one with a month-to-month lease) was the obvious solution.
The rental apartment listings were not half as interesting as the properties
for sale, however, and Phil found himself lingering over the most seductive
descriptions in that category. Sometimes something sounded so good—
grt. lite, trip-mint, 3 expos—that he couldn't resist noting down the address
on a Post-it, and sticking it in his pocket. Not that he was planning on buying a house in Los Angeles, of course. It was just interesting to know what
was out there. *Sizzling opportunity! Have it all!* Perfect houses existed (his
brother's for example), and there was always the possibility that in this
case—*won't last, hurry!*—the broker was telling the truth.

By one o'clock his time, things had slowed down at Aubrey's office,
and on most days she called him then. (Even when they were both in the

same time zone, Phil often felt as if Aubrey were three hours ahead of him.) If he hadn't been hoping that his writing partners would call, he might not have answered his phone.

"Hi," Aubrey would say. "Have they called?"

"Not yet."

"You screenwriters. Living the good life . . . lounging by the pool."

"I've been exercising in the pool," Phil said. "You're hardly going to recognize me."

"What?" Aubrey said (to someone else). And then to Phil: "What's the temperature there?"

When Phil told her, Aubrey repeated it to her officemate, and Phil could hear the two of them groaning enviously together. "They haven't even made him *do* anything yet," he heard her say. And to him: "We have to start figuring out the Thanksgiving plan."

The Thanksgiving plan was for Aubrey to come to Los Angeles and meet his family. More and more, Phil was thinking that plan needed to be revised.

The daily phone call with Aubrey made him feel as if he deserved some reward. Now that Cece took the Nissan Pathfinder to St. Anselm's with Olivia and Yuan Zhao, her yellow Mercedes was available during the day. There were few things Phil liked so much as sliding into the caramel leather interior, which smelled strongly of Cece's Aqua de Gio perfume, putting on Talking Heads' *Stop Making Sense* or anything by Yo La Tengo, and going for a drive.

One afternoon, heading up Coldwater Canyon, he noticed a swinging For Sale sign in front of a high hedge. With more exposed properties, Phil always found something to prevent him from stopping, but when he couldn't see in from the street, he could never resist taking a detour. Who knew when you might stumble upon the perfect match?

The house on Coldwater was almost it. He had not thought he liked modern houses until he had seen this one: double-height ceilings, massive windows, and floor-to-ceiling bookshelves with a ladder to reach the top. The floors were dark polished teak, and from the balcony off the bedroom, you could see all the way down the canyon.

"Are you looking for yourself, or—?" the realtor, Barbara asked. She was an attractive brunette with killer legs. She was wearing a wedding band, but Phil took the flier with her phone number anyway. The flier also had pictures of the house.

"For myself," Phil said.

The realtor nodded in an approving way. "I've had some couples here, but to be honest with you, it's more of a single person's house. This second bedroom is a perfect office—what do you do?"

It took Phil a minute. "I'm a screenwriter."

"Oh, perfect," Barbara said. "It was an architect who designed it for himself—you can see that, I'm sure. Now he and his partner are adopting a child from Burma. Or maybe Bangladesh? Anyway—they need more space. And do you know, it's only ten percent down."

"I've only just started looking," Phil said cautiously.

"I could show you some other things, if you'd like," Barbara said. "But I'll tell you—this is the best bachelor pad I've got. Not that it couldn't be turned into a great place for a couple," she added. "If your circumstances were to change."

Phil promised Barbara he would think about it. He was beginning to doubt that he had the resources to change his circumstances (even the prospect was exhausting), and yet, when he thought of taking his current relationship to its logical next step, there was a problem. He had always thought the problem was Aubrey; she was not quite right. She was too bossy, too demanding; her ideas about what their life should be would swallow his personality, until there was no Phil left. But when he imagined telling Aubrey that he was ready, he knew that her happiness and gratitude would overwhelm any criticisms she had of him, that he would be able to ask for anything in exchange, and she would do her best to indulge him.

The problem was not with this imaginary, satisfied Aubrey, but with Phil himself. When he pictured a wedding, a pregnant Aubrey, a formal abandonment of his apartment in Queens (if not a home, then at least a kind of home base), something in him refused. A second Phil seemed to step out of his skin, like a human being morphing out of a superhero, and say firmly and unequivocally: "No, thank you."

31.

HE HAD NOTIFIED THE STUDIO OF HIS WHEREABOUTS, AND THEY HAD promised that Steve and Keith would be in touch. It was already the first week of October, however, and Phil still hadn't heard from his writing partners. He had looked them up on the computer in Max's room: they had a joint Web page, which listed their extensive television credits, and the fact that they had recently sold an original screenplay, which would be produced by a major studio in cooperation with their own company: Kiss Me, Kill Me Productions. (The Web site didn't mention the adaptation of *The Hypnotist*, which was probably a kind of side project that Steve and Keith were doing for a little extra cash.) According to their joint biography, Steve and Keith had met in college in New Hampshire, and subsequently spent their "entire careers" in Hollywood. Given that his financial future had been secured by a teenager, Phil was not particularly surprised to find himself now desperately waiting for a phone call from people whose "entire careers" were each less than six years old.

Phil had a new cellular telephone, the first he'd ever owned. While he waited for it to ring, he visited LACMA, the La Brea tar pits, and the Griffith Park Observatory—all of the places he had once frequented with Cece and the children. He should not have been surprised to see the changes: the museum had added another wing, the Japanese Pavilion, and the tar pits had been relandscaped to shut out the traffic, which flowed incongruously around the prehistoric black sludge. Only the massive Foucault's Pendulum in the atrium of the observatory was exactly the same. Phil stood above the pit in the middle of the day, surrounded by strange children, watching the pendulum make its mysterious record in the sand.

What, exactly, defined an affair? Certainly not a relationship that had begun during a planetarium show. Not something that had started to the tune of a recorded voice—*"We are approaching the limits of the solar system. We are now eight billion miles from Earth"*—and a five-year-old dropping a Kleenex on the floor. Otherwise it had been an ordinary afternoon: he and Cece and the kids at the observatory, a picnic lunch in the park (sandwiches for himself, Cece and Olivia, and soggy pinwheel pasta for Max); and then the planetarium show, the four of them taking their seats in the darkened auditorium, and Phil jokingly putting his hand on Cece's knee. This sort of flirting had become part of their repertoire several months earlier; it was a bold, but not unprecedented thing to do. Cece had removed his hand. *"The atmosphere around us is four hundred and fifty degrees below zero, Fahrenheit. Bits of rock, ice, and microscopic particles of solar dust seem to float past us, but in fact they are traveling faster than the fastest vehicles on Earth."*

Phil moved his leg so that it touched Cece's from thigh to ankle. "Phil!" she whispered. She was trying not to laugh. Her children's heads were tipped back on the wooden headrests, lulled by the hypnotic voice: *"But most of what you see is dark: the darkest dark you can imagine, a thousand times darker than your bedroom at night, the absolute blackness of deep space."*

As they approached the Sagittarius Dwarf galaxy, Phil could see her glowing profile, the short, "practical" haircut that exposed the tremendously sexy place at the base of her neck. She was staring at the heads of the people in front of her, ignoring him. He put his arm over her shoulders, like a teenage boy at the movies, and then ran his index finger lightly around her ear. Cece turned to him, and her nostrils flared just a tiny bit, a tiny loss of control. *"Even time is different here. We're traveling at the speed of light, one hundred and eighty-five thousand miles per second; according to Albert Einstein's theory of relativity, we are now officially getting younger."*

Phil put his mouth to her ear. "It's a lie."

"What?"

"We're not getting any younger."

She was rescuing something, a program or a tissue, that had fallen on the floor. The space between her sweater and the waistband of her jeans was exposed for a second; he put his hand there. She sat up, and then she did something extraordinary. She bent her head and whispered to her children and, without looking at Phil at all, got up and began edging out of the row. It was the only time he could remember her leaving them alone, even for a second. Her children stared dreamily up. After only a moment's consideration, Phil followed her.

There was a velvet curtain at the back of the auditorium separating the theater from the double doors: a few feet of carpeted space. Cece's hair was red in the light from the Exit sign.

"What are you doing?" she demanded.

"I can't help it. I love you."

"A galaxy is a huge group of stars, dust, gas, and other celestial bodies, bound together by gravitational forces. There are spiral, irregular, and elliptical-shaped galaxies."

"Don't be silly," Cece said.

He thought of grabbing and kissing her; one look at her face, and he could see that it wouldn't work. Her mouth was thin and determined, as if she'd already settled on how to proceed.

"We have to figure this out," she said. "We have to agree, both of us." She was like a child with a plan, touchingly sure of herself. "It can't just be whatever happens."

The theater was dusty. Phil coughed, one of those inexplicable fits that came, at that moment, like a gift from God.

"Sorry," he choked. "Sorry."

Instantly her expression softened. She put her hand lightly on his forearm. "Are you all right?"

"I'm sorry—it's just—this is painful for me."

She took her hand away.

"And I can't sleep anymore," he added quickly. "I'm just so tired all the time—"

"Oh, Phil."

"I don't know what I'm going to do."

"Galaxies radiate a continuous spectrum of energy. This energy may take the form of radio waves, X-rays, infrared, and ultraviolet radiation."

Cece took his hand and kissed him. There were some things you'd been waiting for so long that when they finally happened, you couldn't actually feel them. It took a moment, like a shock or a burn.

She pulled back and looked up at him. "What are we doing?"

"What are we doing?" Phil repeated, just for the pleasure of using the present tense. He slipped his hand underneath her sweater, a very soft lavender sweater, and put his face in her hair. Her perfume was complicated, rich and citrusy: he couldn't imagine ever getting tired of it.

"Cecelia," he whispered.

She smiled: "No one calls me that."

"You are so perfect."

"Oh no," she said. "Obviously not."

"You're everything I want right now."

"Right now?"

"Always," Phil said wildly. "Forever." And to prove it, kissed her a little too earnestly, without the necessary forethought or restraint.

32.

ALMOST IMMEDIATELY UPON ARRIVAL, HE HAD MANAGED TO MAKE HER furious with him. It was the Thursday before Labor Day, the week before his niece and nephew started school. Phil was sitting in the kitchen, waiting for Max to come downstairs. He thought Cece's kitchen was the most peaceful place he'd ever been; he had to refrain from laying his cheek against the caramel-colored Italian marble, which gave him a pleasant graveyard frisson—how interesting that death and cooking should employ the same building material.

It wasn't only the kitchen, or the plush white living room, or his bungalow with its unbelievable Frankenthaler print—a purple wash with a large red splash in the center, the quiet perfection of which struck him, for some reason, like a reprimand every time he looked at it—but the familiar way the air smelled when he stepped out of his bedroom in the morning, the softness of it. Not to mention the fact that when he stepped out of his bedroom *that* morning, right in front of him, there had been a set of perfect tanned and oiled teenage breasts.

The phone shrieked five times, and then he heard Cece's voice on the answering machine in Gordon's study: "You've reached the Traverses. To leave a message for Gordon, press one; for Cece, press two; for Olivia or Max, press three . . ." An unfamiliar female voice was interrupted by someone picking up the phone, and a few minutes later, he heard his nephew tramping down the stairs. Phil felt a funny kind of excitement; he sat up a little straighter, and then tried to look nonchalant. Although he'd sat at the dinner table with Max and even walked through his bedroom (so that Cece could show him the guest room she'd outfitted for the dissident), this was the first time he'd seen his nephew alone.

Max came into the kitchen mid-yawn. He put a tiny, high-tech video camera down on the counter and glanced at Phil.

"Hey," he said, and headed for the refrigerator. He violently shuffled the contents before emerging with half a hero sandwich wrapped in plastic and a bottle of Tsing Tao left over from the dinner in honor of the dissident.

"Hey," said Phil. To his delight, Max sat down at the counter next to him and began silently unwrapping the sandwich. Phil felt a little ashamed of the muffin on his plate—Max was only fifteen, but he was eating such a manly breakfast!

"Cool camera," Phil ventured.

His nephew didn't say anything.

"Is it new?"

Max nodded.

"Are you making a video?"

Max took a swig of the beer and wiped his mouth with his hand. "I can't do anything."

"I know," Phil said. "I can never figure those things out. Anything electronic. Like e-mail—do you have e-mail?"

Max stared at him. "You can't figure out e-mail?"

"I mean, just for example," Phil said.

"I can't do anything"—Max paused and took a swig of Tsing Tao—"because I can't leave the house."

"Oh," said Phil. "Right, yeah. But I mean, if you have to be grounded, this is the place, right?"

Max looked at him blankly.

"I mean, it's great here. At least compared to New York. The weather's great, and your parents have such a great house." Could he say the word "great" one more time? "I always thought I hated L.A., but this is—great. Don't you think?"

"Could you, um . . ."

"Yes?" said Phil eagerly.

"Could you, like, pretend to be drinking this beer? If my dad comes back?"

"Oh . . . yeah," said Phil. "Yeah, sure, no problem."

Max nodded an extremely brief thank-you; Phil was gratified. He decided on the spot that he and Max could be friends. He imagined that Max was in need of a role model, given Gordon's distraction.

"He probably won't get here before Jasmine," Max said. "She's picking me up."

"Oh, I was supposed to make sure—" Phil hesitated: should he be surreptitious about the fact that he was keeping an eye on Max?

"—to make sure I didn't go out," Max finished for him. "You're not going to tell them, are you?"

Phil looked at the clock. Cece had said she'd be back in twenty minutes—ten now. "Won't she notice?"

"But I'll be gone by then."

The question was not, Will you tell? It was, Will you keep me from going? Are you on my side, or theirs? Who are you?

Phil recognized the bigness of the moment: that was the trouble. It was always in big moments that he couldn't figure out what he should do. "If you could just relax," Aubrey often told him, "everything would work out fine." By "work out fine," Aubrey meant that Phil would make some firm and final career decision; they would officially move in together; they would get married and have a baby. Ordinarily, in big moments, Phil simply tried to say "OK." Aubrey, with her quick legal mind, had cottoned on to this strategy fairly quickly. "OK, *what?*" she would say.

"OK," said Phil.

"Thanks," said Max.

"No problem," said Phil. "Jasmine is your girlfriend, right?" Perhaps he could tell Cece that he'd fallen asleep?

"Uh-huh."

"How long have you guys been together?"

"Two and a half months."

Phil sighed. "That's the perfect time. When you're still comfortable, but not *too* comfortable—" He stopped, remembering that his nephew was fifteen. Probably you could never get too comfortable at fifteen. "So what are you guys up to today?"

Max sighed. "I might—" he began, and then took a bite of his sandwich. "Ahmite mekka mooey."

"What?"

Max swallowed. "I might make a movie. With Jasmine."

"What kind of movie?"

"A murder, I guess."

"Do you have a story yet?"

Max looked at him as if he'd just discovered that Phil was retarded. "I just told you."

"I mean, beyond the murder?"

"Oh yeah," Max said. "You're a screenwriter, right?"

"Playwright," Phil said. "That's like a screenwriter, though."

"Not really," Max said.

They heard voices outside; a moment later, Olivia and her friend wrenched open the French doors and made a beeline for the refrigerator. They were now wearing T-shirts and shorts, and the strings of their bikini tops were tied securely around their necks. Their wooden-soled sandals made a racket on the terrazzo tiles.

"Leftover pasta?" Olivia suggested.

"Nothing hot," said her friend. The skin on the back of her thighs had burned evenly: two long, red stripes. "I wish we had smoothies."

"Smoothies!"

"Do you have frozen strawberries?"

"My mom has everything." Olivia cast a disgusted glance in the direction of Max and Phil. "We can make them in the pantry."

"Why?"

"There's a blender there. Then we won't have to be in here," Olivia stage-whispered. Her back was to her brother, who was doing a spectacular job of pretending the girls didn't exist. Suddenly his sister whirled around and stared at him: "Are you drinking a *beer*?"

Phil wondered if he was supposed to pretend the beer was his in front of the girls as well. He didn't want Olivia's friend to think he was drinking a beer so early in the day. He glanced at Max, who had put down his sandwich and was pulling the skin at the corners of his eyes:

"Chinaman dink Chinabee-uh," he said.

"You're hilarious," Olivia said. "Really."

Emily giggled. "I could deal with a beer."

"Take one," said Olivia. "We can go outside after we make our smoothies."

"Watch out," Max said. "The beer will make the smoothie explode in your stomach. Like one of those baking soda volcanoes."

"I remember those!" Emily said. "From science." She opened the fridge and bent over to look for the beer. Emily was the kind of natural blonde you found mostly in Scandinavia; perhaps she was of Swedish origin? (That would explain the toplessness.) Sweden was supposed to have the most beautiful women in the world, and Phil had never been there. He would probably never go either—not unless he and Aubrey got married and decided to go on a honeymoon to Sweden. How ironic that the only way he could think of to see the most beautiful women in the world was to make a promise that he would never, ever try to sleep with one of them again.

Emily stood up and looked at Phil for the first time: "You have the thing?"

"The—sorry—what?"

Max leaned forward and tossed Emily the bottle opener.

Phil looked at his nephew with admiration. Max was the kind of kid who would eventually find his way to Sweden.

Max groaned suddenly.

"What?" said Phil, but just then he heard the front door open.

"Hello?" Gordon called.

Everyone in the kitchen was quiet, as if by prior arrangement. Phil had a pleasant, nostalgic feeling of being caught doing something he shouldn't. He felt the urge to put his finger to his lips—they could scare the shit out of Gordon—until he remembered he was hanging out with his nephew and niece (and his niece's friend), all of whom were more than twenty years younger than himself.

"Hello?" Phil called, but just then the three-tone signal sounded all over the house: Gordon had gotten on the intercom in the living room and was efficiently notifying everyone of his presence.

"Hello, hello. Anybody home?"

"Wow," said Emily, in a theatrically puzzled tone that also expressed her complete scorn. It was brilliant.

"Children, children," Gordon called over the intercom: "Calling all children."

"Oh God," said Olivia, with poignant frustration.

"Maxwell?" blared the intercom. "You have a visitor."

Max leapt up, grabbing his camera, and rushed out of the kitchen, nearly colliding with his father and Jasmine, coming in through the dining room. Phil had just enough time to grasp Max's half-finished beer, moving it over in front of his blueberry muffin.

"Here you are," said Gordon. "Didn't you hear me?"

"Loud and clear," Olivia said.

"That's an amazing system," said Phil.

His brother looked pleased. "I had all the phones replaced six months ago. These are great. You can use the All button to hit every room at the same time, or intercom locally with the numbers: you're number one, in the pool house; two is the kitchen; three, the living room; four's the study—I mean Cece's study, not my office—that's number seven; six is the den; and eight is the deck of the pool. Then upstairs—"

"Thanks," Phil said. "I guess I'll just use the All."

"Dad?" said Olivia sternly. "This is my friend Emily."

"Emily!" said Gordon. "We've heard so much about you."

It was something their own father used to do, whether or not he had heard anything about the person he was meeting. It had usually been accompanied by his idea of a joke: "We've heard so much about you . . . but we promise not to hold it against you!" It was always particularly bad if you brought home someone of the opposite sex. Gordon and Joan had hated it too; how could his brother have forgotten it?

"Nice to meet you, Dr. Travers," Emily said.

"You're the French speaker, if I remember correctly?"

"*Je passais mon enfance en Europe.*"

Gordon smiled at Emily. "*Ma fille ne pratique pas jamais. Peut-être vous pouvez l'encourager?*"

"Are you a French professor?" Emily asked coyly.

"That's very flattering," Gordon said. "I'm a psychiatrist. With a hobby in French—well, a hobby for which I'm required to use a great deal of French."

"I told you that," Olivia said to Emily, but Emily ignored her.

"What's your hobby?"

Olivia sighed: Phil felt sorry for her. Max got to be the black sheep, but Olivia was clearly not the white sheep. In their family Phil and Gordon had taken those roles automatically, and Joan had been somewhere in the middle, a shade of gray. Maybe Olivia was a gray sheep too? It was strange to think that a couple like Cece and Gordon wouldn't have managed to produce even one white sheep.

"Genealogy is like a drug," his brother was saying. "I begin after dinner and often when I look up at the clock—suddenly it's two or three in the morning."

In the dining room, Max was holding a whispered conference with his girlfriend, who was wearing an extremely abbreviated denim miniskirt. Had Aubrey known that his quest for financial stability would send him into this den of half-naked teenagers, she might have had second thoughts.

"Dad?" Max said, but Gordon was explaining about his search for their crossing ancestor, and one particularly exciting dead end: a lone Travers, a bachelor, who had expired on the *Mayflower*, and been tossed to a watery grave.

"A burial at sea," Emily said. "That's so romantic."

"What would it be in French, I wonder?" Gordon mused: "*Enterrement à mer* is somewhat etymologically contradictory."

"Dad!"

"Yes, Maxwell?"

Olivia and her brother exchanged a look, the most sympathetic look Phil had seen pass between them yet. It gave him hope, not only for Olivia and Max, but for relationships between siblings everywhere.

"Could you give us a ride to the mural?"

"We'll take him," Olivia said immediately.

"Most kids want to go to the mall," Gordon told Phil. "My son wants to go to the *mural*."

Max started to say something, and stopped.

"But do you normally go on Thursdays?" Gordon continued.

Max wasn't looking at Phil, but it was the kind of studious not-looking that was stronger than a stare. Phil felt frozen under it. His nephew murmured a sound that had the inflection of "yes," without in fact being that word.

"Dad," said Olivia suddenly. "You're so out of it."

"Why am I out of it?" Gordon put down his racquet and headed for the refrigerator. "Pardon, mademoiselle," he said to Emily.

"Of course they go on Thursdays. Why else would Jasmine be here?"

Gordon held up his hands. "OK, OK. As long as it's fine with your mother." He looked around. "Has anyone seen your mother?"

"She took Mr. Yuan to the library," Max said.

"We'll see you later," Olivia said.

"Where are we going?" Emily asked.

"We'll drop them off at *community service*, and then—whatever. We have the car," Olivia added, lowering her voice. Phil glanced at Gordon, but his brother's head was in the refrigerator, and he did not appear to hear her.

"Bye," Phil said.

But Olivia was herding the other kids out of the kitchen without so much as a glance at him. Nor did his nephew, whom he'd rescued twice over—from his mother's grounding and his father's strictures regarding morning alcohol consumption—even turn around. It was clear, no matter how loyal he was, that from now on he would be playing on the grownups' team. The thought was deeply depressing.

33.

"DO YOU WANT SOME JUICE?" HIS BROTHER HELD UP AN ARMFUL OF OR-anges, grinning. There was a dark tongue of sweat down the front of his polo shirt, which had a little pair of crossed racquets in place of the al-ligator.

"You're in a good mood," Phil said. "Did you win?"

Gordon smiled and deposited the oranges on the counter in front of Phil. "I was annihilated. Six-one, six-oh." He took a knife from a wooden block, impeccably organized according to size, and began slicing oranges. "We were going to play a third set—but what's the point?"

"I'm sorry," said Phil.

"Did you ever read *The Inner Game of Tennis*?"

"I don't think so." Phil listened while his brother explained how he had once been focused on winning to a counterproductive extent. The book had allowed him to change his head game, and replace that results-oriented approach with a method of playing inside each point.

"I've been able to apply that lesson off the court as well. I'm enjoying life now, for the first time in a long time." As if to illustrate his point, Gor-don selected a second muffin from the baking sheet, broke into it with the knife, and inserted a large pat of butter. "Like you," he said, eyeing Phil's beer.

"This is a special circumstance," Phil said, but of course he couldn't explain.

"So when do they start shooting your movie?" Gordon asked. "I hope we're going to be invited to the set."

"We're nowhere near that point," Phil said quickly. "The whole thing needs to be rewritten first." He tried to sound as if he were in daily contact with the film production company, an integral member of the team. He certainly didn't want to tell Gordon that since arriving in Los Angeles, he'd received only one telephone call from his agent, giving him the phone numbers of his "writing partners," whom he had immediately contacted and who had failed to contact him back.

"That's a shame," Gordon said. "I don't think I've ever been on a film set."

"Really?" said Phil, who had never been on a film set either. He could not, in fact, imagine his play (which had two sets: a therapist's office and a one-bedroom apartment on the Upper West Side of Manhattan) as a film. The whole thing was basically just a series of conversations. While he was writing it, he had often thought of his sister Joan, whose stories sometimes didn't contain any dialogue at all. The characters remembered and considered and worried and planned. As soon as they finally did something, the story was over.

It wasn't that he didn't like Joan's stories. (In fact, he liked them a little more than he was willing to admit.) The problem with doing that kind of writing was having to imagine what other people thought. It was easy enough to guess what your characters might *say*, but how could you know what they were thinking? Who knew why other people did things? Phil often felt he didn't know why he did things himself.

"Well, you'll have to keep us posted," Gordon said. "At least this alleviates your financial worries. Cece told me you got quite a nice chunk of change."

"I haven't been paid yet," Phil said.

"She says you're thinking of getting married," Gordon said.

"What?"

"She says you're thinking of marrying Audrey."

"Aubrey," said Phil. "But I'm not. At least not any more than before. I think Cece might have misunderstood."

"*Aubrey*." Gordon said her name as if it were a new kind of French cheese. He seemed to savor it. "Tell me what she does again."

"She's a lawyer," Phil said.

"Corporate or . . ."

"She's a litigator."

Gordon whistled.

"She's very busy."

"She sounds like a catch," Gordon said.

"Aubrey and I aren't getting married," Phil repeated. "I'm not sure we're even going to stay together."

Gordon was frowning at the newspaper. "Look at this," he said, passing Phil the Metro section of the *Los Angeles Times*. "Seventeen-, eighteen-year-old kids."

Phil looked at the paper: someone had been shot in Watts. He thought of Max, and wondered whether he ought to have intervened. Why hadn't he at least found out where they were going? But his brother had been right there. If anyone was to blame, it was certainly Gordon.

Gordon was apparently not thinking of Max. "These gangs are a real problem," he said, taking the paper back from Phil. "Anyway, Au*brey* sounds fantastic. I don't know what you're waiting for."

They were sitting on designer barstools; if he braced himself on the counter, Phil could simply have knocked his brother down. Additionally there was the knife lying on the counter in front of him—not the butter knife that Gordon had used on the muffin, which he was now loudly masticating, but a small Japanese paring knife (the kind that never needed to be sharpened), lying among the juice and seeds and pulp of the eviscerated oranges. He had once seen a French movie about a girls' reform school in which one student stabbed another with an ordinary kitchen fork, pinning her hand to the table in a black pool of blood.

"Hello?" Cece said. "I'm home."

He had meant to be in his pool house, to give the sleeping excuse more currency. How could he have slept through Max's departure, if he was sitting here eating muffins with Gordon?

"There you are," Gordon said. "How was tennis?"

"*You* played tennis," Cece said. "I took Mr. Yuan to the library. Is Max still asleep?"

"I know I played tennis," Gordon said. "I thought today was the day you played with Pamela and Liz and—"

"Carol—no, that's Tuesday." Cece was acting strangely, moving around the kitchen. She opened the refrigerator door, checked the temperature, and then closed it. She put her handbag down on a chair and then snatched it up again. She took out a small pair of scissors, frowned at them, and put them in a drawer. Then she looked at Phil for the first time:

"Where's Max?"

"They went to community service," Gordon said.

Phil looked at his beer.

"*Who* went to community service?"

"Jasmine came to get him," Gordon explained.

"Jasmine was *driving*?"

"If you'll let me finish," Gordon said calmly. "Jasmine was dropped off—presumably by some authority figure—"

Cece made a kind of choking sound.

"—and then Olivia and Emily drove the two of them to the mural."

"You let Max and Jasmine go off with Olivia and Emily?"

Gordon nodded. "I finally met the famous Emily. She's very well spoken. That's the accent I was hoping Olivia would pick up in Paris."

"*How* could you let them go?"

"I just told you. Olivia offered to drive them, and since I hadn't had my breakfast—" He indicated the plate. "These were delicious, by the way."

"Did you forget that he was grounded?" Cece's voice was deceptively calm. "Because I thought we discussed that in detail."

"I didn't forget," Gordon said. "I thought we made an exception for the community service. I mean he's required to do it, isn't he?"

Phil got up and started walking toward the screen door. If he could just leave unobtrusively, as if he were giving them their privacy, he might escape altogether. Cece had a way of storing up her fury, to be released only when something had threatened one of her children. Probably many women were like that—but how could you know until it was too late?

"*You* knew," Cece said, and even though his back was turned, he knew she was talking to him. "Just the way I knew."

"Knew what?" his brother asked.

Phil turned around. "OK," he said.

"OK, *what*?" Cece asked, ignoring Gordon. "Why didn't you say something?"

"Peer pressure," Phil said. Both Gordon and Cece looked at him. He rephrased: "They were pressuring me; I felt like I would be betraying them if I told Gordon."

"Told me what?"

Cece whirled around: "That there's no community service today! *They're finished with community service!*"

"I don't have his schedule memorized," Gordon said. "If in the future you would like me to keep track of it—"

But Cece had picked up her purse and gone out the back. A moment later they heard the car start in the driveway: she was going to look for Max.

His brother looked at him and held up his hands in a gesture that could mean either, "See what I mean," or "What can you do?"

You stupid putz, Phil thought. If you're not going to do anything, then I will.

34.

I HAD AN APPOINTMENT TO MEET THE PRINCIPAL AT TWO O'CLOCK ON
my first day at St. Anselm's, but I had been at school only a few hours before I encountered her. Ms. McCoy was a blond and powerful woman,
with the manner of someone accustomed to doing several things at the
same time. I had been dreading a conversation in which she would demand to see my references, and perhaps a set of lesson plans for the semester, but the principal only tilted her head to the side and gave me a
curious look.

"Professor Yuan," she said. "Walk and talk, will you?"

I knew that to an American the correct application of titles was not
quite so important as it was in China, but I felt awkward being called
"Professor." When I first starting studying English with my mother after
school, she would criticize me for "listening in Chinese." "When you
speak English," she said, "you have to listen in English. When you speak
Chinese, you use your Chinese ear. Why do you think you have two of
them?" I had never thought of it that way, and when I was alone in my
bedroom I would practice: covering one ear at a time while experimenting with different phrases, trying to determine which was which.

"I'm not officially a professor," I corrected her, but Ms. McCoy did not
seem interested in the distinction. Rather, she wanted to know whether
I'd had a chance to examine the still lifes hanging in the Marian Caldwell
Memorial Gallery.

"How would they compare with a similar class in China?"

"Their work is very interesting," I said. In fact I had been shocked by
the sloppiness of many of the drawings, some of which were unfinished.

"Be honest," the principal said. "Do they seem to have a command of their materials?"

"Perhaps some are at a lower level than others."

"If you think they're at a lower level in art, you should sit in on some of the math classes." The principal, to my amazement, laughed. "But we're working on it."

"Art and math require discipline. Perhaps Chinese students are more disciplined." At this moment, as if to illustrate my point, the bell rang; all along the open walkway, which ran on two levels around the rectangular building, doors shot open; students swarmed around us.

"I'm interested that you compare art and math in terms of discipline," she continued, raising her voice above the commotion in the hallway. (I didn't remind her that it was she who had compared art to math. I was glad we weren't talking about what I planned to teach my students, or whether I had any previous experience disciplining untalented seventeen-year-old girls.) "Did you see this article, by any chance, about creativity and the Chinese language?"

I explained that I preferred to watch the news on television, in order to perfect my accent.

"Shoot! Now I can't remember where I saw it. It was fascinating, actually. They've done a study about how the language we think in influences to what extent we're creative." Principal McCoy peered at me in a bright, squirrel-eyed way. "I think it is just ridiculous," she said. "The idea that whole nations would be somehow more or less creative than others. This is the kind of cultural relativism that we thought we'd banished in the eighties; and now here it's back again, in disguise."

I nodded politely. Of course I knew the type of theory she was talking about, if not this particular study: in China there is a great deal of concern about what foreigners, particularly foreign "experts," think of the Chinese. Talking to a certain kind of official functionary, you would think that foreigners spent all their time mulling over the examination scores of our students, the flaws in our national character, and the ways they might take advantage of our economy's tremendous potential. (The latter is certainly the most likely.) They bemoan the fact that so many of our contemporary artists, our writers, composers, and choreographers, even our cutting-edge fashion designers and international star architects, live and work abroad. The foreign experts notice these anxieties, observe our schools, and develop theories. I appreciated Ms. McCoy's good faith, but I'm not sure the conclusions of these experts are wrong. It's their emphasis on language as the reason for our failure that is ludicrous: they see a mental inflexibility in our students, and decide to place the blame on *Chinese*—the language of the Tang poets and Cao Xueqin—as opposed to examining our four thousand years of history.

In the hallway with Ms. McCoy, girls were looking at me curiously. Although they had listened to my talk that morning in All-School Assembly, this was the first time they were seeing the visiting scholar up close. My talk had been called "Believe in the Future," after the well-known poem by Guo Lusheng, and it had been given for the first time by the photographer Zhang Tianming, informally, in our friend Cash's small East Village courtyard, where we had congregated every Wednesday during the winter of 1993–94, to eat a meal and talk about art. Before I left for California, I had gathered several articles and speeches related to human rights in China, particularly the ones that dealt with Tiananmen. "Americans love June Fourth," my cousin had advised me. "Just tell them that was you," he deadpanned, miming the posture of the man in the famous photo, his arms at his sides in front of the line of tanks.

By now I've seen that photo, but at the time I didn't know what my cousin was talking about. In any case, I was in no mood for jokes. I had been having nightmares about immigration for months. In the most memorable dream, a health inspector in a white coat appeared just as I was preparing to board the plane, and asked me to open my bag. When I complied, unzipping my suitcase on a card table in front of which a large crowd had gathered, I found that it was full of bright-colored women's panties.

"We've given you the advanced students—AP Studio Art—if that suits you? I'm afraid the others won't be equipped to appreciate what you have to offer."

"Thank you," I told the principal.

"It's only four classes a week," Ms. McCoy added. "Mrs. Travers cautioned us about leaving you enough time for your work. Excuse me a sec," she said, and bent to take a drink from the fountain.

Although I wasn't thirsty, I drank after Principal McCoy. The water in those fountains always tasted artificially sweet to me, as if they added saccharine in the pipes. Principal McCoy was thanking me (it should've been the other way around) and telling me she hoped I would be able to stay for the entire school year. I began the speech I had prepared about how grateful I was to have a chance to participate in the mission of St. Anselm's: "To educate young women, and to prepare them to confront the intellectual, physical, and ethical challenges of the future with dignity, honesty, and rigor." But Principal McCoy was distracted by her colleague, Laurel Diller, who was disciplining a student at the bottom of the stairwell. Vice Principal Diller had been waiting for me at the gate when I arrived that morning. She was wearing a bright red suit with a large gold starfish pin—evidence, I would learn, of a particular passion. More often than not, if you looked closely, Vice Principal Diller was wearing something of crustacean inspiration: a piece of iridescent abalone on a chain around her neck, a pair of silver sea snail earrings, or a silk scarf celebrating the hermit crab, secret-keeper of the sea.

Principal McCoy excused herself before I could finish telling her how my presence could help guide and shape the burgeoning ethical sense of the St. Anselm's student body. I was relieved that she hadn't asked me more difficult questions, and I went down to see Mrs. Travers, who, in her role as intern coordinator, had a temporary office in the corner of the library. I wanted to tell my hostess that everything was settled: I would be teaching Advanced Placement Studio Art, hopefully for the entire year.

"Olivia's class!" Cece said. "This is wonderful." And then she looked at me in a way she had, which sometimes made me think of my mother (although Cece was ten years younger than my mother, and looked even more so), and ventured: "I just hope they won't disappoint you. High school girls are so often preoccupied."

"I understand."

"Or take too much time away from your project," Cece said, which illustrates one of the lovely things about her. She would not contradict you, or point out the fact that you were making a ridiculous and counter-intuitive decision. Her own suggestions were always couched in terms of your needs.

"I have found that when I have more time, I do less work."

"I know exactly what you mean," Cece said.

What Cece didn't know, and I unfortunately couldn't explain to her, was that I had been effectively "quarantined" from the university by Professor Harry Lin. I didn't understand why the professor was making everything so easy for me, or why no one but my hostess had questioned the decision to spend my precious time in Los Angeles at a girls' high school, when I might have been "crossing borders and challenging my thinking"—not to mention making my name.

35.

OF COURSE, I DID NOT START OUT EXPECTING TO TEACH THE ST. ANSELM'S girls to paint lobsters. Shrimp, maybe—eventually. I imagined we would spend a semester on bamboo first. Bamboo is good practice. The student must learn to roll the brush from side to side to make the segments. The joints between the segments nicely illustrate the concept of negative space. I imagined the concentrated expression on their faces as they labored to reproduce the striated tubes of wood; I envisioned their happiness, the day their leaves attained the quality of translucence possible only with water-based ink. I went confidently into my first day of teaching at an American school, and failed to consider that the St. Anselm's girls might have other ideas.

As at a Chinese school, the St. Anselm's girls wore uniforms—but what uniforms! Short dresses in pastel colors, pink, white, yellow, and violet, with a curly *SA* embroidered on the right sleeve. They wore heavy black-and-white saddle shoes, a design I had never seen (and never did see, outside the white-brick perimeter of the St. Anselm's campus). To my surprise, the students also wore men's undershorts in bright stripes and plaids, hanging out from underneath their skirts. It took me very little time to see that this allowed them to sit in class with their knees apart, gazing out the windows of the art studio, scratching one leg at a time with the opposite shoe.

I will tell you: I was angry. All of that space and all of those fine materials to girls who could not even keep their legs together, as a gesture of respect, in front of a visiting teacher. And their bamboo! It was enough to make you cry. They overloaded the brush with ink, so that it was impossible to get any variation in the stalks—more like the bars of a cage than any living thing—and left soft spots that bled through and sometimes even tore the fine paper.

"Oops," they said when this happened, and giggled; of course there was always more paper.

I had nine students in Advanced Placement Studio Art, including Olivia Travers, none of whom were especially advanced. They were putting together "portfolios." Each portfolio was supposed to demonstrate the students' progress in three specific areas—Drawing, Sculpture, Color and Design—as well as a selection of work on an "Individual Theme." The themes, which they chose themselves, were as follows:

Emily	*The seasons*
Olivia	*The ocean*
Jenna	*The mountains*
Courtenay	*Time travel*
Lizzie	*Time*
Holly	*Outer space*
Katie	*France*
Kate	*France*
Catherine	*Love*

"Love?" I asked Catherine. I didn't mean to be discouraging; in fact my plan was to be as accommodating as possible, so that the students would have no reason to complain. The problem was that I often forgot my plan, and imagined that I was an actual teacher with a responsibility to correct my students' errors and guide their progress. "Do you think love is too abstract?"

"What d'you mean?"

"Too broad?"

"It's not as broad as Outer Space," Catherine said, shooting a glance at Holly, who looked mutely to Emily for support.

"I think Love is *très sympa*," Emily said. "Outer Space is kind of weird—"

Catherine smiled and tossed her hair.

"But deep," Emily finished. "Very deep." Holly looked relieved. As our semester progressed, I would learn that Emily was the final arbiter of all disputes, the judge of who was acting "psycho" or "paranoid," and what was at that moment "*sympa*," "*adorable*," or "*super*." Along with Emily and Olivia, several of the girls had just returned from St. Anselm's Summer Abroad program in France. France was truly *super* that year.

"Should two of you have the same theme?" I asked Kate and Katie.

"They have the same name," Emily said. Others nodded at the truth of this observation.

"I only wonder what will happen when we send our portfolios to the AP board of judges."

"I could make mine, 'French things,' " Kate suggested. "OK Mr. Jow?"

I had tried to correct their misconception of my name; I had little hope of Yuan Laoshi, but Teacher Yuan or even Mr. Zhao would have been fine. However, once Emily had christened me, I was Mr. Jow for good.

Without her connection to Emily, it might have been difficult for Olivia to surmount what in China would've once been called a problematic family background: a Chinese art teacher living at her house, and a mother who volunteered as an intern coordinator right downstairs in the library. It was Cece who came upstairs one day to pin to my bulletin board the announcement of a contest: a ceremonial centerpiece for the celebration of St. Anselm's sesquicentennial.

"The winner's design will decorate the Malmstead Courtyard during the ceremony," Cece told the class. "The vice principal would like you girls to consider the long history of our school in your designs. And we've collected some resources for you in the library, if you'd like to do research."

At this there were some titters, to my mind, inexplicable. I had found in my own schooling that the announcement of a contest was always greeted with great enthusiasm. Perhaps these American girls had gotten too accustomed to the frequent opportunities to prove themselves, and to be rewarded.

"But I'm sure the most important thing is just to be creative," Cece said, smiling at me.

"And think about the dimensions of the courtyard," I added, but no one seemed to be paying attention.

Olivia looked nervous as her mother left the room, her heels clicking on the gray linoleum, but Mrs. Travers was, if not *supercool*, then at least perfectly correct, with her silk twinset and very large diamond earrings.

"You have an adorable mom," Emily told her, loud enough for the class to hear. "Mine is such a bitch."

Instead of reprimanding Emily for her language, I shared Olivia's relief. I am ashamed to admit that on this and other occasions I made use of the Travers glamour, which clung even to me, temporarily, like sweet-smelling rubber cement. At least at the beginning, I coasted through AP Studio Art on a combination of adopted pedigree and novelty value.

Then, one morning in October, we got our tenth student.

This was the same morning that Olivia, working from a model I had taped up on the blackboard, decided to paint a lobster.

"Like this?" she asked. "Mr. Jow?"

Her lobster had fifteen tail segments, like a dragon. It had very short antennae, a cluster of them streaming back behind each eye, as if it were standing in a strong breeze.

"The antennae must move forward," I told her. "The lobster uses them to make his way. He can't see well from his eyes, you know."

"Those aren't antennae."

I confess, I was relieved. "What are they?"

"They're eyelashes."

Emily said: *"Comme c'est vraiment adorable."*

It is possible to accept a position, as a teacher, say, at a high school for young women, intending to do and say nothing that will antagonize anyone, to accept even the strangest customs (why dress adolescent girls in outmoded children's clothing, for example?), but I have found that it's difficult to maintain that posture over weeks and months. It's hard to remember how you planned to act; it's very hard to pretend anything for a long period of time.

"Lobsters do not have eyelashes!" I said, perhaps more forcefully than

I had intended. The other girls looked with concern at Olivia, who was hiding her face in her hair.

"I was trying to make it unique," she said softly. "I was just trying to express myself."

"You do not need to express yourself," I told her excitedly. "You need to express a lobster."

Olivia was crestfallen. I felt sorry. "Pardon me," I said. "May I borrow your chair?"

All of the girls looked at me with surprise. Since I'd arrived, they'd been asking me to paint something like the bold, candy-colored abstraction on the poster Principal McCoy had hung (to my embarrassment) outside my classroom door. The poster was from *DNA-ture*, the 1991 show at TFAM in Taipei—the same paintings that would be shown at UCLA's Fowler Museum in just a few months. Although they were now more than ten years old, my cousin and I had decided that the attention the paintings would get in America was worth the risk of shipping them. Truthfully, X had been more convinced of this than I was; as someone whose greatest artistic influence was a man obsessed with the damage that air and light inflict on ink and paper, I have never been sure that attention is good for paintings.

The paintings I began to make that year in California, ink sketches of lobsters and bamboo, rocks, clouds, trees, and finally mountains, were not what the faculty was expecting. Mrs. Travers and Principal McCoy in particular were perplexed, but as they were Yuan Zhao originals, they were accepted gratefully and hung in the Marian Caldwell Memorial Gallery, where they naturally faded into their environment, becoming as unremarkable as the orange carpet or the plant-filled atrium. Only occasionally you might see a young woman, collapsed on the floor with a textbook, raise her eyes to what I now realize were sketches for my project-in-exile: poor copies of the Tiantai Mountains, where Cangyun Shanren had once wandered, gathering herbs and dreaming of the passage to an immortal realm.

My class was eager to see me paint. Even Olivia seemed to have forgotten her lobster. She stepped back and offered me her easel; you could see she was proud that I would be using her tablet. I admit that I wanted to impress them. Vanity, X used to say, is the downfall of the artist. (He would say this with a wink, swinging his shiny hair.) It was vanity that led me to paint a very large lobster, very fast, in Olivia's Caran D'Ache watercolor tablet. I didn't recognize that at first; I told myself that I was contributing to Olivia's theme of the sea.

I instructed as I painted:

"A light touch on the head."

"The eye is the only time I will ask you to dip your brush directly in the ink."

"The wrist is loose, but controlled."

"Am I going to get to keep this?" Olivia asked.

"Remember, as you make the body, to press the brush, like a stamp. The right amount of ink will leave a mottled texture on the shell. Three segments for an ordinary lobster; four for a big one." I had been watching some television lately, paying particular attention to the commercials. I found them beautiful and reassuring. "Let's make a big lobster," I said now. "Let's supersize it."

My students giggled. I had made a joke in English! Perhaps it was this small success that caused me to reach up theatrically and yank a few hairs from the crown of my head, in the manner of my teacher, Wang Laoshi. The pain was sharp, and my eyes watered. I noticed that my students had stepped back. They were whispering.

"This is AP art," I heard Emily say suddenly, and I was afraid that she had somehow seen what was wrong with my work—that she was calling me a fake.

"I think you can learn from this," I said. But I did not sound confident. Even the stupidest student can hear weakness in a teacher's voice.

"What are you doing here?" Emily demanded. The hairs on my arms stood on end. I stared at my lobster—but how could he help me? He didn't even have his antennae yet. As I was turning to face my students, having lost my face, I heard a voice:

"I'm transferring."

Standing in the front of our classroom was a Chinese girl. Or rather, a Chinese girl with an American voice, what is called a Chinese-American.

She had short hair and a wide face—a country face, but beautiful, like old pictures of my paternal grandmother on her wedding day in Taiyuan. She was wearing the same uniform as the other girls, and also she was not. She was wearing the lavender dress, hemmed just as short as Emily's and Olivia's, but underneath it she had put on a pair of wine-colored corduroy pants, which were spattered with paint, an addition that had the effect of making the dress ridiculous; or rather, since the dress was already ridiculous, making a comment about its ridiculousness. She was wearing a beaded choker around her neck, and a tiny ruby stud in her left nostril, like a Hindu. The stud exactly matched the color of her trousers, which were wide and frayed at the bottom, so that they nearly covered her shoes. There was something strange about her shoes as well: it took me a moment to see that she had painted the stamped leather band on each shoe white, and the rest of the upper black. The inversion was jarring, if you were used to the ordinary model.

My AP artists pinched each other's arms and stepped on each other's feet. There was soft, untraceable giggling.

"I think the class is full," said Emily. "Isn't it, Mr. Jow?"

"I am Yuan Zhao—Yuan Laoshi," I told the new student.

"I'm June," the student said. "I'd like to take your class."

"We have been working together for almost one month," I said. "I'm afraid you might have trouble catching up."

"I could show you my portfolio," June said. "Some of it's old work, but there's some stuff that's OK."

My students exchanged shocked glances. I had only been at St. Anselm's for three weeks, but even I had noticed that my girls shared a particularly Chinese superstition: they didn't admit that anything they'd done was good. A student would come out of a test swearing she'd failed it; another would put on an impressive dance performance after promising her friends that she was going to "fall on her ass."

"Do we even have any extra easels?" Olivia said.

"That's OK," said June. "I've been working on flat surfaces lately."

"Flat surfaces," Catherine repeated, looking pointedly at our new student's petite bosom.

Ordinarily I liked Catherine, our class's defender of love, but that day I wasn't proud of her.

"I would be happy to look at your work," I told June. "You will have to choose a theme, of course." I indicated the whiteboard, where our themes were still written next to our names. Some of the themes, written in whiteboard marker, were becoming faint or indistinct.

June squinted at the board. "Who's Frank?"

"*France,*" Katie said, annoyed. "My theme is France."

"Too bad," said June. "Frank was my favorite."

"You may come to my office hours," I told June. "I'll look at your work then." It seemed like a good idea to separate June from my other students, at least for the moment.

"I have it now, actually," June said, glancing at Emily.

By now I was familiar with Emily's unassailable social position among my students. I knew she lived in the Greek Revival mansion on the corner of Rimpau and Third, drove her brother's "old" black BMW convertible to school, and that the diamond-studded silver heart she wore around her neck was a gift from Jake, her long-distance boyfriend, a senior at a boarding school in Connecticut. Emily was not by any stretch my least talented student, and the mechanics of drawing—proportion, shading, the tricks of perspective—came to her with an ease my other students worshipfully admired. Like June, she had entered the class with some work already completed: four small abstractions, derivative of Mondrian but nevertheless well executed, which she intended to use in the Color and Design section of her portfolio. I had put them up on the shelf above the whiteboard as an example for the other girls, but Emily had suddenly become shy, and asked me if she could put the paintings away.

It was hard to see how anyone could threaten a young woman with all of these advantages—and yet Emily was staring at our new student with such iciness that I was uneasy, as if that look had been directed at me.

"Mr. Jow is doing a demonstration," she said.

June looked at my lobster. She did not say anything disrespectful, or indicate her opinion in any way. Nevertheless, my neck and ears got warm, as if someone other than a student—X or my old teacher Wang Laoshi— were looking at my work.

"Everyone will work on their Color and Design pieces today," I said as firmly as I could. "If you haven't thought about Color and Design yet, today is the time to start."

My students scurried back to their easels, complaining to each other about their terrible senses of Color and Design.

June had already taken her black portfolio from where it was leaning against the wall (it was the same portfolio the other girls used, except that it hadn't been bought new for the class) and was removing some drawings, laying them on my until-now-empty teacher's desk.

The first thing I noticed was that June's drawings were very good. The first were a pen-and-ink series of beds: rumpled and made, pristine and improvised, from a bare mattress with just the suggestion of a cold floor beneath it, to a pristine king that looked as if it had never been slept on (except for an empty water glass on the night table), to a child's bunkbed, full of toys and books and clothing, as if its occupant (absent, as in all of the other drawings) were preparing for a siege.

"These are interesting," I said.

"They're old," June said quickly. "Look at these."

I was surprised to see that my opinion mattered to her. I thought she must have known how good she was, especially in comparison with her fellow students. As the semester progressed, occasionally I would see another student ask her for help, especially when there was no one else around. (June was often in the studio in the mornings before school or after the last bell, when my other students were changing into their St. Anselm Andalusian outfits, getting ready to compete in volleyball and soccer.) Ordinarily when one girl looked at another's work, it was with gasps of awe, followed immediately by a frown, as she professed that her friend's project was "way way better" than her own.

June never commented on the quality of her classmates' work; instead she gave specific suggestions. "Maybe the background should be more purple," she would say. Or: "What about if you did it on a smaller paper?" I noticed that the other students followed her instructions, although they didn't acknowledge her help or include her in any social way.

"These are chairs," June said, showing me four more drawings, this time in oil pastel. She was able to manipulate that difficult material with what looked like ease; any roughness was deliberate.

"These are doorknobs." She removed and replaced the drawings too quickly. I wanted to tell her to wait, except that I was always eager to see the next set.

"Balloons."

"Coat hooks."

"Soap."

Some were graphic, like cartoons; others were more realistic, but none was the same as any other.

"I'm very impressed," I told June. "I think you've already completed a lot of the material you would need for a portfolio."

I could tell June was trying to keep herself from smiling. "I haven't shown you my fruits."

"Are your parents from China?" I asked her.

"Taiwan," June said. "But they died when I was a baby. My grandmother brought me to L.A. when I was two."

I wondered how her parents had died, but I thought it might be insensitive to ask. "Is your grandmother an artist?"

June seemed to find this amusing. "No," she said, but she didn't volunteer any more information.

"So you've mostly studied here at this school?" I tried to speak calmly, controlling my excitement. I wished for someone to confirm what I was seeing; I assumed the other art teachers at St. Anselm's had already discovered June, the kind of student you meet once in a career, if at all.

"I haven't taken art electives here before. I usually like to work on my own."

As she talked, she was laying out several small acrylics: a banana that looked somehow regal, two friendly persimmons, a plum in the first stages of rotting, its skin shriveling into interesting purple rivulets, and a large, resplendent peach, haloed with fuzz. In the bottom, right-hand corner of each painting was a small red mark, like an umbrella with a curved handle, or a child's drawing of a bird.

"What is that?" I asked her. "Your signature?"

June looked embarrassed. "Sort of a signature. Here's the J." She traced it with her finger. "And the W is upside-down."

"What is your family name?" I asked her.

"Wang," she said, drawing out the *A* in an adorable American way.

Now, there are millions of Wangs in China, and the fact that this young woman had the same surname as my old teacher was of no significance. But I could not help remembering how Wang Laoshi used to wear trousers like June's, spattered with paint and coming apart at the cuffs.

"I might be able to accept you," I told her, extending the interview a little longer than necessary. I already knew I was going to let June Wang into my class. "Do you have an idea about a theme?"

"Household appliances," June said.

"Household appliances?"

"Probably the smaller ones: coffeemakers, dustbusters." June smiled. "Maybe a vacuum, if I get ambitious."

I didn't know about household appliances, but knew I wanted those persimmons in my class. It was the same kind of thrill I got the first time I saw X's paintings on the walls of his room in the East Village.

"All right," I said. "You can bring your things and start tomorrow. There's space over there in the corner, next to Katie." I tried to position her as far from Emily as I could, but the other girls were unshakably loyal.

"Um, Mr. Jow?" Katie called from across the room. "The slide projector's here. There isn't really any space."

I hadn't realized my students were listening. "We will move the slide projector," I told them. "Welcome to our class, June."

"Thanks, Yuan Laoshi."

She didn't know how to speak Chinese. Her pronunciation of my name was almost as bad as the other girls'. Still, I was surprised by how happy it made me feel, just to know that she remembered it.

36.

JOAN RESOLVED TO APOLOGIZE TO THE DISSIDENT. YUAN ZHAO MIGHT have forgotten about her error a few weeks ago, but Joan hadn't; in fact, she hadn't stopped thinking about him since the dinner party. At first she planned to stop by Gordon and Cece's, just to say she was sorry, but the thought of Phil observing that visit made her change her mind. She wasn't writing a novel about Yuan Zhao (at least not yet), but she had checked out Professor Harry Lin's book *Experimental Chinese Art: the Tiananmen Generation* from the library, and she'd bought a map of Beijing, to see if she could figure out where the East Village had been.

She decided she would visit him at the high school. She was afraid she might need some sort of pass, but the security guard must've assumed she was a parent; he simply nodded her through the gate. She asked directions from a student and hurried upstairs. If she was lucky, she would avoid running into Cece or her niece.

When she knocked on the door of the art classroom, Yuan Zhao seemed to be alone. He was concentrating on the screen of his laptop computer. The area around him was a pleasant mess: a sink with a coffee can of still-wet brushes, a bookshelf full of heavy art catalogues and magazines (the golden spines of many years of *National Geographic*), and a typewriter precariously balanced on an old metal folding table. The room smelled richly of turpentine and glue.

"Hello?" Joan said. The dissident looked up; his long hair was tied back in a ponytail, and he was wearing Western clothing: a gray sweater that was slightly too big for him, and a pair of pleated trousers.

Yuan Zhao stood up politely and glanced toward the back of the room: a student was working at a large steel table underneath the window.

"I hope I'm not interrupting," Joan said.

"My classes are finished for the day." It was hard to tell whether he was angry, or simply awkward out of shyness. He indicated an empty chair in front of the old typewriter, and Joan sat down.

"I came to apologize about the other night," she said. "I'm so sorry I asked all those questions. I was interested in your life—but I shouldn't have pried. I feel terrible about it."

"Never mind, never mind," the dissident said, blushing.

Joan wondered if there was a Chinese protocol for apologies. Was she embarrassing him? She hurried to change the subject: "I have to admit, I was hoping you might tell me a little more about the artists' villages you mentioned."

"That isn't interesting," the dissident said.

"Oh, it is," Joan said. "To me it is." The studio was quiet except for a faint beat from the headphones of the student sitting at the table.

"We moved to the Yuanmingyuan because it was cheap, and we knew some artists lived there," the dissident said. "That's near the old Summer Palace—where you can see the Empress Cixi's marble boat. Actually a copy of the boat."

Joan was not interested in tourism. She tried to be patient. "When you say 'we' . . . ?"

"Myself, Baoyu, my friend Tianming. Baoyu liked to dress up in women's clothes, and Tianming started to photograph him that way."

Joan had seen reproductions of some of Yuan Zhao's early paintings in Harry Lin's book. One showed police in green uniforms surrounding a young man in a bathrobe, a cornucopia of fruits and flowers growing where his genitals should be.

"One day he was arrested, and—"

"The man in the bathrobe!" Joan exclaimed. "Is that right?"

The dissident looked startled.

"Sorry," she said. "I've been reading Professor Lin's book. You were saying he was arrested?"

"We were often moving from place to place," he said slowly. "We were not supposed to be making that kind of work. Performance art was illegal, you see."

"Why performances but not paintings?"

"A censor can't review a performance beforehand. And so much of our work at that time was done privately, or only for an audience of friends."

"But someone must've taken pictures?"

Yuan Zhao nodded. "An artist named Zhang Tianming photographed most of the projects. Of course, that makes attribution difficult. In the moment, the project belongs to the performer. But if a skilled photographer, an artist in his own right, takes a picture, who does that picture belong to? And who is the author of the performance five years from now?"

"That's fascinating," Joan said. "The idea that the authorship of a work of art could change over time."

Yuan Zhao smiled. "Fascinating, and also a big problem for artists."

"I would love to see those photos," Joan said.

"They haven't been published, unfortunately," Yuan Zhao said. "Only some of them were in a small magazine we started."

Joan had opened one of the thin graph-paper notebooks she always carried, and was jotting things down. "Do you mind?" she asked him.

"I don't mind, but—"

"Just for my own education," Joan said. "Maybe when your show opens, I could do some sort of profile. For the *L.A. Times Magazine*, or even *Art in America*." It wasn't something she'd planned to say (she certainly wasn't qualified to write for *Art in America*) but now it occurred to her that a profile was the perfect excuse. They would have to have several more interviews if she was really going to write an article. "An article would be good publicity for *DNA-ture*," she added.

The dissident looked unhappy. He was the real thing—an artist who didn't care about the press, who just wanted to be left alone to make his work. She was about to apologize again, when Yuan Zhao looked up:

"Yes," he said. "Thank you."

Joan couldn't believe her luck. "Thank *you*," she said. "But I interrupted. You were talking about your magazine?"

"We used to have meetings—'art lunches,' we called them." His voice became more authoritative, as if he'd come to the part of his story he liked to tell. "We talked about Chinese art, the problem of copying."

"Sorry," Joan said. "The problem of copying?" She could hear students approaching the classroom, and wished they would stay outside for at least another few minutes.

"Of copying Western art," Yuan Zhao explained. "Even now it has only been fifteen years since we were first allowed to see these things. Can you imagine, trying to swallow the whole of Western art in fifteen years?"

"I've never thought about that," Joan said. "Did you find that many artists attached themselves to a particular period, before finding their own style?"

The dissident hesitated. He looked at his student, who was bent over some kind of intricate work in her lap. Sunlight glowed orange behind the dirty windows.

"Actually, it seems we began imitating each other," he said.

There was a shriek outside the classroom, followed by giggles. Joan looked up to see Olivia and a friend standing at the studio door. Her niece looked surprised—and not particularly pleased—to find another member of the family at her school.

Joan decided there wasn't any way to avoid embarrassing her. "Hi Olivia," she said. "I just came to see Mr. Yuan for a moment. I was hoping I'd run into you."

Olivia stared at her fingernails, but gave way to her training. "Um, Aunt Joan, this is my friend Emily. Emily, my Aunt Joan."

"Nice to meet you," Emily said, bored.

Olivia turned to her teacher. "Mom wants me to ask when you're going to be done so she can drive you home."

"I'm ready now," he said, to Joan's disappointment.

"Maybe we could set up another time?" she began, but Yuan Zhao was watching Emily, who had wandered to the opposite end of the room. The other girl was still working quietly, wearing her headphones.

"Hi June!" Emily said suddenly. "What're you doing?"

"She can't hear you." Olivia seemed eager to leave the classroom. "I'm going to get my mom now, OK?"

"Don't hurry her," Joan said.

"June!" Emily shouted.

June finally took off her headphones and turned around. She was of Chinese descent: perhaps that explained the dissident's interest. Or it might be that he was simply supporting the underdog. Olivia's friend was clearly one of St. Anselm's social elite, while the other student—with her after-school project, her headphones, and her red-and-white-striped knee socks—was probably not.

"I just wondered what you were working on." Emily pointed one toe in front of her, tracing an invisible line on the linoleum.

"I'm making a net," June said, and indeed there was a heap of netting trailing underneath her stool.

"Come on," said Olivia. "We're going to be late to rehearsal."

But Emily ignored her. "A net for what?"

"It isn't *for* anything," June said, but there was a note of uncertainty in her voice. Joan felt sorry for her. She remembered girls like Emily and the power they wielded: an instinctual, particularly adolescent kind of dominance.

"You are so avant-garde," Emily said. "Isn't June avant-garde?"

Olivia was twisting her hair nervously around her index finger. "Come on," she said. "Let's go."

Mr. Yuan seemed to want to rescue June. He turned suddenly to her tormenter: "Emily, Ms. Travers might like to see an example of our classwork. Would you please show her your Color and Design series?"

Emily gave her teacher a sullen smirk. "I don't have them."

"That's too bad." Mr. Yuan turned to Joan: "Emily has made a good beginning with acrylics."

"I *love* those paintings," Olivia gushed. "Did you leave them at home?"

Emily shook her head.

"I hope you haven't misplaced them," Mr. Yuan said.

"I threw them out," Emily said.

Olivia gasped.

Emily smiled: "I decided they sucked."

"They were very good," Mr. Yuan said. "Your best work so far."

Joan had her first twinge of sympathy for Emily. She'd been in that position herself: having a friend or editor tell her something was good when she knew in her heart it was junk.

June put down her net. "You mean you're not using them, or you threw them away?"

"I burned them."

"You did *not*," Olivia exclaimed.

Emily nodded. "Last weekend, in Lake Tahoe. Our condo has a fireplace." She turned to June. "What do you think? You think I should've kept them?"

June was gathering up her things, and didn't respond.

Emily smiled. "See? *June* thought they were bad."

June slid off her stool, and started toward the door. Then she looked at Emily, and seemed to consider. "They weren't bad. They weren't great, but at least they were better than your other stuff."

For a moment Emily looked startled. She opened her mouth, as if she were going to return the insult, but just as suddenly she seemed to change her mind. She turned to her teacher: "See," she said calmly. "I'm not a good artist. Thank goodness June isn't afraid to tell me." Then she linked her arm through Olivia's and exited the classroom, calling over her shoulder with exaggerated coyness: "*Bye*, Mr. Yuan."

"You may stay," Mr. Yuan told June—he almost seemed to be imploring her—but the girl hurried from the room without acknowledging them. The dissident watched her go with concern.

"Don't worry," Joan said. "Teenage girls are like that. It's when they *aren't* difficult that you have to worry."

It didn't seem to reassure him. If he was going to get worked up about a quarrel between two students, he wouldn't last long at a girls' high school. Joan thought it might be better for him to focus on his own work anyway; frankly, she thought St. Anselm's was a waste of his time.

"I'd love to see what you're working on now," she told him. "Do you think I could stop by some time?"

"I am not very far along yet."

"It doesn't matter," Joan said, getting up to go. "Whenever you're ready."

They shook hands, but the dissident was clearly distracted. He seemed to take the girl's disregard personally. When Joan looked back, he was still sitting there, looking small and young himself behind the massive teacher's desk.

37.

I CAME INTO THE CLASSROOM ONE AFTERNOON TO FIND MY STUDENTS deeply engaged in their work. Jenna ("Mountains") was arranging photographs from a family ski vacation on black posterboard; Holly ("Outer Space") was working on an oil painting of Laika, the Russian space dog, copied from *National Geographic,* while Katie ("French Things") had begun a series of fashion designs.

"What are those?" Kate asked.

"Culottes," Katie replied. I did not recognize the word, but from the horrified murmurs around me, I imagined them to be a sort of medieval torture device.

"Not regular culottes," Katie insisted. "Cool ones. Hey! Cool-lottes."

Emily lifted and lowered her eyes; Katie blushed a burnt sienna. Emily was sitting in the brightest corner of the room, sketching a winter landscape in colored pencil. On a stool facing her, perched at a respectful distance, Catherine was making a charcoal portrait, adjusting her pad to compensate for Emily's frequent sighs, yawns, and shifts of position. With her freckles and kinky red hair, her invisible yellow lashes and unwieldy breasts (breasts were discussed in my class with startling frequency), Catherine was never going to look like any of the women in Katie's fashion designs. Nor did she seem to have any artistic enthusiasm. It was clear even to me that Catherine had joined our class simply to be close to the other girls, a strategy that—to use an expression popular at St. Anselm's, though not found in *Idiomatic English*—had turned around and bit her on the ass.

And yet there was something compelling about this terrible drawing, designed to flatter, with every asset heightened, and each particular smoothed away. Catherine had captured (no doubt unintentionally) a certain imperious expression in her subject's snaky green eyes: I felt as if I had seen it somewhere before. Catherine felt me staring, and looked up.

"What are you working on?" I asked her.

"A drawing of Emily and Jake."

"What does that have to do with your theme?" (I checked the board surreptitiously; I often had trouble remembering which girl went with which topic.)

"Love."

"That's your theme, but . . ."

"She's doing a picture of me and my boyfriend," Emily said. "His name is Jake. He goes to Choate, and he's only here in the summer, so I have no idea how she's going to draw his half of the picture."

Catherine's voice, normally quiet, became almost inaudible. "Maybe at Christmas break?"

"At Christmas break we're going skiing at Lake Tahoe."

The other girls murmured their admiration.

"Just you guys?" Katie asked.

"C'est *super*," sighed Courtenay.

Emily turned back to her work, giving Catherine a supercilious, sideways glance, and suddenly I saw the resemblance. Catherine's portrait had almost nothing in common with its living subject, except for the position of the eyes and the head, which the artist had captured exactly. This attitude communicated the sitter's disdain for the artist—and for me, recalled another young woman (my first imaginary lover) staring down from my former teacher's peeling bedroom wall. For the first time in many years I remembered the majestic, imperious Violante, and from that day on, I could not help but associate her with my student, Emily Alderman.

I hadn't planned to give my AP artists any tasks apart from the portfolio requirements in Drawing, Sculpture, and Color and Design. On the day I found Catherine drawing Emily, however, I decided to give an assignment of my own. I went to the board and wrote in careful upper-case letters: HOMEWORK. When I turned around, three hands were waving in the air.

"Mr. Jow?"

"Mr. Jow?"

"Mr. Jow!"

"Katie?"

"We don't get art homework in America."

"This shouldn't take you very long." Underneath HOMEWORK, I wrote: "Make something that is *not* art."

I looked back at the room to gauge their reaction, and saw that I had finally gotten June's attention. For several days she had been sitting quietly in the corner, tying knots. She spent a great deal of time in my classroom; but no matter how many hours we were together each day, she never said more than "Hello" and "See you." She was wearing her headphones even more often now, and I believed she was living in some private world—a world of art, separate from ours.

Now, however, she looked up.

"But I don't understand the assignment." Catherine looked nervously around the room.

"I only want you to think about what isn't art. That will help you understand what is."

"He means, like, Hallmark cards," Emily said.

"That's greeting cards," Katie helpfully informed me.

"That's a good example," I said. "But everyone must come up with her own idea. We'll discuss the homework in class on Monday."

Soon my classroom was empty except for June. Today she was wearing the yellow dress, and because it was an especially warm day, she had left the paint-spattered trousers at home. The only thing that distinguished her uniform from the others was a pair of red-and-white-striped socks, bunched around her ankles. As she worked, she kicked one tanned and shapely leg against the bottom rung of the chair. I noticed the way she brushed her hair out of her eyes every few minutes, a charming, impatient gesture, and the extra piercing at the top of her left ear, where she wore a thin gold ring.

June must've felt me watching, because she looked up. I immediately frowned at my desk, where there was a stack of announcement cards for my upcoming show at UCLA. These *DNA-ture* paintings had been exhibited at TFAM in Taipei, and would have appeared in Beijing—at no less a venue than the Ancestral Temple of the Forbidden City—had the show not been shut down by the Ministry of Cultural Affairs. Still I had never seen an announcement card as lavish as the one they produced in Los Angeles, on silver metallic card stock, with a sort of double helix design looping around the text:

Yuan Zhao: DNA-ture

The Fowler Museum

Co-sponsored by the Departments of Fine Arts and Asian Studies

Opening Reception: November 22, 2000

6–8 PM

"Is that weird?"

"Excuse me?" I was disoriented by the casual way June had come around to my side of the desk, and was now peering at the card over my shoulder. She smelled like handsoap, with a trace of turpentine.

"Seeing your name like that?"

I explained that seeing one's own name in print is always a strange feeling, intensifying a sensation peculiar to artistic creation: that the work you have created is not your own.

"Uh-huh," June said. "Will we be invited?"

"Of course," I said. "Although you're certainly not required to come."

June looked thoughtful for a moment. "If I come to your show, will you promise to come visit my grandmother?"

"Why would I do that?" I didn't mean to sound rude, but the request startled me.

June was nonchalant. "She wants to make you dinner. You guys can speak Chinese and stuff."

I wasn't sure what to say. If parents in China invited their child's teacher for a meal, it would almost certainly be in order to bribe them. I couldn't imagine that this was the case with June's grandmother, however, since I was not giving the students scores, but only preparing them to be evaluated by the AP Board. Even if I had been grading June, no art teacher could've given her anything less than an A.

"I don't think I can accept," I said.

June brushed her hair out of her eyes. "Why not?"

But I couldn't tell June the reason why not. If there was something wrong with the way I felt about her, I didn't think going to her house would make it any better. At the same time I was very curious, and also very tempted; in a purely pedagogical spirit, I wanted to see the household ~~Please th... ..anced young artist had been raised.~~

~~... for me." I said.~~ "But I—"

"One time," June said. Her insistence surprised and, I will admit, flattered me. "I need your help with something."

"With what?"

"I can't really explain. It's at home."

"I'm sorry," I said. "I'm afraid I can't."

June turned away from me, hiding her frustration. I watched as she pretended to read the assignment on the blackboard.

"You don't have to do that, if you don't want," I said. "You could just continue working on your project."

"I want to do it," June said. "It's a great assignment."

"Thank you," I said shamelessly, as if I'd come up with it on my own.

"I may need a little extra time," June said.

"That's fine." I could hear Mrs. Travers chatting with someone in the gallery outside my classroom. Over the past two months, we had developed a routine: my hostess would come upstairs when she was finished with her work in the Internship Office and pick me up. Then we would drive home together. That afternoon, for the first time, I found I was not eager to leave.

"I mean tonight," June said. "I may need to stay a little later."

"I have to lock up now, unfortunately."

"Why don't you just leave me the key?" June suggested.

The vice principal had drummed into me the importance of keeping my keys on my person at all times. Theft was not unheard of, and there were liability issues if a student were to injure herself on school property after hours.

"I get here early because my neighbor drives me before work," June encouraged me. "I could open the classroom in the morning and leave the key on your desk."

From childhood I have always been the kind of person who obeys the rules, both stated and implied; even in university, I was usually the one chosen to petition the administration in the repeated and futile bids for improvements in our dormitories. When I started spending my evenings and weekends in the East Village, my cousin would sometimes ask me to talk with his neighbors—mostly workers from a nearby automated instrument factory—when they compl̶a̶i̶n̶e̶d̶ ̶t̶h̶a̶t̶ ̶c̶h̶a̶n̶g̶e̶s̶ were suddenly taking place in their neighborhood. Perhaps due to my upbringing as the only child of aging parents, I was good at this kind of negotiation: I had an extraordinary aversion to conflict and a strong desire to please. It was this quality, my cousin told me half jokingly, which made me unsuited for activism of any kind.

"Here," I said, handing June the classroom key and pocketing my desk key as I hurried out of the classroom. "Just don't forget it in the morning."

"Thanks, Yuan Laoshi," she called after me. "Have a good night."

38.

I SLEPT WELL THE NIGHT I'D GIVEN JUNE THE KEY. AS OFTEN HAPPENS with mistakes, I forgot what I had done until the next morning when I was on my way out the door. Due to Ptolemy's diabetes, which necessitated a trip to the veterinarian before school, Cece and I arrived late. I heard the second bell ringing just as I was hurrying from the parking lot around the side of the school, to enter through the back gate.

St. Anselm's is a squat, two-story white building, with classrooms linked by open walkways on both levels. Three sets of stairs (north, south, and east) lead up to the second floor; hiding in the shade of the southern staircase is a slender dogwood tree, which drops delicate white flowers into the Elizabeth Ehlers Memorial Rock Garden. The garden boasts a few stone benches (one of which is shaped like a tortoise, mascot of the class of '56) and a sundial with a brass plaque donated by the class of '29. It was in this pleasant nook, where the students often came to have study sessions, social cabals, or their lunch, that I found my entire AP Studio Art class assembled and waiting for me. The entire class, that is, except for one.

"Mr. Jow?"

"Mr. Jow, Mr. Jow!"

"What are you doing down there?" I asked them. "The second bell has rung for first period."

I saw Emily whispering to Olivia. Then Olivia nudged Catherine, who stood up:

"Mr. Jow, there's a bad smell."

"Excuse me?" I felt ridiculous peering down at my students over the railing; at the same time, I wanted to show them I knew that they should have been waiting upstairs outside my classroom, even if I was late.

"Smell!" Catherine instructed me excitedly.

There was nothing to do but take a deep breath. I inhaled the ordinary aroma of St. Anselm's: cut grass, ammoniac glass cleaner, and carbon monoxide from the traffic around the perimeter.

"Smell what?"

"It's worse outside your classroom," Catherine said accusatorially. "Emily almost fainted."

"Is the classroom open?" I asked them, knowing the answer already.

"It's locked. Should we go get Willie?"

I was not especially eager to alert Willie the security guard, a retired officer of the LAPD.

"Mr. Jow, Katie thinks there's a dead animal in the classroom."

"What kind of animal?"

"A skunk?" Katie suggested.

"Skunks don't smell like that," said Kate.

"It's probably a raccoon," Olivia concluded. "Dead from drinking turpentine."

"That's so sad!" the girls chorused.

"Mr. Jow, if there's a raccoon, can we have class outside?"

"Mr. Jow, can we have a funeral for the raccoon?"

Emily stood up. "Mr. Jow?" she said sweetly. "Where is June Wang?"

"Yes," I said, answering the simplest question. "Sit down, and we'll begin our class here. Courtenay, you may go and find Mr. Willie."

The girls, for some reason, collapsed into giggles:

"*Mister* Willie . . ."

"C'mon Courtenay, find Mister Willie!"

But I wasn't listening. It was one of those moments in America when I retreated into my own language, as on a television show when the noise of a crowd is suddenly diminished so that the principal characters can have a conversation amongst themselves. It wasn't that I didn't understand the English words so much as that I didn't hear them. An image had come to shut them out: June Wang, trussed in silvery net and hanging from the steam pipe, her painted saddle shoes twisting above the aluminum stool.

Did I really believe that June was dead? I don't think so, and yet this improbable scenario got hold of my mind like a night terror and would not let me go. Like a man in a dream I descended the concrete steps; blindly I sat down on the curved stone shell of the tortoise representing the hopes and dreams of the class of '56.

"What is art?" I heard myself beginning. "Philosophers and poets have tried to answer this question for centuries. Often it's hard to come up with a precise definition." Understandably, my students were not paying attention; a few were taking their homework from their matching colored satchels.

"Art is something we recognize, from culture to culture, whether or not we have any training. And so perhaps we've been thinking the wrong way: perhaps art is not the thing itself, but the perception of art, perhaps it resides in the viewer rather than in the object of his attention." I paused to look around the circle, and I could see that my students had fulfilled the assignment. There was a paint-by-numbers clown (Holly), a mail-in art test Indian chief in profile on tracing paper (Jenna), and an advertisement for Australian merlot, employing a detail of Da Vinci's *Last Supper* (Katie). I had a sudden impulse to tell them I was sorry, that these were not my own words, and that in other circumstances, I wouldn't choose to bore them with this sort of pomposity.

"It's easy to determine what isn't art, much harder to say what is." The girls perked up, as if this idea excited them, but it was only Courtenay, whom I could observe from my turtle, coming across the lawn with the security guard. I was unhappy to see that Willie had brought along not only a walkie-talkie and a large ring of keys, but a maintenance man with a mop. For some reason this mop horrified me: I experienced one of those irrational moments that sometimes happen in polite society, when you seriously consider whether it might not be best to run away.

"Willie!" chorused several girls. "Hi Willie!"

"Locked out?" Willie asked.

"Willie, can you smell it?"

"Thank you," I told the security guard. "I'm sorry to trouble you. I seem to have left my keys at home."

"No trouble," Willie said. Then he switched on his walkie-talkie and barked something unintelligible into the microphone.

"Excuse me," I said. "Who is that?"

"Office," Willie said casually. "Just letting 'em know."

As I followed the security guard up the south stairs (my students following me), I wished passionately for an earthquake, a fire, or the Second Coming of Jesus Christ. I wished for an ability I had seen exercised by a teenage alien on television, who could stop time simply by pressing her index fingers together in front of her nose.

I had been cherishing a hope that my students were exaggerating: that June Wang had simply left a sandwich in my room after school, which was rotting in the overheated classroom. The moment we got into the gallery, however, I had to abandon that idea. Although it was usually a popular place for students to study, that morning the gallery was empty—or almost empty: standing in front of my classroom was Vice Principal Diller, wearing a midnight blue suit, a red and blue scarf, and a large pair of clip-on earrings, two spiky gold anemones adrift in the stiff waves of her hair. They seemed especially appropriate in light of the current situation, since there was now no mistaking the smell.

"Fish!" my students cried. "It smells like dead fish!" They covered their mouths and noses and made sounds of disgust. I couldn't help noticing that these gestures were overdone a bit, and aimed in the direction of the vice principal. But Laurel Diller ignored them: she was one of those disciplinarians you find in schools all over the world, who seem to relish their own unpopularity.

"Do you have any idea what's going on, Professor Yuan?" she asked. Both she and Principal McCoy insisted on that honorific, although I had assured them on several occasions that it had not been earned.

"I'm sorry," I stammered. "I seem to have left my key at home."

She nodded, as if this was to be expected. "Line up," she barked at the girls. "You should have been in line for Professor Yuan at 8:14—*as you know.*"

The girls took their hands away from their faces and lined up.

"Teaching is often not the most difficult part of the job," Laurel Diller confided softly, unlocking my classroom door. "If you fail to impress the importance of the rules on the students—and in particular *these* students, Professor Yuan, I know you know what I mean—you may never have a chance to begin your important work." Then she stepped back, allowing Willie and the maintenance man to precede her into the classroom.

The classroom was boiling: the thermostat by the door had been pushed past ninety. In the center of the room, sitting on the aluminum stool, was June Wang, reading a *National Geographic* magazine. This was the first time I had seen her in her own clothes, rather than the school uniform: she was wearing a lime green smock with a border of white daisies, over a pair of bright white trousers. Perhaps inspired by the African ladies in her *National Geographic,* June had looped many strands of bright-colored glass beads around her neck; she was also barefoot, her feet hooked around the bottom of the stool. Although her forehead was shiny with sweat, happily there seemed to be nothing else wrong with her.

I have heard that in moments of great relief people become angry, but my immediate response was embarrassment. I looked at my shoes, which was how I noticed a murky liquid seeping out from underneath my desk.

"Why didn't you open the door?" Vice Principal Diller was demanding of June. "Didn't you hear Professor Yuan knocking?"

"Did you knock?" June asked. "I heard people rattling the door."

I walked around my desk, my heart pounding, as if I were the one being chastised. I was not surprised by what I saw. My key was sitting in the center of the desk, as June had promised; beneath my chair was a large plastic shopping bag, leaking a pungent gray substance onto the floor. I didn't have to look inside to know what was in there, packed (as they say) like sardines. A few ants investigated the perimeter.

This was the second time an important moment in my life had been marked by a piece of performance art involving fish. (How many people can write that sentence truthfully?) Since no record of *Baoyu's Lunch*—performed in the Beijing East Village on June 12, 1994—had yet been published in America, June's use of the material was a coincidence. But that is the thing about art, and performance art in particular. It acts on different people in different ways, depending upon their unique histories.

If you look carefully at Zhang Tianming's photographs of June 12, the last hours of our East Village, you will understand why June's "assignment" affected me so powerfully.

"Why didn't you open the door for the students?" Vice Principal Diller demanded.

"I was wearing headphones."

"Headphones aren't allowed in class, Miss Wang—as you know."

"But class hadn't started."

"I think you had better come see me in the Lower School Office," Laurel Diller said.

Whether the fact that I chose this moment to pick up the bag of fish and place it on my desk indicates that I didn't want June to leave my classroom, I'm not sure. I did, however, succeed in diverting attention from my student: the maintenance man, who had been standing in the doorway with a blank expression, leapt into action, retrieving a garbage bag from beneath the sink and holding it open, so that I could dump the shopping bag inside. He was not able to prevent collective disgust at the sight of the bulging gray bag: several girls screamed, while the more resourceful among them began opening the windows. And there was something disturbing about the bag, something obscene about its softness, its bulging gray wetness, and its smell—of dead things crowded together in a sack.

"Girls!" Vice Principal Diller shouted. She looked from me, cowering behind my desk, to June in her bare feet and beads, to the uniformed girls moaning by the window, barely concealing their thrill at the novelty of the offense. The vice principal did not look defeated. She looked like a racehorse pawing the gate, eager to demonstrate the qualities for which she'd been bred.

"Professor Yuan?" she asked, and there was silence.

"I'm afraid one of our projects has gone awry."

"Was this a class project?"

"Yes," I said, defending June without hesitation. I looked to see whether she appreciated this noble gesture, but my prize pupil was busy sketching a design in red marker on the whiteboard. The design was like an umbrella, or a child's drawing of a bird—a bird with a worm in its mouth.

"Where are your shoes?" Vice Principal Diller demanded.

"In my locker."

"Go put them on, along with the rest of your uniform. If you are not in my office in less than ten minutes, Miss Wang, you'll find that we'll be talking about something much more serious than a few demerits. Incidents like these are particularly unfortunate for someone in your shoes."

June looked thoughtfully at her bare feet.

"For someone on academic probation."

This was the first I'd heard of any academic problems; naively I had assumed that June was an equally stellar student in her other subjects. There were a few titters from my class. I gave them a warning look, but they ignored me; it was only when Laurel Diller turned to them that they began to quiet down.

"I hope all of you are working hard on your Sesquicenterpieces," Vice Principal Diller said. She glanced at the bulletin board, where the announcement Mrs. Travers had pinned up our first week was now sun-bleached and curled in one corner. "I anticipate several strong entries from this class."

June had slipped on a pair of purple plastic clogs, and retrieved her net from the shelf underneath the window. Slowly she made her way out of the classroom, followed by Laurel Diller. Of course she wouldn't have wasted her precious net on "Something That Is Not Art"; it frustrated me to think she might not be planning to use it in my class at all.

"June Wang!" I called suddenly. June and Vice Principal Diller both stopped, although only Laurel Diller turned around. "Please report to me after school. I need to check your homework." I had spoken without thinking: immediately my cheeks flushed. The word "report" was particularly absurd.

June didn't give any indication that she'd heard me, but the sharpness in my voice had an effect on the other students, who finally began to settle into their seats. Even more surprising, Laurel Diller favored me with an approving nod, as if the two of us were engaged in some sort of common enterprise.

39.

NOVEMBER 7, 1993, WAS A BLEAK, LAMPLIT AFTERNOON IN BEIJING, THE beginning of winter, when the air told you the season had changed for good. I followed the directions on the announcement card my cousin had given Meiling, but once I crossed the Third Ring Road and entered the winding lanes and alleyways of the East Village, I was immediately lost. Perhaps it was the cold, or the sudden absence of cars, or the transition underfoot from pavement to dirt, but I felt as if I'd crossed a boundary. As I got farther from the highway, it seemed as if a door had shut behind me: if I turned back, I would no longer find the gates of the Workers' Stadium, thronged with bicycles, or the high walls of the embassies. The city would be cloaked in fog, and there would only be the world before me: silent, old, in black and white.

I was early, and so I walked my bicycle through the narrow lanes, past the dark, falling-down farmhouses, the puddles of brown-green sludge, and a scared-looking yellow bitch, her teats nearly brushing the ground. For a few minutes I followed a peasant who was pulling a cart full of garbage behind his bicycle: occasionally he would glance back, as if to make sure it was still there, but if what he'd collected was salvage, I suspected it was too pitiful even for him to care much about it.

"Grandpa," I called out. "Can you help me?"

The man stopped and looked back warily. I was riding my new black Forever bicycle; my hair was growing out; and I had looped the silk cravat underneath my army jacket, in preparation for meeting my cousin's friends.

"I'm looking for lane number seven."

The old man stared at my bike.

"Do you understand me?"

He shook his head.

"Speak putonghua?" I asked him.

He smiled; of course he had no teeth.

"There are some artists around here," I tried again. "Do you know where they live?"

Perhaps he did understand then, because he responded energetically, in incomprehensible dialect, gesturing vaguely before pedaling off, his wheels squeaking under the weight of the fetid cart. I turned and saw a young man standing against the side of a house, apparently watching our exchange. He was wearing a camera around his neck.

"Hello?" I said. "I'm looking for my cousin's house."

"Who is your cousin?" His face was distinctive, if not particularly handsome, with a high forehead and a bulbous, upturned nose. He spoke quietly, but his expression was noticeably friendly; when I told him X's name, he smiled.

"Do you know him?"

"Everyone knows him, even Old Hua. He was saying you didn't want to find bad people like that."

"I couldn't understand him."

"It's Fujianese. At first he liked talking with me—I'm from Fuzhou—but now that he's seen some of our goings on . . ." The photographer paused: "Hey, are you here to see *Something That Is Not Art*?"

"That's right! My cousin gave me a card for it." I rummaged in my pocket: I was perhaps a little too eager to show off my connection.

"You're not far. Just turn left there, and then right at the public toilet—you can't miss it, although it's much worse in summer. Keep going straight to the second intersection, you'll see a house with a sign on your right. At least I think there's a sign. Better hurry: he'll stop when the photographers leave."

"Are you one of the photographers?"

The question seemed to amuse him. "You could say, well—I am a photographer. But not the same kind. They were taking news pictures. But my kind of pictures? Your cousin didn't want them." The photographer smiled and looked down. "Not that I blame him. I'm a problem for him this time. He's making something that *isn't* art—you see?"

I nodded, although I didn't, quite.

"If I photograph him, then it is art, no matter who's making it. Problem is—without him I'm nothing; without me, his work disappears. That's the big question, see? Whose art is it?"

I must've looked baffled, because the photographer laughed. "Go on," he said. "You can still catch some of it." Then he continued the way I'd come, out of the village toward the Third Ring Road.

At the time, I had no idea that I'd just met the man who'd invented the Beijing East Village, and whose photographs are the only place where it still exists today. Even when the buildings were still standing, before the garbage was covered over and the inhabitants driven away, Tianming's East Village pictures turned this wasteland, with its toilets and junk heaps and falling-down houses, into a place with a name. They were like a map, showing us not only where but who we were. It is ironic, if not particularly surprising, that the pictures that brought our village to life were the same ones that would eventually destroy it.

40.

WHEN I FINALLY FOUND THE HOUSE (IDENTIFIABLE EVEN WITHOUT ITS sign, by the flashes coming from the windows), pushed past the photographers, and joined the crowd of mostly young people standing along the walls of the small room, I thought immediately of my mother. I remembered how many times she had reminded me to contact X; how sure she was that this family connection would eventually secure me entrance at CAFA; and how CAFA would direct me toward the artistic career that had been cut short for her by the accidents of history. She would've imagined an official show at the National Gallery: me and X, a red ribbon, and on the walls, scenes of Yellow Mountain's lofty peaks softened and blurred by mist. Imagining these things, I felt glad that my mother was in Shanghai, more than one thousand kilometers from the Beijing East Village.

I found my cousin suspended between two stepladders, completely naked, his wrists and ankles lashed to the steps with twine. On each rung of the ladder that didn't hold a hand or foot, my cousin had placed either a fan or a small heating unit; electrical cords extended from these appliances to a power strip against the wall. Obviously the circuits in the place were overloading, because the wall socket was sparking dangerously. The way the fans and heaters were arranged (fans on the right, heaters on the left), my cousin was suffering intensely. One side of his body had started to burn; the skin was red and swelling slightly. The other half was in shadow, but I was sure the flesh there was pale and goose-pimpled. Half of his head was wet (at intervals he was being doused with water), and every few seconds, he would shiver violently. The appliances, which had been fixed to the ladders with more twine, nevertheless wobbled in an ominous way.

There were about fifteen or twenty people in the room: I recognized Fang, who waved, and X's girlfriend Lulu, who ignored me. The atmosphere was excited but tense, as if everyone were waiting for something to happen. The spectators were clustered in the warm half of the room. They stared at the red centers of the heating units, which were seductive in the same way that coals are; or perhaps they were avoiding looking at X, whose eyes were glazed and tearing. I could not help noticing that my cousin's uncomfortable, retracted penis was larger than mine in its normal state.

X became more alert when the photographers began packing up their gear: there were still three Chinese and one foreign woman (a Canadian, with a red-and-white maple leaf sewn onto her camera case). They went out silently without making eye contact, as if they were leaving a memorial. Perhaps even the foreigners were nervous about what they had seen?

X waited a few moments after they had gone, and then opened his mouth. No sound came out; immediately, Fang and two other men hurried to untie him. Two of the taller men supported him as he climbed down: he couldn't stand on his own. They wrapped him in a blanket, and someone started to clap. Then everyone else joined in.

"Amazing."

"Fried up like a squid—did you see?"

"He'll catch cold for sure."

"Or something worse."

No one seemed to want to leave. A few people were passing around a thermos of tea. X was in the corner with Fang and Lulu. Suddenly Lulu turned to face the remainder of the crowd:

"Please can I ask you all to leave now?" she said crisply. "This performance has taken a lot out of him, of course. Anyone who would like to discuss it is welcome to come to the art lunch on Wednesday, at Cash's place."

X made a pathetic sound, which only Fang seemed to understand.

"He says there's nothing to discuss," Fang repeated. "Because what you saw today wasn't art." •

At this everyone began to clap again. Then, under Lulu's stern gaze, they reluctantly started filing out. I lingered in the doorway.

"Please leave us now," Lulu said to me. "He's tired."

"He can stay," X said suddenly. His voice was exhausted but clear. "It's just Xiao Pangzi."

Fang grinned, and Lulu looked me over critically. "I didn't recognize you." Immediately I understood that my army jacket and cravat had been a mistake, that I would have been received much more favorably in my ordinary school shirt and trousers.

"Where's your girlfriend?" X asked.

"She couldn't come today," I said. "We have a test next week."

"We must've scared her the other day."

"Oh, no," I said. "She's interested in art."

"Is she? Tell her next time we promise to keep our clothes on."

"You shouldn't talk too much," said a serious-looking young man, who was standing against the wall. "You'll get sick."

"Have you met everyone?" X asked. "This is Cash, our local rock 'n' roll god . . ." I nodded at Cash, who was wearing sunglasses, along with a pair of imitation leather pants and a silver chain belt.

"And this is Yuchen, my doctor."

Yuchen's worried manner first made me think he was older than the others, but in fact he was only twenty-five. He was tall and skinny, with a high forehead and an elegant, feminine neck; he wore thick glasses with brown plastic frames, and a gray nylon jacket not warm enough for the weather.

"I'm not really a doctor," he told me.

"My name isn't really Little Fatty," I said.

Fang laughed, and even Lulu smiled a little. "My cousin must think I'm still eight years old."

"Well, then, you need a new name." My cousin thought for a minute. "I baptize you Longxia Shanren," he said. " 'Lobster' because you used to like to paint them, and 'Hermit,' since you stayed away so long."

That was how I got my East Village nickname, which caught on after my new friends saw me drink for the first time. I much preferred it to Xiao

Pangzi, and it pleased me that my cousin remembered the childish drawings I'd shown him so many years ago.

"You used to draw birds too," X continued. "Do you remember that day I took you to the park in Harbin?"

"I remember you taught me how to fly kites."

X frowned. "I didn't have a kite, and yours were at home. We only watched."

He was wrong, but I didn't want to contradict him. It was possible that the endurance required for his project had taxed his memory.

"That was incredible, by the way," I said. "Thanks for inviting me."

"It was incredibly dangerous," Lulu said. "And for what?"

"For nothing." X smiled at me, and I'm embarrassed to say that I smiled back knowingly, as if I understood exactly what my cousin's project was about. "That was the point."

"The point was that there was no point?" Lulu demanded, looking from one to the other of us.

"I'd like to invite you to my house for lunch on Wednesday," Cash interrupted. "If you have free time, that is." His politeness contrasted with his fierce costume. "Nothing fancy—we do it every Wednesday, to talk about art."

"Or gossip about each other," Lulu said.

"Come over here about noon," X said, ignoring her. "We'll walk there together. Can you find it again?"

I nodded excitedly, no longer trying to conceal my enthusiasm. "I'll be here. Can I bring Meiling?"

X smiled. "If she promises not to be shocked. We may be looking at pictures of our work."

I thought of how that comment would annoy Meiling. I would have to put the invitation very differently, in order for her to accept. Even apart from my romantic hopes, Meiling was the first true friend I'd made in college. I wanted her to get along with my cousin, in part because I already knew that I would spend as much time as possible in the East Village. That dump on the edge of the city suddenly seemed to me the most exciting place in Beijing.

When I left X's house it was already dark, and I was glad for the light on my new bicycle. Two more tiny lights glowed in the doorway of the house opposite; when my eyes adjusted, I could see a pair of men standing in front of the house, smoking. I wondered why they were outside on such a cold night. I nodded in their direction, but like the old man with the junk cart, they stared without acknowledging me.

I pumped hard and fast out of the East Village, trying to keep warm. I was exhilarated, but not afraid: I didn't know that experimental performances like the one I'd seen that evening were illegal. Instead I felt as if I'd crossed over into a foreign country where I couldn't distinguish good from bad, where everything was equally strange. Maybe what my cousin did that night wasn't really art, but it had an effect on me: as I bicycled into the sharp winter wind, my whole long, safe childhood seemed to recede further and further into the past, until it was only a high, bright dot, like a kite.

41.

I DIDN'T EXPECT JUNE TO SHOW UP AT THE END OF THE DAY, AND I WAS locking up my desk (resolving never to let either key out of my sight again) when I heard her clomping toward my classroom in her regulation saddle shoes. She did not have a light step, I noted. I decided to begin a mental list of her shortcomings, but couldn't immediately come up with any others.

June had not only changed her shoes, but was wearing the entire uniform in its most uncomfortable incarnation: a pleated gray flannel skirt (unhemmed, as if straight off the rack) and a starched white blouse with a collar. Even the red rhinestone stud had been removed from her left nostril. Her eyes looked tired, and I wondered how early she had gotten to school in order to pull off her little stunt.

"You wanted to talk to me?"

"Do you have your homework?"

June looked genuinely surprised. "That was it." She pointed to the whiteboard, where you could still make out the J.W. design in red marker. "Didn't you see my signature?"

"Do you feel you've fulfilled the assignment?"

June smiled. "What do you mean?"

"What is art?" I began rhetorically; however, June Wang never allowed me to be rhetorical. She took a pocket dictionary out of her bag and flipped though it, running her finger down the page. We were alone in the studio, still smelling faintly of fish.

"Art," June read. "Old and modern French from Latin *(art, ars)* from a base meaning, 'to put together, join, fit.' The application of skill according to aesthetic principles—"

"You've made an olfactory installation," I interrupted. "Not particularly interesting, compared with your other work, but still art." I thought I saw June suppress a smile, but she continued with her dictionary:

"—especially in the production of visible works of imagination, imitation, or design (painting, sculpture, architecture, etc.). *Visible,*" she repeated for my benefit.

"*Especially,*" I said; "not always."

"A pursuit or occupation in which skill is directed towards the production of a work of imagination, imitation, or design," June continued, tilting her head slightly in the direction of our big table, where the various attempts of the rest of the class lay scattered: "cool-lottes," an unfinished portrait of Emily Alderman, and Laika the Russian space dog. "Or toward the gratification of the aesthetic senses."

"I would say 'stimulation' rather than gratification," I told June.

"An acquired faculty," June shot back. "A knack."

"You have that," I said. "There's no question."

June sighed. "I only did it to bug you. Because you wouldn't help me."

"How can I help you?"

"By coming to meet my grandmother," June said. "Next Thursday would be convenient."

"Why do you want me to meet your grandmother?"

June hesitated. Obviously she was thinking of the answer that might make me agree to come, rather than the truthful one. I added "not particularly honest" to my mental list of June's faults.

"She needs someone to talk to—I mean, someone from China."

"Doesn't she have Chinese friends?"

"Yeah," June admitted. "But she's happy I have a Chinese professor. She wants to honor you."

"I'm not a professor."

June shrugged. "My teacher, then."

I had a strange feeling: there was a part of me that wanted to sit June down and tell her my life story, right here in the classroom, with no exaggerations or omissions.

"In China I'm not even an art teacher."

"I didn't say you were my art teacher."

"What did you say?"

"That you were my business teacher."

"Business!"

June nodded calmly. "My grandmother doesn't like art."

"How am I supposed to pretend to be a business teacher? I don't know anything about business." This was not strictly true, but I would never have told June about the lazy, part-time job in my father's office.

"My grandmother doesn't know about business either," June assured me. "You'll be fine."

But I was not convinced. It was not business, but this business of pretending, that was making me sick to my stomach.

42.

THE BUSH BABY WAS GONE. THEY HAD COMBED THE HUTCH, AND LEFT appetizing bits of food around the garden as a lure. They had tried to determine how she'd escaped—a broken latch, or a tunnel under the wire—but the hutch was secure. Fionnula had simply vanished.

"I asked the children if they had noticed anything," Cece told Phil. "Any changes in her behavior—but of course they don't pay any attention. I even asked Mr. Yuan."

"What did *he* say?" Phil asked.

Cece felt terrible. Fionnula could not have been cheap, nor could it have been easy to transport her. Now the bush baby was loose somewhere in the neighborhood, vulnerable to legions of sharp-nosed neighborhood pets. She was a wild animal, but she'd been raised in a cage; would she be able to find food for herself? Even if some kind person were to find her, and call Animal Rescue, how would they know what she was? It had never occurred to Cece to put a tag on her.

"I just don't understand it. How could she have gotten out of the cage?"

"Someone had to open it," Phil said. They had been standing in the foyer, and he was on his way out. She wondered where he went in the afternoons, but she didn't like to ask. If there was one thing that made him skittish, it was excessive curiosity.

"Maybe she was stolen."

"Stolen—Phil—who would steal her?"

"She's relatively valuable," Phil said. "Or maybe the Chinaman ate her."

"Phil!" Cece said. She hadn't heard Max coming downstairs behind them, but when Phil said that, her son laughed. Cece turned around.

"That's not funny," she told the two of them. But it was hard to stay angry at Phil. He was so often angry at himself that she tried to avoid compounding it. He was also more thoughtful than he used to be; for example, he was the only one who'd noticed that Cece wasn't sleeping again. He didn't say anything, but he left a bottle of Ambien for her to discover in the glove compartment of her car. He had tied a red ribbon around it. Cece put the bottle in the medicine cabinet, next to Gordon's Lipitor.

"Did Dr. Plotkin give you those?" Gordon asked that night, when they were brushing their teeth.

She wondered if he really thought that Dr. Plotkin had given her an unlabeled bottle, with the name of the drug in permanent marker across the cap. Why would Dr. Plotkin tie a red ribbon around a prescription? She might have said they had come from Pam or Carol, or even the nurse at St. Anselm's—but she decided not to bother.

"Yes," she said.

Gordon replaced the pills and closed the medicine cabinet. "Be conservative," he advised.

"I think you were right," she told her husband one evening after dinner, when they were cleaning up the kitchen.

"About the garage door openers? I'm glad, because these new ones won't run out of batteries until the year 2020."

"About Phil," Cece said.

Gordon was consolidating the kitchen and the pantry trash. His voice took on the faintly amused tone he always used to talk about his brother: "What wisdom did I dispense about Phil?"

"About how he's a bad influence on Max and Olivia. The crazy thing is—it's because he wants them to *like* him. He can't say no to anybody. That's his problem."

Her husband was giving her his therapist smile.

"That's the problem for his girlfriend too," Cece continued. "She thinks he's going to marry her. She's thirty-seven, and she wants a baby.

Did you know that? Phil doesn't say yes, but he doesn't really say no. He's willing to ruin a person's life in order to keep her from being angry at him."

"Did I say a bad influence?" Gordon asked.

Cece glanced out at the pool house. The lights were on, and Phil hadn't bothered to draw the shades: she could see him pacing back and forth, probably talking to Aubrey on the phone. She wondered how necessary it had been for him to come to L.A. to rewrite his script; he hadn't even met with his writing partners yet. She hoped it hadn't simply been a way to avoid confronting whatever problems he was having in New York.

"When did I say that?"

Gordon was not a liar. Once, when she had asked him what was the worst lie he'd ever told, Gordon had looked at her blankly and said, "I don't lie."

"But I mean, ever," she had said. "Your whole life." This had been in the early years of their marriage, before Olivia, when she was still working as an assistant account executive at the ad agency downtown. She had imagined that their connection would grow deeper and deeper over the years. At work during the day, she would think of things she wanted to ask him. She had thought that when she happened upon the right question, Gordon would suddenly confess all kinds of things that he'd been keeping from her until then.

"I don't tell lies," Gordon had said impatiently. "I have no need."

Not *I believe in telling the truth,* or *Lying to your loved ones is wrong,* but simply: "I have no need."

"You don't remember," Cece said now. "When we went to see Dr. Plotkin?"

"I remember seeing your therapist, yes." Gordon was standing with the garbage held gingerly away from his body. Cece had a strange urge to laugh. Spock pranced in from the dining room to investigate the soggy bottom of the bag.

"You don't remember when you said Phil was a bad influence on the children?"

"That was ten years ago," Gordon said. "I'm sorry, but I don't remember every single thing I said ten years ago."

"Not every single thing," Cece said. "But just—"

Gordon lifted the bag up away from the dog. "I should take this out."

"Go," Cece said.

She was not upset. She felt that something had been settled. It was as if she'd been attempting for years to solve a particularly difficult puzzle, and someone had told her it wasn't necessary—wasn't even possible. She was released. It was a light, almost giddy feeling.

Olivia came into the kitchen wearing her dance tights, a pair of boxer shorts, and a T-shirt that read, "Fat Jack's: If You Can't Eat the Meat, Then Beat It." It took Cece a minute to get the joke.

"Beat the meat," she said. "That's funny."

"*Mom*," Olivia said, horrified. She took four cookies from the cooling rack. "I can't eat these," she informed Cece. "I'm taking them up for Max and Jasmine."

Ordinarily she would have encouraged Olivia to take a cookie for herself. She would've encouraged Gordon to notice the way that their daughter seemed to be shrinking before their eyes.

"That's a good idea," she said instead. "Should I take a couple out to Phil?"

Olivia looked at her strangely. "I guess."

"OK," Cece said, picking up the plate. "That's where I'll be, if you need me."

43.

ST. ANSELM'S WAS NOT DESIGNED FOR RAIN. THE GIRLS DARTED UP AND down the open staircases, so you were afraid they would slip on the smooth cement. They ate lunch in the auditorium, leaving behind the strong smell of wet flannel and tuna fish. They shivered in their short skirts and sheer navy blue tights rather than don tailored gray slacks, the official cold-weather alternative. The rain was a reminder that the whole concept of a school like this had been imported from another climate, somewhere colder and grayer, with an even longer history.

Cece sat in her office in the library, watching the cold rain drip from the jacarandas. She was supposed to be reading application essays, in which the girls wrote about their internship preferences: child psychology and marine biology were the most popular fields. Next semester Olivia would apply for an internship. Cece was fairly certain that her daughter didn't want to be a marine biologist or a child psychologist, but she had no idea what Olivia would choose instead. She was beginning to wonder whether the internship program was what the girls needed. She sometimes thought they might do better to get ordinary after-school jobs, waiting tables and scooping ice cream.

She was interrupted by a knock on the door, which was usual during lunchtime. The girls would begin with a question about internships or college admissions, and then, with an awkward segue, move on to their problems with boys.

"Come in," Cece called, but she was surprised when the door opened. She hadn't seen Emily Alderman since the incident by the pool. Olivia's friend hesitated, as if she expected Cece to turn her away. In spite of the rain, her hair hung loose and shiny around her shoulders.

"Have a seat, Emily," Cece said, trying her best to be welcoming. "Would you like some hot chocolate?"

"Oh—no, thanks. I have to be careful what I eat, now that we've started rehearsing for the dance concert."

"When is that?" Cece asked.

"Before Christmas," Emily said. "We have so much work to do."

"Well, I'm looking forward to it," Cece said. "We'll definitely be there."

"All of you?" Emily looked concerned.

"I mean, Olivia's father and I, and her brother." It occurred to Cece that Emily might actually be asking about Phil.

Emily looked down, picking at her cuticles. Underneath her Dance Directions sweatshirt, she was wearing a pink Armani Exchange T-shirt, a uniform infraction worth two demerits—not to mention the fact that it was probably stolen. Emily's hair almost covered her face. Cece didn't trust her for a second.

"I wanted to talk to you about something, but I was worried you'd be mad."

Cece's stomach growled, whether from nerves or hunger she didn't know. Often when she was nervous, she got suddenly ravenous. She thought it was her body's trick, to try to make her eat when she wasn't paying attention.

"Mad about what?" she said, as gently as possible. The girl, however unpleasant, was barely more than a child. If she had a crush on Phil, it was simply that. It was no big deal. She looked at Emily, whose face was flushed from the rain. She sat with both feet on the floor, her pink knees pressed together under her skirt.

Let it not be that, Cece thought. Let it be anything else.

"It's about Mr. Jow," Emily said.

It took Cece a minute. "You mean, Mr. Yuan?"

Emily nodded. "I'm in AP art with him."

"Oh, I know." Cece's relief was so great that she felt generous. She smiled at her daughter's friend: "Olivia says you're very talented."

Emily hesitated. "I used to like art. But I'm not very good."

"It's hard to say who's good and who's not," Cece said. "Especially at your age. I would say it's important not to rule anything out."

"I can't concentrate in Mr. Jow's class."

The rain was coming harder now. Outside the girls shrieked as they ran up and down the stairs. The plants on her windowsill released a damp, earthy smell, and Cece had a sudden, thirty-year-old memory: a rainy day in a high school classroom, the fluorescent lights, the smell of chalk, the sawed-off wooden rods propping the windows open for air.

"He makes us feel—" Emily was playing with the hem of her uniform skirt, flipping it up and back, revealing a cluster of freckles on her right thigh. Cece saw herself at that age, preoccupied and distracted by her own body.

"Feel how?" she prompted.

Emily looked up, and Cece was surprised to see that her eyes were full of tears.

"Tell me," Cece said.

"He makes us feel uncomfortable," Emily whispered.

"Uncomfortable how?"

"The way he looks at us."

"What do you mean, the way he looks at you?"

Emily didn't say anything, just stared back at Cece with those doll-like green eyes. Cece was angry, and at the same time aware that she hadn't questioned the same accusation when it had come from Jasmine. When it had been about a man she didn't know, she hadn't hesitated to believe the girl.

Cece thought back to the first time Harry Lin had told her about the dissident, at the Dean's Commencement Cocktail in the spring. They had been talking about the new Japanese wing of the L.A. County Museum, and she'd been flattered that the professor was interested in her opinion. When he asked whether they might like to host a famous Chinese artist, Cece was enthusiastic, but she told him it depended on Gordon and the children. That was when Harry had suggested that Yuan Zhao might agree to volunteer his time at the school. It had been the professor's idea, and so Cece hadn't questioned it. She had assumed that the St. Anselm's girls would make Yuan Zhao feel useful; she imagined that they might even inspire him.

That idea had a different connotation now. But wouldn't Cece know, if something like that was going on? Wouldn't she be able to see it in Mr. Yuan's attitude toward Olivia? (In fact, in the nearly two months Mr. Yuan had been with them, she couldn't remember seeing the two of them exchange more than a few words.) Emily's accusation was exactly the kind of fantasy that an intelligent but sheltered teenager would dream up to amuse herself. Cece thought suddenly of everything that would happen should the girl decide to make this information public.

"Have you told anyone else about this?"

Emily seemed to hesitate a moment; then she shook her head.

"You're sure?"

"Yes."

"You realize that what you're saying is very serious. Mr. Yuan would have to leave the school." It might be a great deal more serious, Cece thought, but she didn't want to suggest that to Emily. She didn't think Emily needed any stronger a sense of her own influence.

Emily had crossed her arms over her chest, and was looking hurt. It didn't matter. Cece was lucky the girl had come to her first. She had an opportunity to fix all of this, before it got out of control. No one else would have to hear about it.

"You would have to be absolutely sure, before you—"

"Whatever." Emily stood up. "I wanted to talk to you before I talked to Ms. Diller. But I guess it was a waste. Forget it."

"I'm willing to listen to you," Cece said, too quickly. "But you're going to have to be more clear."

Emily was moving toward the door.

"You can't say something like that and not explain."

Emily shrugged and opened the door. The weather had driven the girls inside, and the library was noisier than usual. The sound of girls' voices blended with the whirr of the copy machine and the fans.

"Let's handle this together," Cece begged.

"I have class."

"Can you come back tomorrow then? When's your free period?"

Her daughter's friend picked up a pink leather bag and tossed it over one shoulder. She seemed to have regained total composure.

"If you want to know," she said, "you should ask June Wang."

44.

IT WAS TERRIBLE TO BE THE ONLY ONE AWAKE. THE DIGITAL CLOCK FLUT-
tered its eyelids: 2:21. Three and a half more hours until she could plausibly get up. By lifting her head just slightly from the pillow, Cece could
look out the south-facing window: there was a light in the pool house.
Either Phil hadn't come home yet, or he was awake.

He had been out when they'd gotten home, to Cece's disappointment.
She and Gordon had been at a benefit at the museum, and she was wearing a new black cocktail dress. It was an extravagant dress, and she almost
hadn't bought it, but when she'd put it on the salesgirl seemed genuinely
enthusiastic, as opposed to the way they usually acted: forced by economics to help you, but secretly appalled by the brazenness of a middle-aged
person who was not a size four attempting to buy clothing in their city.

"That was *made* for you," the girl had said.

Cece looked in the mirror, and as once happened all the time, she
slipped into Phil's head. It was as if he were standing right behind her, not
touching her but close enough that she could feel his cool presence on the
exposed skin of her arms and shoulders. It was Phil looking at the neckline of the dress, a deep V accentuated by silver beads, and her bare legs in
the shoes the girl had found for her: slate-gray satin, with a very thin black
leather strap around the ankle. The salesgirl had also given her a black bra
to try, and when she adjusted the strap, moving the cap sleeve off Cece's
shoulder for just a moment, she felt a tremor, as if Phil had pushed the girl
aside and was dressing her himself.

She had bought the dress so that Phil would look at her, but the only
person who was around when they left for the benefit was Yuan Zhao.

"That is a very nice dress and pumps," he had said, before shyly escaping to his room. That was at least an improvement on her husband's reaction: Cece was pretty sure that there was no dress in all of Los Angeles that would make Gordon notice her. After nearly two decades of marriage, she couldn't necessarily blame him. When she came downstairs, Gordon had been standing by the door in his suit, with the car keys in his hand.

"Don't you look festive!" he had remarked.

Now Gordon was grinding his teeth. It was an unnerving sound, like a mouse scratching inside a wall, and it was bad for his teeth and jaws. She patted him on the shoulder, as he had instructed her to do.

"Am I grinding my teeth?" Gordon had the amazing ability to speak perfectly coherently from sleep.

"A little." Immediately the grinding stopped.

"Thank you," Gordon said, and the next breath was a whistling sigh.

At 2:47 Cece got up. Her body felt buoyant compared to the exhausted heaviness in her head. She seemed to glide across the rug. All of her clothes were still lying on the narrow loveseat underneath the window; it was no trouble to slip into them again. She picked up her shoes and padded barefoot toward the door. As she crossed the threshold, Gordon began to wheeze, as if her absence had registered and allowed his body to relax. Cece closed the door quietly behind her.

The news had predicted that rain would begin around midnight, but Cece couldn't hear anything yet. She thought of the bush baby: could Fionnula somehow sense the weather coming, and had she found a dry, protected place? Cece switched on only one of the backyard lights, just enough to see by, and took a ripe avocado from a bowl on the counter. Regretfully, she slipped into her gardening clogs, leaving her heels just inside the door.

As she climbed the steps to the garden, the rain started, just a mist at first, from the direction of the ocean. Cece had a feeling that the bush baby was still in the vicinity. She'd escaped from her cage, but she was hiding somewhere in the rich foliage of the backyard. Cece hadn't brought a knife, and so she began peeling the avocado with her nails, dropping bits of soft green fruit around the perimeter of the garden. The only sound was a dry rattle in the palms. The wind was picking up.

She heard a noise behind her, and for a moment she thought it was the animal.

"What a coincidence," Phil said. "I, too, was thinking of coming out here at two-thirty in the morning to eat an avocado in my formal wear. I almost put on my tuxedo, but . . ."

"It's for the bush baby," Cece said.

"That dress?"

"The avocado. The dress was for a benefit."

"It's very beneficial," Phil said. "I feel a hundred times better already. Can I see the back?"

She turned once. He didn't smile or say anything, or hide the fact that he wasn't looking at her face. Nothing's happened, Cece thought, with satisfaction. This is it, and it's enough.

"Do you know what I think about?" Phil asked.

She wished her hands weren't full of avocado. She had to be sure to keep them away from her dress.

"That apartment in Mount Washington. Do you remember the curtains?"

Cece didn't say anything.

"We always used to keep them closed," Phil said. "Remember? I mean, it's not like anyone was going to see us. It was always the middle of the day. Why did we do that?"

"I don't remember the curtains," Cece said.

Phil was wearing an untucked white shirt and jeans. He hadn't even tried to go to sleep yet. He'd probably been reading in bed in his clothes, the worst thing an insomniac could do. If they were together, they would only exacerbate each other's terrible sleep patterns, among many other problems.

"Yeah you do," Phil said. "They were green—some kind of ugly seventies pattern. They made us sort of green."

"How flattering," Cece said.

"It was, though." In this light, you couldn't see that his eyes were blue. They looked black. He pushed her hair away from her face and touched her earring. "Pretty," he said.

It was incredible, and they hadn't done anything. It was perfect. "Phil."

He stepped away. "Sorry," he said lightly. "Here, I have something for you."

Maybe it was not quite enough, Cece thought. She would give herself just a few more minutes, and then she would go inside.

Phil reached into the pocket of his jeans, and handed her a folded piece of paper.

"We should go in," she said.

"At least look at it."

It was a printed flier on high-quality paper, with three photographs and a description: *1375 Coldwater Drive. Modern hacienda w/spectacular park views! Most desirable Coldwater location! 3 BD/2 BA/WBFP/EIK— emotional and breathtaking!*

"What's this for?"

"I met a good broker," Phil said. "I was just looking around."

"You have a broker in L.A.?"

Phil shrugged.

"This is a big house for one person."

"Maybe it wouldn't be for one person."

"Because Aubrey would be here."

Phil stared at her. "That's not what I meant."

Cece looked back down at the flier to keep from looking at Phil. "Emotional and breathtaking," she joked, but it didn't come out right.

"Like you," Phil said.

"How about hysterical and breathless," Cece said. "Do they have anything like that?"

"How about witty and heartless?"

"Neurotic and sleepless?"

"Young and restless?"

"We're not getting any younger," Cece said.

"That's *right.*"

She'd forgotten how it always happened. She would promise herself that it wouldn't, in exchange for allowing other, less serious things to happen. But once she was as close to him as she was now, a sort of impulse took over, more powerful than sex. It was a kind of momentum. Just finish, the impulse instructed, as if the only way to get out of danger was to go straight through it.

"Cece," Phil said. He was holding her now, his arms around her waist. She put her face on his shoulder. All she had to do was look up, and it would begin all over again. She had to decide right now because the moment was threatening to become awkward, and a great deal depended on this moment's being memorable. It was possible that she would spend the next ten years thinking about it.

She looked up at Phil, and there was a noise in the yard. They stepped clumsily apart: someone was watching in the shadows by the pool.

"Who is it?"

But Phil pushed her roughly away, so that she was concealed by the hedge.

"Shh," he said. "Hold on." He took a step forward, so that he was in the light.

"Phil!" she whispered.

"Stay there," he said, and then jogged down the steps. She stepped closer to the hedge, but the eugenia was still thick enough that you couldn't see through it. Please God, she asked, let it not be Max. But who else would be in the yard at three in the morning? What if he had gotten up to go to the bathroom, and seen that the alarm was off? What if he'd seized the chance to sneak out and, hearing voices in the yard, had decided to investigate?

She began offering things to God, in whom she did not believe, and who probably knew it. All of her material possessions first, of course. Their house, their savings, and if that were not enough, her marriage. Let it be Gordon, she thought. Let him finally discover it, in a way that's impossible to ignore, and let him divorce me; only let him not tell the children. The garden was silent. She had the feeling God was listening, unimpressed. If it has to be one of the children, she thought recklessly, let it be Olivia. Her daughter might stop speaking to her, but she would be fine. I will do anything, Cece promised, if only it isn't Max.

Phil's voice called out to someone, calmly, and then, like a miracle, she heard the dissident. His voice was heavily accented and unmistakable. She didn't know what Mr. Yuan was doing in the backyard in the middle of the night, and she didn't care: the only thing that mattered was that Max was upstairs, asleep in bed, oblivious. *Thank you,* she told God, who had already retreated back above the roofs and the purple smog, dissolving into empty space.

She heard the pool-house door opening again, and then Yuan Zhao, politely wishing Phil a good night. Had the dissident seen them embracing? Had he recognized her? And what right did he have to judge them, especially given what was going on at the school? Cece caught herself thinking as if Mr. Yuan were guilty, when she'd already decided she didn't believe Emily's accusation—not even a small part of it. She felt ridiculous hiding in the rose garden, and only the threat of further embarrassment on both sides kept her from going out to the lawn. They were all adults, after all, even if they came from disparate places. How different could it really be? People made mistakes in China; they fell out of love and had to make other arrangements. Maybe the compromises were different, but culture shock could last only so long. At some point, you had to stop being shocked and start absorbing it; otherwise, you would all stay strangers forever.

After what seemed like ten minutes, and was probably less than two, Phil returned. When she saw his face, she knew what she would have to give up, of course: the one thing she'd forgotten to offer.

"False alarm," he said. "Thank God." He collapsed onto one of the stone benches and put his head in his hands. Something about the theatricality of the gesture disturbed Cece. It occurred to her that she would never see Gordon in that sort of pose.

"It was only the Chinaman."

"I wish you wouldn't call him that."

"I thought you'd be glad."

"But did he see us?"

Phil shrugged. "I told him I had a date."

"Did he believe you?"

"Is it beyond the realm of possibility that I might have a date?"

"No." Cece's stomach churned ominously. "But what was he doing in the yard?"

"He saw my light on, and thought I was still up. He came to get one of his books."

"What book?"

Phil shook his head impatiently. "Some art book. Whatever it was, he seemed very excited about it."

"At three in the morning?"

"How do I know? He's a genius—he gets inspired in the middle of the night." Whatever had been between them a moment ago was gone. God had slunk craftily away with it. It was starting to rain for real.

"I should go inside," Cece said, meaning it. Phil didn't argue, which somehow hurt her feelings.

"Good night, Ceece."

"Good night, Phil," she said, but she was the one who stood there and watched him go. Her dress was getting ruined for nothing. Nothing had happened, so why did it feel as if everything had changed? The one thing she wanted to preserve, the possibility, was gone. How was she going to manage without it?

45.

ALTHOUGH IT WAS NONE OF MY BUSINESS, I HAD NOT IMAGINED MRS. Travers as the kind of woman to have relations outside her marriage, not to mention relations with the brother of her husband. At the same time, what drew me into the backyard that night, after I heard the double tone of the alarm system switching off, was a kind of fascinated curiosity, a sense that things in this house were not quite as they seemed. I recognized a pair of high-heeled shoes discarded by the back door, and once I had discovered the truth, I could not get the sight of the couple embracing in the garden out of my mind. On subsequent nights, as I was drifting off to sleep, I found myself imagining, in scrupulous detail, what might have happened if I hadn't discovered them. I had experienced this type of prurient interest once before, at the end of my relationship with Meiling—as if, by some betrayal of my brain, the images most calculated to hurt me had somehow also become my fantasies.

I wondered if Dr. Travers or his children knew the truth. I thought his sister, the lady novelist, must've guessed it. I watched Joan Travers coming across the lawn for our third interview, smoothing her blouse and touching her hair. I had also prepared myself, arranging my ink, brushes and water pan, and changing into the old collarless purple silk shirt, which I now used primarily as a kind of smock, to protect my clothing while I painted.

It was October, and I had finally begun my project. After school and on weekends, slowly and then with more confidence, I was copying one episode at a time from Cangyun Shanren's famous handscroll *Liu Chen and Ruan Zhao in the Tiantai Mountains*. It's true that this endeavor didn't exactly correspond to the Dubin Fellowship's description of an original project, but I had been in Los Angeles almost three months, and I was getting desperate. My teacher had always encouraged me to copy as a way of coming to my own ideas. What is original does not come out of air, he told me, and it occurred to me that I might begin by painting an appreciation of one of those masterpieces. Who knew where it might lead?

It seems to me now that there were several reasons why Zhao Cangyun's scroll in particular was appropriate to my months in Los Angeles, but at the time, the choice seemed arbitrary. I was with Cece one afternoon at Century City, where I often accompanied her on shopping trips after school. While she bought groceries at Gelson's Market, I wandered into the bookstore underneath the multiplex. I was browsing in the Decorative Arts section, looking for a gift for my mother (who has a special passion for Fabergé eggs) when I was distracted by another volume: *Along the Riverbank: Chinese Paintings from the Oscar Tang Family Collection.* I flipped through the index: Dong Yuan, Wang Meng, Bada Shanren, and Zhao Cangyun were all there, a bunch of friendly gods. I stood in the brightly lit store with soothing classical music piped invisibly through the ceiling and cheerful American voices all around me, and began turning the pages, revisiting the great works I had first seen in my teacher's shabby room. When I came upon *Liu Chen and Ruan Zhao in the Tiantai Mountains,* I knew that I had found my project.

I felt purified by this decision, and when I paid for my purchase I was even pleased by its heavy price—the expense seemed to reinforce its value, as if I were buying some rare medicine or tonic. Looking back, however, there are two things I should note: first, that my humble "appreciation" may perhaps have had a core of secret vanity, since *Liu Chen and Ruan Zhao in the Tiantai Mountains* was the longest, most intricate painting in the book. And secondly, there is the fact that I did not announce my project to my hosts. When I met Cece in the Green 7 section of Parking Level Three, carrying my bag from the bookstore, I was for some reason inclined to lie—to say that it was only a gift for my mother: a picture book of Fabergé eggs.

The Traverses had supplied me with an ample store of ink and brushes, but it took me some time to find the right paper: 20 by 564 centimeters, ocher rather than white, thick enough to hold the ink. Once I finally got started, however, everyone was happy with my choice of traditional materials. I knew that Cece had heard something about our East Village from Harry Lin, and I think she'd been afraid that I would end up doing that sort of project: cooking fish in the nude, chaining myself to the ceiling, or emerging newborn from a womblike rubber bubble.

I was far away from such extravagance. I was painting the third episode of Zhao Cangyun's masterpiece, in which two Confucian gentlemen climb up into the Tiantai Mountains in search of medicinal herbs. On their way home they become lost, and bathe their faces in a stream. They look back and see that:

> The air above the mountain is dense,
> The green peaks lofty and contorted.
> Gazing at them you are transported
> To another world.

What Liu Chen and Ruan Zhao don't know is that this moment represents their last chance to turn around, and that this view is a foreshadow of their destiny.

The novelist rapped timidly on my open door. "Oh, I'm sorry," she said. "You're working."

"I was expecting you," I said. "Come in—sit down, please."

"May I move this?" she asked. I helped her move a chair near my easel; she was circumspect about my work, waiting to be invited to examine it.

"This is nothing," I said modestly. I was in fact pleased with what I had produced, the calligraphy in particular. It had been a long time since I had written characters with a brush.

"It's lovely." The novelist glanced at the reproduction. "You're—working in the classical style?"

"That's the first step," I improvised.

"Oh yes, I see," the novelist said. She took a piece of paper from her purse and unfolded it: a poor-quality photocopy from a newspaper, with a picture and some text. The novelist looked from the Xerox to my face, and then back to the copy again.

"You—excuse me—you look—"

"I look older," I said. "I look in the mirror, and I hardly recognize myself."

I remembered the day that photo was taken: it was spring, and I had bicycled straight from school to the East Village, where I found two foreign photographers (a Norwegian man and a British woman) in Cash's courtyard, taking pictures for their newspapers.

The novelist shook her head. "I was going to say the opposite: this picture's six years old, but you're exactly the same."

I stared at that photograph, and I'm embarrassed to say that I was moved: only six years had passed, but it seemed like such a long time ago.

"I feel older," I said, which was absolutely true.

The novelist pretended to scan the article. When she spoke, her voice had an artificial casualness: "You were in jail twice, first in '89, after the democracy protests, and then again in '94, is that right?"

For a moment I was not sure how to answer this question. And then I thought of something the photographer Zhang Tianming had told me, the first time I visited his apartment in the East Village. "An artist can lie and tell the truth at once," he said, and when I saw his photographs, I understood what he meant. Take his portraits of us East Villagers: the photograph of Cash, for example. It shows the musician in his familiar black bomber jacket, black jeans tucked into black leather boots, and a pair of mirrored sunglasses. Tianming placed his subject in front of a window; although it must be evening—Cash never got up early—I like to imagine that the sun is rising behind him. The contrast between his fierce costume (not a lie exactly, but a kind of pose) and the bright light on his glasses was the truth about Cash, who believed he would become a rock star in the new Beijing. That lying to tell the truth was at the root of Tianming's genius.

Thinking of the photographer, I may have told the lady novelist more than I intended.

"I was not in jail in '94," I said. "You won't believe it, but I missed our village's last performance."

The novelist was scribbling excitedly in her notebook. "The article got it wrong," she said, as if this were very unusual, and of great significance.

Something I had noticed about my American hosts was that they tended to believe something was true if they read it in a newspaper.

"So I can't tell you much more about it," I said. I glanced at my scroll, as if I were yearning to return to it.

The novelist looked up. "If you don't mind," she said. "Maybe we could talk a little about your parents?"

"Is this important for the article?"

The lady novelist looked startled and then blushed, making me wonder if I was not the only one telling fibs. "Oh—yes. Although to be honest, I'm not sure I'll use everything. You're welcome to see it before it goes to print."

Here, you see, I tell a real lie. I say this not to excuse myself, but to explain: I was very nervous, and I hadn't expected to be quoted in print.

"We could start with your father?"

"He worked on a cargo boat," I said. "Do you know where Shanxi Province is?"

The novelist nodded. "I looked at a map," she said, but she had stopped taking notes. Clearly I was repeating the information she'd read in her article. Encouraged, I continued:

"My mother sold snacks in a river town, Yichang. That's how they met."

"So your background was considered—"

"Middle peasant," I said without hesitation, as I had on numerous occasions in the East Village. Only X and Meiling knew the truth about my family, about my mother's girlhood in America, her subsequent imprisonment, and my father's rise through the ranks at Daqing. There were other children of wealthy parents in the East Village (X's girlfriend Lulu, and the "doctor" Yuchen), but they did not enjoy the same regard as people like X and Tianming, who had come penniless from the provinces to make their names. I could see this distinction right away, which was why, whenever someone asked, I explained that my situation was similar to that of my cousin.

The novelist asked me a few more questions, including whether or not I had been fairly treated when I was imprisoned in 1989. I suggested that the Taiwanese journalist who wrote that article might have made the story more dramatic, for political reasons. The novelist nodded, but did not look convinced.

"I'm sorry to bring up a painful time—"

"Detention is painful," I said sharply, surprising myself. "What is painful is the water dungeon, the tiger bench, or 'flying an airplane.' Sitting here talking to you . . ."

"Oh I understand," the novelist said, scribbling eagerly. "I so appreciate the time you've taken. If I have other questions—details to fill in—maybe I could come back another time?"

I regretted mentioning the torture. To be honest, I had chosen those particular punishments because of a Falun Dafa demonstration I had observed on Santa Monica Boulevard, when I'd gone to the fish market with Cece. A soft American voice recounted horrors from a tape player, while practitioners meditated on the ground; one young man, apparently of Tibetan origin, was wearing a sandwich board that read, "China Stole My Freedom," on top of a Nike tracksuit.

I have to emphasize that my pretensions here and in the East Village had nothing to do with the dissembling of my parents and grandparents, during the political campaigns of the 1950s, '60s, and '70s. I was eighteen years old, trying on a new identity as a kind of fashion, whereas they had been trying to save their lives. X once remarked on this irony; in general, however, he didn't mind my borrowing his proletarian background if it suited me. My cousin's extreme generosity toward me in the East Village made it difficult for me to refuse later, when I was called upon to be generous with him.

46.

IN JANUARY OF 1994, MY COUSIN X AND I PUT OUT THE DEBUT ISSUE OF
Lu Kou. It began during my first lunch in the courtyard of Cash's place: a
very bad lunch of instant noodles, gray bits of chicken, and a lot of bright
red chili oil. I noticed that Meiling avoided the meat, although my cousin
enthusiastically hunted for it, spitting gristle and bones onto the table.

"The main thing, of course, is distribution," said Cash. "How many
people see it." He was huddled in a black coat: it wasn't windy in the courtyard, but it was cold; I wondered why we were sitting outside.

"The photocopying is going to be very expensive," said Fang. "We're
not going to be able to make many copies."

"I can help with that." Lulu looked elegant in a gray coat with a white
fox fur collar. Aside from X's girlfriend, Fang, and Cash, I recognized the
"Doctor," Yuchen, and the beautiful, aloof Baoyu. There were several
other people I didn't know, including a plump student type sitting next to
Lulu, who introduced herself as Ai Dan. I was sorry not to see the photographer I'd met the other afternoon; I wanted to thank him for directing
me toward *Something That Is Not Art*.

"Depending on when her allowance arrives," Baoyu said, stretching
his arms languidly above his head. He had pushed aside his unfinished
soup, which had immediately been set upon by ants.

"At least I *do* contribute," Lulu said. My cousin observed this rivalry
with amusement, as if the two of them were his children. I was grateful to
X for letting Meiling and me listen in on this important conversation.
Even the courtyard seemed romantic to me, with its dying tree, single table, and extra, mismatched chairs. It faced the back of a small apartment

house, the door of which had been painted bright red. Leaning against the door was a large brown-and-white oil portrait of a young woman's face in broad strokes, looking warily to the left, as if she were expecting someone. I didn't admire the painting so much as its casual placement in the courtyard; when you were with X's friends, you felt that art was the stuff of daily life, present all around you, as necessarily as a pair of chopsticks or a bicycle.

"I think we should start by figuring out the masthead," Cash said. "Who's doing what?"

"I nominate X as editor-in-chief," Fang said immediately.

"I would be honored," said my cousin. It was clear that he'd expected this position and that his nomination was only a formality.

"And you for photo editor," the doctor said to Fang.

"Assistant photo editor," said Fang quickly. "Helping Tianming."

"That's what I meant," said Yuchen.

My stomach was rumbling; I hadn't eaten more than a few spoonfuls of my soup, which had long since turned cold and gelatinous. As much as I was thrilled to be included with X's friends, I couldn't help thinking of the tiny, warm dumpling shop behind the university, with its steamy plate glass and scalding jasmine tea.

"I'd like to make a nomination," X said. Immediately everyone became quiet. I could hear the sound of hammers from the construction site at the edge of the village, and the static barks from the foreman's megaphone.

"I nominate my cousin, Longxia Shanren," X said. "He can be my assistant editor."

I forgot my cold and hunger. I must've let my mouth drop open, because some guys I didn't know nudged each other and laughed. I had heard what my cousin said, but I didn't want to make a mistake: how embarrassing, if somehow I'd misunderstood.

I looked at X, who was smiling at me.

"Are you sure?" I asked. "It seems like a lot of responsibility."

"Oh, you think we're giving you a big position?" my cousin teased me.

"No!" I said. "No, I—"

"Worried you can't handle it?"

"I can handle it!"

X smiled. I looked around the table and saw that everyone was nodding their agreement. Even Lulu didn't raise an objection.

"We already discussed it," said Cash. "You can translate the text into English for the foreign reporters."

"Will there be foreign reporters?"

"There are always reporters when he's around," Cash said, indicating my cousin. "He draws them like a toilet draws flies."

People laughed, and I looked at Meiling, whose cheeks were almost as bright as her scarf. She looked a little like one of those Tibetan children whose faces are permanently reddened from sun and wind and altitude.

"Are you cold?" I asked her.

"I'm all right."

I had been worried about bringing Meiling to my cousin's, but now I was glad: she could see me being honored by actual artists. I thought of how she would describe the afternoon to her provincial roommates, how impressed they would no doubt be by my connections in Beijing.

"What's going to go into this magazine?" Meiling said suddenly, not only to me but so that the entire table could hear.

I looked at her with amazement. I had been trying to think of something to say in response to my nomination, but I'd been too shy even to thank my cousin. Meiling, on the other hand, was boldly offering what seemed to be a criticism.

"Ah," said X. "See? All of you jabbering about nominations and photocopies and distribution, and this young lady tells you what's what."

I was glad that X was defending Meiling. At the same time I wanted to remind him that he'd been "jabbering about nominations" as well. He'd been nominating me!

"We don't even know which works will go into our first issue," my cousin said.

"Yours, presumably."

We all looked up to see who had spoken, and I recognized the photographer who had given me directions to *Something That Is Not Art*.

"Old Hua is right," Tianming said, looking around the courtyard. "You artists are crazy. It must be below freezing out here."

X got up, smiling, and pulled another chair to the table. "Finally," he said. "What took you so long?"

Everyone started standing up, hugging themselves and stamping their feet. Lulu's friend carried the bowls outside and dumped them; a couple of dogs immediately appeared to eat up the leftovers. The party seemed to be breaking up.

"Let's go," Meiling said. "I'm cold."

"Let's wait a little longer," I said. I wanted to thank my cousin privately, but he was talking to Tianming.

"I can't," Meiling said. "I told my roommates I'd help them straighten up."

"Hey, cousin," X called. "Come over here and meet a great photographer."

Meiling sighed. "Just one more minute," I promised her.

I went over and shook Tianming's hand.

"We met already," I told my cousin proudly. "He gave me directions to your place for the performance the other day."

"What did you think of it?" Tianming asked.

I looked at my cousin. "It must have been really uncomfortable. I was worried about you afterward."

"Don't worry," X said cheerfully. "I'm used to it."

"But I mean, did you think it was an art project?" Tianming was looking at me seriously, as if my opinion mattered. I wondered if this was some kind of test. If I said it wasn't art, I might be insulting my cousin; but if I said it was, then the project wouldn't have succeeded. What was the right answer?

"Did my cousin tell you about the project?" X asked Meiling, who was standing beside me but looking out at the road, where the dogs were whining for more handouts. Her breath came in little clouds of warm vapor.

"He described it," Meiling said, and stopped.

I had returned from the East Village that evening and gone straight to Meiling's dormitory. I had to talk to someone about what I'd seen. I had tried to emphasize the aspects of the performance I thought would impress her—in particular the number of foreign journalists present—but Meiling had been skeptical. I assumed she would conceal her doubts now that we were talking to the artist himself; although I think I loved Meiling already that afternoon in the courtyard, I obviously didn't know her very well.

"How did it strike you?" X asked.

Meiling shrugged. "I like art you can use."

I looked quickly at my cousin, and then down at my shoes. I was embarrassed for Meiling, and perhaps also a little bit impressed. How could she talk back to people like my cousin and Tianming—these bohemian, experienced artists—as if she were chatting with her classmates?

"Art isn't useful," X said. "That's the whole point. That's why there hasn't been any of it for so long."

"There hasn't been any because it wasn't allowed," Tianming said. "It still isn't."

"Is that true?" I forgot my nervousness for a minute. "What about at CAFA?"

X shook his head. "I'm talking about experimental art—*real* art. When I got out of detention, I was careful. I went to see my parents, and I didn't make anything. I thought I would never make anything again."

This was the first time I'd ever heard my cousin mention his time in jail, although of course my parents had talked about it when it happened. My mother told me then that prisons had improved a great deal since the 1960s and '70s, and that my cousin would be all right. I remember this as one of the earliest instances in which I knew my mother was lying to me.

"Then one day I saw something," X continued. "I was sitting at the table, and my mother was cooking at the stove. She was talking to me about who knows what, and I was just sitting there, thinking about how many times I had wondered whether I would ever be released and get to go home—to see my mother again, and taste those chive and tofu dumplings."

Even Meiling was listening now; she had stepped closer to my cousin and me, and her left hand in its red glove brushed against mine.

"I was watching the pan, and the smell reminded me so much of being a kid—I really thought I might have traveled back in time. I was afraid to look down: I thought I'd see two dirty little boy's hands on the table in front of me! Then a huge bubble rose up in the pan"— my cousin spread his hands to show the size—"and it stayed for what seemed like forever. I thought it was a message to me." X looked around our little circle, from Tianming to Lulu to Meiling and me. "The pan, the bubble, the steam. There is a whole invisible world, just waiting for people to see it. All of a sudden I thought painting wouldn't work anymore—I would have to find another way."

"That's a great story," said Fang, who had edged into our group. "You should interview him about his inspiration," he said to me. "We could use it for the magazine." Fang glanced at my cousin for approval, but X wasn't paying attention.

"I'd like to see those prints," my cousin told Tianming.

"Which prints?" the photographer asked.

"The ones you took of *Something That Is Not Art*."

"I'd like to see them too," I said. Most of the artists had gone, and I could sense Meiling's impatience. But I was reluctant to leave what seemed to be the inner circle.

Tianming looked surprised. "I wish I'd known."

"What do you mean?" X said.

Tianming shrugged. "I thought you didn't want those photographs. So I destroyed them."

I thought my cousin looked startled, but he recovered quickly. "Good," he said. "Thank you." He turned to me. "Can you be here at the same time next week? That's when we'll have our first official meeting. I promise it'll be inside next time."

That was how I started going to the East Village every Wednesday afternoon at one o'clock. We would alternate between different apartments, depending on whose was most livable at the moment (and who had managed to pay their rent). That winter, my first away from home, was particularly cold, but it wasn't bitter. To me those afternoons in the East Village had all the glamor of an exotic holiday; I was sorry to return to school at night. As I biked west into the city, the Great Wall, Kunlun, and Lufthansa hotels stood out like garish planets in the night. Sometimes I would stop, balancing on my bike with my toes on the ground, and look back the way I'd come: it gave me a pleasant shock of fear to see the nothingness out there. It was like peering over the edge of the earth.

When I got back to the university, I used to bicycle past Meiling's dormitory, count four stories up and three windows over, just for the pleasure of identifying her dim light. If the window was dark, I would go to the library. I would stand outside in the freezing wind, happy to know she was safe and warm inside. The next day, I couldn't help it: I would tell her what I'd done.

My mind returns obsessively to that winter. I can't say whether this is hindsight—knowing what would happen to our East Village the following June—or simply the most perfect season of my youth, when I was falling in love and becoming an artist at the same time. I think of it at night, and try to remember whether I knew I was happy. Did I enjoy those months in the East Village; did I know how fragile it was? Or was the fact that I did not know somehow a condition for my happiness?

47.

WHEN OUR SCHOOL HOLIDAYS BEGAN, TO MY PARENTS' DISAPPOINT-
ment I did not go home, and for the first time I could remember, I missed
the New Year in my hometown. (The Rooster became the Dog that year,
and now incredibly, as I write this, the Rooster has come round again.)
When the dormitories shut down, I went to stay with my cousin and finished the first issue of *Lu Kou*.

The first and only issue is now a collector's item. We made thirty-five
copies, which was all that we could afford. It included some of Tianming's
East Village portraits, a piece by Baoyu called "Instructions for Making a
Piece of Performance Art," as well as photographs documenting a project
that looked nothing like those instructions. We also published my interview with X, about the transformation in his work after 1989. Had I been
born in the year of the Dragon, like my cousin, as opposed to the humble
Rabbit, I might have experienced a similar transformation. But in the
spring of 1989, I was about to turn fourteen. In those days I would hurry
home after school, where I would drink warm tea and study English with
my mother.

I knew I was lucky to have been safe at home that spring. And I didn't
wish to have been a university student at that time. I wanted to be part of
another, newer movement, artistic rather than political. I flattered myself
that X and Tianming needed my youth the way that I needed their experience; together we would let the whole world know about the Beijing East
Village.

That winter we were having a running argument. It took many forms
but always returned to the same issue: who did our work belong to? For

example, there was *Walking Up Coal Hill with Candles*. Wearing a conservative business suit provided by Lulu (as well as tasteful makeup and a pink ribbon in his long, silken hair), Baoyu attempted to climb the hill behind the Forbidden City holding two lit candles. But on that cold and windy day, the candles immediately went out. Even with Lulu and Ai Dan on either side of him, there was no way to climb and shield the flames at the same time. The picture Fang finally took is of failure: Baoyu stands at the edge of the small shrine on top of the hill, looking out over the Forbidden City. We see him from the back, his hair blowing in the wind, holding in his right hand the pair of extinguished candles, like two spent sticks of dynamite.

Fang argued that this picture was his, and should therefore be captioned, "Zhu Fang, *Baoyu on Coal Hill*, February 1994." Baoyu countered that this photograph was simply a documentary recording, if a skillful one, of his own project: "Chen Baoyu, *Walking Up Coal Hill with Candles*, February 1994." Fang looked to his mentor, Tianming, to resolve the dispute.

"Where is this piece going to be shown?" Tianming asked innocently, and the two artists had to concede that until someone was interested in exhibiting *Coal Hill*, it was unlikely to need a caption at all.

Unlike Cash and my cousin, Tianming did not invite the group of us to his apartment, and I was curious to see where the photographer lived. One morning that February, I finally got my chance. It was Saturday, and I was waiting for my cousin in his apartment. (He had given me a key, which I was so afraid of losing that I wore it around my neck, with my citizen ID.) I had arrived early that morning in the East Village, as usual, and my cousin hadn't returned from Lulu's yet.

My cousin's apartment was dirty and cold. One of the windows was open, but there was still a strong smell of cigarettes and mildew. The bed was unmade, and some rusty chains were lying on the floor, which X had obviously been salvaging for a project. A whole collection of empty beer cans and liquor bottles were sitting by the door; since my cousin rarely drank, this was evidence of how many people showed up to hang out with him on a regular basis.

I didn't mind the mess or the cold; it was a luxury to have the place to

myself. After I had finished examining the room, I sat in an old upholstered chair and watched the people going by outside the window: labor-
ers on their bicycles, and the occasional old man with a cart of dried
jujubes and nuts. I imagined that this was my apartment, and that I had
woken up early on a Saturday to jot down an idea for a project—as brilliant and ephemeral as the bubble in a frying pan.

I was so wrapped up in this fantasy of myself as an independent East
Village artist that when I heard a knock on the door, I called out casually:

"Come in!"

It was Tianming. "Have I got something to show you," he said, shut-
ting the door behind him. He turned around, and stopped.

"It's you," he said, as if I'd startled him. "For a second I thought you
were your cousin."

I blushed: could the photographer guess what I'd been imagining before he walked into the room?

"I'm just waiting for him," I said. "He's at Lulu's, but he should be
back any second."

"I had something I wanted to show him, but I had a feeling he wouldn't
be home." Tianming looked around the room: "It's freezing in here—you
should come wait at my place."

"I'm all right here," I said, but I was glad when he insisted.

The photographer led me around the corner and down a long alley to
a run-down farmhouse. His landlady was cooking in the kitchen with the
door open; steam came from a door across the courtyard, in the center of
which was a large jujube tree. A well-fed gray cat was asleep under an old
metal folding chair. Even the drone of construction on the Third Ring
Road sounded fainter here.

"This is great," I said. "How did you find this place?"

"Are you looking?" Tianming asked. In contrast to some of the other
artists, who treated me in an affectionate but condescending way—as if I
would always be X's cousin, Little Fatty—Tianming took me seriously.

"I might be," I bluffed, although I hadn't thought of it until now. "Living in the dorms is really a pain."

"But it's nearly free, isn't it?" Tianming said. "You're so lucky, not having to pay rent in Beijing."

I nodded, embarrassed. I hadn't thought about the fact that the photographer might be struggling to pay for his room, even in this kind of neighborhood.

"I think it's good to live in a dormitory," Tianming said gently. "Otherwise how will you meet people?"

I wanted to tell him that I wasn't interested in meeting other students—that the people I wanted to meet were all right here in this village.

Tianming unlocked his front door. "We can always help you find a place, after you graduate."

I was surprised by the size of the photographer's room, although I tried not to show it. It was even smaller than my room at school: a narrow concrete box with a desk, two beds, and an exposed water pipe running the length of one wall. Tianming's double-lens Seagull camera sat on the desk beside a large black binder; three or four test sheets were taped to the wall next to the mirror. The only other decoration was a dark oil painting of a girl's face, looking over her shoulder.

"My sister's self-portrait," Tianming said. "She painted it the week before she went back home." He touched the edge of the painting, although it was perfectly straight. Then he turned to me abruptly: "So, you want to see some pictures?"

I helped him clear off a space on the bed, and Tianming began laying out the prints one by one. For a moment I didn't understand what I was looking at. When I'd attended my cousin's performance, the electrical equipment—fans on one side, heaters on the other—had seemed to be the most important part of the project; but in Tianming's photos, all of that had been cropped out. My cousin's naked body seemed to be suspended in air, his four limbs extended like spokes of a wheel. Behind him was the banner with the title *Something That Is Not Art:* you could only make out the last two characters, *yishu.*

"That's incredible," I said.

"What about this one?" the photographer asked, holding up a print.

"Of these two, which do you like better?" Tianming was kneeling on the concrete floor. He was wearing his typical faded black jeans and worn cotton sweater, and his hair was cut a little too short. He was skinnier than my cousin, with milder, less distinctive features; if I'd seen him on the street, I wouldn't have thought he was an artist, or even a college student. He looked like someone you might find selling trinkets on a blanket outside Beijing Zhan.

"I don't know much about photography," I said. "But I like this one. It reminds me of Leonardo da Vinci." I was showing off, of course, but the photographer didn't tease me.

"Why Leonardo?"

"*The Vitruvian Man*," I said. Tianming didn't understand the English title, but when I stretched my arms out, he smiled in recognition.

"I didn't think of that—but you're right." He held the photo up: "I like it, especially with that *yishu* in the background." He stood up and taped the photograph to the wall with the others. "You shouldn't be afraid to say what you think," he said, his back to me. "Why's your opinion worth less than anyone else's?"

I didn't say anything, but I was filled with pride. I asked whether I could see some of his other photos.

Tianming seemed to hesitate, and then handed me the black binder that had been sitting on his desk next to the camera. Inside were all of the photographs he'd taken in the East Village, from the moment he discovered other artists living there. There were pictures of Cash in his sunglasses, of Baoyu combing his hair in front of a mirror, and of my cousin—chained to the ceiling, locked in a metal box, and half-submerged in Lulu's glamorous bathtub. There was a progression of intimacy in each set of pictures, as if Tianming were chipping away at his subject's persona every time the shutter clicked.

"Are these for a show?" I asked.

"I wouldn't mind having a show," Tianming said. "Although we'd have to keep it pretty quiet. Mostly I'm hoping to have a book someday."

There was a knock on the door, and I was almost sorry to hear my cousin's voice calling out to us. I was thrilled by the idea of a book about the East Village. The place had a magical quality; every time I left it, I was afraid it might somehow evaporate behind me, and not be there when I returned. A book of photographs seemed to me like a kind of insurance, a promise not only that our village was real, but that it was strong enough to last.

"What would you call the book?" I asked Tianming, who had already taken back the binder, and was putting it away in a drawer.

"Who knows?" he said lightly, but there was something in his voice that made me think he did have a title, and that it was private—the opposite of the communal projects that were starting to make our group famous. Tianming didn't ask me to keep the idea of the book a secret. I seemed to know that without being told.

"Hey," X said, when I opened the door. "What're you two up to in here?"

My cousin seemed to have just gotten out of bed. His hair, normally slicked back in a ponytail, was loose and tangled, and his leather jacket was cracked with wear. Underneath the jacket he was wearing his characteristic black Mao suit. He looked terrible, in a cool sort of way.

"You can come in, but you're not going to like it," Tianming joked. "I've been showing your cousin some pictures."

"I hope they're not dirty. My aunt and uncle would kill me." I could see that he would've kept teasing me, but the photograph Tianming had just taped to the wall stopped him. He stepped past us and examined it, adjusting the lamp to give himself more light.

"You didn't—?"

"Nope," Tianming said. "Sorry."

X stared at the photo, entranced: "Shit," he said finally. "Is that really me?"

The photographer laughed. "No—it's a Leonardo."

"Well, my project was a failure," said X, smiling. "Because this is definitely art. One of your best, I think."

"But the photo can be art even if the project wasn't, right?" I said. "He could've 'carved rotten wood'?" I was excited, and I used an old-fashioned expression of my father's, which *Idiomatic English* might have translated as "making a silk purse out of a sow's ear." I didn't mean to imply that my cousin's project was rotten wood—or a pig's ear—but suddenly I was afraid I'd said something wrong. There was a silence: my cousin stared at the photograph, and Tianming looked out the window at the alley, where someone had started hammering.

I was about to apologize—explain what I'd meant to say—when my cousin turned to me. "Tianming is a genius," he said. "Do you know that? He's invented a completely new kind of photography."

"New in China, maybe," Tianming said.

"There's only one problem," my cousin continued, as if Tianming hadn't spoken. "He needs the rest of us in order to do it."

Tianming finally turned from the window to look at X.

"It's like fucking." My cousin smiled. "You can do it by yourself, but it isn't really the same thing."

I hung out with X and Tianming for the rest of the day. When we'd finished looking at photographs, we sat in the courtyard, talking and playing cards, with the cat rubbing up against our legs. Over a couple of beers, we planned projects that would never happen: covering an East Village house in newspaper, making a giant ice cube in the middle of Tiananmen Square, or walking into the Wangfujing McDonald's completely naked, with the Olympic rings painted on our asses. I might have to wait a little while but I decided I was moving to the East Village, no matter what. I thought this was the beginning for me; I didn't know that what I was witnessing was more like the beginning of the end.

48.

THAT WINTER MEILING BOUGHT A SECONDHAND BICYCLE. SHE HADN'T grown up riding one, but almost immediately after she arrived at college, she'd enlisted a girlfriend to teach her. She would wrap herself up in layers of sweaters and scarves, and pedal determinedly to the eastern part of the city. In my foolishness I attributed that to her feelings for me, although she told me plainly that the East Village was an opportunity for her too. She had found a comrade in Lulu's friend Ai Dan, the plain and quiet girl I had noticed that first afternoon in Cash's courtyard. Ai Dan, who had once worked in a blouse factory, and who owned a large collection of foreign dress patterns, was teaching Meiling to sew. More important, perhaps, Lulu had seen their drawings and commissioned them to make her a coat. Some friends of hers from the Dance Academy were also interested. If Meiling and Ai Dan made enough clothing for those privileged girls—many of whom hoped to become film actresses—someone was bound to notice. It was their dream, Meiling told me, to open up a small high-fashion boutique together.

We went to the East Village on weekends, and sometimes after school. Every Wednesday we went to the art lunch—held in my cousin's apartment, now that the weather had turned really cold. Afterward Meiling would leave with Ai Dan, and I would stay to work on *Lu Kou*. When I was finished, I would go back to pick her up.

At first I thought it was a coincidence that Ai Dan was often on her way out when I arrived. "I have an errand," she would say innocently, or "I have to get something from Tianming," and Meiling would ask me to come in while she got ready to go. I would sit on the rough brown and yellow couch watching her straighten the room, a fascinating activity, especially when she bent to pick things up. She would ask pointed questions about what I was doing at my cousin's (she was skeptical of *Lu Kou,* and particularly of my cousin's role as editor-in-chief).

"Is any of the artwork going to be by people who *aren't* his friends?" she asked. I told her that we were trying to make a community. I explained that the magazine was a kind of manifesto for our group, but Meiling was not convinced.

"You should be spending time on your own art, instead of his magazine," she told me one day. "I'd like to see more of those South American finches." I had shown Meiling some of my bird drawings from childhood, after telling her about Wang Laoshi.

"Those things?" I said scornfully. "Art isn't just sitting around drawing birds." But I was fiercely proud and, as soon as I got back to the dormitory, I took two of the drawings my teacher had praised (the rufous hummingbird and the California thrasher) and inscribed them, "For Meiling," in the top right-hand corner. One very cold afternoon, when we had drawn the heater up next to the couch, Meiling allowed me to take off her sweater. She was wearing a collared blouse over a long-sleeved woolen shirt with a brassiere underneath: the fact that I was only three layers away from actual skin was almost prohibitively exciting. I slid my hand under the fabric, and worked my fingers up to her bra. I was lying on top of Meiling, facing the door, and the right side of my body was burning hot, while the left side was covered with goosebumps. It must've been the same for her, only in reverse.

"Why are you smiling?" Meiling said.

"I was thinking we're like an art project. *Something That Is Not Art,* remember?" But this comment seemed to displease her, and so I quickly changed the subject, asking whether she was warm enough. In response, Meiling took my hand and guided it away from her breasts, down to her belly. "Maybe I can make you warmer," I joked, thinking she was pushing my hand away. Instead, I heard the sound of a snap. I thought it had happened by accident, until I saw that her eyes were closed and her head thrown back; her hand was down near the button of her jeans, working the zipper. In my imagination, I tease her a little, play with the curly hairs escaping the top of her underpants, and put my lips on her belly, running my tongue across that damp cotton and making her cry out, before I push the fabric aside to taste the delicious wetness underneath. What I did, of course, was rush my hand to feel that incredible place I'd been imagining for so long, and gasp, in a voice an octave above my own:

"Won't Ai Dan come back?"

Meiling shook her head, with her eyes closed, as if I were interrupting some private bliss of hers. "I told her not for an hour," she said. "I wanted to give us enough time."

The thought that Meiling had arranged this encounter was perhaps the most erotic thing I could have imagined; I fell on top of her, grinding my body into hers. Meiling laughed and opened her eyes.

"Here," she said, taking my hand and guiding it. "Like this."

After I had touched her, Meiling sat up, smoothed her hair, and said calmly: "Don't you want to take off your jeans?" I shook my head. I was embarrassed to admit that watching her, I'd been unable to contain myself. Of course, when we stood up, she saw the stain on the front of my pants and understood; I was grateful to her for pretending not to notice.

When Ai Dan did return, she wasn't alone. Lulu came in behind her and shut the door. I was always uncomfortable around my cousin's glamorous girlfriend, but in this instance I was especially eager to leave. Lulu was wearing her white fur-trimmed jacket, but her face looked strange, red and white in places, as if she'd been crying. She seemed unhappy to find us in her friend's apartment.

"Still here?" Ai Dan said. "Do you want to stay for some dinner? I think it's only going to be cabbage and noodle soup."

"No thanks," Meiling said. She was putting on her coat, and there was no sign that she'd been doing anything unusual, unless you count the particularly brilliant flush on her brown cheeks, and the clear light in her black eyes. Maybe Lulu was envious of that sheen, because she turned to Meiling and looked her up and down unkindly.

"The two of you need to start making your own clothes if you can't afford to buy fashionable ones. From now on you're a kind of advertisement for your product." People in the East Village were constantly describing the roles they would play, and the renown they would have, in some near and brilliant future, but Lulu's comment was too barbed. I thought at the time that she and X must've had a fight, and that she was simply taking her anger out on me and Meiling.

"Why dress up to come here?" Meiling said casually, but you could see she was angry.

"That's true," Lulu said. "I never wear my best clothes here." She took off the fur jacket and tossed it casually on the couch—the same one we'd gotten up from a few moments before. It drove me crazy to think of that couch one day being put out into the road for scavengers like the Fujianese bicycle-cart man, and I made a hasty plan to save it. I imagined it (re-covered and disguised) in a cozy apartment I would one day share with Meiling, surrounded by our fat and happy children.

"What's wrong with Xiao Pangzi?" Lulu said, breaking my domestic reverie. Even my cousin no longer called me by that name, and Lulu knew it.

"Who?" said Meiling. I was ashamed that she could defend me better than I could myself.

Lulu put on a surprised expression. "I'd think you two would like having little nicknames for each other. He's your boyfriend, isn't he?"

"Why do you care if he is or he isn't?"

"Of course I am." I was facing Lulu, but I meant it for Meiling, whom I'd been hoping to make my girlfriend almost since the day I'd met her. Wasn't it indisputable, especially after today?

"I just meant that you two have been spending some special time together," Lulu said innocently. "That's why Meiling looks so pretty."

"Lulu!" Ai Dan gasped, but I could tell she was trying not to laugh. Meiling glanced angrily at her friend, and then turned back to Lulu.

"At least I don't have to come begging for it in the middle of the night," Meiling said. "At least my boyfriend *wants* me in his bed."

Lulu stared at Meiling, her face that funny mottled color, and for a moment I was frightened of what might happen. I wondered if I would have to jump in and pull them apart, before Lulu began to speak.

"You stupid little country cunt. You ugly black bitch. You filthy slut . . ."

"Come on," Meiling said, "we're leaving," and I followed her like a child who has witnessed something shocking. As we closed the door, Lulu was still insulting Meiling but in a more controlled voice, as if it amused her:

"Greasy whore," and then, as if she were an old granny: "Broken shoe."

When Meiling and I got into the street, I could see that she was shaking, and not from the cold. I wasn't sure she should ride back, and so I locked our bicycles together and put my arm through hers. We hardly spoke on the way to the bus stand, except for me to ask, "Are you OK?" and Meiling to answer impatiently, "Yes, yes." The thing that bothered me most was not her rudeness to Lulu (who deserved it) or even her impatience with me. What disturbed me was her accusation, particularly the phrase "in the middle of the night." Had Meiling heard something specific about my cousin and Lulu that I hadn't? Of course X wouldn't necessarily tell me if he was fighting with his girlfriend, whereas Ai Dan might easily have gossiped about it with Meiling; but the incident gave me the uncomfortable feeling that there was a whole East Village I still didn't know, and that Meiling might be gaining access faster than I was.

49.

THE DAY BEFORE I WAS TO VISIT JUNE WANG'S GRANDMOTHER IN SIL-verlake, I decided to cut my hair. It had been seven years since I'd first started growing it, and when I came out of the old-fashioned barbershop on Larchmont Avenue, where the Anselmites often went to drink iced coffee after school, my neck felt naked and exposed. I kept touching the soft fuzz at the back of my scalp, feeling as if I'd left something behind— my coat or a set of keys.

June Wang lived in a narrow yellow house at least half an hour by taxi from the Traverses'. There was an American flag on the mailbox, and an oversized, misshapen pumpkin resting against the side of the porch in anticipation of the coming holiday. My taxi arrived fifteen minutes early, and I had thought I would walk around the block to clear my head, but June must've been waiting for me. She opened the door before I had finished paying the driver, and called out, "Yuan Laoshi, you're early!"

I'll tell you, I felt cheerful, especially when I saw the grandmother scolding her for being rude, and even more when I stepped into the house and breathed a familiar smell. It was the combination of her grandmother's cooking with something I couldn't quite identify, a heavy sort of citrus perfume. It smelled like home.

"You're right on time," June's grandmother insisted in Chinese. "Please come in." I guessed she was in her sixties, although her skin was remarkably unlined. She was wearing a long-sleeved blouse and matching ankle-length, pleated skirt, but these were of a striking orange and turquoise paisley fabric—brilliant colors that suggested Mrs. Wang had not quite given up her vanity. She kept her hair jet black and wore it short, with a permanent wave.

"Thank you for having me," I said. "June is a wonderful student."

"No, no," Mrs. Wang said, deflecting the compliment and smiling with pleasure. "She's lazy."

"Speak English!" June said. Although it was late October, the weather was still very warm, and June had exchanged her uniform for a summer dress. The dress was white, with green, yellow, and pink flowers embroidered around the hem. I thought June looked especially feminine and very pretty, if a little unlike herself. I guessed that her grandmother had chosen the dress, although I felt sure that the line of silver glitter above each eyelid was her own idea.

"I thought you wanted us to speak Chinese," I teased her.

"My granddaughter doesn't speak Mandarin," Mrs. Wang said. "I tried to teach her, but even when she was a baby she would only speak English." June's grandmother said this with pride: she, a Chinese, had raised a little American.

"I wish you'd tried harder," June said sullenly. And then in adorable, nearly incomprehensible putonghua: "It's too bad!"

Mrs. Wang beamed. "See? You can't understand her."

June's grandmother had the practical habit of buying in bulk; Christmas ribbon, paper napkins, and instant soup were stacked neatly in cartons against the walls, overflow no doubt from a brimming basement. The fireplace was full of miniature potted trees. We were standing in the living room, making awkward conversation, when I happened to notice, hanging next to the television cabinet, a cheap Chinese painting of a mountain scene on silk. Mrs. Wang saw me looking at it:

"The famous Tiantai Mountains," she said. "Have you ever visited?"

All of a sudden I identified the familiar smell I had noticed when I walked in the door: June's grandmother used the same lemon cold cream my mother did. When you're suffering from a crush, anything can seem like a sign; still, the next thing June said gave me a chill, as if there were something about this family that allowed them to see inside my head.

"Do you want to see my birds?"

"Professor Yuan is hungry," Mrs. Wang said. "He can see your birds after dinner."

"What birds?" I asked June urgently, as we followed her grandmother to the dining alcove. Was it possible that June was also a painter of birds? Why had she never shown them to me?

"I'll show you after," June said. I had little interest in food, until Mrs. Wang began bringing dishes from the kitchen: pork and shrimp dumplings, red-braised beef, giant prawns with lotus root, and fiery fried morning glory. There was even a fragrant bowl of sesame rice, under a bamboo lid.

"I wish I had known you were coming further in advance," Mrs. Wang said slyly, switching back to Chinese. "I would have prepared something special."

"You've prepared a feast," I said. The sun was setting earlier now, and it seemed later than it was. Mrs. Wang turned on the lamps in the living room and then fussed over June and me, serving us large portions of everything, and watching as we took our first bites. My pleasure must have been evident:

"Do you get enough to eat with that family?" Mrs. Wang asked me.

"Speak English," June exclaimed. When her grandmother repeated the question in English, June sighed: "Of course he gets enough to eat. They're rich."

"Rich from what business?" her grandmother asked.

I explained that Dr. Travers was a psychiatrist.

Mrs. Wang was unimpressed: "There are still not many psychiatrists in China. Is that right?"

"Not many," I said. "It isn't popular."

"A waste of money," she declared. "What kind of business were you in before you became a teacher?"

I looked at June, who seemed unconcerned by the fact that she'd gotten me into an awkward situation. She was innocently eating a large shrimp dumpling, not particularly gracefully, taking sips of water to avoid burning her tongue.

"My father's business is oil. In Shanghai."

Mrs. Wang frowned. "What oil company is in Shanghai?"

"There's an office there now, but I grew up in Harbin."

"Daqing," Mrs. Wang inferred, nodding her approval: "Harbin, Beijing, and Shandong people are all good people."

"How could everyone in a whole city be good?" June asked.

"Harbin and Beijing are cities," I told her. "Shandong is a province—where Confucius was from."

"She knows, she knows," her grandmother said. "My father—her great-grandfather was from Shandong. He was a marshal under General Chiang. We left the mainland when I was her age." She turned to her granddaughter. "Can you imagine?"

"No," said June. "I never get to go anywhere."

Mrs. Wang appeared shocked by her rudeness, although I had a feeling it wasn't the first time June had made this complaint to her grandmother.

"Are you interested in business?" I asked neutrally. I was trying to smooth things over, and also (I admit) to steer the conversation away from my personal history.

"I'm a businesswoman myself," Mrs. Wang said modestly. "I majored in economics at National Taiwan University. Now I run my own company."

"What sort—"

"Japanese imports," Mrs. Wang said. "Let me show you."

"Oh man," said June. She got up and went into the kitchen. A moment later the back door slammed.

Mrs. Wang also left the room. A moment later she returned, carrying a large cardboard box.

"Do you by chance suffer from carpal tunnel syndrome, Professor Yuan?"

"Excuse me?" I was sure that Mrs. Wang wouldn't have allowed her granddaughter to go out at night, but what was June doing in the backyard? I did not want to leave without seeing her drawings.

"Or any other repetitive stress injuries?" She set the box on the table and began removing thick, elasticized wristbands, headbands, and gloves. As soon as her granddaughter was gone, she had reverted to her own language. "All with a special electromagnetic lining. They're also good for diabetes and insomnia. Take them out of the package."

Mrs. Wang seemed agitated. I examined the socks. "Very comfortable."

"Put them on, put them on," Mrs. Wang said. "I'm sorry my granddaughter is so impolite!"

"No problem," I said. "She's very talented."

"She's been very difficult recently. In fact, that's why I invited you. At first I thought she was worried about college, but now . . ." Mrs. Wang paused, embarrassed. She searched through her carton for another gift.

"All teenagers are troublesome," I said, using some American wisdom to reassure her. "It's when they are not difficult that you should worry."

"Mushroom pills!" Mrs. Wang exclaimed, ignoring me. "Chinese people have had the secret of anti-aging medication since the Three Kingdoms period. In Japan they cost sixty dollars per bottle, but I know how to get them cheaply from Guangzhou. Why do you think my skin looks so smooth?"

"You look very young," I said politely. There was something about talking with Mrs. Wang that relaxed me, as if I were a child again, and could depend on her to tell me what to do.

"Don't flatter me," Mrs. Wang said. "I'm an old lady. My granddaughter is older than she looks as well."

"She is?"

Mrs. Wang lowered her voice, although we were alone. "I kept her out of school," she whispered. "I waited two years, until we could afford a good kindergarten."

If June had been held back two years, that would make her at least nineteen. I thought that explained some of the sophistication of her work. I tried not to meditate any further on the significance of her age: nineteen, after all, was still very young.

"It's my fault," Mrs. Wang confessed. "All my fault. I didn't want her to go to the public school—full of black children."

"Never mind," I said. "June is very advanced, even for a nineteen-year-old. She's the best student I have."

"Professor Yuan, you're flattering us. June has no head for business. I can see that."

"I know," I said carefully. "That's why I think an art college might be better than a business college."

Mrs. Wang nodded calmly. "June likes to draw."

I was startled: had I succeeded in convincing her so easily? "You wouldn't be opposed to that?"

"Any good college is fine with me. The specialty doesn't matter."

"But that's wonderful," I said. "What is she worried about?"

Mrs. Wang shook her head. "You ask her. I can't talk to her. Sometimes I wish I *had* tried harder. I thought I was doing the right thing. But maybe it would have been better?"

"Excuse me?"

"I didn't want her to be confused," Mrs. Wang explained. "I thought that if she only spoke English, there would be no problems. But I wonder if it might be better now, if I could speak to her in Chinese? Maybe in a foreign language we can never say exactly what we mean—do you think so, Professor Yuan?"

There was a rap on the dining room window. A ghostly face appeared in the dark behind the glass.

"Go on," Mrs. Wang said. "Please. Find out what I'm doing wrong."

50.

WHEN JUNE BECKONED ME OUTSIDE, AND HER GRANDMOTHER URGED me to go, I expected we might have a talk. However, my student put her finger to her lips and led me toward the back of a surprisingly large yard, which seemed to end in a chain-link fence. Lights from the dining room and the kitchen did not quite reach this barrier; in the dark June slid back a latch and stepped into an enclosed area, even darker than outside.

"What is this?" I whispered, but June just motioned for me to close the gate. When I looked back, I could see Mrs. Wang doing the dishes behind the kitchen window.

We were inside an open shed, enclosed with chicken wire. At first I took it for some kind of outdoor studio; I was expecting to see drawings, and even after I heard a few querulous notes and breathed the sour sharpness of guano, it took me a moment to understand that we were standing in an aviary. My student did not paint birds—she raised them. Parakeets, cockatiels, Australian finches (not only the common Gouldian, zebra, and owl varieties, I would later learn, but a rare South American warbler and a skittish pair of violet-eared waxbills). June switched on a battery-powered lantern. In the dim light, the bewildered birds began to welcome a premature sunrise.

"You keep birds."

June gave this observation the attention it deserved. "Hold this," she said, handing me the flashlight. Then she began filling the feeders with seed and suet.

"Do you have any thrashers?" I asked.

"What are thrashers?"

"Mockingbirds are the most well known, but there are different types—the brown, the American—"

"You can't keep native species in an aviary," June said. "It's against the law. I'm going to get an African gray parrot, though. Not for here—he would murder the others. But for my room. I'm going to teach him how to say, 'Go away and leave me alone.' " June paused. "How do you say that in Chinese?"

"In Mandarin: *Ni chuqu ba.*"

"Is that impolite?"

"Not really. It's more like, 'Please go out.' "

June sighed. "What about 'Leave me alone'?"

I had to think for a moment. "You could say: *Bie xiao wo.*"

"What does that mean?"

"Literally, 'Don't laugh at me.' "

"That's even worse!"

The birds clustered around the feeders in the dim light. There was a clicking sound, like beads on a string.

"I have an aunt and uncle in China." June tilted her head toward the kitchen. "Did she tell you that?"

I shook my head.

"My aunt looks just like my mom did," June said. "She has two kids— their names are, like, Yee and Yin or something. They invited me to come visit them in Wuhan."

"That would be interesting for you."

"My grandmother doesn't think so."

"I think you underestimate her," I said. "She just told me that she would be happy for you to go to an art college."

I think I expected June to be stunned and grateful, perhaps even to thank me, and so I was surprised to see her expression of genuine disgust. "An *art* college? Who wants to go to an art college?"

"I thought you did. You should," I told her. "You're very talented."

But June was already shaking her head. "I want to go to China to see my family. I don't want to go to art college. I'm not sure I want to go to any college."

"What can you do in America without college?"

"I hate it here," June said. "My grandmother doesn't understand me."

I was afraid her Wuhan relatives might be even less likely to "understand" her, but I didn't want to tell her that.

"She thinks I miss my parents. But she's the one who misses them. How could I miss them? I didn't even *know* them."

I wanted to tell her about my grandfather, and the stories I'd heard all through my childhood. I wanted to tell her how I had imagined him, coughing up blood in a freezing cell, and how those images (handed down carefully by my mother, like an inheritance) had made me angry for all the wrong reasons. I was not indignant on my grandfather's behalf, nor did I admire his patriotism and sacrifice. I did not long to have known him. When I thought of him at all, I resented the tragedy that forced me to share my mother's love with this noble ghost, who would always trump my father and me in her affections.

"How did they die?" I asked June. I had trouble reading her expression in the dim light from the lantern, but her voice, when she answered, was matter-of-fact:

"My dad had a friend who was a tourist pilot—you know—taking people to the islands. My dad wanted to go with him, but my mom was afraid of flying. Then one day they convinced her. The pilot survived, but both my parents were killed."

I was not sure whether to touch June's shoulder or take her hand, or pretend to be casual, and so I did nothing. Maybe that was what made her continue.

"They were going to a place called Orchid Island, to look at birds—isn't that funny? Did you know that Taiwan is the winter home of the blackfaced spoonbill?"

"No."

"Also the whistling green pigeon. Is it true that there are hardly any birds in China because Mao killed them all?"

"Some species have died out," I told her. "I think it has more to do with pollution than with Mao Zedong."

June nodded, filing this information for future reference. Then she looked at me and, as if this question followed from the last, asked:

"What's your real name?"

"What do you mean?" I asked, but my heart was pounding.

"I mean, in China. Besides Teacher Yuan." We were sitting on plastic chairs, unsteady on the gravel. The lantern hung from a hook above our heads. June was sitting on her hands; when she leaned forward, I had a glimpse of a bit of a white lace bra. I looked away, but in that moment, I wanted to tell her everything.

"My parents used to call me Xiao Pangzi," I said.

"Show Pongsy," June repeated.

I couldn't help laughing. "Xiao *Pangzi.*"

"How old are you, Show Pongsy?"

"I can't tell you that."

"Well then, what's your sign?"

"I'm the lobster," I said.

June frowned. "There's no lobster. Do you think I'm stupid?"

Before I could answer (an emphatic no!) June did something that surprised me. She took my hand and flipped it over, as if she might find the answer in my palm. She frowned, and traced the head and heart lines with one finger. It was as if she'd thrown her arms around me and put her lips against my neck. My chest constricted, and my face got hot.

"Well, I won't tell you my sign either," she said.

"I bet you're the rooster."

June looked startled. "How did you know that?"

I almost told her what her grandmother had said, and then thought better of it. I shrugged. "You're outgoing, for one thing. Roosters say what they think. They're not very good at trusting people—but it's supposed to be a lucky sign."

June smiled, and suddenly all of her childishness was gone. "Tell me yours," she said, putting her hand on my arm. She was looking at me clearly, asking me to trust her, and I felt like crying. Even if things might have been different, under other circumstances, I was her teacher. I was not free from consequences, simply because I was in a foreign country. I was here for a particular reason, playing a particular role. Not to mention the fact that I was sitting in her grandmother's backyard.

I removed June's hand. "I'm sorry."

"I won't tell anyone," she said.

I looked at June, who was smiling at me as if she already knew my secret. If she wanted to know, and I wanted to tell her, what could the harm be? I couldn't tell her everything, of course, but I could give her this one, inconsequential piece of information, as long as I made a promise to myself. I would never again spend time with June outside of school, and therefore things would have no way of going any further. I would have this dreamlike moment in the aviary to remember, and she would satisfy her curiosity—or at least a piece of it. As long as I stuck to my resolution, everything would be fine.

"I'm the rabbit," I said. "Intuitive and creative. Also, honest. Not that I subscribe to this stuff."

"Of course not," June said, smiling, and I couldn't help it: I put my palm against her face and kissed her. It was only a couple of seconds; her mouth was soft and hot, almost feverish. I never felt that we were doing something wrong. I was so happy when we pulled away from each other that I laughed. It seemed appropriate there should be birdsong.

"Ni choo-choo ba," June said.

"You want me to go away?"

"No," June said. "I just felt like saying something to you in Chinese."

I'd been afraid she would be angry, or upset, but it was just the opposite. It was as if she'd experienced the same feeling I had. I thought: *She knows me.*

"We have to be careful!" I said ecstatically.

"OK," said June.

"I think we should go inside now!"

June picked up the lantern. The birds seemed to follow her movements, making small nighttime sounds and shifting on their perches. They had finished gorging themselves at the feeders; yellow seed was scattered in the gravel under our feet. June unlatched the gate to her aviary and then paused, holding up the light.

"Can I ask you a favor?"

"I won't say anything," I promised. "And even though I'm very—fond of you, and I think you have a terrific future" (what was I talking about?)

"I want you to know that *this* doesn't—have a future, I mean. It won't happen again, no matter what—"

"OK." June smiled. "But that's not what I was going to say."

I felt like an idiot.

"I was going to ask—could you teach me to speak some Chinese?"

I could think of few more pleasurable activities. But I had to be cautious. Language lessons, although they could occur on-campus, would certainly involve individual instruction. Under those circumstances, would I be able to stick to my resolution?

"I'm sure your grandmother would be happy to teach you," I suggested.

"She wouldn't teach me the right words," June said. "I would learn to speak like a *lao taitai*."

"That's good. You know some Chinese words already."

"That's the name of a cake," June said.

"Do you like those?" I had a sudden craving for one of the flaky "old wives' " cakes, filled with melon paste and stamped with a cheerful red seal.

June made a face. "They look cool," she said. "But they taste like soap."

51.

TWO MONTHS AND THREE DAYS AFTER HE ARRIVED IN LOS ANGELES, Phil got the phone call. Or rather, he got a brief message from Kiss Me, Kill Me Productions (he was in the shower, the only time he didn't have his phone nearby) with directions to a house in the fashionable district just east of La Brea, where Keith and Steve would be "hanging out." If "by any chance" he was free next Thursday, he was welcome to show up and help. If not, "no worries"—they'd do it another time. Phil felt it was better not to call right back, and managed to wait seven minutes before dialing Steve's number, which went straight to voice mail. Thursday, it turned out, was good for Phil.

The night before he was supposed to meet them, Phil had trouble sleeping. He finally drifted off at three o'clock, and was woken two hours later by Aubrey, who had forgotten (or pretended to forget) the time difference.

"Were you sleeping? I'm sorry," she said. "But we have to figure out Thanksgiving. If I'm coming out there, I have to give Bruce at least three weeks notice, and the ticket's going to be expensive."

It was still dark out. He had slept for exactly two hours and fifteen minutes. "Who's Bruce?"

"The partner on the AT&T case. If you don't know that, you haven't been listening to me for the past six months."

"Look," Phil said. "I don't know if Thanksgiving is going to work out."

"Hold on, hold on—I'm getting some coffee."

He heard the morning rush at the local nonfranchised place, and Aubrey saying, "Excuse me, sorry," in a sweet, friendly way. She was probably talking to a man. Probably a man in a suit, with a perky, bright-colored shirt. A hedge fund manager who lived downtown and did interesting drugs in his fabulous duplex. Phil wasn't jealous so much as envious of the opportunity the stranger had, to notice the mysterious, original Aubrey who had first captivated him, before everything became so complicated.

"Sorry," Aubrey said in her ordinary voice. "It's going to be expensive, but you coming here would be the same thing, and I feel bad I've never done it with your family, since you've done it with mine a million times—"

For a woman talented with numbers, it was amazing how twice could suddenly become "a million." She had manufactured a million dollars for him, however, out of the air; perhaps it was silly to fight it.

"Unless you wanted to just come here, and we wouldn't have to go to my mom's. Maybe it would be nice to have it just the two of us—in the apartment?"

Phil thought of the two of them in the apartment: candles, a meal that referenced Thanksgiving without in fact being a Thanksgiving dinner, a pregnant pause, a pause in which Aubrey thought about pregnancy . . .

"I don't know what you had planned?"

"I don't have anything planned." Perhaps he sounded too insistent.

"What a surprise," Aubrey said.

There was a long silence. There was no way he was going to go back to sleep after this.

"Well, I'm going into the subway now," Aubrey said. "I need to know by the end of the day."

"What a surprise," said Phil, but she had already clicked out.

52.

WHEN HE ARRIVED AT THE ORANGE BUNGALOW, THE HOUSE WAS DARK, but as he approached, he heard a steady bass beat coming from somewhere inside. His heart sank—the fact that he couldn't get into hip-hop was a serious failing. He heard it coming from Max's part of the house, and felt envious. (Another failing was his affection for Billy Joel, especially the ballad "The Longest Time," which Aubrey had gleefully caught him humming on more than one occasion, after they'd had the misfortune to hear it in a taxi.)

Phil rang the bell, knocked, and then noticed that the door was ajar, an intimidation tactic that forced a visitor to wander through your house like a thief until he found and inevitably startled you, ensuring an unpleasant beginning to whatever social interaction you were about to embark upon. Phil shut the door behind him: there was no point in calling out over the furious music. He could see how inner-city youth could be this furious—but a couple of twenty-nine-year-old Ivy League graduates, making upwards of a hundred thousand dollars a year in a city full of aspiring actresses? He didn't get it. When he had lived here, in his tiny studio in Mount Washington, coming to West Los Angeles always made him feel like he had wandered onto a movie set, a place where the bartenders, the salesgirls, and even the parking attendants were all played by actors.

"Hello," he shouted.

The music was lowered to an outraged whisper. "Yeah? Jorge?"

"It's Phil—Phil Travers."

"Phil? We're in here."

He went through the living room, large, empty, and shuttered, and stepped down into an open kitchen, also dark, where two sleepy-looking young men were sitting at an island with a black marble top, facing an enormous television hooked up to a slick video game console. A box of Cap'n Crunch was on the counter between them.

"Sorry," said the taller, blonder one, getting up. "We thought you were our gardener." He was wearing a T-shirt that said "Sailing the Seas of Cheese," and a pair of board shorts. "I'm Steve, this is Keith."

Keith raised one hand and turned back to the screen. At least they didn't look alike. Keith was more what Phil had expected, with curly dark hair, freckles, and a squint, whereas Steve looked like some kind of teen-age pop idol.

"Sorry about the dark," Steve said, nodding his head toward the TV. "Glare."

"This is so awesome," Keith said. "Ghost in the Shell was awesome, but this Korean action is something fucking else. Fucking Kiss Me, Kill Me? Shit."

Phil was confused. "That's your company, right?"

Keith emitted a kind of strangled laugh; the screen exploded in green fire.

"Also a Korean comic book," Steve said gently. Of the two of them, he seemed the more sympathetic. "Are you a fan of *manhwa*, by any chance?"

"Is that this band?"

Keith looked away from the screen for the first time. "What?"

"Sorry," said Phil. "What's *manhwa*?"

"Korean comic books," Steve explained. "A lot of them have been turned into cartoons. It's kind of a cult thing."

"Manga!" Phil said. "I've heard of that."

"That's Japanese," Keith said, disgusted.

There were footsteps upstairs, and a pair of long, tanned legs appeared on the spiral staircase, followed by slim hips, large but perky breasts, dra-matic dark eyes, and thick, honey-colored hair: in short, a knockout. She was carrying a rolled-up exercise mat under one arm.

She looked from Keith to Phil and Steve to the television and sighed.

"This is disgusting."

Keith flipped off the TV, and Steve started opening the drapes. Two sets of French doors were revealed, leading out to a backyard with a dark blue, kidney-shaped pool.

"I'm Leona," the woman said, pronouncing it in an appealing South American way. "You must be the other writer for the movie without a name."

"It's called *The Hypnotist*," Phil said. He didn't want to stare, but he was finding it difficult to look away.

"We were thinking of changing that, actually," Keith said.

"Changing the title?"

Steve and Keith exchanged a glance. "It's just that—"

"That's cool," Phil said. "I never really liked the title."

"Yeah?" said Steve. "Because we were thinking of punching up the shrink a little."

"Making him more of a kind of cult leader."

"A cult leader?"

"I'm going outside for stretching now," Leona said. "Please don't drink my kefir, Keith."

"Of course not," said Keith.

"Bye," said Leona, giving Steve a little wave: she was dressed entirely in loose white cotton, with a black leotard underneath—the kind of outfit that made you want to become a cult leader.

"What's kefir?" asked Keith.

"It's like yogurt," Steve said.

"Shit," said Keith.

"Leona is from Rio," Steve said proudly. "But she's interested in the California lifestyle—you know, yoga, organic food, shiatsu." Outside, Leona had taken off everything but her leotard and inverted her body on the purple mat. The pool sparkled in the background like an advertisement for a vacation. How stupid people were, choosing to live anywhere besides Los Angeles.

"We're supposed to make it a little edgier." Keith reached into the box for another handful of Cap'n Crunch. "A little more dangerous."

"We need to find the MacGuffin," Steve said.

"That would be OK," said Phil. "I think a MacGuffin would be good."

"Yeah?" said Keith. "Because maybe it could be a kind of survivalist cult. Maybe on an island—like Catalina?"

"*Catalina?*" Steve said. "How could there be a survivalist cult on Catalina? There's a fucking ferry twenty times a day."

"OK, OK." Keith looked annoyed.

"It has to be more remote," Steve said. "What's that island in New York called?"

"Manhattan?"

Keith laughed. "Hey—this guy's funny."

Phil felt wonderful. They were bonding. The age difference didn't matter. He imagined the three of them inhaling Cap'n Crunch, punching up *The Hypnotist*—terrible title anyway—and talking about girls. He pictured them doing whiskey shooters in a Hollywood dive bar with Leona and a couple of her friends. He saw himself with a Brazilian on each arm, discussing *manhwa*.

"Not Manhattan," Steve said. "The other one."

"Long Island!" Keith said. "That's good."

"Long Island isn't actually—" Phil began and stopped. It would be a shame to interrupt, now that they were really rolling.

"A survivalist cult on Long Island," Steve suggested. "Darcy gets lured out there by the guru—"

"What's her name?" Keith asked.

"Celine," Phil said. "But we can—"

"Change that," said Steve. "Right."

"And he's experimenting with her head," Keith continued.

"And it's after Y2K, so everyone thinks the world is totally fucked."

"Dude? Maybe you missed it? Y2K didn't *happen*."

"That's the point." Steve smiled. "They don't know. It's after Y2K, but they still *think* everything's fucked. Only the guru knows, and you see him going into town and having a beer or something—"

"Wait," said Keith. "Does Long Island have towns?"

"Quite a few," Phil said.

Steve turned to Phil with concern. "Is this getting too far away from your play?"

Phil had hung out with Steve, Keith, and Leona all afternoon. They had taken a swim (except for Phil, who didn't have a bathing suit), drank a pitcher of sangria, and debated various names for the cult leader.

"We want something evil," Keith said. "Like Colonel Moon."

"I don't think this one can be Korean," Steve said.

"*Your* name is evil," Leona told Phil. She was standing in the shallow end, rippling the surface of the water with her fingertips. The lower half of her body wavered underwater, like a fantasy on TV.

"Mine?"

"It sounds a little evil—in Spanish." Leona smiled. "*Travieso, travesura.*"

"That means evil?" Phil asked. Was she flirting with him?

"Leona speaks Portuguese, Spanish, and English," Steve remarked. "She's only twenty, and she's already written a telenovela."

Leona splashed some water at Steve. Then she turned to Phil, and made an inch with her fingers: "A *little* evil. A mischief—like a little monkey." Then she sank down into the water, her hair floating for a moment before dipping beneath the surface.

"I'm going to ask her to marry me," Steve said, once Leona was underwater. "What do you think?"

The afternoon had ended with plans to meet up over the weekend in a pool hall off Sunset where Steve knew the bartender, so that they could "spitball" about the new storyline. Leona would join them, in order to offer the female perspective.

"Where's the bar, exactly?" Phil asked.

Steve looked at Keith.

"Dude—if you want to come, be our guest," Keith said. "But you might be kind of—uncomfortable."

"He doesn't want to hear us mutilating his art." Steve smiled companionably at Phil. "Better to take it all in one blow, at the end. Then you can offer suggestions."

"It was nice to meet you," Leona said. "I hope your movie is a big success."

Probably the fact that Leona was underage would be no problem at the pool hall. Probably it was only overage drinkers who had to worry.

The three of them saw Phil out, watching while he backed Cece's matronly Mercedes into the narrow street. He felt ominously tired. What was wrong with him? He forced himself to recall the sight of Leona, climbing out of the pool in what must have been a genuinely Brazilian bikini, and instead saw Keith's pale, underdeveloped chest and self-satisfied leer. His lust, he was horrified to discover, was directed not at Steve's girlfriend but at his house and his pool, his palms, red hibiscus, and birds-of-paradise. The door closed behind them, and Phil idled for a moment, straining to see through the thick front hedge, but except for a flash of chlorinated blue, sparkling in between the leaves, that lush landscape was completely hidden from the street.

53.

THE WEEKS LEADING UP TO MY SHOW PASSED QUICKLY, EACH ONE
faster than the last. I tried to ignore it—teaching my class, working on my
scroll, and, on Tuesday and Thursday afternoons, staying late at St. Anselm's to instruct June in Mandarin Chinese. I clung to the resolution I'd
made that night in the aviary, and was even a little cold with her, but what
had happened between us had removed a boundary. Although there was
no more physical contact, June now felt free to address me as a peer. Her
questions became more personal, about my family and my life in China,
and were therefore more difficult to answer. The single subject that seemed
to be off-limits was my visit to her house; she mentioned it only once—
and that was in order to correct me.

"Xiao Pangzi isn't a name," she said one afternoon in early November,
when we were alone in the classroom.

"It's a kind of family nickname," I said. "More personal."

But June shook her head. "My grandmother says there are a million
'Little Fatties' in China."

I was impressed that she'd been able to remember the name "Xiao
Pangzi" well enough to repeat it to her grandmother. "You already know
my name," I told her. "There are a million other Yuan Zhaos, too."

June looked at me critically. "But I wasn't asking about them."

On afternoons when I didn't see June, I worked on my project in the Traverses' pool house. Many afternoons, Cece or the lady novelist came to
look at the scroll, which had extended now to six panels. I didn't mind
their visits so much anymore. To be honest, I was proud of my work. I had

ideas about my painting when I was doing other things: looking over my students' portfolios, doing my exercises in the morning (on the floor of my bedroom, now that the weather had finally turned chilly), or even soaping my body in the luxurious shower. Sometimes in my head I added things that were not in the original, a few saplings on the bank of the stream, or a teahouse high up on a distant mountain, with a tiny pilgrim making the steep ascent.

These additions were fantasies, of course, and when I sat down at my easel, I didn't depart from Zhao Cangyun's masterpiece. It was only that my mind returned so often to the painting that the world inside it seemed to expand; I couldn't help thinking of what lay beyond the last hill, or behind the half-glimpsed gate. I almost wished it were the scroll I would be exhibiting at UCLA in two weeks, rather than the famous *DNA-ture* paintings, which I had transported so carefully across the ocean.

"Why did you call it that?" June asked me one afternoon, peering at the announcement card on my desk. We were supposed to be studying from a textbook June's grandmother had supplied. Each chapter began with a list of vocabulary words related to a subject, such as "Sports," "Talking About the Weather," or "At the Beijing Post Office."

Since none of these subjects was especially interesting to me or my student, we were not making very speedy progress.

"The paintings are based on cells," I told her. "The smallest units of life."

"Cells aren't the same as DNA."

"But they're a pattern that represents human life. That's what the paintings are too."

"What about the 'Nature' part?"

"I made these paintings a long time ago," I said. "I barely remember."

"Not that long," June said. "Ten years, right?"

The way she was pestering me about my show, it was almost as if she suspected something. I dreaded the thought of June in the gallery looking at the paintings. Whatever humiliation I might suffer in front of Harry Lin, I thought June's presence would compound it. It was the same feeling I'd had the first time she looked at my work, the lobster I had painted in

Olivia's sketchpad: I was sorry that I hadn't spent my whole life trying to become the kind of person she'd admire.

"Let's focus on the lesson," I said, perhaps more sharply than necessary: "Celebrating a birthday."

But June had got up, and was examining her classmates' creations, displayed on the fancy wooden easels. She stopped in front of Emily Alderman's workspace, and began flipping through a sketchpad of dully competent watercolor landscapes.

"Did you really like those Color and Design paintings?" she asked.

"I thought they were very good," I said, perhaps overstating the case. I thought June had been harsh with Emily regarding those paintings, and that no matter how advanced she was, it was wrong of her to put down the other students' work. "They showed she'd been looking at art."

"They showed she'd been looking at Mondrian," June said. "She copied."

"They weren't exact copies," I said. "And anyway, copying is one way to learn. Just like with languages."

June made a skeptical noise, but she returned to the desk and sat down next to me. She leaned on her arms, allowing her elbow just slightly to touch mine. I was better prepared than I'd been the other night for the feeling her skin gave me; if June noticed, she pretended not to, staring dutifully down at chapter 3. Flipping forward, I had noticed with apprehension that the subject of chapter 17 was "Dating." Luckily, we were moving extremely slowly.

"Listen and repeat," I said, moving my arm away from hers. "*Jintian shi Xiao Lin de shengri.*"

"Jin-tian-shi—"

"Xiao Lin," I prompted.

"Show leen."

"*Xiao Lin* de sheng ri."

"*Show leen* de sheng ri." June looked up: "But I bet Emily didn't destroy those paintings."

"Focus on the lesson," I said.

June gave me an innocent smile. "How do you say 'fish' in Chinese?"

54.

CECE HAD INFORMED THE PRINCIPAL ABOUT MY SHOW, AND MS. MCCOY
had obtained her own stack of printed announcements from UCLA. She
had posted these on bulletin boards throughout the school, so that by
Monday everyone knew where and when my work would be displayed.

"We're all coming to your show on Friday, Mr. Jow," Holly said that
afternoon. "We can't wait to see your paintings!"

"You should only come if you've finished your homework," I said.
"Please don't make your parents go out of their way."

Emily raised her hand, but didn't wait for me to call on her. "We have
a show too, Mr. Yuan. Our dance concert is December 11. Will you
come?"

"Of course," I said. "That's the same day your Sesqui—" I stopped; for
whatever reason, I never succeeded in saying this English word. "—your
projects for Mrs. Diller are due."

"Sesquicenterpieces," June supplied. I was surprised to hear her take
an interest in the sesquicentennial contest, which I would've expected her
to scorn. I was sure that the other girls had ignored it, and in this case I
couldn't say that I blamed them.

Still, I felt an obligation to produce some entries. "That's right," I said.
"Vice Principal Diller asked me to remind you."

June returned her attention to her net, which seemed to be going
through a repetitive cycle. One day it would be small, covering her lap
like an old lady's crocheting. A few days later it would be a skirt, and
after a week it would be hanging all around her stool, gossamer puddles
on the dirty linoleum. I thought she was doing the same project again

and again, until one day after school I saw her knotting two pieces together: in fact it was a very large net she was making, one small section at a time.

I had seen artists who became involved in this kind of mind-numbing mechanical labor as a way of postponing their real work. If June really needed an enormous net, she might have bought one in any hardware store. Emily seemed to agree with me, because she suddenly turned and addressed June directly:

"Is that what that is?"

"What?"

"Your *Sesquicenterpiece*. Are you making a big net for Mrs. Diller?" There was giggling at this admittedly appealing thought.

"No," June said.

"I'm sure you'll win, if you are." The girls covered their mouths, emphasizing rather than hiding their amusement. I had the urge to intercede, but something stopped me. Ever since I'd seen the shadow of Violante in Catherine's portrait, I couldn't help seeing it on Emily's face as well. The analogy wasn't comforting.

"I'm not."

"Well then, what is that?"

"It's a net."

"Uh-huh," Emily said. "But what's it *for*?"

I was accustomed to thinking of June as something special, a kind of genius, and I couldn't believe that these girls had the power to disturb her. I was therefore surprised to see her edging off the stool, one toe on the floor, allowing her net to fall from her lap and a whole row of knots to slip loose, a half hour's labor. She blushed in cartoonish spots, like a Roy Lichtenstein; if she could have escaped from the studio at that moment, I believe she gladly would've abandoned all of her work behind her.

What I did next, I did to help her—which illustrates how little I had learned from my fellowship in Los Angeles.

"It's for the birds," I said. I did not mean to speak idiomatically, but the moment the words were out, my English ear heard them that way. I didn't really think that June was making the net for her aviary: I believed she was doing it because she had to, even if she wasn't sure what she would eventually use it for. I didn't think that "for" was particularly important to June.

"For her aviary," I corrected myself. "June keeps birds."

This time I didn't understand the giggling. Ornithology seemed a perfectly innocuous hobby, even an admirable one. It had occurred to me that I would never have had the patience for the daily monitoring, feeding, and sweeping of shit that the aviary required; I'd always preferred photographs and Audubon's renderings to the messy, frenetic creatures themselves.

"Her *aviary*," someone said. "Can June do birdcalls?"

And, "June, can we come over and see your zoo?"

If Mrs. Diller had entered the art studio at that moment, she would've found unacceptable chaos. Of all the girls, only Emily remained calm, raising her hand and looking seriously in my direction.

"Emily?" I called, hoping the class would quiet down out of respect. And sure enough, Emily waited until she had their attention:

"How do you know?"

"Excuse me?"

"About the aviary. Have you seen it?"

I must've hesitated too long. I watched this error register on Emily's sharp features, and a second later, on the cluster of faces around her. The idea that one of their classmates had been socializing with a teacher after school, particularly a male teacher, was too suggestive to ignore. Even if my visit with June had been completely innocent, the other students wouldn't have seen it that way.

"June's grandmother is an old friend of mine, from China," I said quickly. "I saw June's aviary once while I was visiting her." But the bell was ringing, and no one was listening. I hoped that the girls would forget the little scene, the way they seemed to forget what they had been doing at the end of every class period, as if each bell erased the previous hour and allowed them to begin again from scratch.

Of course that had never been true of June, who hurried out of the classroom, for the first time leaving her net in a heap on the floor. I had to restrain myself, waiting for the chattering pack of girls to leave the room, before bending down to smooth and fold it up.

55.

I WAITED UNTIL THERE WERE ONLY A FEW WEEKS BEFORE THE ART SHOW to begin worrying in earnest. (That is typical of me.) I hadn't heard from Harry Lin since his letter in early September, and all that time I'd been hoping that something would happen to get in the way of the show. Maybe the professor would decide that ten-year-old work was too stale for an American audience after all, or perhaps he had discovered an exciting new painter in the months since my arrival, who would preempt me. Even when I saw the fancy announcements, I still didn't believe I was going to be honored. Perhaps the professor could simply exhibit *DNA-ture* without me? He would apologize to the audience, and explain that the artist had been forced to return to China (leaving them free to imagine some vague and ominous political persecution), or he might describe the decision as my own choice, a personal passion to "Keep Chinese Art in China."

As November 22 approached, and Harry didn't call, however, I became more and more anxious. I will not bore you by recounting my dreams during this period, except to say that many of them took place in cavernous white galleries, where a tall, thin Chinese man performed introduction after introduction: *May I introduce the world-famous artist, Little Fatty! I give you, ladies and gentlemen, the Lobster Hermit!* The night before my show, waking up from a particularly unsettling version of this dream—in which Harry Lin, disguised as a PLA soldier, turned from the podium to embrace June Wang—I could not fall back to sleep. After lying there for more than an hour, I turned on the light and dialed the familiar number.

"I can't do it," I said, when he answered.

"Do what?" X asked.

It was three in the morning, L.A. time, three in the afternoon in Beijing. Fourteen hours later, *Yuan Zhao: DNA-ture* would open at the Fowler Museum of Art. I would be the guest of honor, and my cousin would be asleep.

"I can't do the show."

"The what? You're breaking up."

"The *show*."

"What time is it there?" X said. "You sound tired."

"I'm wide awake," I told him. "There are going to be dozens of people there—maybe a hundred."

"I hope at least a hundred," X joked. "Otherwise, what've you been doing over there?"

"My hosts will be there," I said. "Also my students." There was one student I thought of in particular, but after the incident in class the other day, I wasn't expecting her. I wished that were more of a consolation.

"It will be inspiring for them," X said gravely.

"It will be humiliating," I said. "They're expecting someone else—an artist."

"You have no confidence," X said. "How can you be an artist without confidence?"

"I'm not an artist."

"You've been painting, haven't you?"

"Not anything Harry Lin would be interested in," I said. A part of me wanted to tell X about *Liu Chen and Ruan Zhao in the Tiantai Mountains*: how I could lose myself in the roots of a tree, or an outcropping of mossy rock. But I restrained myself. My cousin would want to know why I cared to spend months copying when I could be making something new. It was the same question June Wang had asked, and I'd had only the most pedagogical of answers. Perhaps the truth was that copying was what the talentless did. It was up to the real artists to make new things.

"I'm not sure how much longer I can do this," I told my cousin.

"I'm having trouble hearing you," X said.

"I'm thinking of disappearing into the mountains," I told him. Longxia Shanren, I thought, the Lobster Hermit—going back into his shell.

"Don't go anywhere before tomorrow night," X warned. "Everyone's expecting you."

I hung up the phone. I could feel rather than hear a beat coming from Max's headphones in the next room. I was listening to that sound, the house's pulse, when something occurred to me. It wasn't a new or particularly original idea; in fact it was a version of the same thought I'd been having since I sat on the fountain outside Beijing Normal so many years ago, and watched people streaming past the gates. The difference was that now I was prepared to act. People's expectations didn't matter. First thing tomorrow morning I would go to UCLA and find the professor. If Harry Lin wasn't going to call off the show, I would do it myself.

Why did I suddenly feel confident enough to betray my hosts, not to mention my illustrious academic sponsor, Harry Lin? I wasn't sure, but as my mind finally decelerated into sleep, I seemed to see a kind of billboard, hovering over the intersection between wakefulness and dreams. Although I couldn't remember the words of its message the next morning, I retained an image: my two travelers, Liu Chen and Ruan Zhao, ascending a mountain, accompanied by a young female companion who bore a striking resemblance to my student, June Wang.

56.

WHEN I ARRIVED AT THE GALLERY ON THE MORNING OF MY SHOW, SOME
students were busy painting the walls. One of them was standing on a ladder, stenciling large letters in a deep vermilion: "Yuan Zhao: DNA-ture."
For a moment, I stood in the hushed interior, watching him work, savor-
ing the experience of walking into the preparations for my own show. The
feeling was so intense that it took me a moment to notice another person,
a man sitting with his back to me in a glass-enclosed office at the back of
the gallery.

The student on the ladder paused and looked down: "Can I help
you?"

"I'm here to see Professor Lin," I told him.

"Is he expecting you?"

"No," I said, glancing toward the office. This was it: the professor had
heard us talking and was getting up. "I don't have an appointment.
I'm—"

But at that moment the glass door opened, and I saw I had made a
mistake. The one thing I remembered from my brief conversation with
Professor Lin years ago in Beijing was his height; by contrast, the man
coming toward me was short, handsome, and solidly muscled. He was
much younger than the professor, and was wearing a blazer over a T-shirt
and jeans, with a university ID on a cord around his neck.

"Mr. Yuan? I thought that might be you!" He continued formally, in
Chinese: "I am Martin Lu. I'm pleased and honored to meet you. I will
serve as your interpreter tonight."

"My interpreter?"

"I am extremely sorry that Professor Lin is not here now. He is sick in his—" Martin struggled, and resorted to an English word: "Sciatic. I'm sure he will be sorry to have missed you, but he wants to be very healthy for your opening."

"Never mind," I said. The two students working on the stencils were watching me while pretending to keep busy—as if I were some kind of celebrity. I felt defeated. I'd been steeling myself for the meeting, which would be difficult, but would at least remove the primary difficulty of *DNA-ture*. Now I was back where I started: how could I cancel the show if the professor wasn't even here?

"I apologize for my putonghua," Martin continued. "I understand better than I speak."

"You speak very well," I said. "Although I suspect you might find better uses for your time. I would be perfectly comfortable speaking English at the reception." That is, I thought, if the reception were going to take place at all.

Martin stared at me. "That's incredible," he said, switching to English. "Don't tell me you've picked that up in the last couple months?"

"You know what they say: you have to immerse yourself."

"Wait until I tell Harry. I'm sorry he's not here, but selfishly I'm glad to get a minute with you before the show. I have to tell you—I love your work." Martin suddenly looked shy. "Actually my dissertation is about the East Village, your performances in particular."

"My performances?"

"My favorites are *Something That Is Not Art* and *Drip-Drop*. I wanted to ask about the Ping-Pong table, whether that was part of the project from its initial conception, or something you came up with later . . . ?"

"It came from the hospital where a friend of ours was working," I said. "We got it at the last minute."

"From a *hospital*," Martin repeated, as if I'd just confided the identity of the *Mona Lisa*. "That's *terrific*. Harry absolutely forbade me from getting in touch with you before the show, but I've been dying to talk with you. Maybe next week sometime, if you could spare a half hour?"

"Next week would be fine."

"Great!" Martin was staring at me in a way that made me feel uncomfortable, as if he knew more about me than I knew myself. I imagine that's something celebrities have to contend with all the time: their fans have an unshakable impression of them before they've even met them. Even if the reality doesn't conform to those expectations, a true devotee won't be disappointed by the discrepancies. He simply won't see them.

"I love *DNA-ture*," Martin continued. "But I have to admit, I wish we were showing the performance work instead."

I should have been concentrating on how to find Harry Lin, but I enjoyed talking with Martin Lu, who reminded me of myself as a university student. I don't mean in his dress or mannerisms, which were completely American, but in the way he sounded when he asked about *Drip-Drop*. It seemed to mean something personal and concrete to him. I was curious to know more about what Martin thought of the East Village artists, especially of my cousin X.

"How could we have shown my performance work?" I asked him.

"We could've shown the photos?" His tentativeness suggested that he was aware of the controversy surrounding Tianming's photos of the East Village.

"Where did you see those photographs?" I asked him.

"Oh—I've practically been living with them for the last year. I'm Harry's research assistant for *Tianming's East Village*."

"Tianming's East Village?"

"For the book. We've gone through so many arrangements with the plates, but finally we decided that a chronological—" Martin saw my expression and stopped.

"Harry is working with Zhang Tianming on a book about the East Village?"

Martin blanched. "Oh—I . . ."

"Is it called *Tianming's East Village*?"

Martin sounded desperate. "Mr. Yuan—I'm so sorry. I had no idea you didn't know about Harry's book, or I wouldn't've said anything. I know he meant to tell you himself, but maybe he was waiting until after the show, so that you . . ." Martin's voice trailed off, and he looked as if he were becoming increasingly frightened of what he had done.

I thought of the first time I had met the photographer, that cold November afternoon on my way to *Something That Is Not Art.* Tianming had seemed to appear out of nowhere, from the cold fog of the village, to send me on the right path. There had been no stream to cross, no peach tree, and no stone arch, but when I followed the photographer's directions I had indeed found myself in another world.

"The book is just one perspective," Martin continued anxiously. "Your performances are another. And even these paintings—"

"I think *Tianming's East Village* is a great title."

Martin hesitated. "You do?"

"The East Village only exists in Tianming's photographs. Where else is it? It's a kind of legend now—who knows if it was ever there at all?"

Martin smiled, but I could tell he didn't like this kind of joke. He was a scholar—shy and deferential, but with an academic's vanity. He wanted all of the precise details I could give him about the groundbreaking community and the radical activities of its inhabitants in the years 1993–94. He didn't want airy speculations or stories, and who could blame him? You could hardly write a dissertation about a place that was never there.

"I want you to know," he continued seriously, "I don't think there's any question of authorship. I mean, the portraits are one thing, but the photographs of your performances? *Modern Dance,* and *Drip-Drop,* and *Something That Is Not Art?* How could those be anything but yours?"

"Thank you," I said.

"Harry might feel differently. And I know I'm just a graduate student, but . . ."

"That doesn't matter," I told him. "You shouldn't be afraid to say what you think—why should your opinion matter less than anybody else's?"

Martin beamed; the student-painters looked on enviously; and all of a sudden I wondered whether I might not attend this art show after all. Once a work of art is finished, the artist is in any case superfluous. He may follow the work around a few paces behind, like an abandoned lover, but his claim is nostalgic at best. Tonight I would return to stand beside these paintings and, if there was sufficient interest, perhaps say a word or two about the dramatic time and place in which they were conceived. What artist could do more?

"It's so great to finally meet you," Martin said. "And I have to admit, I'm relieved I'll be speaking English tonight." He shook his head: "Is Harry ever going to be surprised!"

"Yes," I said. "He certainly is."

57.

WHEN I ARRIVED, THE GALLERY WAS ALREADY FULL OF PEOPLE. THE TRA-
verses had dropped me in front of the entrance while they parked the car,
and I'd thought I might slip in unnoticed, but I was wrong. Everyone recognized me as the famous dissident, in spite of my haircut, my conservative dress shirt and plain black trousers. On this one point, I reflected, my
cousin had been mistaken. In Los Angeles there was no need to keep your
hair long or wear silk pajamas; in fact, the less noteworthy you looked, the
more authentic people were likely to find you.

Congratulations. A woman touched my arm. *I love your work,* said
someone else. *I so admire your political commitment . . . your use of
color . . . your unique emotional style . . .* In that moment, I wished for my
mother. I wanted her to see the table with its symmetrical cups of red
and white wine, its cubes of orange and white cheese, its twin heaps of
green and purple grapes. I thought the bottles of Californian wine and
imported water were at least as beautiful as the paintings, a few of which
I could see behind the immaculate white wall. This was exactly what she
had always imagined for me, and as people swarmed in front of that wall,
obscuring the text in tall, red letters, all of my mother's dreams were
realized.

"Mr. Yuan!"

I looked up to see Martin Lu, waving frantically and making his way
through the crowd. Right behind him was a tall Chinese man, with
thinning hair, sloping shoulders, and a shy, oval face dignified by a pair
of wire-rimmed glasses. Harry Lin hadn't changed since his visit to the
East Village in the spring of '94. We had been eagerly awaiting him—a

Chinese professor from a distinguished American university—and we all had been a little disappointed when he finally arrived, by his modesty and his shabby clothes. Of course we warmed up right away when the professor raved in print about our collaborative performance piece, *Drip-Drop,* and called *Lu Kou* "the best new journal of Chinese experimental art."

Harry's eyes met mine, and the blood rose to my face. Did he remember me? Shouldn't I have known for sure? His smile implied recognition, but it had been seven years since he'd met me, and I'd been naked at the time, apart from a pair of satin boxing shorts.

"Here you are!" Martin exclaimed. "Say something to Harry—he doesn't believe me!"

"Hello," I said.

"Hello," Harry said. "Welcome."

"I was afraid you wouldn't recognize me," I said.

"It hasn't been that long," said Harry.

"He just picked it up, staying with the Traverses," Martin said. "Isn't that amazing?"

Harry did not comment on my incredible English. "How are you enjoying your stay?" he asked instead. "You're still comfortable?"

From across the room, I could see my hosts talking with some of Dr. Travers's colleagues. Next to them, the lady novelist was trying to catch my eye.

"Very," I said, turning back to Harry. "I'm afraid I don't deserve their hospitality." I was waiting for some sign from him, but the professor was unreadable. Martin Lu might have been praising my English, but for the first time since I'd arrived in Los Angeles, I felt at a real disadvantage speaking that language. A few words from Harry in our own tongue, and it seemed to me I would've known immediately where I stood.

Harry put a hand on my arm (he was several inches taller than I was) and steered me toward another group. "Let me introduce Dr. Mandelbaum—also from Visual Art," he said. "And Dr. Khan from Asian Studies."

Dr. Khan shook my hand.

"It's a tremendous pleasure, Dr. Yuan," said Dr. Mandelbaum.

"I can't pretend to be a professor," I said quickly. "Especially with so many real ones around."

"Nonsense," said Dr. Mandelbaum. "Who would want to be a professor of art, when you could be an actual artist?"

"That's right," Harry said. "I still think about one of his first pieces, in its debut performance in Beijing. It was called *Drip-Drop*."

"It was a collaboration," I mumbled. If the professor was making fun of me, he was doing it very subtly. He seemed to be studying me: it was almost as if our positions were reversed, and he was trying to figure out how much I knew about *him*.

"You should see the photographs," Martin told Dr. Khan. "They're going to be published in Harry's new book."

"Martin thought you would object to the title," Harry said, turning to me. "I told him I thought you were more thick-skinned than that."

"Are you still doing performance-based work?" Dr. Khan asked politely.

This was a question I could answer: I explained that there would be no more projects like *Drip-Drop*, *Something That Is Not Art*, and *Walking Up Coal Hill with Candles*, since that work was decidedly site-specific. Even when they didn't take place in our neighborhood, those projects grew out of the East Village, like misshapen vegetables from toxic soil. Once their substrate was destroyed, the performances stopped; even the artists who were still prolific were not doing collaborative work anymore. That kind of art seemed to belong to another time.

To my surprise, Harry Lin disagreed. "I'm not sure about that. You may have turned away from performance-based work, but have all of the East Village artists?" He paused and looked around, including the others in the debate. "What about your cousin?"

In that instant my heart began to slam against my chest, so violently that it seemed impossible no one else could hear it. The crowd around me appeared to press closer.

"He also works alone," I said, but it came out sounding like a question.

"Who is your cousin?" Martin Lu asked eagerly. "Would I have heard of him?" The room, which had been very loud before, now quieted dramatically, as if everyone were waiting for me to answer that question.

I looked at Harry, and then I saw the reason for the sudden calm: the professor was about to make a speech.

"Excuse me a moment. It's time for me to introduce you." As Harry made his way to the podium, everyone in the room turned to look—not at him, but at me. I fought the urge to close my eyes, like a child who hides by covering his own face. Instead I stared at the floor: it was gray concrete, marbled with white, exactly like the one in Tianming's old apartment. I wished, more than anything, to be back there.

I heard Harry Lin welcoming the guests, and thanking the benefactors of the Dubin Fellowship. Then he began to give a brief history of Chinese experimental art. Now everyone was paying attention to the professor, and so I was able to look around for my students: I saw Olivia standing with Katie and Holly, holding plastic cups of wine surreptitiously at their sides, and Catherine standing with her redheaded family near the door. As I'd expected, there was no sign of June, nor was Emily Alderman anywhere in evidence.

At first I allowed Harry's speech to wash over me, grateful for the respite from questioning. But as he continued, I began to listen more carefully. Although this was a show of acrylics, painted before 1989, Harry spent very little time on that period. In fact he raced ahead to the early 1990s, when I was a college student just starting to visit my cousin in the fledgling East Village, and then to even more recent exhibitions.

"In particular, I'd like to talk for a moment about a show of experimental self-portraits at the Ancestral Temple of the Forbidden City, in November of 1998. *Shi Wo,* or in English, *It's Me,* was not less important because it was canceled by the authorities," Harry said. "In fact, the cancellation of the show contributed to its significance."

I had heard about the preparations for *Shi Wo,* and the dismay when it was shut down, but by that time I was living in Shanghai, working for my father, and I'd had no intention of attending myself.

"We might contrast it with Zhang Yimou's expensive production of *Turandot,* which took place in the Forbidden City only a few months earlier. Zhang Yimou had said that his goal was 'to attract an international audience through adopting an Oriental pose.' " Harry adjusted his glasses and coughed softly. "The *Shi Wo* artists claimed the same object for their exhibition. However, the spectacles they were presenting turned out to be quite different."

The audience, who had perked up at the mention of censorship, were whispering now that Professor Lin seemed to be talking about opera. Several people made their way stealthily toward the cheese.

"*It's Me* was eventually reinstalled in the Smart Museum of Art at the University of Chicago. But by that time it had become a show about the cancellation of experimental art exhibitions in China, and was therefore not the same show at all. The original *It's Me* could *only* have taken place in the Forbidden City."

I stared at Harry as he spoke; I didn't want to look around me. I felt as if the professor was trying to tell me something, which I was just beginning to understand, and I was afraid that dawning understanding might appear on my face in an embarrassing way.

"Just tonight," Harry continued, "Yuan Zhao has corrected my misunderstanding of certain performance pieces by the group of artists who lived for a short time on the outskirts of Beijing, in an area they referred to as the 'East Village.' Those performances are impossible, he told me, now that the East Village community no longer exists."

Now, for the first time during his talk, Harry Lin looked directly at me. "I wonder," he said. "By transposing this show from China to Los Angeles, is Yuan Zhao giving us *another kind* of experimental self-portrait? Although the work hanging in this gallery was created before the artist became interested in performance, could we say that the presentation of this show tonight is in fact another *performance*? One in which Yuan Zhao has resolved the *central paradox* facing the Chinese experimental artist? That in order to establish himself he must show abroad, while in order to remain authentic he must *keep Chinese art in China?*"

Harry was excited, almost tripping over his words, and suddenly I did not want to be in the gallery. I looked toward the exit, but the way was blocked by bodies. There was no means of reaching the doors without causing a dramatic disruption.

"If you asked me to choose a title for this show," Harry projected (he was no longer using the microphone), "I would not choose *DNA-ture*. I would call tonight: *Yuan Zhao in America*, and I would not hesitate to call it his best and cleverest performance to date."

There was a flash, and then another. The student photographer was taking pictures. All around me people were clapping. I was photographed with my hosts, board members of the Dubin Fellowship, and a curator from the Armand Hammer Museum, who slipped me his card and whispered something about "having a chat."

"Thank you," I said, "thank you."

Finally the photographers brought Harry Lin to stand next to me.

"Here we are," Harry said, switching for the first time to Chinese: "My only regret is that Zhang Tianming isn't here to capture it on film."

"You found a willing substitute," I said, nodding to the student photographer.

Harry laughed and put his hand on my shoulder. We smiled for the cameras.

58.

IN THE FALL OF 1987 A TRAIN TRAVELED NORTH FROM THE PROVINCIAL
capital of Wuhan to Beijing. Yuan Zhao was sitting in the hard-seat compartment. He had been expelled from the Hubei Academy of Fine Arts for a daring piece of performance art. In *Buried Alive No. 1,* ten art students had interred themselves in a pig farmer's field, breathing through flexible rubber tubes. Photographs were taken of the artists burying each other, one at a time, and of the finished field, empty except for its strange crop of stalky yellow rhubarb. No photographs were taken of the performance's aftermath, in which plainclothes policemen "resurrected" the participants and dragged them off to be interrogated, like ghosts, their hands, clothes, and faces still dusty with the whitish, anemic earth.

Yuan Zhao was content to be expelled. Beijing was the only place in the country for real art: an artist might become known there. He found a place to squat in the artists' village near the Yuanmingyuan, the old Summer Palace, where the Dowager Empress Cixi had once mortgaged her country's future for the sake of a marble boat. After several unsuccessful applications, he was finally admitted to study at CAFA, Beijing's famous art school. It was at CAFA that he became involved with the student protests, which would send him to prison for six months.

After being released, Yuan Zhao went home to his parents in Shanxi, where (in a transformative moment the artist describes in *Lu Kou,* volume 1) he decided to give up painting. He didn't know what medium he would use; only that it would no longer be colors on a flat canvas. Almost immediately he was back in Beijing, where he moved from place to place before settling in a slum on the eastern edge of the city. To his surprise, Yuan Zhao found that the neighborhood was inhabited by other artists.

Because they had nothing—no paints, no brushes, no canvas—these artists began experimenting with themselves. One cut himself with a knife; another cooled himself in a freezing lake; a third locked himself in a metal case and nearly suffocated. One day a beautiful young man who wore his hair long (whose silky mane, along with his slim hips, sleepy eyes, and bow-shaped lips, would have been envied by the most ambitious starlet at the Beijing Academy of Dance) covered his naked body with melon paste and walked outside wearing only a woman's bathrobe. He sat on the lip of an open sewage canal where the mosquitoes were breeding, and was almost arrested for the first time.

Neighborhood workers saw the young man on the concrete canal, and immediately called the police. Friends warned him just in time. Yuan Zhao, who had watched the police arrive, went home and painted a picture of a mysterious young man with a white face, wearing a woman's bathrobe. He painted the police lifting the bathrobe, jumping back in surprise, and the young man nude under the bathrobe, his body covered with star-shaped red sores. In place of a penis, he painted a cornucopia of vegetables and fruits, a horn of plenty borrowed from the disarming painting by Giuseppe Arcimboldo, whose peculiar portraits of Hapsburg emperors—their brows, noses, eyes, and lips composed of fruits, flowers, burning faggots, fuses, candle wicks, and cannons—had sparked his imagination.

It was the last painting he would ever make. When it was finished, he paid the young man a visit, and presented it as a gift. The two artists proceeded to become friends, collaborating on strange performances. Later they met a young photographer, also an immigrant from the provinces, who began to document their activities with a double-lens Seagull camera.

59.

JOAN HAD SPENT MOST OF THE ART SHOW WATCHING YUAN ZHAO. HER suspicions about the dissident and the professor had been confirmed: Mr. Yuan had seemed extremely nervous around his old friend, and had escaped as soon as the speeches were over. You would think they would've gone out to celebrate the success of *DNA-ture,* but Joan had seen Professor Lin leaving the gallery afterward with a few of his colleagues. Yuan Zhao had not been with them.

She had to admit that Cece had been right about the professor. Harry Lin was modest and intelligent, and there was even something pleasing about the combination of his serious face with a lanky, almost boyish frame. For the art show he had been wearing a well-worn, conservative suit with a pair of surprisingly stylish wire-frame eyeglasses. When Joan told him how much she'd admired *Chinese Experimental Art: The Tiananmen Generation,* the professor offered to show her the galleys of his new book. They had arranged a time for her to stop by the university the following week.

The professor's office was in the basement of a new Fine Arts Department complex. There were two casement windows at ground level, which let in a modicum of natural light and offered a view of some grass and a rusted storm drain. The walls were painted a sedate blue-gray, so the only color was provided by the spines of Harry Lin's books, a vast library of exhibition catalogues and fat critical studies displayed on cheap, stackable shelves. Many of the titles were in Chinese. Hanging above the professor's desk was a bilingual poster advertising Zhang Yimou's *Turandot,* performed in 1998 in the Forbidden City.

"Welcome," Professor Lin said, standing up. "I'm sorry it isn't more glamorous. My old office was in a lovely building, but a long walk from the classrooms. And—as my students remind me—I'm not getting any younger."

"I think this is nice," Joan said. She was biased toward people who did not did make a production of their offices; she thought the ability to work anywhere indicated seriousness. "I'm sorry to interrupt you."

"Not at all," Professor Lin said. "I know you're a novelist—you have to forgive me. I'm not much of a fiction reader."

She hated it when people apologized for not having read her books, as if they thought she would expect that they had read them. "This doesn't have to do with fiction," Joan said quickly. "I'm writing an article about Yuan Zhao, and I thought you might be able to help."

"For which magazine?"

"I'm not sure yet," Joan said.

Harry nodded politely. She knew he'd only agreed to see her because Gordon was a colleague.

"How long have you known Mr. Yuan?" she began, trying to sound like a journalist. The thing she most wanted to ask about—the girlfriend who'd died at Tiananmen Square—was probably not within the bounds of an ordinary interview, and yet she had the feeling that the story was somehow the key to understanding Yuan Zhao.

"The first time we met was in the winter of '93, although I was aware of his work before that. I was in Beijing writing a book on the Southern Song—specifically, those noblemen who left the court after the Manchu conquest. I don't know if you know: there's a tradition of dissenters retreating to the mountains or the countryside. They often became monks, and in some cases, poets and painters."

"Like in his new painting."

Harry smiled. "I haven't seen his new work. It must be quite a departure, though."

Joan was struck by the warmth in the professor's tone. If there was any ill feeling between him and Yuan Zhao, it was clearly one-sided.

"Maybe his new painting has something to do with coming to Los Angeles?" she suggested. "With responding to the Western fascination with ancient Chinese culture?"

"That's an interesting idea," Harry said. "I also shifted my focus during the year I spent in Beijing." He indicated a set of bound galley proofs on the desk at his left elbow. It was a large-format art book, with a grainy urban landscape on the cover. In bold letters, above the photograph, was the title *Tianming's East Village*.

"This is about to be published," he said. "I first proposed it to the photographer seven years ago in Beijing."

Harry opened the book to a particular photograph: two young men dressed in satin boxing shorts, crouched on the surface of a legless Ping-Pong table. The picture was obviously meant to be funny; Yuan Zhao scowled theatrically at his opponent across the three-inch net. But there was also something ominous and arresting about the roughly hung flags in the background (Chinese and American) and the shininess of the men's bodies, as if they'd really been fighting.

"Do you recognize him?"

Joan studied the photo: Yuan Zhao was on the left, in front of the Chinese flag, while his opponent was on the right. She could feel the professor watching her closely. "Yes," she said. "But it's as if he's transformed himself. I mean, I guess that's the art in it. I've never been very excited about performance art. Or maybe I don't understand it."

"A lot of it is bullshit," Harry said. "And a lot of it depends on the context. At that time in Beijing, experimental artists were working in a kind of crucible; their actions inspired reactions from the powers that be. They in turn were inspired by the government's actions." He paused: "Of course many of the artists now would disagree with me. The younger ones aren't even interested in 1989 anymore, much less the '60s and '70s. They criticize me for preferring work that deals with the China I know." The professor shrugged his shoulders. "I can't help it. I think I'm right. I believe that, in order to be successful, this kind of art must be political—must be socially engaged."

"Like these East Village artists."

Harry nodded. "Some of them, anyway. Several were arrested during one performance, in June of '94." He flipped through the book to show her another photograph. A naked young man, wearing makeup and silver earrings, was cooking fish on an outdoor stove.

"That's Baoyu, isn't it? Am I saying his name right?"

Harry hesitated. "That's right. How did you know?"

"I saw that painting in your book: the man in the bathrobe. And then when I mentioned it to Yuan Zhao, he told me about Baoyu. He's beautiful, isn't he?"

"That didn't help his case with the police," Harry said. "After he was arrested, along with some others, all of the artists had to move out of that area."

"How sad."

"But you have to remember, the East Village was their invention. They named it—you could say that it only existed in their imaginations anyway. Now I hear that the whole area is going to be turned into a park."

"You're kidding," Joan said. "That's a tragedy."

Harry shrugged. "Not really. It's gone already; if it still existed, bulldozing it wouldn't be enough to destroy it. The community was already falling apart that spring, in '94."

Joan became aware that she was jiggling her knee, an anxious habit she had retained from adolescence.

"The first thing was attribution," Harry continued. "It became very complicated, but basically, it's difficult to determine the authorship of some of these works." He indicated the open book on the table. "That one, for example. Is it a photograph by Zhang Tianming? Or a performance by Yuan Zhao?"

Joan looked back at the boxers. She noticed Yuan Zhao's well-developed physique—something he'd apparently let go in the intervening years. His skin was darker, sleek with sweat; he looked tougher than he did today.

"Well, it seems like an academic distinction," she said. "I mean, it's both—isn't it?"

Harry smiled. "And therein lies the trouble. Of course, once it becomes worth something, the question is somewhat more immediate. This particular photograph is part of a series that recently sold in Berlin for fifty thousand U.S."

"Gosh," said Joan.

"You can imagine, our friend was not pleased."

Joan nodded, but she had a hard time imagining Yuan Zhao fighting over money. He seemed like the kind of person who would give way—and then maybe stew about it later.

"It's much harder to collaborate once you have to determine the percentages. Those of us who work in a solitary way probably can't imagine," Harry said. "I complain about it—this little underground bunker—and pretend to be grateful for the teaching. But in fact I think solitary work suits me."

"I know what you mean," Joan said. "I think he's the same way—I mean, he seems to enjoy working alone." She decided to take a chance. "And in his personal life . . . I guess he's been single for a long time?"

"Did he say that?" Harry asked casually. He opened a drawer in his desk, as if he were looking for something.

Joan didn't want to seem as if she were desperate to hear the story. She thought Harry would tell her more if he didn't think she was planning to write about it.

"He told me about his fiancée," she said.

Harry looked up from his desk. "I wasn't aware that they were engaged."

"He said they were," Joan said. "He said they had just gotten engaged when she died."

"Died!" The professor started. For the first time, she felt as if she had his full attention.

"In the detention center?" Joan said.

"Which detention center?"

"I don't know the name of it. But Mr. Yuan said it was very dangerous—it was summer, and there was a lot of sickness."

Harry smiled, and for a moment even seemed to be trying to keep from laughing. She couldn't imagine what she'd said that could be funny.

"I don't know about that," he said. "But the woman I'm thinking of is very much alive. I believe she's having a child."

"Perhaps I misunderstood," Joan said, although there were few conversations she remembered as clearly as the one that first night with the dissident. She looked back at the photograph of the boxers: Yuan Zhao was in a defensive posture, as if he were waiting for the other guy to throw a punch. His opponent was in motion, warming up: that was why you couldn't see his face.

"Who's that?" she asked, pointing to the other artist. She obviously wasn't going to find out anything more about Yuan Zhao's fiancée from the professor.

"I did meet him," Harry said. "The name escapes me—but I remember that we had a very interesting conversation about the twelfth-century monk painter, Fanlong."

"Yuan Zhao mentioned that painter the first time I met him."

Harry raised his eyebrows in a kind of mock surprise. "Did he? That's interesting, because Yuan Zhao isn't much interested in these old painters. Actually, not many of the young artists are. That other young man was the exception." Harry glanced at his watch. "I'm sorry to say that I have to teach. A 'research methods' class." He smiled. "Never imagine that tenure frees you from this kind of thing."

"Thank you so much for your help," Joan said.

Harry Lin stood up and removed a neatly pressed sports coat from a hanger behind the door. "I don't think it would be a bad idea to write something about our friend," he offered. "An article or even a piece of fiction. You might start by asking about this performance."

Joan could feel herself blushing. It seemed that Harry had known what she was up to all along.

"Feel free to stay and look at the books if you'd like. The door will lock behind you."

Joan waited until she heard him climbing the stairs. The interview wasn't what she'd expected, for several reasons. She began flipping through *Tianming's East Village*, hoping to find a picture of Yuan Zhao's girlfriend, the fashion designer (now, only questionably dead). There was one group snapshot, of maybe twenty artists around a long table, but there was no way for Joan to guess which young woman she might've been.

There were no captions on the photographs, and the titles were given at the beginning of each section: *Drip-Drop, Something That Is Not Art, Modern Dance*. Although the names of the other artists appeared in the text, the book was clearly one photographer's vision of a specific place and time, rather than a documentary of the performances that took place there. Joan didn't see anything wrong with that, although it was some-times hard for her (an uninitiated viewer) to tell the performers apart. Maybe that wasn't important? Even Harry Lin, who had actually attended some of the performances, couldn't remember the name of the second boxer. Did it matter if that name was nowhere in the book?

It was the kind of issue that made you glad to work alone. Even if you were inspired by other people, no one could claim that the thing you'd written somehow belonged to them. People lived their lives, carelessly dropping information as if it were trash. The writer moved behind them, like a ragpicker. She cleaned and separated their garbage, culled and col-lected it. She made something of their leavings, and afterward they could not say: "Wait, that was my love affair," or "Hey, give me back my child-hood memory," any more than they could demand the return of their soda cans from the man who gathered them from the neighborhood trash.

60.

THE BEIJING EAST VILLAGE "ENDED" ON JUNE 12, 1994. OR THAT'S THE date that Harry Lin has put down in his book. It's been my experience that anniversaries are not fixed; they wobble, depending on who is telling the story. I suspect that if you were to ask each artist when they knew it was finished, you would get a succession of different dates. Some might argue that the name "East Village" didn't refer to a community, but only to a random collection of people brought together by cheap rents in a changing city. Others might even say that there was never an East Village in Beijing, except in the imagination of one photographer, and that those pictures are the only place it existed at all.

For me, the end came almost two months before the official date, April 21, 1994: as it turned out, my nineteenth birthday. We had just finished our performance of *Drip-Drop*, which was attended by the Chinese-American scholar Harry Lin, in Beijing that year on a Fulbright. After the performance, there was going to be a party at Lulu's beautiful apartment, up by the Asian Games Village.

Drip-Drop was my first artistic collaboration with my cousin, apart from the magazine, and the only time I performed as an artist in the East Village. Like *Something That Is Not Art*, it took place in X's apartment and was crowded with journalists and other spectators. My cousin and I stood on the surface of a legless Ping-Pong table, one of us on each side of the ragged net. Yuchen had got us a discarded table from the staff room of the Concord Hospital. We were wearing knock-off Thai boxing shorts, an idea of my cousin's that I enthusiastically supported, since I had been afraid we would be performing naked. Behind us were two flags—Chinese and U.S.—and in front of the flags X had placed the same heaters he'd used before, only this time there were no fans. My cousin set the timer for twenty minutes, and the two of us crouched down, facing off like sumo wrestlers. Soon, we began to sweat.

In the dramatic photographs of this performance, my cousin's body and my own are slick and dripping. The flags and the Ping-Pong table comprise the background; nothing else is visible, and X and I are giants tramping on a puppet stage. What was most extraordinary about this performance (I will brag a little, since I was only an actor in my cousin's show) was not captured in the photographs. It was the sound of our sweat hitting the table in that silent room, faster, slower, and faster again, like the sound of the ball in an actual match. My cousin had originally wanted to use blood for this purpose; it was only with great difficulty that Yuchen and I persuaded him of a more practical alternative.

Afterward, like marathoners, we were allowed to stand outside in the cool night, wrapped in blankets, while the journalists asked us (asked X, mostly) questions about the significance of the piece. Meiling had brought us both thermoses full of cold green tea, which I drank greedily, and my cousin left politely untouched until he was finished with the reporters. The three of us took a taxi and arrived early at Lulu's place, where she and her grandmother were setting out a spectacular buffet.

I had been nervous about Lulu's reception of Meiling, but my cousin's girlfriend was more than polite. In fact, they seemed to be trying to outdo each other with friendliness. Meiling had brought a bottle of expensive whiskey for the party, as well as a flowering plant for Lulu's grandmother; Lulu complimented Meiling extravagantly on the silk tunic she was wearing over her jeans, which she'd designed herself. I could see that they hadn't resolved their quarrel, only transferred it to another arena, as women so often seem to do. Under other circumstances this behavior might have made me nervous, but that night I was just glad for the appearance of peace.

The guests arrived in twos and threes until the apartment was hot and crowded. In Lulu's living room, with its brightly painted traditional furniture and its photographs of X's performances on the walls, we sat on the floor and had dinner. Sometime around midnight, when we were all pretty drunk, my cousin gave me a happy-birthday toast:

"Way back when we were kids—when we used to call him Xiao Pangzi—I never imagined my cousin and I would be making art together. Now I can't imagine the East Village without him. Welcome to Beijing," my cousin said: "Happy nineteenth!" Everyone cheered and raised their glasses, and Meiling gave me a public kiss on the cheek. Lulu had even gotten me an American-style cream-filled cake, decorated with candles.

"Make a wish," she told me, at the same moment that Meiling took my hand. I must have sat there for half a minute, trying to think of something else to wish for. In the end I just blew gratefully, extinguishing every flame on the first try.

After the cake, we rolled back the rug and started dancing. Cash brought out his electric guitar and amplifier, and I danced with Meiling, and then with Ai Dan, Lulu, and even Baoyu. A beautiful exchange student from the French island of Réunion had brought purple and silver glitter; we made a game of dousing our friends. I noticed that Lulu was getting angry about the mess and the commotion, and I saw her shouting at my cousin, who seemed unconcerned. When he and Fang lit a joint on the couch, however, I saw Lulu grab her bag and go out. I raised my eyebrows at X, but he was busy getting high, and I don't think he noticed.

I didn't plan on falling asleep, but it was four-thirty when I woke up on the couch. My mouth was dry, and my head predictably throbbed. When I sat up, it seemed that most of the guests had left: Cash sat on the floor, not playing but simply cradling his guitar as if it were a baby. A couple made out in the doorway; behind them in the kitchen, Yuchen was cleaning up. I got up and squeezed by the couple, blinking in the fluorescent light.

"Can I help?" I washed and then filled a glass from a jug on the counter.

Yuchen shook his head: "I just wanted to get the bottles picked up. I'm going home."

"Have you seen Meiling?"

He nodded: "A while ago. I don't know if she's still here, though."

"She would've woken me up if she were leaving," I said. "She's probably asleep somewhere." I noticed a pot of Lulu's grandmother's fried rice on the stove, and was suddenly ravenous. I decided I would take a plate into the living room and eat; then I would find Meiling and take her home.

The main room was so smoky, however, that I ended up carrying my plate of rice down the corridor, looking for another place to eat. I passed Lulu's bedroom, where the party was continuing: I peeked around the door, in case Meiling was there, but it was only some guys, drinking and gambling with cards. I continued to the end of the hallway, a part of the apartment I had never seen, where there was a closed door. I assumed that the room belonged to Lulu's grandmother, who had gone to spend the night with some relatives.

I debated about whether I should enter this room, which was certainly off-limits to the party. I was hungry, however, and even cold, my rice smelled delicious, rich with pork and scallions. I was slightly worried about Meiling, but I assumed she must've gone home, after finding me asleep. I thought of joking with my cousin tomorrow, about how both our girlfriends had left in disgust.

I expected Lulu's grandmother's bedroom to be dark, but when I turned the handle, I saw that I was mistaken. There was a bedside lamp, on one of those fancy dimmer switches, turned to the lowest setting. The couple on the bed were so wrapped up in each other—quite literally—that they didn't stop what they were doing right away. She was on top, her hands pressing down on his shoulders and her head thrown back. His eyes were shut, and he was holding her hips. They were moving very slowly. Her T-shirt was pulled up around her neck, exposing her familiar breasts: the dark nipples were pointed and hard, like a picture in a magazine. His black cotton trousers were tangled with her fashionable new jeans on the floor. I wondered if my cousin had unzipped those jeans or if she had done it for him, as she had the first time for me. I suspected that my cousin would not have needed to be guided.

When Meiling finally saw me, she pulled her shirt down—as if she were shy. My cousin's eyes were closed, and he was perhaps too stoned to notice that anyone had come in, but I could see that Meiling was sober, as usual. She sat still on top of him, staring at me. Neither of us gasped or cried out, the way it happens in the movies, and after a moment I simply pulled the door shut behind me, being careful not to spill my plate of rice on Lulu's grandmother's rug. I set it down carefully on an ornamental table, and walked out the front door into the hallway, past the clay horses and the bouquet of silk flowers in its imitation porcelain vase.

Only once I was outside did I realize that I didn't have my jacket or my wallet. But nothing could've made me go back into that apartment. Nor could I stand the idea of going back to my dorm room, where I imagined Meiling might come to find me in the morning. I walked around the traffic circle until I found an old man sleeping in his motor-rickshaw. He was unhappy when I gave him directions, and I thought of how much grumpier he would be when he found I had no money. I did, however, have the key to my cousin's apartment, where there were always a few yuan hidden in a box underneath the sink.

Had the police come to X's apartment that night, they would have found all the evidence they needed: the mess, the magazine (our manifesto), and the crumpled Chinese flag, not to mention one of the perpetrators, naked under a blanket, suffering from more than a hangover. I would've been the one to answer for the Polaroids lying carelessly on the table, the suspicious books, the videotape of *Something That Is Not Art* that was eventually produced for Belgian television.

But I was lucky, as usual. No one came that night, and when I woke up later that morning, parched again and shivering, it was to the loudspeaker of a man selling nuts and dried jujubes from a cart outside the window.

61.

AT THE MOMENT POLICE FROM THE CHAOYANG BRANCH ARRIVED IN THE
East Village to interrupt *Baoyu's Lunch*—a performance so famous I will
not describe it here, except to say that (by coincidence with our own story)
it involved several dead fish—I was sitting in the library at Beijing Normal. I hadn't spoken to Meiling, although she'd left me notes and even
waited one day outside my dorm, practically begging me for a chance to
talk. I brushed her off: what was the point? Spitefully, I refused to go to
the village for Baoyu's performance, where Meiling and my cousin would
certainly be among the spectators, but I couldn't help imagining everyone
gathering in the courtyard: the festive atmosphere in which I would've
been included, if not for the treachery of my two best friends. I wondered
if anyone had ever suffered so unjustly.

I was supposed to be participating in a review session in the library.
Instead of listening to my classmates expounding on Hemingway's *The
Old Man and the Sea*, however, I was daydreaming about Meiling and my
cousin, imagining them in various romantic scenarios: climbing the Great
Wall, visiting the Da Jue Si, paddleboating on Houhai Lake. I envisioned
the storm that might come up at just the wrong moment, tipping their
fragile craft and revealing the tragic fact that neither could swim. While
my classmates compared theses, I imagined the headline in the student
newspaper: "Undergrad's Untimely End in Tryst with Untrustworthy
Artist."

The above illustrates my state of mind a month after the incident at
my birthday party. On Sunday, June 12, 1994, my review session lasted
from eleven to one. Sometime in the last half hour, four armed policemen

arrived in the East Village and arrested everyone in Cash's courtyard. By six o'clock that evening—when I was heading to the dining hall with my roommate, Little Gao—most of the bystanders had been released with warnings. Only three people remained in detention: Baoyu, my cousin, and Meiling.

I learned the details from Fang, who came to see me two days later. He had spent the whole day waiting outside the detention center in Changping, trying to get in to see our friends, and in the end had only been able to send some cigarettes through the guards. Fang told me how on Sunday he had attended *Baoyu's Lunch,* but had left early to grab something to eat himself, along with Cash, Yuchen, and Tianming. As it turned out, that lunch was the thing that saved them. Ten minutes after they'd left, the police had arrived in the courtyard.

As soon as he got home from the detention center, Fang had telephoned Harry Lin at his apartment on the Qinghua campus. Harry said that the police had searched all of the artists' rooms in the East Village, where they'd found photographs, our first issue of *Lu Kou* (as well as plans for the second), and several videotapes. They had also found our country's flag: dirty, crumpled, and stashed in the corner of X's bedroom. According to Harry, the police had shown the videotapes to some university professors, and asked whether they were art. Those professors, whoever they were, had said no.

Harry had told Fang that the rest of us might receive visits from the police in the next few days. He advised us to lie low, and avoid meeting each other in public. Most important, we should not go back to the East Village.

It was summer, and the detention center would be hot. I thought that there would be vermin there, maybe even rats, and remembered how Meiling used to complain about the conditions in our dormitories, especially the smell of the toilets. I thought of the people she would be imprisoned with; I was afraid she wasn't important enough to be put in solitary. I was surprised she hadn't been released the evening of the twelfth, along with the others not directly involved. I knew Meiling's habit of saying what she thought, and I wondered if she'd somehow insulted the police. Either that, or she had bravely refused to leave my cousin.

Meiling and X were in real trouble. My revenge fantasies stopped, but instead of thinking logically about what I might do to help them, I continued to dream up unrealistic scenarios. Now I imagined myself as their savior, calling on my father's connections to rescue them. I would wait outside the building for the two of them to stumble into daylight, and nod solemnly as X took my hands, begging: "Can you ever forgive me, cousin?" Meiling would throw her arms around my neck, and whisper, "I made a terrible mistake."

It's true that women do not tend to rush into the arms of people whose fathers have made important telephone calls. Ordinarily they reserve that type of behavior for genuine heroes, such as people who've been persecuted for their beliefs. I'm glad to say that I did try calling my father, who was worried but helpless. (He was especially concerned about the flag the police had found.) Perhaps in Shanghai he would've been able to do something, he told me, but in the capital he had no power. Even though I'd been circumspect about my involvement in my cousin's activities, I still got a lecture about staying away from X once he was released.

In spite of Harry's warning, Fang and I met a week later, in the dumpling shop behind the university. Fang hadn't returned to the East Village himself, but he'd talked to Tianming. The photographer couldn't help going back to his old neighborhood, where he'd found his room sealed off with tape. Tianming's landlord told him that the same thing had happened to X, Baoyu, and Cash's rooms. The police had fined the landlords each 1,000 RMB, and warned them not to rent rooms to artists anymore.

"He knows it's risky, but he keeps going," Fang said. "He even took some pictures." Fang reached into his backpack and removed one of Tianming's snapshots, holding it reverently between his palms, so as not to touch the print.

The picture showed my cousin's place, from across the street. Perhaps Tianming hadn't dared to get closer. The photograph was characteristically black-and-white, although there was no white in the picture: the sky was dark, and the only pale spots were the pieces of litter blowing in the road. You could see the remains of posters for *Baoyu's Lunch*, torn away from my cousin's door; for some reason the hand-lettered sign X had left that afternoon for the photographers was undisturbed. He must've written it just before leaving for Cash's courtyard, taking care to translate for any foreigners who might be attending the show. In Chinese, the sign read "Back Soon," but in English X had striven for something more elegant: "Closed until further noticed." I couldn't help ascribing meaning to my cousin's grammatical error.

"Where's Tianming now?" I asked.

"Hiding," Fang said. "No one knows where."

Something in Fang's tone told me he was lying. I couldn't understand why he would keep Tianming's whereabouts a secret from me, unless it was simple jealousy. I knew Fang idolized the older photographer, and guarded their particular friendship, but the extraordinary circumstances in which we found ourselves should have canceled out such petty emotions.

"The question is, who tipped off the police?" Fang continued, uncharacteristically ignoring the plate of steaming jiaozi in front of him. "How did they know to come to that courtyard, on that Wednesday, precisely at that time?"

"There were those fliers," I said. I still had several of the fliers in my dorm room, which someone had dropped off a few days before the performance, and I knew they would've been pasted around the village as well. Posting directions to our performances had been my idea, after I'd had trouble finding *Something That Is Not Art*. I told Fang about the two men I had seen after that performance, smoking cigarettes outside of X's apartment.

"They could've seen *Drip-Drop* a couple months ago, and then gone to the police with one of the fliers for *Baoyu's Lunch*."

But Fang was not convinced. "We've had fliers before," he said. "Nothing like this has ever happened."

Several days later, Fang telephoned from a public call shop. Two cops had come to question him in Tongxian, where he'd been staying with his aunt since the arrests.

"You're next," he said. "Be careful. Don't give them any more information than you need to, and make sure there's nothing in your room. If they didn't take me, you'll be OK."

I got rid of my fliers for *Baoyu's Lunch,* as well as the old ones I had saved from *Drip-Drop* and *Something That Is Not Art.* I couldn't bear to give up the first issue of *Lu Kou,* and I knew the police had copies of our magazine anyway. Since my name was on it, they would be able to use it against me if they felt like it. I waited another week in a state of jumpy anxiety, and Fang called two more times. Each time I told him no one had come.

"I didn't live there, after all," I said. "Maybe they don't think I'm important enough to question."

"Uh-huh," Fang said. Then, calmly, as if he didn't know how important this would be to me, he said: "I talked to Professor Lin again. Your cousin and Baoyu are still being held, but they've released Meiling."

My heart was so loud, I was afraid Fang would hear it over the phone line. It was like the feeling I had every morning waking up, before I remembered what had happened. For a moment it was as if the old Meiling was out there somewhere, and all I had to do was find her.

"Where is she?"

"Home with her parents in Chongqing," Fang said. "Her dad came to get her."

At least I knew she was safe. My first thought was of writing her a letter, telling her I never wanted to see her again. My second was of getting on a train to Chongqing.

"Who knows if she'll ever be able to come back to school," Fang said. "This could ruin her life."

In my self-absorbed state, I thought Fang was trying to console me.

"I may be angry at her," I told him. "But I hope she gets to come back to school. I'm glad she's not in jail anymore—I was really worried about her."

"Uh-huh," Fang said.

I knew Fang was still working part-time in the office at CAFA, where Meiling and I had first met him. Two weeks later I called him there, to see whether he'd heard anything more, but a young woman answered the phone and told me he was out sick. I tried several more times over the next two weeks, but Fang was always out of the office when I called. I left him messages, but I never heard anything back.

Why would they have come for me when they already had my cousin? I had never rented a room in the East Village, nor had I been anything more than a bit player in someone else's performance. Fang should've known me well enough to realize that no matter how upset I was, I wasn't the kind of person to go to the Chaoyang police station and file a complaint. Even if it had occurred to me to do such a thing, I would have hesitated, considered, and turned them in a thousand times in my head, until it became too late.

In the weeks after the arrests I dreamed again and again of the East Village. I dreamed of the police, and of horrible prisons—like a Piranesi etching—levels and levels of bricked-up rooms, from which I heard screaming and the clanging of equipment. In my dreams I descended circular stone stairwells, ignoring the cries for help, until I found her—stretched out on a couch in a cold village room. I woke up with my hand in my sweatpants, and once, with tears on my face.

Bie xiao wo: don't laugh at me. I was nineteen years old, you're thinking: what did I know about love? And maybe you're right. But I have never been sure that we are all talking about the same thing when we talk about love. Perhaps real love is too boring to talk about. Heartbreak is so much easier to understand that I think we might sometimes employ it as an understudy, a stand-in for the real thing.

62.

CECE DID NOT BELIEVE IN GOD PER SE, BUT SHE HAD FAITH IN SOME
large system of accounts. If you did something good for someone, interest
would come back to you; if you did something bad, your balance de-
creased. She had even been thinking, just a few moments before the doorbell rang, that it would be nice to have one more person. The table was
designed for eight settings; with seven she had to fudge things, and still it
looked awkward, as if they were hiding something.

It was two-thirty, and she was waiting for the rolls to come out, so
that she could put in the apple pie. She'd done the pumpkin early this
morning; it was cooling on a rack on the breakfast-room table. In fact she
should've reversed the order and done the rolls last, so that they would
come warm from the oven, but the rising always made her nervous (what
if you got bad yeast?), and she liked to start anything that required baking
early. She could always warm them up in the oven before everyone sat
down.

When the doorbell rang, Cece ignored it. There were four other people in the house, not counting Mr. Yuan (who was upstairs typing on
Max's old computer). Joan was supposed to arrive at four for cocktails,
and Cece hoped to sit down at five exactly. No one was helping her in the
kitchen; there had been some halfhearted offers from the children this
morning, but truthfully Cece preferred to do it alone. She had allowed
Gordon to peel the sweet potatoes, and then sent him off with the children until it was time to carve. Max was probably in his room, listening to
his headphones. She had encouraged him to invite Jasmine today, and
then was relieved when he said that her family wanted her at home.

The doorbell rang again. Had Olivia gone for a run?

"Gordon?" she called. When she looked out at the pool, she saw some-one swimming laps. That would be Phil, of course.

Cece sighed and wiped her hands on her old Williams-Sonoma apron. She used a paper towel to blot her face and moved the unbaked pie toward the center of the island, just in case Salty knocked against it. As she hur-ried through the dining room, she took pleasure in the spicy pumpkin smell, the ticking of her grandfather's grandfather clock, and the center-piece of decorative Indian corn. Maybe Olivia had forgotten her keys, Cece thought, glancing through the bubbled glass peephole (you could never see anything), yanking the heavy door the way you had to, and step-ping back as it swung wide open.

The woman on the doorstep was thin, with dark hair, heavy-lidded black eyes, and a slightly aquiline nose. She might have been of Middle Eastern descent, or even something more exotic; she was wearing an ex-pensive red cashmere sweater with three-quarter sleeves, hip-hugger jeans slightly flared at the bottom (the way Olivia liked them), and a pair of high-heeled leather boots. She was holding a large white shopping bag, and looking at Cece with a panicked expression, as if she were thinking of scurrying off into the undergrowth like the bush baby, and never being seen again.

"Can I help you?" Cece asked.

"I think so," the woman said, and at that moment Cece knew. Of course she knew. She was surprised she hadn't recognized her immedi-ately.

"I'm Aubrey? Phil's friend? I'm sorry to disturb you—it was sort of a last-minute thing."

"Aubrey! How wonderful. We've been waiting to meet you for so long. And I was just thinking we needed an eighth tonight, or we were going to have way too much . . ." But Cece couldn't continue. Her whole upper body was hot and prickly, and for a second she worried she was having an allergic reaction: her breath was coming shallowly, as if her throat had suddenly swollen.

"I've been waiting to meet you too," Aubrey said shyly. "I'm really sorry to barge in on you—I know you have a full house. I'm staying at the Beverly Wilshire, but Phil and I could definitely go out to dinner tonight—"

"Of course not," Cece said, recovering a little. "It's such a pleasure to have you. If I'd known it was a possibility, I would've done something special. I'm afraid we're just having the old standbys—although my daughter would like it to be carbohydrate-free, and my husband doesn't eat turkey." Cece heard her own laugh and thought of her mother: laughter that had nothing to do with pleasure or amusement, but was simply a nervous placeholder.

"I brought a little something," Aubrey murmured, holding out the heavy white shopping bag. Cece glimpsed the neck of a bottle of red wine, a box of marrons glacés. She felt the subtle shift of power, as if she were exchanging it for the gift. Aubrey stepped inside.

"It's just that this case I'm working on suddenly seems as if it might settle," she said. "And I got an extra day off, and I was going to call, but then I just thought I would surprise him."

"He's going to be thrilled!" She sounded so strange, she thought even Aubrey would have to notice. But Aubrey was blushing and looking around, as if Phil had given her the compliment himself.

"I think he's in the pool," Cece said. "I'll just go—"

"Or maybe I should go?"

The red sweater set off Aubrey's olive skin. Cece noticed how delicate her bones were, her upper arms and clavicle. She was wearing an unusual necklace—an ornate, filigreed cross on a fine gold chain.

Aubrey saw her looking at it. "It belonged to my grandmother. I'm not religious, but she was Greek Orthodox. It's a little fussy."

"It's lovely," Cece said. "The pool is just through there."

"Thank you," Aubrey said.

Cece let Aubrey out the sliding doors. Then she went back to the kitchen. Gordon was crouched by the oven, getting ready to baste.

"Who was at the door?"

"Phil's girlfriend. It's a surprise."

Gordon turned at looked at her. "The famous Audrey!"

"Aubrey," Cece corrected. "She's working on a case. It suddenly seems as if it might settle."

"Terrific," Gordon said. "What can I do?"

Cece gave him the beans to string. Through the French doors, she could see Aubrey at the edge of the pool. She saw Phil hoisting himself onto the deck (he did look better since he'd started swimming), holding her by one shoulder, since he was wet. Aubrey threw her arms around him anyway.

"Is she pretty?" Gordon asked.

"Can't you see?"

"I'm not wearing my distance glasses," Gordon said. "I was looking up the Ottawa Traverses online. This branch has been involved with lumber for a century, but I e-mailed one woman who mentioned that she believed there was an ancestor who traded furs with the Algonquin Indians, when it was still New France. That would have been before the Revolution."

"The American revolution?"

"French," Gordon said. "This is all pure speculation, of course."

There was a scream from outside. Phil had grabbed Aubrey's shoulders and pretended he was going to push her in the pool. She pretended to hit him; he playfully defended himself. It was lucky Mr. Yuan was working upstairs, since they would certainly want the pool house to themselves for a while.

Gordon squinted out the window at Phil, who was holding the door open for Aubrey: "She doesn't look thirty-seven."

"No," Cece said.

"Why haven't they gotten married? Doesn't she want to?"

"I believe so," Cece said.

"What is he waiting for?"

"I don't know."

"No one's getting any younger," Gordon said.

63.

THEY PUSHED DINNER BACK TO SIX-THIRTY, TO GIVE PHIL AND AUBREY
some time together, and everything had to be reheated. The stuffing and
the rolls were fine, but she'd left the turkey in too long.

"I apologize for the turkey," Cece said. "It's a little dry." She noticed
that Mr. Yuan had eaten everything else on his plate, but left the meat in a
fastidious heap.

"Jasmine's family deep-fries their turkey," Max volunteered.

It was perhaps the first thing he'd contributed to the conversation,
and Cece wanted to encourage him. "Maybe we should've done it that
way."

Olivia made a gagging gesture.

"Some friends of ours were having a tofurkey this year," Aubrey joked.
"Thank goodness we came here."

"I think tofurkey sounds good," Olivia said.

"Which friends are those?" Phil said. He looked stony, closed up; in
this mood, there was no way you could reach him. She wondered if that
bothered Aubrey, or if it was only Cece's special perspective that made her
notice it. Aubrey seemed like a very nice person—but there were limits to
everything. If Phil's girlfriend knew what had been going on for all those
years, she would certainly not sit here making polite conversation, trying
to ingratiate herself.

"Chris and Alison," Aubrey prompted Phil. "You know, she's my yoga
instructor?"

"Do you do yoga?" Olivia asked.

"She's very good at it," Phil said.

"You're not really *good* at yoga," Aubrey explained. "You do it at your own pace, so you're not competing against anyone else." She turned to Olivia: "It's a great thing to get into while you're still young. You can get very flexible."

"Mm," said Phil.

Aubrey rolled her eyes and elbowed him under the table.

Gordon turned to Cece. "I bought you that yoga tape," he said. "Whatever happened to it?"

Olivia bounced childishly in her seat. "Do we still have it, Mom?"

"I could look," Cece said. "I'm sure we do." Why was it only now, in front of Aubrey, that she felt this deep regret? Shouldn't her husband be the person who inspired feelings of shame and remorse?

She looked at Gordon, motioning to Lupe to refill the water pitcher. He seemed perfectly at ease, leaning back in his chair so that you could see the slight curve of belly over his belt. It was not the belly that she minded, not at all. She had welcomed the changes in his body, partly because they corresponded to her own, and partly because they were the first signs of vulnerability he had ever shown her. Nor was it the fact that right now he was perhaps sixty percent present at the dinner table, and forty percent still shut up in his office, hunting down stray Traverses in remote corners of Canada. Cece couldn't understand why your ancestors who lived two or three hundred years ago were any more interesting than, for example, your neighbors, who weren't related to you, but who lived next door right now. Did this family he was researching have anything to do with their real family—with their worries about Max, or about the two of them—or was Gordon just using "Travers" as a random sample?

"It's a practice," Aubrey told Olivia, and then addressed the rest of the table: "I hope that doesn't sound pretentious."

"I think the word *pretentious* is overused," Joan said. "It's not pretentious if you're not pretending." She looked at Mr. Yuan, as if she were waiting for him to argue or agree. Cece noticed that Joan's cheeks were flushed from the wine.

"It's not pretentious if you're not pretending!" Phil exclaimed. "Somebody write that down!"

"Oh, shut up." Joan turned to Aubrey: "Phil still teases me, but I do think that in America our anti-intellectual bias is becoming stronger and stronger. It begins in high school."

Mr. Yuan laid down his fork. "Is that the case?"

"Poor Joan was too smart for high school," Phil said.

"At least Joan was *successful* in high school," Gordon remarked.

"What do you mean by successful, Gordo?"

"I wasn't popular like Olivia, that's for sure," Joan said. "And Max," she added, a second too late.

Joan was trying to help, but she had made it worse. Cece looked at Max, who had pushed his turkey to the side of his plate.

"I'm not popular," he said. There was a silence.

"I'm sure you are," Joan said lamely.

Leave it, Cece thought. For God's sake, let's move on. She would've liked to move right past dinner, past dessert, past books and bedtime, into the middle of the night. Once everyone was sleeping off their dinner and she was the only one awake, then, finally, she would be able to breathe.

"I wasn't popular either," Aubrey said.

"Aubrey's mother died when she was ten," Phil told them. "She had to take on a lot of responsibility."

That was too personal to share with strangers, but Aubrey didn't seem to mind. Everyone looked at her sympathetically. Cece realized they had forgotten to say what they were thankful for.

"The death of a parent is perhaps the most intense trauma a child can experience," Gordon said.

"Oh," Aubrey said modestly, "I don't know about that."

"Can I go upstairs?" Max asked.

Cece didn't blame him. "Don't you want dessert?"

"Can I take dessert upstairs?"

Cece said yes. She felt they owed it to him.

"I'm so sorry," Joan whispered to Cece, when Max was gone. "About the popular thing. I think I've had too much wine."

"It's fine," Cece said, more sharply than necessary. She looked up and noticed Mr. Yuan watching her. His expression was sympathetic, and at the same time there was no question that he knew exactly what was going on.

After dinner Olivia uncharacteristically offered to help with the dishes. Max was upstairs on the phone with Jasmine (she could see the red light next to line two), and Mr. Yuan had gone with Gordon to walk the dogs. Phil and Aubrey had left for the Beverly Wilshire, Phil carrying an unfamiliar overnight bag on one shoulder. They had said good night in the hall. Cece had encouraged them to come back over the weekend, for a swim, and Aubrey had agreed politely. (Of course there was a beautiful pool at the hotel.) Phil had held the door for Aubrey, who disappeared out into the driveway, where her rented black Acura was just visible in the shadows. Phil had paused for a moment, and Cece had shrugged, idiotically, as if to say, "Don't worry, I'm fine! Have a super time!" Phil had stared at her a moment too long, letting her know *he* knew it was just an act, and then shut the door behind him. She heard laughter from the driveway, and Aubrey, in a different voice from the one Cece had heard before:

"Could I use a drink . . ."

She stood in the foyer, listening while the engine started and the car backed out of the driveway. She heard it brake at the stop sign, and then fade away into the rush of Sunset traffic.

"Mom, there's a hole in this trash bag!" Olivia called from the kitchen.

"Then put it in another one." But she hurried back anyway, through the dining room, the napkins like crushed white flags abandoned on the table.

"I did it already," Olivia said, when Cece reached the kitchen. "Do you think Uncle Phil will ask Aubrey to marry him?"

"I don't know."

"Why not? She's so cool."

"I agree," Cece said, setting the dishwasher to the scrub cycle.

Olivia twirled around on the terra-cotta tiles, stopping expertly on one toe. "Do you need any more help?"

"No," Cece said. "Thank you. I think I have it under control."

64.

PHIL STAYED AT THE BEVERLY WILSHIRE ON FRIDAY AND SATURDAY
night. He and Aubrey didn't come over to use the pool, and Phil didn't call
to let her know when he'd be coming back. Part of her hoped he would decide to go home to New York with Aubrey on Monday; that would probably
be the best thing for everyone. She could picture getting the call from New
York, a bad connection, a payphone, because Phil wouldn't have wanted to
call from Aubrey's apartment: "Can you hear me? Ceece, are you there?"

She was sleeping now, but only four or five hours a night, and she got
tired early. A little after ten on Sunday night she knocked on Max's door
to check on him. She tried to remember exactly when it was that things
had been reversed, and it had become accepted that the parents would go
to bed before the children.

"Hi," Cece said, and waved at him: Max was wearing a pair of enormous headphones, which he lowered just slightly when he noticed her
standing there. The beat was so loud that it seemed as if the music would
make a bruise on the very pale skin below his ears. From Max's room she
could see that Mr. Yuan's bedroom was dark; the dissident was probably
out in the pool house, hunched over his extraordinary scroll. His concen-
tration these days was impressive: one hundred and eighty degrees from
when he'd first arrived. She thought it must be that way for all artists: they
had slumps, followed by periods of furious creativity.

"I just wanted to say good night," Cece said. "I'm turning off the
ringer now—unless you're expecting a call?"

Max shook his head.

"I'm a little tired," Cece said. "Maybe from all the cooking. I'm glad you liked the pumpkin pie; your sister didn't touch it."

She never knew what to say to him anymore, but she wasn't sure it mattered. She felt like quantity of communication was more important than quality, at least for the time being; you never knew what might prompt a response.

"I enjoyed the weekend, though."

Max tilted his head in the direction of the pool house. "Is he coming back?"

"You mean, up here?" Cece said. "I don't think so. He seems to prefer the pool house now that Phil's gone, which makes me wonder—"

Max gave her an uncomfortable look, as if she had something stuck in her teeth.

"Oh," she said. "Were you talking about Uncle Phil?"

Max took the headphones off completely, flipped onto his stomach, and began fiddling with the treble and bass. Gordon had said that the new stereo was a way of showing Max that they trusted him, and that they weren't punishing him for what had happened. Cece liked that idea. The only problem was that when she looked at the stereo on the floor by Max's bed, she saw the Beretta Cougar. The transformation had happened so easily: toy to gun and back to toy. What was to keep it from happening again?

"If you minded having him, you should have told me," she said. "Or your father. How are we supposed to know, if you don't say anything?"

Max sighed.

"I should've asked you and your sister. It's just—I didn't know he was coming."

"You didn't?"

"You remember," Cece said. "He just showed up."

Max was still facing the stereo; she had to talk to the back of his head. She loved the way the black waves of his hair folded one into the other, like weaving. Gordon had once had hair like that.

"I thought you knew," Max said, turning finally to face her. It surprised her.

"Why wouldn't I have said something if I had known he was coming?"

Max shrugged. Didn't he believe her?

"It wouldn't have even made sense to invite him, while Mr. Yuan was here."

"O-*kay*," said Max, clearly exasperated by the conversation.

"I don't think Phil is coming back," Cece said. "I'm pretty sure that was about it."

Max barely nodded, then sprang up toward the bathroom.

"Max?"

He turned around. He was taller than she was, of course. His features were his father's, but he got his fair, sensitive skin from her. She remembered the way it had looked when he was an infant, and she would bathe him in a plastic tub in the sink. It was like rice paper, with the green veins forking just under the surface. The pimples on his neck now made her want to kiss him. She wanted to tell him that everything would be fine, if he could just get through the next couple of years.

"Good night," she said instead.

65.

PHIL CALLED ON MONDAY NIGHT, RIGHT AFTER DINNER. IT WAS STRANGE to hear Lupe summoning her to the phone, as if the last four months had been a dream, and she had suddenly woken up to find everything the way it was before.

"Are you in New York?" she asked.

He didn't say anything.

"Phil?"

"Why would you think I was in New York?"

"I don't know. I thought——"

"You don't think I would've called you?"

"I just thought you might have gone back today." Why did she sound apologetic? "But you're still in L.A.?" Cece caught herself hoping that the "you" was singular, that Aubrey had gone back alone.

"That's why I called," Phil said.

Now that Phil was gone, Mr. Yuan had moved his things back down to the pool house, his allergy mysteriously cured. Cece was about to offer Phil the upstairs bedroom, and then she thought of Max. "What are you going to do?" she asked instead.

"Aubrey's staying another week. She has some friends in Pacific Palisades."

"Oh, uh-huh," Cece said. "I see."

"She has her laptop," Phil said. "So she can work from here."

"Great!"

Phil hesitated. "We have some things to work out."

"That's good," Cece said. "I mean, I hope you do. Work them out.

She's lovely." Cece heard the bright fakery in her own voice, but she couldn't stop. "Olivia thinks you should get married!"

Phil was silent, but she wasn't going to prompt him. She'd done her part—gone above and beyond the call of duty.

"What do you think?"

"What?"

"What do *you* think I should do?"

Cece was standing in her study, which smelled of guinea pig. Ferdinand rustled in his shavings. There were running footsteps overhead, and then the sound of a door slamming shut. How could he ask her that?

"Ceece?"

"I think if you love her, you should."

"Should . . . ?"

"Go home. Get married. I mean, we loved having you—it isn't that. But I'm not sure it's been good for Max and Livy, having so many people in the house."

"They're the most important thing," Phil said solemnly, as if he were making a sacrifice—as if they were making a sacrifice together, each giving up an equivalent thing.

"And Mr. Yuan," Cece heard herself saying. "Because I do think he was just being polite about the cats. And it didn't matter so much before, of course. But now that he's getting so much work done—"

Phil was silent.

"I'd like to let him just have the space. You understand?"

"Cece?"

"Yes?"

"Don't be mad at me—"

"I'm not mad at you." Her voice was pitched higher than normal.

"—when I say this." Phil paused. "I think Mr. Yuan might be taking advantage of you."

"What?"

"I'm not sure he's here just to paint."

You think *Mr. Yuan* is taking advantage, Cece thought. But she couldn't go that far. "He isn't here only to paint," she said. "It's also about experiencing another culture."

"I know. I just think you should be careful."

"You think he's dangerous." She was joking, but Phil responded seriously:

"Not physically. Aubrey didn't have a good first impression of him, which is strange."

"It is strange," Cece said. "Since Mr. Yuan barely said anything during dinner. It was Aubrey who was doing most of the talking, if I remember correctly." She was having trouble seeing. Her body felt jerky and detached, like the wooden manikin out in the studio.

Phil laughed. "OK. I just wanted to say thank you for the other night. But now you're mad at me."

"I'm not *mad*."

"I was just telling you what I think, Ceece."

"Don't call me that," Cece said. "It's inappropriate."

There was a silence—not one of their typical, loaded silences, but simply a freeze.

"Wow," Phil said. "I guess that's it."

"Probably we shouldn't talk for a while," she said.

"Probably not."

"Take care, Phil."

"You too, Cecelia," he said, taking it a step too far. When had she become so unaccustomed to the sound of her given name?

66.

CECE WAS SITTING IN THE INTERNSHIP OFFICE ONE AFTERNOON, AD-
dressing permission slips, when she had a visitor. It was after three-thirty,
and she was waiting for Mr. Yuan to be finished. The Internship Office
was pleasant at this time of day, and it was still warm enough to leave the
window open. She could hear girls' voices coming from the picnic tables
outside the library. They were working on their centerpieces for the sesquicentennial. From the side lawn outside the auditorium, you could hear
the tinny hammers of the men building a stage in front of the Claire Mof-
fet (class of '38) Memorial Reflecting Pool, where they would make the
sesquicentennial speeches, and release the balloons and the doves.

She was glad to hear the knock on her door. The fact that other people's children still wanted to confide in her was a small consolation, in the
face of recent failures with her own.

"Come in," Cece called, but it took her a moment to recognize the
woman who opened the door: a slim shadow with the sun slanting in from
the atrium behind her.

"Am I interrupting? I was just here to get Emily, and I thought I'd stop
in—"

"Felice," Cece said. "It's so nice to see you—I was going to call, actually. We would love to have you to dinner after everything settles down."

"With your houseguest," Felice suggested, sliding into the seat normally occupied by Cece's interns. "You must be overwhelmed."

Cece had not forgotten her conference with Emily, but she had been
able to put it out of her mind successfully. When she saw the girl in the
hallways, she tried to smile, but Emily purposefully avoided eye contact.

Cece assumed that Olivia's friend had thought better of her accusation, or had simply been making an idle threat. Perhaps, if asked, she would pretend not to remember it at all. This was a strategy both of her children used, and she did not consider it lying. As a teenager, your whole personality was a kind of rough draft. You made a lot of mistakes, and Cece felt that you ought to be able to do as much revising as necessary, without being penalized for it.

Now, however, as she faced Felice Alderman across the desk, Cece had the uncomfortable feeling that she had not behaved completely correctly either. Had the best course really been to forgive and forget? Or had she perhaps been under some obligation to reveal Emily's accusation (however groundless) to school authorities—an obligation she had ignored, in order to protect Mr. Yuan?

"Olivia and Emily are so close," Cece began. "Olivia adores her. It's been Emily this, Emily that, ever since they got back from Paris."

"Yes." Felice sighed. "Emily is certainly popular."

Cece smiled graciously, a skill she had developed through charity work. There was no point in allowing things to become unpleasant, just because you didn't happen to like a person.

"Now we just need to get those grades up," Felice continued. "I know she hasn't come to see you yet, but she *says* she's interested in art."

Cece took a deep breath of the sweet, grassy air (outside the gardeners were mowing). Apparently Emily Alderman had kept their chat to herself. Any damage the girl had done might still be repaired.

"Of course they have this Chinese teacher this year. Thanks to you."

"Oh no," Cece said firmly. "Thanks to Mr. Yuan. He volunteered, you know."

Felice looked surprised. "I didn't know. You mean, he isn't officially a teacher?"

"Well, he has taught a great deal in China," Cece said. It occurred to her that she didn't know whether this was true. "The certifications are different there, of course."

"Of course," Felice said.

"The important thing is just that the girls have this wonderful opportunity."

Felice gave her a noncommittal smile. Cece glanced out the window: the students were shooing some pigeons away from their project, a sesquicentennial banner stretched out on the cement.

"Personally I've always thought she ought to study psychology. That's what I did in college, and I never regretted it."

"My husband is a psychiatrist," Cece said, gratefully steering the conversation away from Mr. Yuan. "Where did you—"

"Oh I know," Felice interrupted. "Emily mentioned that."

"I'm arranging for some of the girls to go to one of his lectures, if only to see what a college lecture is like. If Emily is interested—"

"How wonderful of Gordon to help."

"Oh, well, he doesn't have a choice," Cece joked. "I psychologized him into it."

Felice smiled. "You know what they say."

"Sorry?" Outside, the girls were screeching about something. A siren wailed up Third Street, shattering the peace of the afternoon.

"They can't do it on their own families," Felice said. "Isn't that right?"

Cece looked at the stack of envelopes on her desk, still waiting to be addressed. Joan had said that Cece was a "people person," but Cece was beginning to doubt it. These days all she ever wanted was to be alone.

She looked up from the desk, and tried to summon her sister-in-law's intimidating reserve: "It's not that he couldn't," she said. "Only that it wouldn't be appropriate. Gordon is a wonderful father."

"No, no," Felice exclaimed, leaned forward and put her left hand on Cece's desk. Multiple diamonds flashed there, like warnings. "You're misunderstanding me. I just meant that cliché—you know—about psychiatrists and their families. No doubt Gordon is the exception that proves the rule."

Outside, the girls continued yelling: why couldn't they be quiet, even for a minute?

It's in her hair.

Ew, ew.

"Obviously he's wonderful with Max," Felice said.

"Max?"

"After everything he's been through."

Gross. Get it OFF.

"What is going *on* out there?"

Felice's voice maintained a casualness, but the emphasis betrayed her: she knew she'd gone too far. How dare she bring up Max, as if everyone knew all about it?

"It sounds like some kind of *crisis.*"

"A bird shit in someone's hair." Cece was surprised this wasn't obvious to Felice. She was surprised to hear herself use the word *shit.*

Felice laughed again. "It's supposed to be lucky."

Shut up, Cece thought. *Get out—go.*

"Isn't that what they say?"

Cece stood up. "Unfortunately I have to run. Mr. Yuan is waiting for me." She felt Felice watching as she rifled through the piles of paper on her desk. She was sure to forget something.

"Maybe it's a Chinese saying? About it being lucky?"

"We said that when I was a girl," Cece said, stuffing the permission slips into her purse, where they would get crumpled. Never mind—she could Xerox them at home. She had a powerful desire for home: the dim, silent foyer, the stained-glass window dropping chips of colored light onto the ivory-carpeted stairs.

"That's right," Felice said. "So it couldn't be, could it?"

"Be what?" Cece said, opening the door.

"*Chinese,*" Felice said softly. "Back then—we barely even knew where China was."

67.

Cece gave me a message that someone had called for me.

"He didn't speak very much English—or maybe it was the connection," she said politely. "He said to tell you he'd spoken to Harry, and to congratulate you on your big success." Cece handed me a sheet of paper with a number, and the words *DNA-ture* and *Big Success* in enthusiastic red ink. "I'm sorry that I didn't get his name."

When I called my cousin back the next morning, he was in the middle of packing. I could hear voices, and a good deal of banging in the background; friends were helping him clear out his things, he explained, in preparation for a move to an apartment in Chaoyang, near the Kerry Center.

"It's expensive," X said. "Like everything these days. Do you remember how much I paid for that room in the East Village? Eighty kuai! Isn't that incredible?"

"That was a long time ago," I said.

"You're right!" my cousin exclaimed. "It's stupid to live in the past. And this new place is a lot better than that room, that's for sure. Everything new, two bedrooms, even radiant flooring in the bathroom. And there's an office for me to keep track of my work." X laughed; he was notoriously bad at any kind of bookkeeping.

"It sounds perfect," I told him.

"How is Los Angeles?" he asked. I was surprised to hear a new tentativeness in his voice, as if he were being careful to humor me. He was waiting to ask about the art show until he found out whether I was angry.

"Oh, fine," I said, allowing him to squirm a little. "The weather is great."

"And the, um—*DNA-ture*? Was it boring for you?"

"Boring!" I said. "Why do you say that? People loved it."

"They did?"

"There must've been two hundred of them there." (I exaggerated a little, for effect.)

"Really?"

"And a curator from the Armand Hammer Museum—he said something about wanting to talk."

"Great!" said X.

"There should be some gallery interest, maybe even in New York."

"Wow," my cousin said. "You're incredible." Then he repeated the news to someone else. I heard a female voice.

"Who's there?" I asked.

"A lot of people are helping," X said. And then, as if casually: "Meiling is here. Not helping, of course. You should see her—like a house!"

I heard Meiling chastising him in the background. My cousin paused, and then, with extremely uncharacteristic awkwardness, made a joke:

"Lucky the new place is so big."

I understood so quickly that I thought I must've always known. I wondered how I could've doubted it. There was the way my cousin had encouraged me to visit her, and the way Meiling had avoided the question of a father. How could I have imagined that the post might be vacant? My ex-girlfriend was, above all, practical; she would not have allowed herself to drift toward motherhood without a firm plan in place. I had no doubt about who had insisted on the comfortable apartment in Chaoyang: Meiling's child would not grow up in a rickety hutong house, or a drafty studio at Dashanzi, with a loft bed and a toilet down the hall. Most important, he would not grow up without a father. In fact he would have a famous father—one who had prestigious international shows, but preferred staying with his family in a large apartment with radiant flooring to traveling all over the world. Knowing Meiling, I was not surprised it had all worked out so elegantly.

My cousin and I were both quiet for several moments. It didn't hurt as much as I would've expected. In fact there was a kind of lightness, a sloughing off, as if I had completed some particularly onerous task.

"So, do you know what you'll do now?" X asked. "Thinking of coming home?"

"Probably not," I said. "I have to finish my project."

X hesitated. "Right, of course."

In spite of his encouragement, I knew it hadn't occurred to him that my "project" would be anything but a distraction. My teaching job would've seemed to him an onerous responsibility. It was only recently that those things had begun to mean something more to me. I decided, on a whim, to confide in my cousin.

"And there's this girl," I said.

"Really?" X said. "That's *great*. Who is she?"

"Not a girlfriend," I told him. "A student. She particularly needs my help—she's very talented."

"Mm-hm," X said. "How old is she? Sixteen, seventeen?" I heard Meiling again in the background, and I couldn't help being a little bit gratified.

"She's nineteen," I told him, "and she's really just my student. I should get going, actually—so I'm not late to class."

"Hold on," X said. "Meiling wants to talk to you."

For a moment, I had the familiar excitement: a tunnel opened into the glistening past. But for the first time, the present was stronger.

"I actually have to go," I told my cousin.

"We'll be around if you want to call back," X said. "Your time tonight would be tomorrow morning for us."

"I'm going out tonight."

"A date," X guessed.

"A concert," I said, not exactly correcting him. "Give my best to Meiling. Tell her the Lobster Hermit sends his regards."

68.

MALMSTEAD HALL WAS DIMLY LIT AS PARENTS, SIBLINGS, AND TEACHERS
(as well as a large contingent from the William O. Douglas School for
Boys) filed in for the Dance Directions concert. Although we were early,
there were not five seats together; Cece and I sat on the left side of the
aisle, while Dr. Travers, Max, and his girlfriend sat a few rows back on the
right. I looked around at the audience filling up the tiers of plush orange
seats, like the ones in a particularly fancy movie theater, and spotted a few
of my AP artists who were not members of Dance Directions. The one
student I was looking for, however, did not seem to be in attendance.

I hadn't really expected to see June and her grandmother in the crowd,
but as I scanned the rows of faces, I was disappointed anyway. After my
slip in the classroom two weeks ago—letting the other girls know I had
seen June's aviary—our Chinese lessons had abruptly ended. That, I supposed, was my punishment. But June had also stopped working in my
classroom during her free periods. Had she finished her net, or was she
simply trying to avoid me? I had spoken to her only once since then, when
we'd encountered each other at the snack bar on the south side of campus.
It was the middle of the morning, when most students were in class, and
we were practically alone.

June hadn't smiled when she saw me approaching, but she hadn't
walked away either.

"How have you been?" I asked her. "Have you finished your project?"

June collected her change before answering me. "Which project?"

"Your net." I lowered my voice, as if it were a secret between us.

"I'm throwing it away." Just like that: casual.

"Throwing it away!"

"You were right—there was no point to it."

"But you must have *something* to do with it. You spent so much time."

June shrugged, like she didn't know what I was talking about. I was desperate to continue the conversation, although I didn't know what I wanted to say.

"Are you bringing your grandmother to the concert on Friday?" I asked, trailing after her to the communal microwave. "I know several of your classmates are in Dance Directions."

"Talk about 'something that is not art,'" June said. Then she called out to another girl, one I had never seen before, with very long black hair and an armful of colorful leather bracelets. I should have been glad to see that she had her own friends; instead I was tremendously jealous.

"See you, Mr. Jow," she said casually, giving me (as Batty would say) the cold shoulder. I was still standing there when a voice startled me: Vice Principal Diller peered down over the railing on the second floor to ask whether my students would be delivering their Sesquicenterpieces to her office the following Monday.

"I believe so," I said, careful not to promise anything.

My hesitation had not seemed to please the vice principal. "I certainly hope so," she said, withdrawing her head like a turtle.

I could see Vice Principal Diller now, standing at the back of the auditorium, wearing a whistle around her neck. It occurred to me that she might intend to monitor the content of the show: to shut off the lights and blow her whistle, were anything inappropriate to appear on stage. Then I remembered that I was in America, where that sort of thing did not occur.

The lights went down further, and a spotlight appeared in front of the curtain, a pleated fall of burnt orange velvet.

"It's starting," Cece said. "Oh I'm so nervous!"

I wondered what Cece had to be nervous about.

"You never know what could happen," Cece continued. "She could forget the steps or—God forbid—fall down. I'm worried about her. She—"

But before Cece could say what else she was worried about, a woman in the next row half-turned and shushed us. The dance teacher, Ms. Kirschgraber, entered stage right, her hair pulled into a ponytail so tight the skin on either side of her face appeared stretched. She was wearing tights underneath a long, cotton print skirt; when she walked, her feet pointed out at angles, like a duck's. I had seen the same walk long ago on some of the lovely creatures exiting the Beijing Academy of Dance, the one time I had been allowed to accompany X to meet Lulu there.

"Not since I was a principal in the Irina Ivanovna Dancers, auditioning student associates," began Ms. Kirschgraber—who was not a lovely creature, in part because she was wearing so much green eyeshadow— "have I seen such a talented group of young dancers."

"I'm afraid she's lost too much weight," Cece whispered, and for a second I thought she was talking about Ms. Kirschgraber, whose collarbones did poke out sharply above the neckline of her leotard.

"In addition to choreographing their routines, the girls have spent hours rehearsing until late in the evening—as those of you who drive carpool know." (There was knowing laughter from the parents, although it seemed to me that almost all of the girls old enough to have a license had their own cars as well.) "And since tonight is about the girls, I'm going to get off the stage and let them show their stuff. They've been working very hard, so if you'll please give them all a big round of applause . . ."

Ms. Kirschgraber was drowned out by a terrific wave of clapping, foot stamping, and (from the young men of William O. Douglas) wolf whistles. Then the lights went off altogether; the curtain flew up; and we were looking at an illuminated, electric blue set. There were two chairs placed at angles in the center of the stage. We heard the opening bars of a catchy song, and four girls cartwheeled onto the stage, two of them impressively manipulating bright pink scarves.

"That's her," Cece whispered, and I saw Olivia, upside down, second from the left. A row of background dancers entered with the same cartwheels, while the girls in front enacted an up-tempo tug-of-war with their scarves.

"She's on the beat, isn't she?" Cece said.

I gestured to Cece that we should keep our voices down, but the woman in front of us was also whispering to her companion; everyone was pointing out daughters, sisters, and friends to everyone else.

As we watched, I couldn't help being mesmerized by the scenery, which was changing from the bottom up, bleeding one color into the next, blue to turquoise to green. The effect of the students leaping and spinning in their black unitards made the background seem to pulse, and I found myself concentrating less on the individual girls—I could hardly tell Katie from Lizzie from Holly at this distance anyway—than the shapes of their flexed black limbs against the glowing scenery.

Those colors, changing now from lime green to yellow, made me think of Matisse's chapel at Vence, which I'd first seen in one of my cousin's books (all of which had been seized and "lost" when the police raided our East Village). For a moment I shut my eyes, and it was as if I were back in that apartment, magically reconstructed in my memory, on the afternoon my cousin and I spent translating his interview for *Lu Kou*. Or rather, I was translating while X sat on the bed under the window, chain-smoking Honghe cigarettes.

"What if there could be a city where every building was made by artists?" my cousin had speculated, looking at Matisse's chapel in the book.

"No one would be able to cook or sleep or use the bathroom," I said. "The elevators wouldn't work, and there would be no place to park your car." I thought I was being clever; it was the kind of thing Meiling might have said. Like the Bauhaus-inspired architects of Factory 798—where my cousin established his studio after the East Village was gone—Meiling believed that there should be a purpose for every part of a design, whether for a building, a salt shaker, or a cocktail dress.

But my cousin was shaking his head. "I don't think that's what would happen," he said. "I think the buildings would work all right. I think it would be the artists who would change."

I thought that sounded good, and I decided to insert it into the interview, although I didn't really know what he meant. This was at the beginning of April, just as the weather was starting to warm up again. My toes no longer froze on the long bike ride from campus to the East Village, and the jujube tree outside my cousin's place had started to bloom. Even slightly warmer weather felt so good after the long winter that I don't think I could've imagined anything bad happening to the artists living there. I thought they would just keep going, getting more and more famous, happier and happier. I would graduate from college, find a bohemian apartment like my cousin's, and begin to do the same sorts of projects he was doing (already our first collaboration, *Drip-Drop*, was in the works). Eventually Meiling would move in with me. She would start her company, and we would become rich. Perhaps we would even have a baby.

Certainly my cousin was wiser than I was (it would've been hard not to be). But I wonder if he knew what was going to happen, or—this is going to sound strange—even in some sense wished for it. Not that he wanted to go back into detention, of course, or take any of his friends to jail with him, but I think that X had recognized a contradiction in the East Village that spring. As strangers were becoming a regular fixture at our shows (art critics, journalists, and foreign exchange students), my cousin's performances were evolving. They required more hands to assemble, for one thing. Almost every performance he did that spring (the water tank, the "pit of snakes," and *Two Buddhas,* to name a few) was photogenic. There were fewer failures. And yet there was also something less moving about these later works. Perhaps this is only because I know the story, but when I look at the simple portraits Tianming made of X, when he first discovered he was not the only young artist living in that village, they touched me in a way that those later collaborations did not.

Were my cousin's circumstances changing, or was he? That's what I think he was wondering that day, as he sat smoking by the window. After the arrests, X might even have felt a kind of relief in breaking free of our little crowd. Yuchen finished medical school, and Lulu finally obtained her Hong Kong visa. I know that Cash opened up a DVD shop–cum–rock 'n' roll bar, just outside the west gate of Qinghua University, and Baoyu (contrary to everyone's expectations) got married and had a baby. After he was released from detention, my cousin finally had some peace in which to make his work. The question, of course, was whether he had gotten too accustomed to the attention, whether he would shut down when the microphones and cameras went away: *Closed until further noticed.*

There were more dancers onstage now, circling their arms like so many skinny windmills. I had an urge to laugh, and suppressed it. The music was so loud that I didn't notice Vice Principal Diller until she crouched next to my seat and laid a pale, veined hand on my arm. She whispered, so as not to interrupt the performance:

". . . small problem . . . put our heads together . . ."

I must've been listening with my Chinese ear, because my first thought was literal: I didn't want my head any closer to Vice Principal Diller's than it already was.

". . . come with me . . ."

"Is everything OK?" Cece asked, tearing her eyes away from the stage, where her daughter had stretched one leg high above her head and was holding her foot in her hand. The music had changed to something softer, involving flutes.

"I'd like to speak to Mr. Yuan for a moment," Vice Principal Diller said, more distinctly this time. (I noticed that no one asked her to be quiet.) "Please continue to enjoy the concert."

"Please stay here," I told Cece, who nodded, transfixed by the dancing. The rest of the audience didn't look up as I followed the vice principal out into the hallway. I blinked in the fluorescent light, but I was hardly surprised to be called out. I had been expecting it for months.

"Perhaps it would be more comfortable in my office," the vice principal suggested, and I agreed immediately. I found the empty hallway creepy; somewhere above us was the lonely sound of footsteps, and the music was faint through the thick auditorium walls.

The vice principal's office was oddly intimate. The only light came from a lamp on her desk, where a spectacular giant conch was prominently displayed. I thought there was something garish about that combination of colors, orange and dollhouse pink, as if a polluted sea had left a radioactive trace on the shell.

"I'm sorry to take you away from the show," the vice principal said, once we were seated. "But you see, there was no other choice."

I did not see. But I remembered what my old friend Fang had once told me: that if I were ever detained, the most important thing would be to avoid talking any more than necessary. No matter what they threatened, what documents or proofs they offered of my guilt, I was not to defend myself alone. Anything I said without a witness might be twisted into a kind of confession.

"A group of parents has complained."

"We were talking during the performance," I began, but I stopped when I saw the way Laurel Diller was looking at me. For a moment I had a strange fantasy: of myself as some kind of soft arthropod or mollusk, a bit of dumb muscle gummed to its glorious house, and of the vice principal as a shrewd collector, who wished to extract me from these spectacular lodgings.

"The reason I was forced to remove you is unrelated to tonight's concert," the vice principal said slowly, as if I might have trouble understanding her English. "Or rather, your presence aggravated a complaint I received from a parent last week. I had intended to complete my investigation before taking action, but you see—"

I heard a burst of static from a walkie-talkie outside, and my heart began to thud. Had this whole nonsensical conversation been a stalling technique, to keep me here until the police arrived? I was terrified of the American police, and at the same time disgusted with myself. Didn't I know people who had faced much worse with bravery, and even honor? I recalled the stoicism of my mother and grandfather in the 1960s, of my cousin in 1989, and even of Meiling in the spring of '94. And yet, when the door opened, I whirled around and clutched the arm of my chair. It was only Willie the security guard, sticking his head into the office.

"Beg pardon," he said. "We've got a situation in the Malmstead Courtyard."

"Is the concert over?"

Willie shook his head. "Five, ten minutes. I'm short-handed tonight. No *way* are we getting it cleared up by then."

Vice Principal Diller was already up and out of her seat, motioning for me to accompany her; perhaps she didn't want me out of her sight. We hurried toward the auditorium, Willie communicating by walkie-talkie with Maintenance in truncated language I couldn't understand, but even before we reached the steps leading up to the garden—a concrete pavilion, with ornamental trees and a fountain containing oxidized green cranes, gift of the class of '67—I knew we were too late. The audience had already exited the auditorium, and as we ascended the steps (at a jog), I could see the crowd pressed back against the building, staring up at the majestic purple jacaranda, which had undergone a strange transformation.

In the hour and a half of the concert, the tree had blossomed. But what blossoms! Heavy, inverted flowers—ten, fifteen, twenty times the size of the ordinary blooms—weighing down the delicate branches and releasing a powerful odor. These appendages had been hastily attached with twine: you could see how the knots were strangling the fragile, pinnate leaves. Over the entire display, with loose folds to spare, a large net had been cast, as if the tree had been apprehended on its way to commit some crime. From the fountain the copper cranes took in the scene, frozen in stalk-legged wonder.

There was a pop and a whistle: the crowd gasped as something small and black shot up in the dark, exploding over our heads. Three more fireworks followed, raining white sparks. The fireworks illuminated those pale and scaly flowers, as well as a small figure crouched beneath the tree. There was a familiar, fishy smell.

"It reeks!" someone cried—there are always critics—but most of the audience simply stared, watching the performance unfold in front of them.

For the first time, the vice principal seemed absolutely speechless. Perhaps because Willie had gone to apprehend the culprit, Laurel Diller turned to me.

"*What* is that?" she asked, and I'm ashamed to admit that I answered without hesitation, implicating myself even further.

"I believe it is a Sesquicenterpiece," I said.

69.

BRIGHT LIGHTS FLOODED THE COURTYARD, AND THERE WERE NO MORE fireworks. The fish shivered and were still. Willie and his crew had surrounded the figure under the tree, and the curious crowd edged closer. But I did not need to see the artist in order to identify her.

"Please wait for me in my office," Vice Principal Diller said. She started to hand me a key from the ring at her belt, and then thought better of it. "The art studio will be more private," she said. "Give me just a few minutes to clear this up."

I didn't want to leave. They had taken June a kind of prisoner, and I wanted to argue. I was developing a half-mad plan to offer my services, pleading the special influence I had with my prize pupil, when the Dance Directions girls streamed into the courtyard. They had heard the commotion, and (afraid of missing something) hurried from their dressing room in their makeup and tights. I turned and found two sets of eyes: Emily Alderman's, and their exact replica, staring out from a gaunter, older version of her face. Mrs. Alderman put her arm around her daughter and said something I couldn't make out.

I left the courtyard then. I crossed the front lawn, climbed the stairs to the studio, and turned on the lights. My classroom was far enough from the Malmstead Courtyard that you couldn't hear the din, and it was warm: St. Anselm's excellent central heating intensified a complex aroma peculiar to art rooms all over the world: oils, newsprint, turpentine, dust, gesso, and glue. It was funny that I'd had to come all the way to Los Angeles in order to remember it.

I was still thinking of those two pairs of eyes, and maybe that was what led me to the AP storage racks. I found Emily's portfolio, sat down at my desk, and began removing the finished canvases one by one. June had said that Emily hadn't destroyed those Color and Design paintings, and I meant to search the art room until I was sure they weren't there. It wasn't only curiosity; I had the feeling that whatever had happened to the paintings was connected, however obliquely, to my fate.

I hardly thought I would find the missing paintings in Emily's portfolio, and as I expected, there was nothing like the Mondrian-inspired acrylics. I remembered the disciplined excitement of those paintings, their formal (if slightly rigid) charm. They had convinced me of Emily Alderman's aptitude and led me to expect something from her—an expectation she had not yet fulfilled. I went through landscape after landscape: well proportioned, in pleasing colors, and completely dead on the canvas. Why had Emily decided to destroy her best work?

I was stacking each canvas facedown upon the frame of the last; I had got to the final painting, and was about to return them to the portfolio, when I noticed something very faint in the lower, left-hand corner. I turned over the canvas: it was a winter landscape, a copse of delicate black trees in the snowy foreground, but underneath the snow was something unmistakably red, as if an animal had died there. I held the painting up to the light, and only then did I see the mark. It looked something like an umbrella, or a child's drawing of a bird, a bird with a worm (or a fish) in its mouth.

There was a rattling at the door, and I hurried to replace the canvases. I was expecting the vice principal, but thinking of my student, and so I was doubly startled when June walked into the room. She had dressed up for her performance in a sort of Scandinavian peasant dress, blue with red rickrack piping, on top of the same wine-colored corduroy trousers she'd been wearing the first day I met her. A red-and-purple silk scarf held her hair off her face, and she was wearing intricate copper wire earrings—if I wasn't mistaken, homemade. I thought she'd never looked so pretty.

"Yuan Laoshi!" she said, and then she laughed. She had a full and beautiful laugh, which she tried to hide by turning her head to the side. "I'm in trouble."

So am I, I wanted to tell her.

"How did you know I was here?" I asked instead. I noticed that Willie was waiting for her outside the classroom.

"I didn't," June said. "I'm supposed to get my stuff."

"Why do you need your stuff?" I asked, but June had noticed the paintings on my desk. She feigned casualness:

"Why are you looking at Emily's portfolio?"

"How do you know it's Emily's?"

"Emily's theme is 'The Seasons.'" June pointed to the winter landscape. "So of course those must be Emily's."

"June," I said sternly, "did you make these paintings?"

"Those paintings? Are you serious?" June pretended to be shocked, but whatever her talents, she was not an actress.

"Not these paintings," I said. "You know what I mean."

"Did I make paintings that happen to be underneath those paintings, do you mean?"

I nodded. "Why?"

"Who knows?" June said. "Like I said, they weren't great, but they were better than her other stuff."

"I know why she painted over them," I said. "I want to know why you gave them to her in the first place. Was it for money?"

For the first time June looked genuinely scornful. *"Money?"*

I was glad to hear she hadn't succumbed to financial pressure so early in her career, but I resolved to remain stern. "Plagiarism is a serious offense—no matter why you do it. Passing someone else's work off as your own will corrupt the very part of you that makes your own art. It's—" But I couldn't continue. I coughed artificially, stealing a moment to catch my breath. June was looking at me with a funny expression.

"I didn't plagiarize," she said.

"But you allowed someone to do it to you. Why would you do that?"

June went to the storage rack and picked out her own portfolio. She put it under her arm and retrieved her can of brushes from the shelf above the rack. Then she began to walk the perimeter of the room, scavenging small items—paper clips, adhesive gum, a pack of sewing needles—and dropping them in her bag.

"June?" I prompted.

"I wasn't even in your class yet," she exclaimed. Then she opened a drawer and took a handful of beads. "But I sometimes used to make things in this studio—and one day Emily was in here too." June shrugged. "She saw those paintings, and she wanted them."

"So you were flattered."

"*No,*" June said. "Who cares what she thinks?"

I couldn't help smiling. "But you gave them to her?"

June shrugged. "I didn't need them. I wasn't even going to *take* AP Art. I just got annoyed when I saw that you'd put them up there." She indicated the shelf above the whiteboard, where I'd displayed the paintings after Emily first showed them to me.

"That's when you decided to join our class?"

"Yeah."

June was examining a still life I had arranged on top of a broken potter's wheel. I had covered the wheel with a purple velvet cloth to set off the objects I'd chosen: a wineglass, a wooden flute, a ceramic bowl filled with oranges sitting on a black-and-white-lacquered chessboard, inlaid with mother-of-pearl. I had drawn these items from an impressive stockpile expressly for this purpose, which was kept in a tall filing cabinet labeled "SAS Dept. of Art."

June looked up at me. "But then she painted over them. I guess she was embarrassed."

"But what if you hadn't noticed she was using them? What if you hadn't joined the class, and Emily had won a prize, or an art scholarship? They have those, you know."

June tried to keep from smiling. "They weren't *that* good."

"But you were afraid to find out yourself."

June didn't say anything. She lifted the bowl of oranges and removed the chessboard. Then she replaced the bowl casually on the potter's wheel.

"Someone might be painting that," I said, but June ignored me. There were noises in the gallery; people were coming toward the art room.

"I finally have an idea for Color and Design," she told me. "But I might not see you."

I wondered how she knew.

"Maybe I could send a slide?"

"Of course," I said.

"I wanted to ask you—"

Someone was hurrying toward the art room.

"—what you thought?"

"Of what?"

Mrs. Diller knocked and entered at the same time. She flipped on the overhead lights and examined June.

"What are you doing here?"

"You told me to get my things," June said.

The vice principal shook her head. "Your grandmother is here. She's waiting for you in the parking lot—she's very upset, as you can imagine."

June did not seem to hear her. She was looking at me, holding the chessboard against her body, waiting for my answer. I didn't flatter myself that my opinion was so important to her. It was simply that I had seen her project from the outside. No one had taken a photograph, and of all the people in the courtyard, I might have been the only one to see the tree and immediately understand it as a piece of art.

"Put that away, and let's go," Mrs. Diller said.

June held her chessboard tighter. "It's mine," she said. "I brought it from home." The vice principal looked to me for confirmation: we were still colleagues at that point, and she expected support.

"It's hers," I said.

"Willie will walk you down to the parking lot," she told June.

June was still waiting for my answer. I hadn't allowed myself to think that I might not see her again. I had to say something—but what could I say in front of the vice principal? Not, When will I see you again? Not, certainly, I love you.

June sighed. "Well, then, see you, Show Pongsy."

I had an inspiration: "*Wo zhen ai ni de shu,*" I blurted out.

June smiled at me blankly.

I repeated it more slowly, the way you might address a child. But had June even learned the word for tree?

"*Shu,*" I said, desperately. "*Shu de yue.*" It occurred to me that the sentence—"I really loved your tree of fish"—wouldn't make much sense, even to a native speaker.

The vice principal was looking from me to June.

"June is learning Chinese," I explained.

"June is going down to the parking lot," Vice Principal Diller said. "Right now." She put a hand on June's shoulder, not gently.

"I really liked your class, Yuan Laoshi," June said. "Or whoever you are." Then she turned and followed the security guard out of the studio, through the gallery, down the stairs, and out of my life. I noticed she was wearing her school shoes, painted gold.

"Good-bye, June," I called after her, and at that moment I thought it might not matter whether or not she had understood. Perhaps it was the kind of thing that loses its shape when you try to put it into words, like dreams, or like fireworks in a tree full of fish.

Mrs. Diller had already shut the door behind her.

"I think you know what I'm going to say," the vice principal said.

And in my distraction, my thoughts of June, I forgot all of my friend Fang's advice.

"I think I do," I said.

70.

PHIL AND AUBREY STAYED IN THE IMMACULATE GUEST BEDROOM OF AU-
brey's friends, the Barnetts. Patrick Barnett was a partner in the L.A. office of her firm; he lived with his family in Pacific Palisades, in a house
perched on a cliff two hundred and fifty feet above the sea. Their street
was a cul-de-sac lined with verdant magnolias. A thick marine layer
burned off each morning by ten o'clock, and then descended again each
evening at about six, when the housekeepers were out walking the dogs.
The guest bedroom was beige and white, decorated with photographs of
the Barnetts in exotic locales: the Taj Mahal, Angkor Wat, Machu Picchu.

Aubrey waited until their third evening in the Palisades to get to the
point.

"I think about the future," she said. She was sitting up against the
headboard, her legs curled underneath her, wearing a very fetching black
nightgown. "I can't help it."

"Me too," said Phil. What did he do besides think of the future? He
thought about it constantly, minute by minute. It was terrifying.

"I'm afraid."

"I know," said Phil. It was the rare conversation in which he felt they
were on the same page. Aubrey's breasts looked lovely, lolling in cups of
black silk.

"I try to picture things. Like, I don't know—like getting breakfast."

"Getting breakfast?"

"Like that old couple we see at Murray's Bagels? Who read the Travel
section?"

"We could read the Travel section," Phil offered, but he was starting to feel nervous.

"Or—can I say this?"

Why did people ask if they could say something before they'd said it? How could you give your permission, Phil wondered, before you knew what they had in mind?

"OK," he said.

"I try to picture getting married." Aubrey didn't look at him. She traced the pattern on the beige-on-beige duvet cover with one finger. She had very small hands with very bitten fingernails. Her hands looked like they belonged to a ten-year-old kid.

"Even having a baby." She looked up suddenly, with the kind of manic attention she ordinarily reserved for case briefs. He almost expected her to put on her glasses:

"I try to picture you *holding* the baby."

Phil attempted to picture holding a baby, but he was distracted by Aubrey, who was smiling in an unsettling way. She was smiling as if she'd finally understood some hidden truth about life, perhaps religious in nature.

"Dr. Harris asked if I could picture you holding the baby, and I can't. It's like trying to superimpose something where it doesn't go."

Exactly, Phil thought. He felt grateful to Aubrey's therapist, Dr. Caroline Harris, for the first time.

Aubrey had sat up, and was speaking excitedly, gesturing with her hands: "You just sort of float away, into the ether. And I've tried, but I finally realized—I think it was when you left to come out here that I realized—it isn't going to happen."

"Really?" Phil said.

Aubrey nodded. She looked calm and gorgeous. "I can't picture it."

"I agree!" said Phil. "That's exactly—"

"And that's why I think we have to end it now."

"A lot of people don't get married and are very happy," Phil said. "Like Susan Sarandon and Tim Robbins. They support all of those good causes."

"When I picture doing those things—I always picture Bruce."

Phil had been looking at the Barnetts on Machu Picchu, feeling vindicated. He had been thinking that he would never have to go to Machu Picchu, which was probably full of fat, sweaty tourists, moving out of the way for each other so that everyone could get their picture with the stone and the vegetation and no one else in the frame. If he and Aubrey went somewhere, it wouldn't have to be a place like that, a once-in-a-lifetime kind of place. It wouldn't have to be so far. They could go to Long Island, for example, and have a wonderful time.

He had been feeling vindicated, and he had missed something Aubrey had said. She had said something important, and now she was picking at her cuticles, which were starting to bleed.

"Don't do that," Phil said. "What did you say?"

"I said—" She was almost whispering: "I picture doing them with Bruce."

"Doing *what* with Bruce?" Phil said. "Who is *Bruce?*"

Aubrey's eyes were wet, but she seemed to be yelling at him: "Bruce is the partner on the AT&T case! If you don't know that—"

"Isn't he married?"

"Divorced," Aubrey said.

"You're having an affair with *Bruce?*"

"You don't even know him," Aubrey said fiercely. A tear made its way attractively down one cheek. "And I don't see how it's an affair. You're not even here."

"I am here!" Phil said. "I'm right here!"

"But you're not there."

"How can I be here and there at the same time?" Phil asked, but Aubrey got up and went into the bathroom. She shut the door, but he could hear her in there, sobbing and blowing her nose. He didn't understand how sadness came so easily to people. For him it was like a pile of rocks that had to be moved one at a time. Just thinking about it made him tired.

He waited a moment, until it was silent in the bathroom.

"Aubrey?" he said, but there was no answer. He was getting up to knock on the bathroom door when his cell phone rang. He could feel Aubrey in the bathroom, tensing, waiting to hear whether he would answer.

He wouldn't answer, but he would look. He took the phone out of his pocket and looked: it was Steve.

"I'm not going to get it," Phil said.

A muffled voice came from the bathroom: "You should get it."

"I'm not going to," Phil said. The phone was quiet. Wasn't Steve going to leave a message?

"Did you get it?" Aubrey asked.

A moment later, a text message flashed across the screen: "Lunch tomorrow, commissary @ 1?"

"No," Phil said. Y-E-S, he keyed into his phone. He was proud that he could use the text message function. It had taken him a while to get the hang of it.

Phil put the phone back in his pocket just as Aubrey opened the door, pale but no longer crying. She had put a robe (presumably Samantha Barnett's) over the black nightgown. Phil wondered how much the Barnetts knew about his and Aubrey's situation.

"You can stay here," Aubrey said. "I'm going to go downstairs and sleep in the den."

"I'll sleep in the den," Phil said.

"No," said Aubrey. "I already told Samantha."

"You told Samantha before you told me?"

"I should tell you that I'm leaving tomorrow," Aubrey said, a non sequitur that suggested to Phil that she was following a script: *The Break-up,* original screenplay by Aubrey Harmanci, based on a concept by Dr. Caroline Harris, Ph.D., in cooperation with Barnett & Barnett, Ltd.

"I'm taking a really early flight, so I can go into the office tomorrow night."

Phil couldn't believe how much seemed to be happening without him. From somewhere in the house he heard the Barnetts' toddler, Gabriel, shout, and then the sound of heavy footsteps hurrying to give him comfort.

"I can't go tomorrow," Phil said. "I have a meeting with the production company."

Aubrey looked at him as if he were crazy. "Well, I don't think we should go back *together.*"

For the first time, a kind of panic gripped Phil. His head and his extremities felt light, and at the same time there was something heavy in his abdomen, as if a magnet were sucking all of his organs into one solid mass. Once Aubrey was gone, he wouldn't be able to stay with the Barnetts, and he certainly couldn't go back to Cece's.

The child cried out again.

"But where will I go?" Phil said, but Aubrey was already halfway down the stairs and she did not turn around.

71.

PHIL ARRIVED AT THE STUDIO EARLY. BOTH BARNETTS HAD BEEN AT work when he left, and he'd been able to slip out easily, throwing his few things in the back of the car. (Aubrey had agreed to leave him the rental, although the firm would of course no longer be paying for it.) The guard spent a long time looking for his name on a list, and then waved him through reluctantly, toward the visitors' lot. He passed the eyeless, dun-colored soundstages, a "New York Street" with a yellow cab and a garbage truck parked at one end, and a fleet of billboards for spring 2001 releases, including Darcy Feyth's new romantic comedy: *Live a Little,* about a small-town beauty pageant queen who dreams of becoming Miss America, and her improbable friendship with the town dwarf.

Phil found the commissary, and sat down to wait at a table by the window. He assumed the revision was finished, and that now was the time he would be called upon to "take it all in one blow." Of course, he wouldn't have a sense of what he was going to have to take until he got home and read the script. Got somewhere and read the script, he corrected himself.

At one-twenty, Steve appeared in the commissary. He lifted a hand and waved to Phil. Phil was surprised to see that he was alone.

"Where's Keith?" he asked. A bevy of young women immediately occupied the other end of the table, casting covert glances at Steve. They looked to Phil like production assistants, some of them only a few years out of college. Of course the executives and the stars did not eat in the commissary.

"Couldn't make it," Steve said tightly. They got their sandwiches and Diet Cokes (Phil was not a diet soda drinker, but there didn't seem to be any other kind) and found a table in the corner, by the window.

"I have some bad news," Steve said, pushing his sandwich to the side like a prop. "We broke up."

"You and Leona?" Phil tried to look concerned, but he couldn't help feeling more cheerful. Steve was going through the same thing he was! And Leona was single!

Steve frowned. "No—of course not. Leona and I are a done deal."

"Oh, well, that's good."

"Me and *Keith*." Steve leaned close to Phil, as if communicating a secret: "Keith's brilliant, but he's so fucking immature. This fucking computer shit is all he talks about now. He wants to design *video games*." Steve shook his head. "He thinks *gaming* is going to be a big deal."

"I'm sorry," Phil said. He thought of Leona, and could not feel too terrible for Steve.

"So *I'm* sorry," Steve said. He took the screenplay out of the pocket of his orange messenger bag, and handed it across the table. Phil glanced reflexively at the first page, and it was not until then that it was clear to him. The title—*The Hypnotist*—was exactly the same.

"Maybe you want your copy?" Steve asked.

"You mean—they're not going to do it."

"Of course they could've hired new writers," Steve said dismissively. "But my theory is, they were looking for an out. It was only, you know, Darcy who wanted to do it in the first place. My money says that's why Keith and I got it. You know"—he glanced around and lowered his voice to a whisper—"we're not really as big-time as we seem."

Phil stared out the window, to keep from looking at Steve. Of course it was bound to happen. *The Hypnotist* was a long shot to begin with. He ought to have been relieved that there would be no movie, no matter how small, about a psychiatrist whose brother has an affair with his wife.

He looked out the window at the streaming secretaries, the gaffers, best boys, script girls, sound men and wardrobe mistresses, hurrying by in the relentless Los Angeles sun. He did not feel that they were real. They were an illusion, a projection designed to make him feel a part of something he was not.

"You still get your money, of course," Steve said. "You know that, right? That's the great thing about this business."

Suddenly there was a glint of golden hair, a parting in the crowd, and from the tinted glass door of a nondescript gray office came a luminous and oddly familiar form. Phil only glimpsed her profile, but in a second he knew: it was Darcy Feyth.

"What is it?" Steve said. "Are you OK?" But from his vantage, he couldn't see the star.

Phil thought quickly. "I'm not feeling very well," he said. "Can you excuse me a minute?"

Steve nodded sympathetically, simultaneously looking around at the other tables. By the time Phil was halfway to the door, Steve was waving at someone, getting up and melting into another table across the room.

"Excuse me," Phil said, as he pushed through a knot of people and out into the bright sunlight. Everyone but him was wearing dark glasses, not only for style, he was convinced, but as protection against melanoma and macular degeneration. He was as little prepared for this climate as he was for a meeting with an underage movie star, who would probably not even deign to speak to him.

She was about to climb the steps of a trailer, but had been stopped by a man in a dark blue suit, too heavy for the weather. The people passing by inclined their heads to one another, glanced at her, and kept walking, neither awestruck nor indifferent, as if the star were a prize in a video game you collected as you went along, with a satisfying *blippity-blip:* Darcy Feyth, 500 points. He was going in the wrong direction; in fact, the entire crowd seemed to be coming toward him, but at this point Phil didn't see what he had to lose.

"Darcy!" he called out. Now people stopped to stare. The man in the blue suit turned and gave him a look of horror, the kind of look one might bestow on the town dwarf.

"Miss Feyth!"

She was smaller even than he'd expected, and prettier. Her appeal on the screen was a sweet, girl-next-door sort of ordinariness, but it struck him now that she was distinctive, almost odd-looking. Her cheekbones were unusually high, for one thing, Her hair was the variegated shade of blond you saw so often in Los Angeles, the product of years of expensive experimentation, but her eyes were a deep, unfaded cobalt, like an infant's. Although he could remember her in sexy scenes—most notably one in which she was pulled from a river, her demure cotton dress sopping—she was not sexy in person. She was like a tiny queen: you wanted to bend down and touch her toes.

Darcy did not seem fazed by his attention, and even smiled at him, although the suit (an agent, he was certain) had stepped in front of her and was holding up his hand in warning, like some kind of bodyguard. Clearly he had seen too many movies.

"Excuse me," Phil said. "I'm sorry to bother you. Could I just take a moment of your time?"

The agent noticed the script in his hand and visibly relaxed. It was clear that Phil was a garden-variety pest rather than a viper; the man's expression of alarm was replaced by one of confident condescension.

"Miss Feyth is late for a meeting," he said. "May I ask what this is regarding?"

"A movie she's doing," Phil began: "Was doing."

"Which movie would that be?"

"Well, I'm not sure—" Phil began.

The agent rolled his eyes.

"—because it had a couple of titles. *The Hypnotist* was one?" He was pleading.

"Maybe you should get in touch with Miss Feyth's junior management," the agent began. "I have a card—"

"It's OK, Greg," Darcy said. She held out her hand to Phil.

"I'm Darcy Feyth."

"Phil Travers."

"Are we working on a movie together, Mr. Travers?"

"We were going to," Phil said. "I'm a writer—not really a writer, more of an actor-writer."

"There aren't many of those." Darcy frowned and lowered her voice: "Most of us can't read."

It took him a second to realize she had made a joke. She was charming!

"I'm sure you *can* read," he said. "You're wonderful! I'm a big fan."

"Thank you," Darcy said, in a practiced yet sincere-sounding voice. "That means a lot to me. I have great respect for writers."

"Darcy," the agent reminded her.

"I do have a meeting," she apologized. "Do you want me to look at something?"

He had almost forgotten what he had to ask her. "I—no. The movie is, um, canceled." The agent smiled, for the first time. "I was just wondering if you could tell me why you liked it. I mean, it was such a surprise for me—I was just wondering what made you decide, because it changed some things." There was no point now in holding back: "My whole life, really."

The agent opened the door of the trailer.

"And I'm wondering whether it was just that you liked the title, or the paper it was printed on . . ." His voice trailed off.

"I'm really sorry," she said. "I read so many things. *The Hypnotist*, you said it was called?"

Phil nodded. He shouldn't've been surprised. Relationships were never equivalent: that was why it was so hard to find permanent ones. When two people depended on each other, they each had their own reasons. Sometimes the reasons balanced each other out temporarily, and the two of you were suspended gently in air. Then inevitably, one side came crashing down. What had been for him a turning point, an epiphany, was for Darcy Feyth a moment like thousands of others, too ordinary to recall.

"That's OK," he said. "Never mind."

"Wait!" Darcy said suddenly. "I *do* remember. About the guy who falls in love with his brother's wife?"

He couldn't believe it. "That's right," he said. "That's it!"

"You know we're not doing this picture, right?" Darcy said. "You're clear on that?"

Phil nodded. He even liked the affectation of "picture" instead of "movie."

"But if you really want to know—"

"I do," Phil said. "Was it that you had some connection to the material?"

"Was I married to a shrink I cheated on with his brother, you mean?"

She giggled, and then suddenly got serious: "Actually I'll tell you what it was. I liked that woman—wait, don't tell me—Cecelia. Was that it?"

Phil felt as if the breath had been knocked out of him. "Celine," he said.

"Right, her. I thought you did a good job with her character." Darcy shrugged. "A lot of men don't know what women are like."

There were crowds of people going by. Phil knew they were looking, but he felt protected from them—protected by her. For the moment he was inside Darcy Feyth's private force field, and it was like having a mask or a cape or a pair of wings: nothing could happen to him as long as she was there.

"I have to go now," Darcy said, extending her hand. "It was nice to meet you, Mr. Travers."

"Thank you," Phil said. "Thank you for telling me that," he called, but Darcy was already up the steps of the trailer, half-waving without turning around. There were people going by, but now that Darcy was gone, they didn't give him a second glance. They didn't give him even a first glance, and so he joined the crowd, in the common direction, making his way slowly back to the visitors' lot.

72.

JOAN WAS NOT INTENDING TO BREAK INTO HER BROTHER'S HOUSE. SHE parked her car across the street only so as not to block the driveway. She knew that the whole family would be at the dance concert, since she had declined Cece's invitation on the grounds that she had other plans. She hoped Yuan Zhao had also turned it down, and that she might find him at home tonight, working on his scroll. She wanted to ask him about *Tianming's East Village*, and especially about the performance *Drip-Drop*.

The lights were on in the living room, as a deterrent, but Joan assumed that the housekeeper was in her room behind the kitchen. There was no point in disturbing her. She opened the combination lock on the gate, which was set to Max's birthday, and made her way around the side of the house to the backyard. To her great disappointment, Mr. Yuan's room was dark.

She thought about knocking on the kitchen door. Lupe certainly would've let her wait in the house. If they had all gone to the concert, however, they would probably go out to dinner afterward. She could hardly be waiting for them when they got home, especially after saying she had plans for the night.

As she was debating what to do, Joan wandered around to the pool house. She found herself idly trying the knob; it was locked, as she'd expected. She glanced back once at the housekeeper's window, obscured by a thick osmanthus, before reaching into a stamped tin lantern hanging above the door: there was the spare key, resting in the empty glass chamber.

The last time she had seen the dissident's scroll, the two wandering scholars had just encountered the immortal women. Joan had admired the folds in the women's garments, the drift and whip of their ribbons in the wind. The men stood stationary on the opposite bank, unruffled, eager, baskets of herbs on their backs. Now, however, the scroll had extended by several scenes; time moved in the Chinese fashion, from right to left. The herb-gatherers had crossed the stream, and the women had led them up a path to their dwelling, where a lavish banquet was set out on straw mats. The men lounged and ate, attended by serving women. Musicians strummed strange long-necked guitars.

Joan took out her notebook, planning to write a rough description of the scroll. As usual, she was missing a pen. She opened the top drawer of the desk; along with an impressive selection of pens was a large-format catalogue: *Along the Riverbank: Chinese Paintings from the Oscar Tang Family Collection.* When Joan picked up the book, she saw that one page was marked by the jacket flap.

Two woman stood by a riverbank, beckoning two men to cross. In the next panel, the men were being led up a stone path, past flowering peach trees. Joan looked back at the dissident's scroll, but she was not mistaken: the only difference between the painting on the desk and the one in the book was that the book provided an English translation:

> *After a brief rest the women prepared a delicious meal of sesame rice and mountain goat, after which the men were no longer hungry. They inquired about the women's families, but the ladies only laughed and made small talk, refusing to reveal anything. The two men eventually stopped asking. They realized these were strange women, and they observed that there were no men in the house.*

Harry had said that he hadn't seen the dissident's new work. Did he have any idea of what Yuan Zhao was doing? What would he think if he found out that his visiting artist had become a plagiarist?

She heard a noise outside and looked up, expecting the housekeeper.

"Lupe?" she called, and was startled when the artist himself pushed open the unlocked door.

"Mr. Yuan!" she said. "I thought you were at the concert."

The dissident looked wildly around the room, as if he expected things to be missing.

"I'm so sorry." She was standing up, clutching the book in front of her chest. "I came to see you, and the door was unlocked, and so I just thought I'd wait and see if you came back."

Yuan Zhao was staring at her. She thought he was going to challenge her—certainly he remembered locking the door himself—and then she noticed where his attention was focused. She realized that she was still holding his book.

She wanted to tell him that it was all right, that she understood. She wanted to say that you couldn't produce things on demand, just because people wanted you to, and that nothing you made would ever live up to their expectations anyway. Even if by some miracle you wound up pleasing a few people, you would never satisfy yourself.

"How was the concert?" she asked idiotically. "Is everyone back?"

The dissident bent and pulled a red suitcase from underneath the bed. Then he went to the closet, and took an armful of clothes from their hangers.

"Pardon me," he said. "I have an appointment." He was moving efficiently, transferring his clothes from the closet to the suitcase. She could hardly ask where he was going.

"I'll leave you alone, then," she said. She was wondering if she could slip out without meeting her brother and Cece, and whether they knew about the dissident's "appointment." It was possible that there had even been a quarrel. If only she hadn't done something so absurd, she could've invited Yuan Zhao to come and stay with her.

She was almost at the door when he stopped her.

"They went out to dinner."

"Without you?" Joan asked.

"I had some business at the school."

"But how did you get home?"

"Vice Principal Diller was kind enough to call me a taxi." The dissident was packing his books, distributing them the way you were supposed to, for weight. He zipped the suitcase and retrieved a black drawing tube from underneath the bed; obviously he was planning to take his scroll with him. For the first time it occurred to Joan that he might be leaving for good.

"I'm worried about how you'll get to your appointment," she said. "You could call another taxi, but it might take a while to come. In the past I've waited over an hour."

"Excuse me," Yuan Zhao said. "Could I—"

"I'm sorry," she said, handing him the book. She thought he would put it in the suitcase with the others, but instead he opened it on the desk and began writing something on the flyleaf. She noticed that he'd taken care with his appearance for the concert: he was wearing one of his black, collarless jackets over a crisp white shirt and tailored gray trousers. His new short hair suited him, she thought, and made him look even younger than before.

Joan waited while Yuan Zhao wrote his inscription. It took several minutes; he seemed to be concentrating hard. Finally he closed the book and stood up.

"If you want, I could drive you," she offered.

The dissident shook his head, but he glanced at the clock. It was already almost nine, and the concert had finished at seven-thirty. She saw him calculating in his head.

"Wherever you need to go."

"I have to leave a note," he said.

"My car is just across the street," Joan said. "I'll wait for you."

"My note will say that Professor Harry Lin has invited me for the weekend. When you speak to them—"

"Of course," Joan said. "You can trust me."

73.

THEY HEADED EAST, YUAN ZHAO DIRECTING HER. THERE WAS NO TRAFFIC
on the wide and silent stretch of Sunset that ran beneath her brother's
neighborhood; they drove in silence, flanked by spindly palms. She waited
until they'd reached the cheerful seediness of the strip before she asked
whom he was visiting. But Yuan Zhao refused to reveal anything.

"A friend," was all he would say.

He had the address written on a slip of paper, but Joan didn't recognize the name of the street. They stopped at a gas station at the corner of
Crescent Heights, and Yuan Zhao insisted on going in; she watched him
struggling to communicate with the clerk through the lit-up window of
the mini-mart.

"Now I will direct you," he told her when he got back in the car. "Go
straight across, up that hill." The farther they'd gotten from Beverly Hills,
the more cheerful he had seemed. Now he was positively excited. She
knew that this would be her only chance to ask him about *Tianming's East
Village.*

"Now go right."

They turned onto Hollywood Boulevard and drove for some time. "I
went to see your friend Harry," Joan said. "He showed me his new book."

Yuan Zhao didn't register any emotion. He was staring fixedly out the
window, as if this were his first car ride in America.

"I liked the photographs a lot," Joan continued. "Especially *Drip-
Drop.*"

"Mm," said Yuan Zhao.

"He was surprised to hear about your project though." She was glad for an excuse to keep her eyes on the road. "He was talking about his last book, on the Southern Song. He said that your generation isn't interested in any of that. But I told him how your new painting—"

"Excuse me," Mr. Yuan said. "Please turn here."

Joan made a left onto a side street. They were in a quiet residential neighborhood of modest houses, each separated from the next by a well-lit driveway. Joan slowed down. "I've been reading some Chinese history: the Song are conquered by Mongol invaders, but then they have to rename themselves to become a ruling dynasty. They call themselves 'Yuan'—is that right?"

"Yuan," Mr. Yuan said.

"That's what I said."

"You said: *Yuan*," the dissident corrected mildly. "Different tone, different Yuan. Yuan, *Yuan*." He craned his neck to see the house numbers. "Excuse me. It's this one."

Reluctantly, Joan pulled over in front of a neat bungalow with an American flag painted on the mailbox. A string of red and green Christmas lights outlined a wide picture window, and an illuminated plastic Santa lifted one arm in greeting from the front step.

"If you were never interested in those paintings, what made you choose to"—she did not want to use the word *copy*—"to study that one?" She looked at the dissident, who hadn't wanted to put the drawing tube in the back seat. He was holding it carefully across his knees. According to Harry, the only young artist who'd wanted to talk about the classical scrolls was the unnamed boxer in the photo. Something occurred to Joan, so unlikely that she almost laughed.

"Why not?" Mr. Yuan said lightly. He opened the car door, and a light went on inside the house.

"Wait," she said, putting a hand on his arm. "Could you just tell me— who was on the right?"

"Excuse me?"

"In the photograph, *Drip-Drop*. You're on the left, but who was on the right?"

Mr. Yuan hesitated. A woman had stepped out of the house, and was standing on the doorstep.

"Do you mean, on the right in the performance, or on the right if you're looking at the photograph?"

"Sorry?" Joan said.

"From our point of view, during the performance, I am on the left and he is on the right. In the photograph, of course, it is the reverse. I am on the right, and my cousin—the author of the piece—is on the left."

"Your cousin," Joan repeated dumbly.

"My father's older brother's son," he said slowly, allowing her to get it. "The artist—"

"Yuan Zhao."

The man who was not Yuan Zhao smiled. He retrieved his suitcase from the back seat, and put his bag down on the grass. "Thank you for the ride," he said. "If you would only not mention—"

"Yes," Joan managed to say. "Of course not." She watched him walk up the flagstone path to greet a motherly figure waiting at the door. She heard the modulated clip of Chinese being spoken before they disappeared inside the house.

The newspaper photo of the dissident was still hanging on her bulletin board when she got home. She reread the caption: "Yuan Zhao, a leader in the June 4th student protests, ten years later in Tiananmen Square." Looking closely at the photograph, she didn't know how she could've made the mistake. There was a family resemblance, certainly, but the two men had completely different builds. This dissident had short limbs and a broad, muscular chest, while the man Joan knew was slim, with effeminate, sloping shoulders. The features were similar, but even from this badly printed picture, the difference in their ages was clear. Joan turned on the desk lamp, but the photograph continued to con her: the closer she looked, the more completely it dissolved into its discrete gray dots, the facsimile of a face she'd never seen.

74.

THE MESSAGE FROM THE PRINCIPAL'S OFFICE CAME ON MONDAY MORN-
ing. Cece had met periodically with Elise McCoy over the past few months
to talk about the internship program, though always on a Tuesday or
Thursday. Cece thought Elise must've forgotten that Monday wasn't one
of her days, and almost rescheduled, but in the end she kept the appointment. She was eager to stop by the art room and talk with Yuan Zhao.

His note had been on the kitchen counter when they'd gotten home
from the dance concert, underneath the fruit bowl. It hadn't indicated
when he would return. On Sunday morning she wanted to call—just to
see whether he would be joining them for dinner—but Gordon had argued against it. Her husband had suggested that the dissident needed a
break, an idea Cece resisted. She considered Yuan Zhao a part of the family now, and family members did not take breaks from one another.

When she arrived at school, Cece discovered that she was already fifteen minutes late. She would have to postpone seeing the dissident until
after her meeting with Ms. McCoy. It was only a few weeks before Christmas, but the sky was a cloudless summer blue, the temperature near seventy degrees. In anticipation of the holidays, the girls had become more
liberal with their uniforms; as Cece hurried through the crush of students, she noticed sneakers and ratty T-shirts peeking out from underneath the regulation dresses, worn simply to test how far they could go.

When Cece arrived at the principal's office, the receptionist ushered
her right in.

"I'm sorry I'm late," Cece said.

The principal dismissed her apology, coming out from behind her desk. "Thank you for coming in on a Monday. I didn't want to wait until tomorrow."

The secretary stuck her head in to ask whether Cece would like a cup of tea, but something in Ms. McCoy's expression prompted Cece to decline refreshment. They sat down in the social corner of the office: a mock living room with a carpet, a pair of easy chairs, and a mahogany coffee table, on which a pair of miniature crystal ponies were frozen in mid-gallop. "Class of '86" was etched in a contemporary font across the base.

"I don't know whether I'm right in talking with you," Ms. McCoy began. "One of the surprising things about this job, for me, is that after ten years I still come up against situations every day that perplex me. That's the pleasure and the difficulty of working with real people, I suppose."

Cece smiled and nodded. She wondered if there had been a problem with one of the internships: for example, Ilana Levy's involvement with the Arab-American Institute's Middle East peace initiative. It was Ilana's idea—a wonderful demonstration of her generation's commitment to tolerance and diversity—but would Ilana's father, Rabbi Levy, see the situation the same way?

"I've received some complaints from the parents. Well, to be honest, one set of parents."

"The Levys?" Cece guessed.

McCoy looked confused. "No. I'd rather not name names, if that's all right. I already feel that I'm crossing a boundary in discussing this with you. But since you're so much a part of the school now, I decided that in this case it makes sense."

"Thank you," Cece said, but she was starting to feel as if she were one of the girls, brought in on a disciplinary offense. She felt the urge to defend herself:

"Not all of the girls wound up with their first choices," she began. "There just weren't enough marine biologists. Actually there weren't any marine biologists—"

"It's nothing to do with the internship program," Ms. McCoy interrupted. "It's about Mr. Yuan."

Cece looked down at her hands in her lap. She folded one over the other. She was aware of the principal's gaze.

"Are you surprised?" Ms. McCoy asked.

For the majority of the dance concert, after the stern and (to Cece's mind) somewhat threatening vice principal had materialized next to their chairs to summon Mr. Yuan, Cece had not been able to keep her mind on the performance. A worry kept resurfacing, like blight on the eugenia, poisoning her enjoyment of each successive dance. Half an hour later, however, when they had exited the auditorium to find an astonishing spectacle—a jacaranda festooned with silver mackerel, emitting a fountain of sparks—Cece had been relieved. There seemed to have been a clear reason that Mr. Yuan had been called out: to legislate a matter of artistic discipline.

Cece had not put this incredible display together with the name "June Wang" until the next day, when Olivia had returned home from a slumber party at Emily's. Olivia, who had not seen the spectacle herself (she'd been backstage taking off her makeup at the time) was nevertheless certain which of her classmates had been the perpetrator.

"But how do you know it was her?" she had asked. "Did you see her?"

Olivia shook her head: "She did something like that before."

"That's happened *before*?"

"Not with the tree," Olivia had explained. "I just meant the fish. She's into fish."

Cece realized that the principal was waiting for an answer.

"Sorry," Cece said. "What?"

"I asked if you were surprised."

"No," Cece said. "I mean—yes. Very surprised." Ms. McCoy did not look convinced. "What is the complaint?" she asked.

"One set of parents believe that Mr. Yuan has behaved inappropriately toward their daughter, as well as toward another girl in the Advanced Placement class." Ms. McCoy paused to allow the word *inappropriately* to take on its full implications. Cece remembered Emily hesitating in the doorway, the solemn expression on her rosebud mouth. *If you want to know, you can ask June Wang.*

"But what was inappropriate?" Cece demanded. "What do they say he *did*?"

Ms. McCoy nodded. "I think the most important thing is not to get ahead of what we know. Which is not much. The second student hasn't complained. Apparently the first girl—the one who did complain—didn't say anything to her parents until last week. According to this student, Mr. Yuan also mentioned that he had visited the second girl at her home."

"But Emily talked to me *months* ago," Cece exploded. "Why would she have waited all this time? If anything really happened, wouldn't she have spoken out right away?"

"Emily Alderman talked to you about Mr. Yuan?"

"Yes," Cece admitted.

"That was how long ago?"

Cece realized she had made an error. She ought to have heard the principal out before speaking herself. Now there was no going back.

The principal was staring at her.

"I was concerned," Cece said. "I asked her to come back and speak to me again—but she never did."

"You should've told me!" Ms. McCoy exclaimed. "You should've sent her to me immediately!"

It had been a long time since another adult had raised her voice at Cece. She was startled, not least by the change in the principal. Elise McCoy's habitual mantle of political reserve had fallen away; her face was pink, in sharp contrast to her lacquered blond hairstyle. It was as if another person were emerging from the principal's familiar form. Cece tried to summon the appropriate response—anger, contrition, or fear—but she had no precedent for this situation.

"I'm sorry," she said. "I forgot—"

Ms. McCoy took a breath. "Excuse me. The last few days have been very stressful."

"I made a mistake," Cece said. "I thought—" But what had she thought? That Emily was inventing things? That she was lying? That a girl who shoplifted at Nordstrom's was automatically untrustworthy on all counts? "There's been so much going on this fall," she told the principal. "And I was so surprised to hear her say it. I thought she must've been mistaken—I know she must've been. Still, it's inexcusable not to have mentioned it. I don't know how I could've forgotten something like that."

But had she really forgotten?

"I'm as surprised as you are," the principal said. "I only wish this hadn't gone so far already. The Aldermans—" She paused and looked at Cece: "I suppose I can say that now. Felice Alderman has already hired a lawyer."

Cece stared at the principal. "A lawyer?"

"We've set up a meeting with the school's counsel. But I assume Mr. Yuan will want independent representation."

Was this her fault? Was there something she could've done? And if she was to blame, was there any way to fix things now?

"The second student—" Cece ventured. "Was that June Wang?"

"Yes." Ms. McCoy sighed.

"But what about her? Before we go any further—couldn't she help explain?"

Ms. McCoy shook her head. "June Wang has been expelled. To bring her back for questioning at this point is complicated."

"Expelled!" In all of Olivia's years at St. Anselm's, Cece had heard of only one expulsion: an eighth grader who came to school so drunk that she had thrown up on the floor of the vice principal's office. To Olivia and her friends this girl had acquired a mythic stature; they spoke about her in the past tense, as if she were dead, instead of only a few blocks away, attending Fairfax High and scooping ice cream after school at the Double Rainbow on Melrose.

"I was sorry to do it," Ms. McCoy said. "But illegal fireworks on school property . . . Someone could've been killed."

"Do the girls know?"

Ms. McCoy shook her head. "And if I could ask you not to mention it to Olivia. They'll know soon enough. I'd like to keep the two incidents separate as long as possible."

"But what if they *are* connected?"

"That will be something for the lawyers to determine," Ms. McCoy said. "Do you know whether that will be possible for Mr. Yuan? To hire a lawyer?"

Cece was trying to concentrate, but she felt as if she were watching the events of the past few months on a tray of mixed-up slides. If only she could have a moment by herself, a few minutes to put everything in order.

"Mrs. Travers? Are you all right?"

"Yes," Cece said. "I'm sorry—it's a lot to take in."

Ms. McCoy nodded. "Olivia is in Mr. Yuan's class, isn't she?"

Cece glanced up. The principal was looking at her with a sympathetic expression. It was infuriating. "This is—" Cece began, but her voice was untrustworthy. She took a deep breath. "This is a mistake," she said, more quietly. "I'm sorry, but you don't know him the way we do. If there were anything to worry about, I would be aware of it—if not from him, then from Olivia. I spend so much time with my children."

"I understand," Ms. McCoy said, in a tone she must have perfected over years of dealing with hysterical parents. "I'm very sorry to involve you in all of this. But we have a responsibility to take the Aldermans' concerns seriously, even if they turn out to be completely baseless."

Cece sensed that the principal thought that unlikely. "But do they know he's a political dissident? Do they understand what's at stake? It was very difficult for him to get permission to come. His government might even put him in jail again." Cece had no idea whether this was true, but then, how could you know?

"I understand," Ms. McCoy said.

"What are the charges?" Cece demanded. "What do they say he *did*?"

"That's the problem," Ms. McCoy said gently. "That's what we would need the lawyers to determine."

Cece stood up. "Thank you for bringing this to my attention," she said, and then wondered where that language had come from. "I'll discuss it with him immediately—I think we'll both go home now, if you don't mind."

"Excuse me?" said Ms. McCoy.

"He usually stays a little later than this to—" But in spite of her resolution to be completely honest with Ms. McCoy, Cece could not bring herself to mention the private Chinese lessons. She was fairly certain which student it was who was being tutored.

"He stays to clean up," she said. "But maybe we should leave early today?"

The principal gave Cece a strange look. "But he isn't here now."

"Yes he is," Cece said. "He stayed with a friend for the weekend, but I'm sure he would've been dropped off this morning."

"Well, he certainly didn't arrive at school," Ms. McCoy interrupted, as if the suggestion offended her. "Willie wouldn't have allowed it."

"Do you mean you turned him away?" Cece couldn't keep the anger out of her voice. "Why not just give him a sabbatical until the confusion is resolved?" Why would they treat him like a criminal—before they were even sure?

Ms. McCoy looked confused. "We did give him a leave of absence. Laurel Diller spoke to him on Friday night, during the concert. We hadn't thought he would come to the dance concert, although of course it makes sense—I mean, it makes sense because he's staying with you." Ms. McCoy hurried on: "But the Aldermans were furious, and Laurel felt the best course was simply to ask him to leave."

Cece felt lightheaded, as if she'd forgotten to have lunch. The sun coming through the blinds seemed very bright. The principal was looking at her with concern:

"He didn't tell you that?"

75.

CECE DROPPED HER BAG ON THE FLOOR IN THE FRONT HALL. SHE HEARD the housekeeper calling her, but she ignored her, hurrying through the living room and out the sliding door to the lawn. She'd hoped to find the shades lifted in the pool house, the door slightly ajar, and Yuan Zhao quietly working inside. She loved the way he bent over the scroll, holding the brush near its base, making the hair-thin lines.

She knocked on the door of the darkened pool house, but she could see immediately that he wasn't there. She took the key from the tin lantern and opened the door. The bed was made, the closet door open, and the clothing gone. Although it was clear to her immediately—he would hardly take all his clothing for a weekend with Harry Lin—she looked methodically, opening drawers and cabinets, searching for some sign that he planned to return. Even the scroll was gone. The desk was empty except for a solitary art book, a volume of Chinese paintings.

"Missis!" The housekeeper appeared in the doorway behind her. "Guess what!"

"He's gone," Cece said. "He left on Friday night, and we didn't even *know*." She couldn't help sounding accusatory, although Lupe had been off all weekend. No one else had any reason to go into the pool house.

Lupe glanced around the empty room. She shook her head gravely, as if she'd always expected something like this from Yuan Zhao, and then brightened immediately.

"But Missis—a surprise for you!"

The last time Lupe had prepared a surprise, it had been to "shine" the leaves of the two potted ficus trees with margarine: a trick from the old country, presumably, which had left the living room smelling of sour milk for weeks.

"In the garden. Guess who?"

Cece had an instant of hope. "Not Mr. Yuan?"

Lupe shook her head, barely containing her merriment. "You go, Missis."

Cece pushed past the housekeeper. She crossed the lawn, climbed the steps at a jog, and stopped. The rose garden was empty. Had he come and gone? Her first emotion was embarrassment, as if she'd been the victim of a practical joke. She took a few steps into the garden, out of the housekeeper's line of sight, and sat down on a stone bench.

The sky was overcast, and there was a breeze. Most of the bushes were bare. The cabbage roses hardly seemed to last through August, and the supposedly stalwart Félicité Parmentiers had been temperamental even in July. Her favorites, the Penelopes, were gorgeous all summer but were now long gone: it was hard to imagine that the cluster of brown and gray sticks at the end of the bed contained instructions for those blowsy white and salmon blooms. Only the Cherry Meidilands and the hardy Great Maiden's Blush were still thriving.

Cece started at a sound from the corner of the garden. A raccoon, she thought, or a possum (they had called Animal Rescue on more than one occasion) had broken into the bush baby's empty hutch, and was thrashing around in the vegetation. She went closer and knelt by the cage, but even when she saw the dark ringed eye peering at her through the ferns, she hesitated to believe it.

"Fionnula?" she said, as if the animal might confirm her own identity. Had the bush baby returned home like a lost cat, doubled back on her own trail, miles through the neighborhood to find the place where she'd last been cared for? Had she missed the security of her cage? And if so, how had she gotten in through the mesh?

The bush baby had backed herself into the vegetation, and was feeding on the curled brown head of a fern.

"You're back," Cece said. "Are you all right?"

The bush baby stared at her with those oddly human black eyes. Fionnula couldn't have returned on her own. Someone had to have opened the cage, set her inside, and then fastened the latch. For a moment, Cece thought of Phil, but for all she knew, he was already back in New York.

"Where were you?" she demanded, and then felt foolish. She looked behind her, in case someone was listening, but she was alone.

Cece found the housekeeper waiting for her in the den. Max and Jasmine were sitting on the leather couch, having a snack and watching television.

"Fionnula is back!" Cece could not help telling them, although she was sure they didn't care. "It's like a miracle. She just appeared in the hutch."

Lupe smiled. "You see, Missis?"

"Lupe—where did she come from? Did you find her?" It was not until then that Cece noticed the housekeeper was glaring at Max's girlfriend. Jasmine uncomfortably picked the salt from her pretzels.

Lupe said something angrily in Spanish. Jasmine gave Cece a nervous look. Today her eyes were an uncanny turquoise.

"It's OK," Cece said. "Tell me what happened." But Jasmine seemed close to tears.

"It's my fault," Max said. "I said we should set her free."

"Set her free!" She wasn't questioning Max's explanation, but as sometimes happened, he credited her with more insight than she actually possessed.

"OK—it wasn't *exactly* to set her free," he admitted.

"But how did she come back?"

"Jasmine didn't want to let her go. She said a dog would get her."

"I didn't steal her," Jasmine said.

"Of course not," Cece said. "No one said you did." She looked at Lupe, who was suddenly very busy dusting the stereo.

"Jasmine saved her," Max said. "She's been taking care of her."

"But where was she?"

"At my house," Jasmine said. "My stepfather's good with animals."

"I thought you didn't get along with your stepfather," Cece said automatically. Max winced and shook his head just slightly, but whether he meant to say that he'd been wrong about Jasmine's stepfather, or that things had changed, or simply that Cece shouldn't have mentioned it, she didn't know. Had Jasmine actually said that her stepfather made her "uncomfortable," or was that Max's word? And if it was Max's, had he chosen it, consciously or not, because he knew it would make his mother respond? How could you ever know the truth if each successive person translated it into a new vocabulary?

Jasmine seemed relieved that Cece wasn't angry at her. "My stepdad's OK. He fed her a lot." Jasmine giggled. "Did you know Fionnula likes carne asada?"

"Well, you'll have to thank him for us," Cece said calmly. "Max, can I see you in the other room?"

Max looked up lazily. "Now?"

"Now." Max seemed surprised by her tone, but he got up and followed her, through the living room and into her study, crowded with pets. Cece hadn't changed the cages this week, and of course no one else had bothered to do it.

"Tell me why you let Fionnula out."

Max reached into his pocket and extracted a rubber band. He began stretching it between his fingers, almost to the breaking point.

"Was it because Uncle Phil gave her to me?"

"*No.*" The rubber band sailed across the room. "I just didn't want her."

"But the thing is, it doesn't matter whether you wanted her or not," Cece said.

Max looked up for a second, confused.

"Because *I* wanted her. She was *mine.*"

Max didn't say anything.

"What if I didn't want your stereo? Or your video camera, or your comics—"

"I don't like comics anymore," Max began, but Cece ignored him.

"And so one day when you were in school I just went in there and threw them out?"

"OK, sorry," Max intoned. "Jeez."

"It's not OK yet."

Max exhaled a short, exasperated breath. "Are you going to ground me again?"

"No," Cece said, making a snap decision. "I hate grounding. No, I want you to take these animals up to your room. I'll keep the birds, but you take Ferdinand and Freud."

Max gave her a disbelieving look. "Why?"

"Because I don't have space for them here."

"But I might kill them. Not on purpose, but, like, I'll forget to feed them and they'll die."

"That's your decision," Cece said briskly. "Love them, kill them—just get them out of here, so I have some room."

Her son picked up one of the cages and shook his head, as if he suspected she'd gone completely crazy. Cece didn't have time to reassure him. She put the other cage in the hall, and closed and locked the door. Then she sat down at her desk. The first thing was to come up with some kind of plan.

76.

WHEN GORDON GOT HOME, HE INSISTED SHE CALL HARRY LIN. AS SHE'D expected, the professor hadn't seen the dissident since *DNA-ture*.

"I can't understand how he could just disappear," she said. "He hardly knows anyone besides us."

"I'm sure he has a good reason," Harry reassured her.

That Mr. Yuan might have a good reason was exactly what Cece was worried about, but of course she couldn't confide that to Harry Lin. Didn't Mr. Yuan understand that the last thing to do was run—that, at least in America, it was always the guilty person who fled the scene?

"Xiao Pangzi wouldn't want to worry you, unless it was absolutely necessary."

"What did you call him?" Cece asked.

Harry laughed. "It's a nickname—from when he was young. Younger, I should say. It means 'Little Fatty.' "

Cece didn't see anything amusing in the situation, but Harry's casualness reassured her. Only when she mentioned that Gordon wanted to contact Missing Persons did the professor sound concerned. Harry was adamant that they should wait a few days, since the police were sure to contact the Chinese consulate, and that could cause problems for Mr. Yuan at home.

"I'll let everyone here know," Harry said. "And of course you've notified your daughter's school?"

"If they see him, I'll hear about it," Cece had said, which was as truthful as she could be under the circumstances.

Gordon had reluctantly agreed to wait until Friday to notify the police of Mr. Yuan's disappearance. At breakfast on Wednesday morning he reminded Cece that they would need a current photo, as if he had already lost hope of Mr. Yuan's returning on his own. Cece berated herself silently for not having taken out the camera a single time since the dissident had arrived, even at Thanksgiving. If they did have to go to the police station, she would be forced to take the newspaper clipping she'd Xeroxed for Joan: the grainy photo of Yuan Zhao in Tiananmen Square, with his long hair whipping in the wind.

Cece didn't sleep on Wednesday night, and by early Thursday morning, when the palm trees in the backyard were just gray shapes, and the first birds had begun sounding uncertainly, she was sitting at her desk in the study. When she heard Gordon's alarm, she went upstairs and dressed as if she were going to St. Anselm's. Then she made her family breakfast. It was not until they were all off to their various destinations that she got into her own car, took Mountain Drive out to Sunset, and headed east.

She had copied the address from the student directory, and it took her some time to find the house. Olivia had once had a friend who lived up the hill alongside Griffith Park, but Cece got turned around in the grid-like streets of the flats. She stopped twice to consult her Thomas guide, noticing each time the pleasantness of the neighborhood. It seemed to be an area full of young families: a pair of Indian women crossed in front of her with strollers, and on every block were lawns littered with bright-colored plastic toys.

The Wangs had a dry but neatly clipped lawn, with gray concrete stepping stones leading up to the front door. Although it was daytime, Cece noticed the red and green lights around the living room window, like the ones they'd used to decorate the old house in Westwood. For the new house they'd purchased strings of flame-shaped white fairy lights, planning to illuminate the trunks of the trees along the driveway. When Gordon had tried to install them, however, he'd taken a bad fall from the stepladder (onto grass, thank God) and Cece had put a stop to the whole project. The smaller, more elegant lights never seemed as festive to her anyway.

It occurred to Cece, as she touched the doorbell and put on a preparatory smile, that this visit was a gesture of faith. Mr. Yuan would return, and as soon as he did, he would need to defend himself. Or to be defended: Cece was not at all confident that the dissident could handle this situation on his own. That was why she was beginning to gather evidence on his behalf. The question of what sort of evidence, for or against, she brushed from her mind. It would be Emily's word against June's, and whatever June's shortcomings (the fact that she'd been expelled from high school, or her tendency to make artwork out of seafood), she was nevertheless a quiet Chinese student, who lived in an up-and-coming part of town with her old grandmother. How could you help but trust her?

Cece had been expecting a tiny, white-haired old lady, perhaps wearing a traditional silk blouse, and so June's grandmother was a surprise. Mrs. Wang was dressed in a purple velour pantsuit, accessorized with a large moonstone pin, pink ballet flats, red socks, and, most incongruously, a set of navy blue sweatbands around her wrists and her neck.

"May I help you?"

"Mrs. Wang?" she began. "I'm Cece Travers. I hope I'm not disturbing you."

"Hello," Mrs. Wang said, but she did not open the door any farther. "Are you from the school?"

"Yes," Cece said, and then corrected herself. "I mean, I'm a parent at the school. I also volunteer in the internship office, but only three days a week. I'm here on my own—is what I'm trying to say." How was Mrs. Wang going to understand her, if she kept going on like this? Cece forced herself to slow down. "I didn't have your phone number," she lied. "I wonder if you might have a minute to talk?"

"Please come in," June's grandmother said, but it was not an effusive welcome. Cece stepped directly into a dim, carpeted living room, decorated with a type of 1950's Americana that made her nostalgic for her childhood. Pale blue wall-to-wall complemented the mustard-colored upholstery and matching drapes. A brick fireplace (apparently unused) housed potted bonsai with smooth, twisted trunks and lanceolate leaves. Behind the trees were several large bags of birdseed. An eclectic assortment of packaged goods was stacked along the other three walls, still in their boxes or plastic wrappings.

"Please excuse the mess," Mrs. Wang said.

"Not at all," Cece said. Given the sheer number of things being stored there, the Wangs' living room was remarkably neat. "You have a lovely home."

Mrs. Wang brushed the compliment aside. "It's been a difficult time." She lowered her voice and put a hand on Cece's arm: "They've made a *terrible mistake*."

Cece was startled: she had been thinking so much about Mr. Yuan that, for a moment, she assumed Mrs. Wang was talking about the accusations. But of course June's grandmother couldn't know about the Aldermans' complaint. She was completely focused on her granddaughter's expulsion, and what she had to do to get June back in school; if she was interested in Cece at all, it was as a potential ally in this fight.

"I know," Cece said carefully. "That's why I came here today."

Mrs. Wang smiled and seemed to relax. "How embarrassing, I have nothing to offer you. Maybe you would like an iced tea? Before you arrived I was showing my granddaughter how to make sesame cakes. June has been interested in Chinese cooking lately. But maybe this type of cake is not your taste?"

"I'd love to try it," Cece said. "Probably just a small piece though; I try to watch myself with cake."

"So skinny!" Mrs. Wang said, appraising her. "Like a girl. Anyway these cakes are not fattening, not like American cakes."

Mrs. Wang disappeared into the kitchen, and Cece was able to look around. Most of the cartons along the wall were open: there were more sweatbands and slippers, water purification filters, shower caps, thermometers, eye cream, and vitamin packets with Japanese writing on the box. The ceiling in the living room was low, and there were footsteps moving back and forth upstairs. A moment later a door slammed, and Cece heard water running. The visit wouldn't be a success unless she was able to talk to June.

Mrs. Wang returned with a bowl of round, golden cakes, and a pitcher of iced tea with flowers in it.

"Oh," Cece exclaimed. "How beautiful."

Mrs. Wang frowned, barely concealing her pride: "The food June makes always *looks* nice, but how it tastes . . ."

"Will she come down and join us?"

Mrs. Wang set the tray down carefully on an antique table, polished to a high gloss. Except for a scroll painting hanging next to the fireplace— a cheap one, Cece thought, like a tourist souvenir—the table was the only explicitly Chinese thing in the room.

"I'm afraid June isn't feeling well," she said. From the curt way Mrs. Wang delivered this information, Cece had the feeling the complaint was psychological rather than physical.

"I'm so sorry about everything," she told June's grandmother. "I firmly believe that children shouldn't be punished for any kind of creative enthusiasm, even if they sometimes go a little far."

But Mrs. Wang was shaking her head. "Not creative," she said. "For an assignment. For the one hundred and fifty years."

Cece was momentarily confused. "For the sesquicentennial, you mean?"

Mrs. Wang nodded slightly, coughing discreetly into her sleeve—as if she was reluctant to say anything unpleasant. "For the center of it."

Cece had taken a bite of cake, and her mouth was filled with a sweet, gluey paste. She struggled to chew and swallow: "For the Sesquicenter- piece. Oh, I didn't understand at all!"

"June was going to win the prize."

Cece thought of the Sesquicenterpieces she had seen: the felt banner, for example. It was impressively done, the result of careful planning and hard work, but the fish-blossom tree was on a different level. It was hard to imagine a project less like the Sesquicenterpieces Laurel Diller or- dered, and yet Cece thought that if it were up to her, June would indeed have won the prize.

"The other parents were envious," Mrs. Wang confided. "That's why they expelled her."

"I don't think it was the parents," Cece began, and instinctively looked up: June was standing at the top of the stairs. She was wearing rainbow- striped wool knee socks, a pair of navy surplus culottes, and a yellow vintage T-shirt that read, "Mr. Yi's Karate Palace." She had done her hair in tiny braids, each secured with a red band.

Cece felt herself blushing, but Mrs. Wang didn't seem bothered by the fact that her granddaughter had overheard their conversation.

"Feeling better?" she asked her granddaughter. "Look, Mrs. Travers is eating your cakes. Much tastier than last time."

Cece stood up. "You must be June. I'm Cece Travers, Olivia's mom. I've seen you in Mr. Yuan's class, but I don't think we've really met."

"Come down here," Mrs. Wang said. "Shake Mrs. Travers's hand. She's come all the way here to help you go back to school."

"I don't know how much I can do," Cece began.

Mrs. Wang was looking at her expectantly.

"I'll certainly try, though," she heard herself saying.

June was making her way very slowly down the stairs, running her hand along the banister behind her. The gesture reminded Cece of Max, and the way there always seemed to be two of him: one who would do your bidding, and at the same time another who vehemently disobeyed.

"Hi," Cece said, taking June's reluctantly extended hand. "Your grandmother tells me there was some misunderstanding about your Sesquicenterpiece."

June let go of her hand. "Did you see it?"

"It was very original," Cece said. "I think the only problem was the firecrackers, but maybe if I—"

"They were safe firecrackers!" Mrs. Wang interrupted. "Made in Japan! I imported them myself."

"Maybe if we explained that to Ms. McCoy?" Cece suggested.

June was drawing a triangle in the carpet, going over and over it with her toe. "Thanks. But I'm not going back there."

"June!" her grandmother said.

"I understand why you would feel that way," Cece began, but this was clearly between June and her grandmother. Neither one was paying her any attention.

"I want to get my GED," June said. "And then I want to go to art school."

"Well, well," said Mrs. Wang. "*Now* your heart is stuck on art school?" June groaned. "*Set* on. Not *stuck*."

"Mr. Yuan says you're very talented," Cece said.

"You don't need to tell her." Mrs. Wang feigned exasperation. "She knows."

At this June could not suppress a small smile.

"I would love to see some of your artwork," Cece said, feeling only slightly dishonest. She did want to see June's artwork, and she also wanted to go upstairs, where the two of them could talk in private.

"Here," said Mrs. Wang, piling two more of the heavy, fried cakes on Cece's plate. The old lady gave her a gentle shove in the direction of the stairs, as if she were a friend of June's, rather than a parent. "Take your time," she said. "You can enjoy."

June's bedroom was at the end of the hall. One wall was on an angle and the ceiling sloped; it had probably been designed for storage. The room was very light, however, and from the bed you would be able to watch clouds and planes against the muted, smoggy sky. Cece thought of how her children had fought over the smaller room in their current house. There was something about the coziness that they liked; it was a myth that children needed lots of space.

"Come in," June said formally, as if she were inviting Cece into a Manhattan gallery, rather than a small child's bedroom in Los Feliz. Cece stepped into the room and immediately sensed someone behind her. She whirled around: standing behind the door was a life-sized white papier-mâché figure, wearing a yellow turban.

"Oh, that surprised me!"

"That's Raja. He's old," June said. "Look at this." On the wall opposite June's bed was a chessboard, mounted like a painting. Pieces of black and white velvet were pasted onto the wood, at random intervals, so that some of the dark squares became white, and some of the white ones, black. Pinned to each of the velvet squares was an extraordinary butterfly. The butterflies were not protected by any kind of glass, as they were in the Natural History Museum, and Cece was afraid to get too close, for fear of damaging them.

"Those are gorgeous," Cece said. "And what an unusual way you've mounted them. Did you catch them yourself?"

June looked puzzled, and then suddenly smiled. "They're not real," she said. "Did you think they were real?"

Now that June pointed it out, Cece could see that the butterflies were too dramatically colored, too perfectly whole, to be real specimens. They were exquisitely painted bits of silk, pinned to the board in such a way that, when a breeze came through the room, twenty pairs of wings gently fluttered. Cece had to remind herself that June was still in high school.

"I can't tell you how important I think it is—that you finish at St. Anselm's," she said. "You want to get into the best art school you can."

June shrugged, but Cece could tell she was pleased.

"Your work is really very special—not that I'm an expert. But I used to be a docent at the L.A. County Museum. And I do collect art." She noticed a pile of netting in the corner.

"There's nothing in there," June said quickly.

At first Cece thought June was talking about the net (she was relieved to learn the fish had been discarded). Then she noticed a black storage tube, half hidden behind the closet door.

"I was just looking at your net," Cece said. "I was wondering what you meant by it, what you were trying to express?"

June seemed hesitant and eager at the same time, as if she wanted to talk about her project and also keep it a secret.

"I wasn't trying to express anything," she said. "I mean, I was trying to express the tree. I didn't think it belonged there, because the rest of the courtyard was all cement." June blushed. "I thought it looked wrong."

"Like a fish out of water," Cece said.

June half-smiled. Then she began to chew on the inside of her cheek, a habit Cece recognized because she occasionally did it herself. The girl took a step toward the closet and picked up the storage tube, holding it against her chest.

"I guess I can show you." June uncapped the storage tube and pulled out a roll of ivory paper. Cece watched as she unrolled Mr. Yuan's scroll calmly on her bed, and began searching for heavy things to pin down the corners. She found a basketball sneaker under the bed, and a biology textbook on the night table—the same edition Cece had picked up dozens of times from Olivia's floor. June used an enameled jewelry box to secure the third corner and, with a sheepish smile at Cece, reached under her pillow to extract a beanbag crocodile. A crocodile, Cece thought, but a stuffed toy all the same.

Mr. Yuan was born in the year of the dragon, which made him (Cece had looked it up that very first day) almost thirty-six. She remembered she had thought he was very young to have accomplished so much, and had felt inadequate. Now his age had a completely different connotation.

"Did Mr. Yuan give this to you?"

"No," June said. "I'm just keeping it for him for a while."

Cece swallowed and forced herself to continue. "June, did Mr. Yuan ever do anything to make you feel uncomfortable?"

The girl had turned her face away, and was looking at the scroll. There was no way to tell what she was thinking, but from the length of time it was taking her to answer, Cece knew she'd understood the question.

"I won't tell anyone," Cece said. "Unless you want me to. But it's very important that I hear it from you."

"No," June said.

"No?"

She looked right at Cece. "He never made me uncomfortable."

"Oh," Cece said. "Good. I mean, that's what I thought." It was exactly what she'd been hoping to hear. Why didn't she feel more relieved?

June switched on the bedside light: in the most elaborate scene, the men were picnicking with the immortal women. Intricately rendered plates and serving bowls were set out on a cross-hatched bamboo mat: a dish of tofu, a pot of soup, a curling heap of ferns, and a large basket of new peaches, the long green leaves still attached to their stems. Serving girls bent their heads to pour the wine and tea from two-handled ceramic pots. Each scene was separated from the next by a webbed curtain of Chinese characters.

"Do you want to hear the story?" June asked.

Cece was surprised. "Can you read that?"

"Not yet. But I'm learning." She handed Cece a packet of pages, photocopied from a book: *Along the Riverbank: Chinese Paintings from the Oscar Tang Family Collection*. "He gave me the translation."

The title was vaguely familiar. "So he used the story from another painting?"

June frowned. "The story *and* the painting."

"The story and the painting," Cece repeated. She was missing something.

"Of course," June said. "You know about art. But some people at our school thought this was just the way he painted. Like, just because he was Chinese, he had to be really old-fashioned. Can you believe that?"

Cece glanced at the Xeroxed pages, but there was no doubt about it: the scroll was a perfect copy. The only difference was that Mr. Yuan hadn't quite finished. The last scene he'd completed was of the two men taking leave of the women, their baskets on the ground near their feet. Musicians surrounded them, playing a guitar, a flute, and a strange mouth organ with a cluster of vertical pipes.

"See," June said, pointing a bitten fingernail to a paragraph in the translation. "Read here."

The two women persuaded Liu and Ruan to remain for more than half a month, but then the men asked to return home. The women responded, "Coming upon us and living here is your good fortune. How can the herbal elixirs of the common world compare to this immortal dwelling?" So they begged the men to stay for half a year.

"Look, they're so short. And they have weird beards." June giggled: "Why do the immortal women like them?"

Every day was like late spring, but the mournful cries of the mountain birds caused the two men to plead once more to return home. The women said, "Traces of your karma have remained here, which is why you still feel this way." So they summoned the other female immortals to bid them farewell with music, saying, "Not far from the mouth of this cave is a roadway leading to your home. It is easy."

June was squatting, froglike, on her bedroom floor, waiting for Cece to finish reading.

"Have you gotten to the part where they go home and find out that they've been away for seven generations?"

"Not yet," Cece said.

"It *seems* like they've been away for half a year," June explained. "But actually everyone they knew at home is dead. Isn't that creepy?"

"Like Rip Van Winkle," Cece said.

June frowned. "Is that the guy the kids follow around?"

"I think that's the Pied Piper."

June moved the scroll carefully aside, and sat down on the bed. "Anyway this is much older than any English stories," she said. "It's from the Song dynasty."

Cece felt as if she were still several steps behind. "But why would he bother to copy it?"

"Why not?" June said.

"His own work is so well known," Cece said. "You would think he would want to make something new."

June shrugged. "I don't think Xiao Pangzi is that well known."

"What did you call him?" Cece asked.

"It's a nickname," she said. "It's pretty common in China."

"I know," Cece said. "That's what Harry Lin called him. But Yuan Zhao *is* famous. Not only for his art, but—"

"You don't get to see the seventh-generation descendents," June interrupted. "Even the real artist doesn't paint them."

"Yes," said Cece. "But why do you say—"

"I bet they wouldn't even look that different. I bet seven generations was nothing in China."

"You're probably right," Cece said. "But June?"

"What?" She finally looked up. "Why are you asking me? Who cares if he's not a famous artist, as long as he's a good teacher. He's the best teacher we ever had." The girl's voice threatened to break; she scowled at the scroll.

"I'm sorry," Cece said, as gently as possible. She didn't want to upset June, but she had to understand. What the girl was suggesting was impossible. "Are you saying that Mr. Yuan isn't—Mr. Yuan?"

June shrugged. She replaced the scroll in the tube, and sealed it firmly.

"But who is he," Cece exclaimed, "if he isn't Yuan Zhao?"

"Not anyone famous," June said.

"But I don't even know his name!"

June stuck the drawing tube under the bed, where it was concealed by the dust ruffle. "I could tell you," she said. "But I'm not sure you could pronounce it." She sat down on her bed and began playing with a loose thread. She picked up the beanbag crocodile, and let it slide, Slinky-like, from hand to hand. She was only a high school student, or rather, a former high school student, who'd been expelled. There was no reason to believe anything she said—except that only a few moments ago, Cece had decided to trust her.

"He might still come back," Cece said. "He might be staying with a friend."

June looked skeptical. "A friend *where*?"

"I'm not sure," Cece said. "But I'll let you know when we hear something. I'll give your grandmother a call after I speak with Ms. McCoy." She hesitated. "I can't promise anything, but I'm going to try to help you finish the year. Your AP portfolio is quite simply—" But June wouldn't let her finish:

"I don't want to go back without him."

"Without Mr. Yuan?" She had to use that name: she didn't have another. "I'm going to do my best," she said. "That's all I can do."

She had her hand on the bedroom door, under the watchful eye of Raja, when June spoke. Her voice was so soft that at first Cece thought the girl was talking to herself:

"Can you give me that?"

Cece realized she was still holding the Xeroxed packet. "Oh," she said. "Of course. Let me just—do you mind if I write down the name of the book? I'd like to read the story."

June shook her head. "But you have it already. He left it for you."

Suddenly Cece remembered the volume on the desk in Mr. Yuan's room. She'd thought he'd forgotten it; it hadn't occurred to her that it might be a gift. "How do you know about that?" she asked.

"He told us," June said. "He felt bad that he hadn't finished the painting. He wanted to give it to you, as a present. He thought you might've hung it in the living room, next to the Diebenkorn." June smiled. "He's kind of vain, even if he pretends he's not. He pretends you can't be vain if you're just copying." June looked down at the banquet scene. "Who cares if it's a copy, anyway, if it's beautiful?"

"When did he tell you that?" Cece asked. "About giving us the painting."

"On Friday," June said. "After the concert. Do you really have a Diebenkorn?"

"Did he stay with you last weekend?" Cece asked.

June nodded. She got up and went to the chessboard, adjusting a pin in one of her butterflies. Its purple wings shivered for a moment, and were still.

"But then he left," she said.

"Do you know where he went?"

June nodded, as if it were obvious: "He went back to China."

"China!"

"Lucky him. I *always* wanted to go to China."

"But when did he leave?" Cece asked.

"Sunday night," June said calmly.

Sunday night! If they had only called Harry on Sunday morning, Cece thought, they might've stopped him. But even if Harry had confirmed he was missing, no one would've known where to look. It suddenly occurred to her that the professor had to know a great deal more about their houseguest than they did. Could he have known from the beginning?

"Flights to China leave late at night," June said. "Did you know that?"

Cece shook her head.

"You have to get to the airport around dinnertime, and then you have to wait. You fly for ten or twelve hours, and then you have to land somewhere, like Hong Kong or Seoul. The plane can't get there without stopping for fuel. But that's good, because when you finally get to China, it's early in the morning." June smiled. "That way, you have the whole day to look around."

77.

SHE FOUND GORDON IN THE STUDY ALONE. HIS STUDENTS WERE TAKING their exams this week, and his work for the semester was nearly finished. She stood for a second outside the half-closed door, watching him. His hair, now that it was thinning, stood up sometimes in little peaks, giving him a boyish quality. The freckles on his forehead became a kind of sunburn up near the hairline, where the newly exposed skin was still delicate. Gordon was frowning, and the creases in his forehead were pronounced, but she could see that he was happy. He was transcribing information from a document at his left elbow. Every few seconds, he shifted his focus from the screen to the desk, or from desk back to screen.

Cece couldn't see the document from where she was standing, but it would be like all the others: the slightly greasy yellow paper, cracking at the folds, the script so antiquated it was almost foreign. The capital letters tilted like sails across the page. It was one kind of person whose narcissism led him to purchase family trees and take trips to ancestral villages, and another who actually tracked down these old charts and letters, census records and indentures, and took the time to copy and compare them until they yielded up their secrets. She felt a wave of protectiveness toward him that was much stronger than the feelings she'd called love when she married him. She wondered whether she wasn't making a terrible mistake.

She knocked lightly on the open door.

"Hello, Wife," said Gordon cheerfully. "How dost thee?"

"We weren't Quakers," Cece said. "Were we?"

"Lutherans," Gordon said. "I'm just in an eighteenth-century mood."

THE DISSIDENT ▍ 411

Cece went over to the desk and looked at the document, pinned down by two of her glass paperweights. "General Warranty Deed," read the heading, in a font Cece associated with Wild West cartoons, and under it, in stranger type (some of the letters were backward): *Witnesseth. That the said parties of the First Part, in consideration of the sum of* ("three hundred dollars" was written in) *to* (illegible) *paid by the said parties of the Second Part, the receipt of which is hereby acknowledged . . .*

"I don't know how you can read that," Cece said.

"Very slowly," said Gordon. "This is connected to the Lancashire Traverses through a letter I found last week. They were Protestants who settled in Newfoundland. It's much more convincing than the Travestère material from Normandy, I'm afraid. The case for the Canadian branch is becoming stronger and stronger."

"But you still haven't found the crossing ancestor, right?"

Gordon sat back in his chair. He took off his glasses and wiped them on his shirt. "Believe me, when I find him, you'll be the first to know."

Cece moved away from the desk and sat down on the sofa. The blinds were closed so that Gordon could see the screen; light was concentrated in the small interstices between the slats, bright needles in the dark room. She didn't know where to begin.

"Or her," Gordon amended. "Of course it's unlikely that an unmarried woman would cross alone."

"I found something out today," Cece said.

"What's that?" Gordon's face was a long shadow; she couldn't see his expression.

"Could you sit over here?"

Gordon got up obligingly and came over to the sofa. He was wearing an old pair of khakis and a checkered, button-down shirt. Unless he was exercising, Gordon did not wear T-shirts. He didn't own a pair of jeans.

"About Mr. Yuan."

The computer made the automatic-save noise, and Gordon glanced reflexively at the machine. No matter how much they used them, their generation would never be completely comfortable with everything the computer did for you. They would continue to insist on the value of simple intellectual labors—basic calculation and spelling—even as they became unnecessary, the same way her mother had made soup stock from scratch, and her father had repaired the two boatlike old Lincolns, until he had to pay to have them towed from the garage to the wrecker.

"You didn't find him," Gordon said.

"Not exactly," Cece said. "He—"

But she couldn't say that she'd brought a con artist into the house. She wasn't even sure whether Mr. Yuan *was* a con artist. Were you a con artist if you'd perpetrated a single con? If yes, almost everyone she knew had been a con artist at one point or another. And if that was true, didn't it depend on the seriousness of the deception? Were you a con artist if all you pretended was to be a real artist?

Gordon waited patiently. He had accepted a long time ago that Cece would slow him down. Now he was used to it. He had a relaxed but interested expression she imagined he used on his patients, meant to encourage them to take their time. She wondered what he thought of in those moments. In many cases, he probably already knew what the patient was going to say. She imagined a background of soft classical music going on inside her husband's head.

"He left," she said. "He went back to China."

"How do you know that?"

"One of his students told me," Cece said. "The one he was tutoring in Chinese."

Gordon nodded, as if he'd expected it. "I was always afraid that this arrangement might not work out. The reason I suggested that on-campus housing might have been more comfortable for him—mentally, if not physically—is because of the international community. I thought he might have felt grounded enough to complete his project there." Gordon paused and smiled at her. "You seemed so set on having him, though."

"I made a mistake," Cece said.

Gordon patted her hand. "No harm done."

"Some harm," Cece said.

"What's that?" Gordon glanced at the desk: he was eager to get back to his General Warranty Deed.

"I'm afraid I might have been postponing the inevitable," Cece said.

Gordon gave her a sharp look, and then turned away. He squinted at the window, as if he were puzzling out some problem, but she knew he had understood immediately—another helpful thing about him. She didn't have to spell things out; in fact, he preferred that she didn't. That was probably something that was different with his patients. Gordon had explained that you sometimes had to force people to say things they would rather not articulate, just so that they could hear their own words. It was interesting the way that people could know things and not know them at the same time. Denial, he said, was like a thick stone wall.

"Do you think now is the time?" He was sitting on the couch in his habitual posture, one leg crossed over his knee. Now he put his foot on the floor, but otherwise he didn't change his position. Even so, he seemed to be moving away from her, his whole body getting smaller but more distinct, the way his eyes did when he took off his glasses.

"I was thinking that we should wait until after the holiday," Cece said quietly. She was starting to cry. It would be wrong to expect comfort from Gordon in this situation.

"I don't think that's quite right," he said.

She knew what he meant, but she hadn't imagined doing it now. In her mind they were just discussing it, not acting on anything. It was only a couple of weeks until Christmas; everyone's gifts had been bought and wrapped and secreted deep in her closet (although the children had stopped hunting for them long ago). Still, some things had to be protected. There had to be a last Christmas together, so that they would have it to remember. Otherwise what had all of the years of ornaments and cookies and stockings and gifts been for?

"Please," she said. "Let's wait until the new year."

"*You're* the one—" Gordon began, and stopped himself. It was the closest he was going to come to anger. "I do think you're making a mistake."

"This is something we're doing together," Cece said, but Gordon got up and returned to his desk. For a moment she thought he was going to continue with his record—noting down price and acreage, births and deaths, military service and marriages of those once, twice, and three times removed—but instead he replaced his documents in a manila folder, saved his file, and shut down the computer.

"I'd like to stay in this house," he said. "Until the end of the school year. It's a convenient commute."

Cece was startled—not because she minded him staying, but because she hadn't thought of even the most basic practical arrangements until now. Perhaps she had had a vague idea of Gordon moving to a condominium, as Pam's husband had, and coming to take the children out to dinner on Thursday and Sunday nights. She had gotten so used to the way Gordon spoke; when he said the house was "a convenient commute," what he meant was that he loved it. What would he do, if he couldn't go out every afternoon and check the temperature of the pool?

"Of course," Cece said. "That makes sense."

"And then I would move out in May."

"Or September," Cece said. "When Olivia goes away." Would that make it harder or easier, she wondered, to send them both off at once? She had the absurd idea that she would have to buy her husband the same basic supplies she would buy her daughter: a wastebasket, a desk lamp, two sets of hardy, dark-colored towels.

"The Hobermans have just bought a condominium in Venice Beach. I'll ask them about their broker."

"Venice," Cece said. It was amazing how quickly her husband was able to formulate a plan.

"Not necessarily."

"I just heard of someone," Cece said, without thinking. "A broker—I mean." Was she trying to be helpful, or simply to stay involved? There was something about the thought of Gordon in a condominium in Venice Beach that terrified her.

"Who?" Gordon said.

"She was Phil's broker—when he was here."

"Was Phil thinking of buying real estate in L.A.?"

"I don't think he was serious."

Gordon smiled.

"I would want to move, too," Cece hurried on. "After Max goes away, of course."

"You would live alone?"

"Well, I'll have to, won't I? Once the kids are gone."

Gordon studied her. "I would think you would be lonely."

"I would have to find something to keep me busy."

"At the school." He said it as if it were a foregone conclusion. What else could she do?

"I don't think so," Cece said. "I think I would have to find something else. Something—"

But Gordon didn't want to continue the conversation, and she didn't necessarily blame him. *She* was the one who was doing this, as he had pointed out, and he wasn't especially interested in what she planned to do next.

He took off his glasses, wiped them on his shirt, and replaced them. He stood up.

"I'm going to Gelson's," he said. "Do we need anything?"

"I'm going to do a big shop tomorrow," Cece said.

"So just for tonight."

"I think so."

"All right," said Gordon. He veered slightly toward her on his way to the door, as if he might do something wild and unexpected, some touch that would change everything. He seemed to decide against it.

She waited until dinner was finished and the children were upstairs to go out to the pool house. Lupe had cleaned, and the room was returned to its crisp perfection. It was as if he'd never been there, except for the wooden drawing manikin—one arm lifted, as if to say, *What can you do?*—and the art book sitting on the desk, just where June said it would be. The cover was a view of a mountain dotted with tiny pavilions, minutely rendered in brown and black ink.

Cece found the chapter on Zhao Cangyun (active late thirteenth–early fourteenth century) and his single surviving masterpiece, *Liu Chen and Ruan Zhao in the Tiantai Mountains.* She was reluctant to turn on the lights; there was still enough daylight. She opened the blinds and flipped to the end of the chapter, which showed the last panels of the scroll, the only ones she hadn't seen, along with a translation of the Chinese text:

The two men exited the cave and reached the roadway. They looked back, but saw only the brilliant glow of peach blossoms and the layered greens of the mountain. When they arrived home, they recognized no one. Greatly perplexed, they made inquiries until they realized that the villagers were their seventh-generation descendants.

Cece wondered if it sounded less abrupt in Chinese. The last panels would probably have been the most difficult to copy (maybe that was why Mr. Yuan hadn't gotten there yet). The penultimate scene showed a path leading away from the realm of the immortals, with only a thin shaving of light to indicate the passage between the two worlds. In the final illustration, Liu Chen and Ruan Zhao stood regarding a solid stone wall. Only a person looking at the scroll could see both worlds at once. For the men in the picture, time moved from right to left: they had passed through the cave, but it seemed to have closed up behind them. The rock face was grown over with delicate, knobbed branches, like the trunks of Mrs. Wang's bonsais.

Finding that their homeland held neither close relations nor a place to live, the two men decided to reenter the Tiantai Mountains and seek out the roadway that they had just followed. But the way was obscured, and they became lost. Later, in the eighth year of the Taikang reign era of Jin Wudi, the two again entered the Tiantai Mountains. What became of them remains unknown.

A colophon by a later admirer revealed that Zhao Cangyun, in his youth, had been more famous than his contemporaries, Zhao Mengjian and Zhao Mengfu. Zhao Cangyun, who was also called Cangyun Shanren ("Gathering Clouds Mountain Man"), had never married or served as an official, however, preferring to live as a hermit in the mountains. This colophon, written directly on the scroll, was therefore the only record of the painter's life; the painting was his only surviving work.

Cece flipped idly through the rest of the book. Was it possible that he could just disappear among the hundreds of thousands of Yuans in China, and that they would never hear from him again? Of course she could always call Harry Lin: the professor had no reason to keep secrets from them now. The fact that the dissident had left the scroll with June suggested that he planned to keep in touch with her. Cece wondered whether the girl would share his news.

She was about to close the book when she discovered it: there, on the title page, was an inscription—as if he'd left a colophon of his own. "Dear Cece," it began:

> I am ashamed of the inadequacy of this gift, which is meant to symbolize another (perhaps equally inadequate) token of my gratitude, to be delivered at a future time. Certainly nothing could repay the hospitality you and your family have shown me this year. Here in the painting you see how the two Confucian gentlemen, although they miss their home, gracefully accept the kindness of their hostesses. I am afraid I have not followed their example. I feel that my own journey home is overdue—though I will be very surprised if I find my seventh-generation descendants there!—and I want to say that I am sorry I lied to you. Do you remember when I told you that I belonged to the . . .

[Here, Mr. Yuan had sketched a dragon]

> It was, instead, the humble:

[Here a lovely, long-eared hare]

> That was the first of several untruths—I hope in the future to have an opportunity to correct them all. Please apologize to your husband and your children, and to the rest of your family, for the trouble I caused them. I wish for you and for them all of the happiness in this world. Your friend,

[Here he had signed his name, in Chinese characters]

It was an eloquent note, Cece thought, better than most native speakers could have written. Her main regret was that he hadn't signed his name in roman letters. Perhaps he'd done it on purpose, for authenticity's sake? The characters were beautiful, of course. It was only that this way, to her eyes, it could be any name.

78.

I RETURNED HOME JUST BEFORE CHRISTMAS OF THE YEAR 2000. I STAYED
with my parents for two months before finding my own place on a quiet
street in the French Concession, near the library. Meiling and my cousin
knew I was back in Shanghai, and they must've been waiting to hear from
me. Some days I thought I would do it tomorrow, or over the weekend,
but the weeks passed and I didn't call.

Although I did not make contact, it would be a lie to say I didn't follow them. I scanned the culture pages of the papers and the listings magazine, where I saw that they had started working together, mostly on
performance and photography pieces. When the reviews appeared, I read
critics who panned the new work, saying that Meiling was just a fashion
designer, and that X had sabotaged his career for the sake of a woman.

Once, wandering into a small gallery in the corner of Fuxing Park, I
happened upon an image of myself facing my cousin across a makeshift
boxing ring. We were crouched in front of two hastily hung flags, sweat-
ing rhythmically on the top of a dismembered Ping-Pong table. I was surprised to read the caption under the photograph: "Zhang Tianming,
Drip-Drop, 1994." Not that I'd expected to see my own name—I'd been
proud of what I'd contributed to the project (sweat, instead of blood), but
I had always thought of my cousin as its author. The only part of the project that had survived, however, was the photograph, and that photograph
had indisputably been taken by Tianming.

I thought of Zhao Cangyun painting in solitude for all those years.
Liu Chen and Ruan Zhao in the Tiantai Mountains was his only surviving
work, and if not for the colophon by Hua Youwu, we would never have

been able to identify it. "Gathering Clouds Mountain Man" would have remained anonymous: the scroll, authorless. I wondered if that mattered.

I knocked on the door of a small office at the back of the gallery, and a sullen assistant came out to see what I wanted. When I asked the price of *Drip-Drop*, she escorted me into a back room, where a young man in a pinstriped suit with a pink silk tie was talking on a tiny phone. The photograph, he was happy to tell me after he'd hung up, was priced at seven thousand dollars, U.S.

"That's some of his finest work," the curator told me. "You see, it's from the East Village period."

The East Village period! I almost smiled. Instead I asked whether the gallery also represented the performance artist Yuan Zhao.

"We do have a few of his paintings, if you're interested," the curator said, sizing me up.

"Do you have any recent work?" I asked, in the tone of voice I imagined a person who would spend seven thousand dollars U.S. on a photograph might use. I was wearing a T-shirt and a pair of cargo pants, but one thing I had learned from living with the Traverses is that you can't determine how wealthy someone is by looking at his clothes.

"I'm interested in something from the last year or so," I added firmly. "Price doesn't matter."

The curator gave a small smile and looked away: "Unfortunately I only deal in the work before he began collaborating with his . . . partner," he said, letting me know by his tone what he thought of Meiling's influence on my cousin. "For the new work, I'm afraid you'll have to look elsewhere."

Although the remark at one time would've pleased me, I was offended. I thanked him curtly and left the gallery, as if I'd been the one insulted.

Plenty of galleries are happy to show the work of an art-star couple, of course, and I've seen their latest photographs: a series of the two of them, completely naked, on the Huanghua section of the Great Wall. I remember one in particular, shot from a distance with a tripod. (My cousin learned the lesson of the East Village, and these days always takes his own pictures.) They are climbing up to one of the crumbling guard towers, which has a large diagonal crack across its southern face. You can tell it's winter from the dry, terraced fields around the wall, and I wonder how they can stand the cold. Meiling has stopped to look up at the square tower: her hands are at her sides and her hair hangs straight to the middle of her back. Her bottom is like a white heart against the gray stones.

My cousin, characteristically, cannot stand still. He seems to be jumping, and beckoning his lover at the same time toward the tower. The contrast between his silliness and her steadiness makes my heart ache, and I wonder whether the critics who dismiss this work might just be envious. My cousin still has the inventiveness that was evident in his "East Village period," but when I am honest with myself, I have to admit that love has added a new dimension to his work.

79.

IT WAS THREE YEARS BEFORE I SOUGHT THEM OUT. I WAS IN BEIJING, on business for my father, and it was an unusually clear spring day, warm but with a breeze. On a whim I took line two to Dongzhimen, and then got on an airport bus. I knew they lived just adjacent to a new gallery, out past Dashanzi, and I'd looked up the address long ago. Still, it was difficult to find the right road. I got off the bus near the Nangao police station, and had to stop and ask the way: a policeman, of all people, gave me directions to X's place.

I arrived at their house, tucked away on a dead-end street, in a quiet area I suspect will soon become an "art village." The house was huge—one of the sleek live-work spaces that are now so popular—but built of old-fashioned brick, which blended in nicely with the smaller houses around it. It was lunchtime, and I thought they might not be home, but when I rang the bell, I heard footsteps coming toward me from behind a solid gray metal gate.

"Who is it?" my cousin called, and it took me a second to decide how to respond.

"Longxia Shanren," I said. It's the Lobster Hermit. "Open up."

The gate rolled back, and there was my cousin, his long hair pulled back in the habitual ponytail, but wearing ordinary clothes, just like mine.

"Cousin," he said, and put his arms around me. Standing behind him in the courtyard, as if they'd been waiting for me, was Meiling, along with their latest collaboration. Although he was only seven months old, he was very strong: while I watched, he pulled himself triumphantly to his feet, using the edge of the table for support.

"That's his new trick," Meiling said, taking my hand. "He's been out here for an hour practicing. He must've known you were coming."

The baby sat down with a thump, screwed his face up as if he were going to cry, and then changed his mind. I was confused for a minute, imagining that this was the child I'd seen in Meiling's belly more than three years ago, before I left for Los Angeles. How was he still so young?

"This is our second," my cousin explained. "Ruyang—say hello to your uncle." He looked at me carefully, to gauge my reaction. "His older sister is with her grandmother this afternoon."

"Congratulations," I said, and this time I meant it. I sat down on a stool at the low beechwood table (a real antique, I suspected) that complemented the ultramodern glass tea set.

"May I?" I asked my cousin, who nodded. I took the baby in my lap. Ruyang was not yet at an age to be fussy about being picked up by strangers. As soon as I lifted him, he began pedaling his feet, as if he were trying to bicycle.

"How are things?" my cousin asked. "How is your work?"

"I do a little, here and there," I said. "I'm thinking of starting a gallery." It was not an idea I'd articulated to anyone yet, but my cousin nodded enthusiastically. I told him my impression of the galleries in Shanghai, and described some of the terrific spaces I had seen, in the old warehouses by the river.

"But I didn't know I was entertaining a curator!" my cousin joked with me. "Let me tell Meiling to bring out the whiskey."

"You'll be hearing from me," I said. "Don't worry."

Meiling pushed open the front door with her hip, balancing the heavy tea tray. "Worry about what?" she said.

"Did you hear?" my cousin said. "There's finally going to be a first-class gallery in Shanghai."

Meiling looked at me, but before I could explain, the baby stood up in my lap, pushing his fat little feet into my knees. He uttered a string of nonsense syllables in a loud, clear voice—not crying so much as imitating the sound of speech, the same way he was trying to stand.

"He has strong opinions about art," my cousin said. "Don't get him started."

424 ||| NELL FREUDENBERGER

The three of us laughed, and for a second I felt we were back in that other courtyard, outside of Cash's house. But this time it was spring, and no one could have compared the fine Wulong tea we drank, or the French crepes we had afterward at a chic new café in their neighborhood, to one of our meals back then.

Our old East Village is now buried under massive Chaoyang Park. You can wander through that park for hours (I have done it), trying to identify trees or mounds of dirt, or remember the placement of courtyards, but it's no use. There is no passageway back. Perhaps that is for the best.

80.

I HAVE FINISHED MY RETELLING OF THE LEGEND *LIU CHEN AND RUAN Zhao in the Tiantai Mountains.* I've changed the title slightly. Look closely among the characters in the top right-hand corner, and you will find the English letters X, Y, and Z. "X and YZ in the Tiantai Mountains," it reads now. As in algebra, however, the values of X and YZ have changed. Now that X = YZ, there is a new unknown. I've written my own name in the bottom left-hand corner, and yet I don't think there's any point in copying that name here. I think it has nothing to do with this story, and there would be the further problem of how to present it: as a combination of strokes, dots, and hooks that I would have to cut and paste into this English text, or as an English transliteration: an approximation, a stand-in, a copy.

I am finished being an artist. When I do go into the studio that's supposed to be for the two of us, it is mostly to admire her work. Now she is making fishing nets with objects caught in them: baseballs and hubcaps, as well as glazed cherries on sticks, bright paper sparklers, and fur earmuffs in the shapes of hearts and stars—things she acquired on a trip we took this past winter, to see the Ice Lantern Festival in Harbin. To be clear: there was nothing improper in this traveling. It has taken me six years to write this story. I am a lazy writer, and only the fact that I am writing the truth—a kind of copying of events, in prose—has made this record possible.

It has been six years since I left Los Angeles, not knowing whether I would ever see her again. Fortunately for me, June was an excellent correspondent. (Not that she always sent words. Sometimes it was a photograph—of her work, not herself—a pair of Japanese electromagnetic socks, a pink plastic fish, or a feather.) Our relationship was an epistolary one for several years, on and off, while June took her high school equivalency, and then got her degree in studio art at the prestigious Wesleyan University in Connecticut. When she finally arrived in Shanghai to meet her cousins, it was on a traveling fellowship similar to the one that brought us together in the first place. (Although June's fellowship was absolutely earned, and she arrived at Pudong Airport as no one but herself.) I held a sign with her name in English and Chinese. She said:

"You know I can't read that chickenscratch, Yuan Laoshi."

I no longer paint very often, and I've also stopped working for my father. Mostly now I spend my time at the gallery, which I have sentimentally named "Mountain," in honor of Cangyun Shanren, as well as a certain street in Beverly Hills, California. I had thought of naming it for my old teacher, but there is another Wang in my life now, one who refuses to be honored except in the wall text next to her work. In the middle of the day, I often come home to cook: shrimp and chive dumplings, red-braised pork, sesame rice, and cold cucumbers dressed with sauce. These things are ready for us when June comes home from her studio, hungry and excited. After eating our big meal of the day we nap, and after that June sometimes wakes me in the best way imaginable.

Our apartment is charming, but hardly large: there are dozens of galleries in Shanghai, and hundreds of curators, all struggling to survive. June says I have better taste than the others, and I tell her that soon her work will be keeping us both in luxury. Who knows? Maybe it will happen: maybe we'll make some money, and go back to visit America in style. It would be nothing like before. For one thing, Cece has written to me that they plan to sell their big house. I would like to walk through the rose garden one more time before that happens, and present her with the finished scroll: she should at least have the original copy. I would like to show June the bush baby, still alive, I suspect, safe in her landscaped hutch. It would be nice to go back to California as myself.

It is exhausting pretending to be someone you're not; June says that's part of the reason it's taken me so long to finish this account. (There aren't even any pictures, she mocks.) It is a relief, in any case, to write these final words. June sometimes teases me, calling me "Old Man." Maybe not in years—we are, in fact, only six years apart—but in spirit. She says I am a conservative or even a reactionary (using the word in the American way, of course, as someone who isn't culturally up-to-speed), and it's true that I have trouble letting go of the past. I was certainly never meant to be a dissident. I was never meant to be an artist, or at least not the same kind of artist as my cousin X—the groundbreaking performer Yuan Zhao. I am someone who paints rocks and birds and lobsters, again and again the same way, because the repetition of these forms gives me solace. They make me feel that I am home.

And yet occasionally there's something more than that. Sometimes there's a tree or an arrangement of clouds that makes me think I'm doing something—not new, perhaps, but something of my own. June has said that she recognized that I wasn't who I said I was right away, that first day in the studio at St. Anselm's.

"How?" I asked her. "How did you know?"

"Because I was expecting to find Yuan Zhao, and you weren't him."

"How did you know I wasn't him?" I said. "There were people who'd seen us both who still didn't know for sure."

"I recognized you."

"Because you're an artist," I said.

June shook her head in a particular, frustrated way that is so dear to me—when I think of how I almost allowed that gesture of hers to slip away forever, my skin puckers and I am, for just a moment, cold.

"Because you were for me, Old Man. How could you be anybody else?"

Acknowledgments

I would like to thank the Whiting Foundation, the Pen/Malamud committee, and the American Academy of Arts and Letters for their generous support. I'm also indebted to the U.S. State Department for sponsoring my first trip to China, especially to Michael Bandler and Paul Thomas. I'm enormously grateful to Rong Rong and inri for taking the time to talk with me in Beijing, and welcoming me into their home, and to Karen Patterson for translating our conversation. And I stayed too long with Sommer and Alex in Beijing: thank you.

Wu Hung's lucid writing about contemporary Chinese art was invaluable to me, especially *Rong Rong's East Village*. I was very lucky to have editors like Daniel Halpern and Lee Boudreaux, who read this book many times. Amanda Urban is simply the best agent a writer could imagine. Finally I'm grateful to Paul for agreeing to spend his vacation in Harbin (in January), and for his faith that it would be worth it.